*Tx for buying my book*

*♡*

*Susie*

# The Lost Wisdom of the Magi

## Susie Helme

*The Lost Wisdom of the Magi*

Published by The Conrad Press in the United Kingdom 2020

Tel: +44(0)1227 472 874
www.theconradpress.com
info@theconradpress.com

ISBN 978-1-913567-37-8

Typesetting and Cover Design by:
Charlotte Mouncey, www.bookstyle.co.uk

The Conrad Press logo was designed by Maria Priestley.

Printed and bound in Great Britain by Clays Ltd, Elcograf S.p.A.

# Contents

# Acknowledgements

Thanks to John Mullen for giving me the idea of writing a 'revolutionary historical romance'; to my fellow Bounds Green Book Writers Group for their valuable feedback; and to Laura Proffitt for her scholarly eye

# Chapter 1
## Genesis

Sisters of Alexandria, you have requested an account of my years in Palestine, and so I pledge these scrolls to you, a gift from sister to sister, in appreciation for all your works. Some of you, my Sisters, are interested in the war, and want to hear heroic tales of Zealots. Some of you mourn *Churban HaBayit* (Destruction of the Temple), and wish to join my grief with yours.

I know that some of you, too, yearn for the Lost Wisdom. You are curious about magic; and I will teach you what I know. As my most beloved disciples, these things are for your eyes alone.

Our Academy is dedicated to the womanly promulgation of all the jewels of civilisation. This work must be part of that goal.

In my memory, the story began on that night when I came to my senses on the sandy hill west of the ruins of old Babylon. Everything before that seems a far distant past. It was on that cold ground that my destiny was cast, the Evening Star shining down upon my dusty shawl and bloodied robe, a magical fox questioning my actions with a probing gaze. I've had to trace the story backward from that moment, as for many years my mind blocked the memories of what had gone before.

I cannot report to you that event, Sisters, other than by starting from the beginning. I cannot confess to you my behaviour on that night before I tell you the story of who I was, for I was very different then as a girl from the old crone you know now.

As you know, I was born in the Land Between the Rivers, in the city of Babylon, which is called Seleucia on the Tigris by the heirs of Alexandros (Alexander the Great).

My father, Itamar son of Nebazak, was a keeper of the royal archives of the Parthians. It has been the tradition in our family for eighteen generations by virtue of our scholarship. We are in Babylon since the Captivity.

My mother, Sherah, suffered a grave illness in the years after my birth, and there are many years between me and my younger brothers.

Some moons passed her with no moonblood, other moons she bled so heavily she took to bed. Sometimes when she lifted something heavy, she would cry out in pain and curl into a ball on the kitchen floor. Father was so careful when he embraced her, it seemed as if he was afraid even to touch her. Of course, no one ever explains such things to children, but I later described the symptoms to Ima Devorah, and she said it sounded like scarring on the womb. When Mother conceived and delivered the first boy, Adam, the birthing must have cleared away the scarred tissue from her body. When she recovered, she had three more sons in a row, each born before the elder was weaned.

My father gave me a Greek name, Sophia. It was the fashion in those days among Babylonian Jewry to have Greek names, and Father, a Pharisee of the old school, had ever a soft spot in his soul for the Greek arts. Sophia is a Greek word. It means wisdom. I believe my father saw the true course of my spirit when he so named me. Mother was too ill to dispute it, though I think she would have done.

Grandmother lived with us as nurse all during my mother's illness, remaining as minder to the boys, and as she aged, I was expected to replace her in that role. She constantly scolded me to do this or that 'for Mother' or 'for your brothers' and scolded me with the same words she scolded the slaves. The boys saw me as a maidservant. Not only did I have to do all the work, but I got no respect for it. My brothers asked me to fetch them things without saying 'please' or 'thank you'.

When my first brother was born, Mother told Father, 'no more Greek names'. The babe was to have 'a proper patriarch's name, like their father', as if her hitherto son-less condition had been the result of some foreign curse worked by her husband's choice of name for a daughter. Adam was the name he chose, and the brothers that followed were Yonah, Mikha'el, and Ya'akov—proper patriarch's names.

My mother having much on her hands with the boys, I was taken most days by my father to the archives, where in idle moments he taught me to read, to write, and to hunger for the knowledge stored therein. Tucked quietly into a back corner with a codex or scroll; few of the scholars even knew I was there.

It was in those days that I developed the habit of reading silently, which many scholars find strange. It was of necessity in order to disappear into the shadows as I did, so as not to be a nuisance to the men, but also, I liked to think upon the meaning of the texts inside my head and not be distracted by the sound of the words. There is something very sacred, I feel, about the written word. While I'm reading something, I don't want anyone else touching it. Spoken words have their power, of course, but when it is written, it is forever.

My father was a quiet, bookish person, as besuits an archivist, and he was not dismayed to have a daughter for a pupil. My uncle, however, was not happy about the matter. He oft complained to his sister my mother of the unsuitability of a girl's devotion to such pursuits.

I worshiped my father's quiet nature and took refuge in it. My mother, though, bewailed my special love for him. At home, he was her devoted husband, but during the day he belonged to scholarship and to me. My uncle thought my filial love unnatural, and he was always attacking our peace. When I was younger, it was ever to urge me to go home to my mother. He came to the archives so many times, my timid father had to ask the governor's guards to stop him at the gate.

My mother was terrified of him. My father, however, could usually shrug him off. He had such a gentle character he could rarely even see conflict. He would defend me, in his own mild way, usually by saying something like 'let the child develop the talents HaShem (God) has given her' or 'she causes no harm, let her follow her own path'. And surely, he could outquote my uncle on any matter of Scripture or the Law.

My mother and uncle had been inseparable, it seems, before her marriage; even his own wife was second to her in his attentions. The only two offspring of aging parents, they had done everything together since infancy. Uncle, being the elder, had the last word on everything. When Grandfather died, Uncle had already taken in hand the running of the family property, so Father was free to enter his own father's occupation.

The real separation of brother and sister, though, came when Mother took ill. The experience brought my parents to cling to one another in worry. Since then, Father has obeyed Mother's every wish, to the dismay even of Uncle. Since she recovered and has been producing for him sons, Father's admiration for her knew no bounds. Uncle was jealous.

His wife my aunt was one of those extraordinarily competent housewives, bursting with sons, three of them, who worked the fields and animals with their father. Our household's status in the Jewish community was due to my father's position–and his father's before him–in the archives; but our prosperity was due to the richness of my grandfather's land, the strong arms of my uncle and cousins, and the keen husbandry of my aunt.

She always had everything firmly in hand, and Uncle, at a loss as to his role in his own household, was always meddling in ours. Father was too gentle to protest; and Mother, tied down with the boys, would usually welcome the intrusion, and leave him to it. If ever I complained, it was 'he is your uncle' or 'he is only doing his duty by you, child'.

I have few memories of good times with my mother. I picture her constantly big with child, her face always busy around the hearth surrounded by constant noise and the smell of babies' dirty rags. Once she began having all those sons, she saw it her duty to pull me into the women's world, and whenever she had a moment free, she showed me how to make barleycakes, to cart wool and to weave, but she rarely talked to me about things I wanted to talk about. She would joke with Grandmother, 'the girl would rather bury her head in a scroll and bid the rest of the world to fly away.' But I did not laugh. The more fastidious she was in her instructions, the more I pulled away.

I search back through my life to find a picture of my mother to cherish, and my mind goes all the way back to an afternoon when Adam was asleep and Yonah yet unborn in her belly. The house was quiet.

Mother called me into the courtyard under the citron tree and poured us both a cup of pomegranate juice, her long sleeves brushing gently against my hand. There were no men around; we were alone and uncovered in our female intimacy.

We Jews were no different in our style of life from the Parthians. Our house was alike theirs, three stories high and made of sun-dried bricks–for there is little stone in the region– faced with glazed or enamelled tiles of brilliant colours. There were no tiles on the roof, and the beams and pillars of the vaulting were made of palm wood due to the scarcity of timber in the land. We twisted ropes of reed around the pillars and adorned them with colourful designs and painted our doors black with tar. In our courtyard, the corners were adorned with rows of six-petalled rosettes of sculpted plaster painted bright colours.

We Jews of property dressed more like our rulers than like our cousins in Palestine with their stiff embroidered woolens. The cloth of my mother's robe was fine and loose and a long belt tied it between her breasts and around the waist above her swollen belly. Outside our gates, she would wear an elaborate turban tied with strings of beads with a veil covering her hair. In the courtyard she wore only an underveil, which lifted in the breeze, and I looked upon her face.

The tree was full of fruit, and they reflected a yellow light upon her cheeks and the black ringlets of her hair. The breeze gave me a breathful of her perfume. The blossoms were still abundant, and the buzz of bees somehow accentuated the silence of the quiet afternoon. The six-petalled plaster rosettes in the corners had been freshly painted by the slaves in vibrant blue and yellow, still wet enough that I could smell the linseed oil in the paint. All the columns had been given a fresh coat, as well. Never would Grandmother have suffered a single barleycorn's-span of the house to fall into disrepair.

I feared Mother would put me to labour picking citrons, but she was too tired to think of work. She stroked my hair and asked me, 'Daughter, what is your favourite fruit?'

I lifted my cup and said, 'pomegranate. It is the fruit of knowledge.'

'My thoughtful daughter, I should have known you would choose for meaning rather than taste.' There was not the reproach in her voice then that there would be in later years.

'And yours, Mother'?

'The citron. By itself the taste is bitter, but with a spoon of honey it is a drink for lovers.'

'So, you, Mother, too, choose for meaning.'

She laughed, and began plaiting my hair. We spent the rest of that delicious hour in silence or chatting of this or that while she gently fixed my tresses.

Whenever I think of my mother, it is that face, ringed in yellow light, I see.

Father, of course, I picture at the archives, and there are many tender memories.

When there were no enquiries from scholars, we would sit together at a table, each at our copying. He would let me roll and store scrolls and called me his 'apprentice', which made me feel so proud. I was not supposed to refer to 'our little game' at home, of course, which would never have occurred to me to do. But for me, it was no game.

Father bathed in perfume, too, a different scent from my mother's. He wore a white linen tunic reaching to the ankles, a woolen robe and a white mantle, and *tzitzit* (ritual fringes) in blue and white wool on the four corners of his hem. We were not strict about mixing linen and wool. He walked with a staff with a carved wooden head, and from his girdle dangled the impressive clay seal of the government with his name and title on it. He wore the wrappe turban appropriate for his age, entwined with red ribbons to indicate his rank, and long hair and a full beard, though Parthians are often clean-shaven. We dressed like our rulers, but we were not ashamed to wear the evidence of our faith. Jews are highly respected in Babylonia. Once Uncle stopped intruding, I never once at the archives heard a word of disrespect spoken to my father.

When not safe at the archives, I escaped when I could from the household and from the town, though it was entirely forbidden, to a cave I had discovered in the hills beyond the walls, where I went in search of healing herbs and other treasures. Here, I would read scrolls surreptitiously borrowed from the archives, some my father would not have approved of. I always returned them—all except one.

As our house was located just inside the southern wall, it was close to the Antioch Gate, where traders entered when they came from the east. I could easily slip in and out with the crowd, as long as I never left it too late. The gates would be closed an hour or so after sundown, and often traffic in the hours just after dusk was slighter and the guard less vigilant. I was skilled at making myself unnoticed by intermingling with the throng. A few times he spotted me, but he must have considered me to be with someone.

The regular grid-like streets of Seleucia emptied into the valley where the bed of the old Tigris touched the edges of town, where the docks were. A canal connected the two rivers at this point, and a bridge at the end of the canal crossed the

Euphrates. Further to its south was the old Babylon and the ruins of the Temple of Esagil behind Nebuchadnezzar's walls. The Euphrates was no longer navigable this far north, but there was much foot traffic. South of the walls and the old city, there was a smaller, older bridge. My cave was on this side of this bridge, before crossing the river, directly south of the Uras Gate where the hills began.

The cave was my sanctuary, and no one, no one knew of it but me. There, when I was not called to chores and my parents believed me elsewhere in the compound, I would gaze at the sky and say aloud the prayers that were in my head. Inside, I built a chapel from the rock, adjusting the walls with boulders and setting up stones in the interior to catch the light and to reflect the tones of Holy Songs.

I kept my scroll there. I call it a scroll, though it is only a fragment, because it is part of a larger work. It is ancient, and I know belongs by right in the archives; for that reason, I never told my father. HaShem took my hand to it, and I know He means for me to have it.

The story of that night, when I left the warmth of home and set off into the wilderness with a merchant caravan–the night the angels came for me–traces back to that cave, singing with the Elohim, and a magic spell gone wrong.

# Chapter 2
## The magician's quest

Day after day, left to my own devices, I discovered new treasures in the archives. As I grew older, despite the scholars' frowns, I conversed when I was allowed with the priestly students of the Pharisees. They were scholars of Holy Scripture, but they had little knowledge or interest in the old tongues, which was my passion.

As keepers of the foreign language works at the archive, it has been a tradition for the scholars in my family to learn the languages of the peoples of the Land Between the Rivers. So, I learned to read and write not only the languages of the Hebrews but also those of our rulers, and to recognise the symbols of ancient Shinar and Chaldee. Anything ancient was amusing to me, and I loved the antiquities because they were old. My father, having only a daughter for so many years, schooled me in the knowledge, and despite my youth, I was able to read some small documents.

My study of languages, nourished by my father's tutelage and encouragement, was sharpened by the practice of writing, every chance I could get. I had writing materials aplenty at the archives, as mud from the two rivers provided an endless supply of clay tablets. I have always felt a great desire to express my thought and to safeguard that thought forever, as if each piece I recorded would someday be joined together with the thoughts of others to construct something–Wisdom.

But my writings were all disjointed, unconnected. My

knowledge was a pile of unorganised scraps, bits of information that answered the question what? but not the question why?

Once I saw a dream. I saw Avraham standing next to 'the Chaldees' atop a mountain. He spake not, but I understood that he wanted me to join them on the mountain.

What could it mean? The story is that Avraham came from 'Ur of the Chaldees', though the kingdom of the Chaldees was not for many generations after. Which did my vision invoke, the myth or the history?

The Saints of the Yachad (the Community [of Essenes]) would say it is the Feeling Self that sees a dream. But in those days, having no one else to turn to for guidance, I asked my father to read it for me. 'Think upon what it is that the Chaldees represent to you,' he suggested, 'and what was your heart's feeling about this when you saw it.'

All day long I ruminated upon this. Was there something Avraham, the Chaldees, and I had in common? What was it that was beckoned to on the mountain? And how did I feel about it?

I wrote:

> Chaldee is in our blood. Avraham came from the land of the Chaldees, and when I hold in my hand the tablets from Ur or Eridu, I transport into the past; I hear His voice as He must have first spoken to the forefather of all. The patriarch, who understood the language of trees and of birds, knew the True Name of God. He must have known the right words with which to answer.

I told Father of my thoughts, and he said, 'You are guided to the languages of the ancients. Now in your life, you must find out why.' I knew that my Dreaming Self, as I would later describe it, referred to the myth.

Then at the archives one day, when all the scholars were elsewhere, I was rummaging through the tablets and parchments on the shelves, and my eye hit upon two covers of parchment, containing between them an ancient fragment of clay. I lifted the covers to see glyphs I knew to be from those times. It was only a partial document, a small shard, appearing to be perhaps the upper right-hand corner of a larger tablet. The text was composed of old Amorite words written in Shinar wedgewriting.

Almost all of the words I didn't know, and there were many words missing from nicks and scratches in the parchment. I focused on the top line, the title of the document. The last part of it was clear to me, and drew me like a lodestone to a sacred rock. It said ...true name.

I reached for the parchment and felt at once blessed. I knew what it was. It was a magic spell for learning the True Name of God.

I pleased myself to imagine that the inscriber of this cuneiform fifty generations ago in ancient Ur or Eridu had been a female magician, and fancied myself in mystical communication with this Chaldee *maga* (female magician) from the past. I would continue her quest. I would conjure her to know the secret that she once knew. I would devote myself to the study of Chaldee magic and uncover the missing letters in the spell, the missing bits of the tablet, in the language the forefather spoke, to learn the True, most ancient Name of God.

I copied the notches of cuneiform onto a piece of parchment and kept it in the pocket of my sleeve as a talisman, the shard itself I kept in my cave.

I should have been ashamed to commit theft, especially from my father's royal patrons, but I was certain that the document had fallen to me by divine will. I suppose I intended to return it once I had studied it sufficiently. If everything hadn't happened that night, perhaps I would have done.

The Chaldees were the most excellent of astronomers. They told Alexandros they had been observing the stars for 473,000 years and possessed the ancient knowledge therein. They made great magic by harnessing divine energy from the firmament.

Just so are the names of the ancient gods of the Hebrews recorded, and they are said to have their movements in the heavens. But I knew no magi in Babylon to consult.

I did enlist my father's willing tutelage to further study the languages of the Amorites, but I had to guard secret my interest in magic. No one in my family would have approved. Sorcery is forbidden according to the Law, and Pharisees like my father were suspicious of witchery.

Though I had no teacher and no supplicant, I read about magic, collected recipes for simples, and especially memorised the words of power to drive out demons. My desire, though, was not for performing tricks like those you see at market.

A mountebank may cause you to remark, 'That was a fine trick; wonder how he did that?' Only real magic can make you throw your arms and head to the sky and sing praise to the Elohim. My search was for the Lost Wisdom of the Magi, the magician's quest for God.

The True Name of God

In ancient times each land had its god, whose name was called in their own tongue. But the one God, whose true name is unutterable, had no land. He was wherever the sun shone and wherever the breeze blew upon the water. By what name was he called? When the great magus Moshe spoke the Name before Pharaoh, Pharaoh fell speechless to the ground. The trumpet blasts of the *shofar* (ram's horn) and the sound of the Name brought down the walls of Jericho. By what name was he called before Moshe, before the languages of the people were scattered at the Tower? What was His name then?

YHWH is not the true name of God. It means 'I am'–the magician's calling card. God said to Moses from the acacia tree: 'I am what I am'. To know the Name is the magician's challenge.

The gods of other peoples were called by different names. Or were they all the same god called by a different name in different tongues? Before there were all of these, there must have been an older god, from whom all others sprang and whom our God consumed in his greatness. In the beginning was the Word, and in the Name is Power, so before there were all of these, there must have been a Name.

For powerful magic like our forefathers possessed, the God of Avraham must have been addressed by his true name and in the original tongue of the forefathers. I made lists of holy titles; magic we still know invokes them accordingly. Ba'al Shamem, El Elyon, Elohei Shamayim, Iao Sabaoth, Shem HaMeyu–names of the ancient gods of the Hebrews, and of the goddesses–Succoth-Benoth, Ashtaroth, Lilith the Bird-footed, Ashima of the Doves, Anatha of the Lions. I invoked them by name according to the prayers I presented, for they each have unique energies.

Much of magic involves names, letters and numbers and geometric proportions which are qualities of the deity. I counted the letters by their numerical values in Hebrew, or Akkadian for the older ones, as magical forces respond to certain values, and the old names of God are embedded within secret alphabets. I made notes on the meaning of the numbers derived, notes such as this:

> The word of the Four-Letter Name of God–YHWH, whose numbers total 26, which can be reached by total-ing the values of Love-13 and Unity-13. Thus, is God Unity manifested as Love.

The ancient belief that God had created the world via words, combinations of letters, was directly linked to mysterious ideas concerning the various names of God. It was said, for example, that the Torah consists entirely of permutations of these names. Bezalel, who constructed in the desert the Tabernacle that housed the Ark containing within it the original Tablets of the Law, it was said that he knew how to combine the letters of the Divine Names with which heaven and earth were created.

A treatment for melancholy:

Recite the names of the tribes of Israel, in reverse order
to that which is on the High Priest's breastplate of Urim
and Thummim—as the last shall be first and the first
shall be last.

Benyamin, Yosef, Asher, Gad, Naftali, Dan, Zevulon,
Issachar, Yehudah, Levi, Shimeon, Reuven

So doth God love us as he loved our forefathers.

In those days, I knew nothing of Rome, I knew nothing even
of Jews beyond Seleucia. Now, my every thought is of how the
world should be and how we might create it thus. But then,
my every desire was to discover the secret Name of God. Even
my dreams were preoccupied with this pursuit.

I filled dozens of scrolls with notes such as these. I even wrote
some exercises on tablets in Chaldee, though I haven't included
any of those here. In truth, with all the sheets of papyrus, the
cowskin scrolls or scribblings on pieces of ibex leather, notches
on clay tablets or ostraca (pottery shards) piled in corners, on
shelves and in jars wherever was my domicile, I never went back
to read them again. Most of the ones I gathered with me on my
travels ended up burned at Secacah (Qumran) or Jerusalem,
anyway. And, Sisters, you have seen most of my writings since
my arrival in Alex (Alexandria), the ones I'll admit to.

It is only now that I am old and spend so much of the day
seated on this bench, overlooked by the precious shelves of our
Academy, that I have looked back through the old scratchings.

So, although I cannot avow to have uncovered any miraculous mystery during these childish years, I do include a few

writings I made when I was that age. My father kindly sent them to me in his aging years with a delegation from Babylonia. When I received the shipment, I did finally believe myself truly loved. It was as if he were returning a lost, hitherto unacknowledged, part of me to myself.

I had to tell Father about my secret cave, whereby he discovered all the evidence of the childhood secrets I had kept from him, even in our intimacy. Alas, by then he had suffered so much hurt on my account, perhaps he was not loath to set things straight between us, no matter how painful. I never told him about the scroll, though.

Forgive me for skipping ahead in my story. An old woman's mind skips backward and forward in time, at once seeing her own babes in her grandchildren's faces or recounting an afternoon of decades ago as if it were yesterday.

Yet over the shoulder of her youthful memories lurks the shadow of her future, wiser, tireder spirit. It casts its shade upon even the bright spots from the days of her innocence. Thus, her wisdom is not spent, as God requires, in bringing the lessons of her past to the problems of the present. Instead, she wastes her spirit in berating herself for every little act, every little word, every little thought.

For the benefit of my younger audience who do not share an elder's transcendence of time, I will try not to jump forward in my story by impressing upon you my judgments from the point in my life at which I write. I will instead try to portray to you the mind of the girl I was then, flawed but sincere. Thereby you may learn the heart and soul of a young girl, knowing so little but wanting to know so much.

You see, I believed myself far more knowledgeable than all

the Pharisees and more even than my scholarly father. Many of these writings are from when I had no more than twelve or thirteen years. A child is most pretentious at that age. The boys all seek active sport in which to excel in front of the other boys, while the girls cling together in gossipy circles and consider themselves better than those outside. I had no playmates, so I created my own internal theatre as I pledged my heart to God alone:

> I free my mind, letting God's universe in through my nose, my throat, my fingertips. I become part of that universe and throb with humble joy. When I sing Sacred Songs, the rhythms of His universe fall into line. I become filled with wonder and capture the power. HaShem speaks His will if I listen. I hear His voice in my dreams and when I pray.
>
> My uncle says that too much holiness is unseemly for a girl, and the scholars will not answer my questions, but I could tell them things that I know. There are things that I can see that they do not. Though I am weak and sinful, I fear not, for so God has called me, and so will He equip me for the Work.

Though I shared with my father everything about my studies and readings, my pledges to God I kept to myself, and I told no one about the magic.

In secret I read the Treatise of Shem, the Book of the Watchers and the Songs of the Sage; and foreign works such as the Chaldee Book of Numbers and the Oracles of Gergis. I read the works of Manetho, Berossus and Bannus; learned the cures and causes of disease in the Prayer of Nabonidus and how to sing in the language of the angels in the Testament of Job. I read about the magic of sacred songs, once accompanied by the wailing blast of the shofar and the tinkle of the sistrum, its strings tuned to the vibrations of the four elements—air, water, earth and fire.

Magical energy

Everything the maga does should have relevance to the energy desired. So, she can also employ actions—lying motionless, casting arrows, breaking a rod in pieces—to symbolise a desired effect, thereby to achieve the purpose through the performance. She can assume in her person a godform as a device, assuming a personality that may be in keeping with the conjuring.

She may likewise use the dead, or pieces of the corpse or the person's implements, once safely consecrated, to transport her power. So, Rachel carried forth the head of Adam—the original *teraphim* (domestic cult objects)—when she left her father Laban. With it she performed great magic, and our forefathers heard through it the voice of their progenitor. None of this knowledge remains to us. The head of Adam disappeared in the mists of the forest.

Though strictly banned nowadays, such skulls were once used for magic. Before the Flood, magicians would plaster over the skulls of enemies taken in war for warriors to use as charms. You may see them in antiquities shops in Alexandria and Palmyra.

The maga sees the numerals, reads the letters, and hears the words from hidden works by opening her heart to the sacred vibrations.

Knowledge becomes emotion becomes an act of will; the three enemies of will are dispersion of energy, laziness, and sensuality.

Moshe the Lawgiver knew how to seize an element from its group soul and imprison it within an object of power.

When an element is released: fire goes south, earth goes north, air goes east, water goes west.

The maga knows that the progress of time is an earthly illusion.

Much of the power of magic comes from the spectacle and the resulting impression evoked from the supplicant. Scholars and men of science and women of mysteries possess knowledge that can easily astound the onlooker into a blessed state.

A statue can 'speak' by means of a pipe inserted near its mouth. Hecate can be made to fly though the air by wrapping some poor bird in cloth and setting it alight. Objects can be moved by steam or by magnets.

Much though magicians desired to keep the knowledge hidden, the first schoolboy to figure it out rushed his stylus to the task of revealing the secret to all and sundry. The ancient miraculous devices are clearly illuminated in diagrams in numerous works. But people are still impressed. They may know that the heavy bronze temple doors, which seem to spring open of their own accord upon the utterance of formulae by the priest, are actually powered by steam from the priest's fire, but the spectacle still fills their hearts with the power of the divine.

The study of magic has much to do with the physical realities of the universe. The older I become, through all my adolescent romance with magic, my later sophistication with the Yachad, and everything I saw during the war, the more I believe that all magic lies within the reach of Man and within the realm of the earthly plane. I will go to my deathbed believing that one day we will know the answer to absolutely everything.

## Chapter 3
## Betrayal

Now I may begin to tell you, Sisters, of how it came to pass that one night I was sitting at my family's table and the next day setting off into the wilderness with a troupe of gypsy merchants.

Many pressures and confusions were coming to a climax inside my head at that time—the constant persecution from my uncle, my studies and the influence they had on me, my emotional reliance upon my father. Maintaining the solitary secret of my magical studies, not to mention the clandestine trips to the cave, was also a strain. I would later explain it as my Acting Self incurring stress that my Dreaming Self would not acknowledge.

In the household, all was disharmony. No one seemed to fit in their proper place. Grandmother did all the work of wife, as Mother was too busy with the boys. She strove to order the family according to her will before she should die, and constantly told us so. Mother never had a moment for herself, missing Father's companionship during the day, and wishing for anyone else for a daughter but me.

Whenever anyone wanted me, I had sneaked away to my cave, and when I was at home, I was constantly scolded. The boys, ever ignorant as youngsters are of anyone else's concerns, constantly caused havoc. Father always had his head in the clouds.

Uncle sought to upset the balance of my parents' bond. Since

Adam had begun his schooling, he had become particularly critical of my inclinations. He was increasingly jealous of the refuge I found with Father, and angered by my deference only to him. He spoke increasingly to my mother, and she, hearing what she herself wished, would listen.

One autumn afternoon, I was unlucky enough to run into my uncle on my way home after enjoying the sunset at my cave. I didn't notice him until he was right in front of me. It was typical of the sort of altercations we had.

'Sophia, what are you doing outside the gates? At this hour, you should be with the women.'

'Yes, I shall be late.' Fortunately, my basket was full of juniper berries I had picked, so I was able to seem as if I had been undertaking a chore for my mother, but still he frowned fiercely. Another maiden might have been suspected of having a boy hidden in the brush. He looked at me as if I were hiding a scroll–which I probably was. I moved the basket of berries forward in my arms as if to imply that my mother was in a great hurry to receive them.

He cast a manipulating eye. 'You would do anything to avoid chores, wouldn't you?'

'It is not so, Uncle. Mother and Grandmother have much to do, and it is my pleasure to help them.' I lied.

'Where have you been this afternoon?'

'In the juniper groves.'

'Does your mother know you went beyond the gates? Does she know your mind?'

He knew this would anger me. 'Only the angels know my mind. And why should she heed, if I've completed my chores?'

He spoke angrily. 'I know you. You've never completed your

chores. And your responsibility does not end with the chores. Do you not think that your mother wants you at hand?'

'I shall go to her immediately and ask her what she requires.' But he wouldn't let me go.

'It's time you were married, Sophia. You are the only daughter; it is your duty to your father to marry. Itamar married well; it is because of the wealth of your mother that he is able to pursue his scholarly idleness.'

He well knew that to insult my father would make me angriest of all. 'Father is not idle. He never ceases in his work. Besides, if Mother is so wealthy, she will have no need for a rich son-in-law. Mother knows I have no wish to be married, and so does Father.'

'You do not know what is best for you,' he said.

'I know that I am too young to marry.'

'You're no younger than was your mother when Itamar came along.' I was startled by the way he emphasised the name of my father, as if cursing him.

'Marriage matures a maiden,' Uncle said. 'If he may grant that you are young, you must at least begin preparations for betrothal.'

I should be learning 'the society of women', he said. I should be studying 'the womanly arts', he said. By this he meant cooking and embroidery. I was not about to let him know of my pride in knowing of lost womanly arts—herbs and magic.

There was something he often said when he spoke of his intentions for my future. 'Itamar would miss your company at the archives,' he often said. But this day he spoke it differently, and with a sneer, 'Itamar will lose his little disciple. You may be sure of it.'

'Father is glad to have me at the archives,' I said. I was tempted to tell him how he called me 'apprentice', but that would have given him a weapon to carry back to my mother and grandmother.

Usually this conversation was in front of Grandmother, where he could garner support. This time it seemed more ominous, but I tried not to worry about him 'making sure of it'.

There had been an incidence at the archives which caused me some unease. I'd overheard one of the scribes saying to my father, 'How fares your wife, Sofer (Scribe)?'

'Completely recovered, *baruch HaShem* (Thank God).'

'I'm so happy to hear it, but I had thought...' and he indicated his head in my direction.

'Just until she marries,' he said.

'Oh, I meant no criticism. She's ever so well behaved, so quiet one would barely know she was there, and quite as scholarly as the boys.'

I didn't know whether to be flattered by the scholar's compliment or hurt by my father's keeping 'our little game' secret even at the archives, but I wasn't apprehensive about the reference to my marrying. As far as I intended, that 'until' would be forever.

I read Scripture very intensely during the winter months of sowing; and I had been even more inattentive to the family than usual, escaping to my cave whenever I could. The angry conversations between my uncle, grandmother and father had been increasing, my mother trying to voice her wishes while tending to this baby boy or that, my father deflecting all rancour with geniality, and I, my nose in a scroll, had ignored them.

My thoughts were of God and prayers and scrolls and Holy Songs and incantations. I paused in my zeal only long enough to say 'No' when the subject of betrothal was raised, usually by Grandmother. With my father's protection, I thought, I would be safe.

One night at the beginning of Purim, as I had long feared, all the tensions around me coalesced into one big argument.

I had spent the daylight hours in my cave, practicing a ritual called the Equilibrium, and some strange things had happened.

As soon as I rattled at the gate, Grandmother yelled, 'Where have you been, as usual, girl? And scarce two hours till sunset,' as Mother dumped into my hands a steaming cloth full of tiny, smelly reed warblers, still warm from the blanching. Without waiting for an answer or to instruct me in the plucking, they moved on to scolding the slaves–'the other slaves,' my Feeling Self grumbled.

One sliced citron and arranged it on a plate. Another took the bread from the oven and poured spiced olive oil into a saucer for dipping. The freedwoman helped Mother begin carrying things out to table.

At this point Yonah and the other boys, accompanied by one of my cousins, burst in carrying a huge ray-finned mangar he'd caught, all chafing in one breath to tell Mother and Grandmother of their angling adventure and to boast of his prize. We females, the slaves and me, too–he was my darling baby brother, after all–we all fell over ourselves with praise for the young fisherman. How 'all thanks to him' we would have such a fine meal. So enormous was 'Yonah's big fish', we joked, that we were relieved it did not 'swallow him whole'.

The two rivers had poured their spring riches upon our table. As well as the mangar dressed with citron slices and warbler meatballs and the bread and olive oil, there was barley mixed with seeds and herbs, eggs, nuts, beans, leeks, lentils, onions and garlic, figs, apples, grapes, cow's and goat's milk, butter, goat's cheese and yogurt from the cold room.

I had picked a basket of blackberries from the woods around my cave, a contribution which did not, needless to say, invite the same laudits as Yonah's had done. At the end there would be sticks of sugar cane which the boys would fight over and apricots with date syrup.

The family meal, though usually less eventful than on that fateful night, was always agony. Aunt, Uncle and Grandmother did most of talking, with Father and Mother contributing the occasional mild comment. I only got deeper into trouble when I joined the conversation, so I tended to stay as quiet as possible.

After the reciting of the Shema (the Shema Yisrael prayed twice daily), the meal began as usual, me lost in a cloud thinking other thoughts. Grandmother sat at the table, leaving Mother to fuss over the boys, while the freedwoman and I served the men. As usual I remained as silent as the servant while I served, and as silent while I ate as one who knows an attack may come at any moment.

As well as an amphora of wine for Father and Uncle there were great jugs of pomegranate juice, which I drank greedily because the day had been warm but also in hope that no one would say anything to me.

My aunt and cousins were not eating at our table, and I wondered if that fact bode ill for me. Surely enough, my uncle introduced the usual topic: I was 'far too holy for a proper maiden'.

My uncle brought up the marriage issue, addressing my

mother but for my ears, saying 'it was time I was betrothed' since I had reached a marriageable fourteen years.

A friend of his had spoken for me for his son, a boy a few years older than I, and my parents agreed him to be a good match. I knew the boy, Huna, and he was goodly enough, but I wanted to spend my days reading books and loving God, not washing clothing and sweeping floors. I wanted to spend my evenings in study and prayer, not caring for a husband.

If Adam took to his schooling, he would go into the archives, and if he showed an aptitude, he would follow in Father's position, Uncle was explaining. In any case, as a girl I knew it wouldn't be me. But I did think I could yet accompany them. Father had never pressured me about marriage or about staying home from the archives, so I hid behind him and ignored everyone else.

I kept looking at my father. I was not such a fool as to expect him now to reveal 'our little game' to the company. But I did expect him to mention my scholarly nature. I expected some words from him asking what may be my own desire. He said nothing.

The rest of the family, however, never had everyone had so much to say. They all had some dirt to throw. Grandmother, Uncle, Mother, Father–even Adam and the little ones had a few arrows. Here was their opportunity to chide the maidservant who never finished her chores.

First, they started on 'what was good for me'; then it became 'what was wrong with me'. Everything I had ever done wrong, every fault and failing, was reviewed and examined in loud voices. I had no sooner answered one accusation than another would be flung in my face.

As each family member cast their stones, it seemed they had all saved everything they ever wanted to accuse me of, or make me do or stop doing, to bombard me with them all at once. I was even blamed for things that were not of my making; everyone aired their grievances against everyone, while aiming their poison at only me.

I had nothing to respond. I was guilty of it all. Everyone had their place and their role in the family but me. I was not in the home when I was needed, and I was bothering serious, important men at the archives. I was selfish, sinful, a wicked girl. The only justification I had for my behaviour was the belief in my Calling, but how could I speak of that to them? They would think me mad.

However, at the point in the evening when Uncle would usually turn toward me and begin a long lecture, backed by Grandmother, instead, he was silent. It was my father who spoke.

'Sophia, now that Adam has begun his schooling, he may begin apprenticeship at the archives. Grandmother is infirm, and you are needed at home to help Mother with the younger ones.'

He barely stopped for me to gasp. 'Your betrothal has been agreed with Huna's father.'

It was from Father's mouth I was hearing these harsh words, and the finality of his tone indicated that the decision was immutable. I looked at him, but he simply smiled silently in that passive way of his, as if thinking 'there is no reason anyone should be distressed'. He had even used the word 'apprentice-ship', as if to dig further deeper into my heart his betrayal of 'our little game'. I was stunned to the core, struck without a word to reply.

Now as I recount it, I realise that matters had been leading up to this; there had been indications all around showing me that things were not going to stay the way they were. But at the time I was completely overcome. It was like a seizure of the earth. I couldn't believe my father would betray me. All my young life I loved learning and read scrolls while others played in the alleys. And now my entire family, my father too, wanted me to give that up for the sake of a boy? Should all my reading have gone to waste? Should my knack for magic and ancient scripts be tamped down, replaced by the mundane skills of the hearth?

Feeling attacked to the very depths of my being, I became increasingly distraught, crying and beating at my robes. The missiles fell so fast and unrelenting; I began to say things I later regretted; incoherent things spilt from the depths of my gut.

'I am a Nazirite like the *Nevi'im* (prophets) of old, fed with the wine of ancient learning,' I announced. 'You cannot make me to break my vow.'

It was not only that I was too young and desired to read the Torah rather than sweep floors, I screamed at them. God wished for me to remain chaste. 'I am the Lord's bridesmaid,' I railed. 'He calls to me. I cannot belong to a man.'

I even screamed at my father, my sweet father, 'Why do you not defend me?'

'Daughter, this is how it must be,' he said. 'You are grown, now. This is the way of the world.' I think he intended it kindly, but I did not take it so.

The last thing I can clearly remember is standing up in front of my father, mother, my uncle, Grandmother, brothers and everyone, shouting something that ended with 'the angels have come for me'.

Sisters, I avow that ever are the hopes and dreams of young people scorned in this world, be it Babylon, Jerusalem or Alexandria, and I have heard many tales of discord among families. But, can you not pity me? Whatever may have further transpired that night, after an evening meal such as this, any girl may have suffered to awaken in that house.

My eyes swollen with tears, I ran so fast into the alley I fell in my haste on the step at the gate.

There was more than that, though, more than the horrible meal—in the alley. I was in such a state I believed it was my Dreaming Self that lived it. That must be why for so many years I didn't remember.

My shoulder burned; there was blood on my leg and pain in my groin. Among the tears swam a vision of my uncle's face, victorious, and the phrase 'proper maiden, proper maiden' rang in my ears. My heart shouted back, 'I'm no proper maiden, and I don't belong here.'

The Antioch Gate was still open, and I got out easily. The guard is more mindful of who comes in than who goes out.

I ran across the hills to my cave, too fast for anyone to follow, and never had I been so glad of its secrecy. Not intending to offer excuses for my absence, no bundle had I left in my bed. My family knew I was gone. They did not know I was not coming back.

In a state of heightened sensitivity, I spent many hours through the night there in prayer, my emotions rubbed raw. I made an infusion to call myself, and I included a bit of oil of kerm-oak—the scribes in the archives made ink from the galls, but the oil from the bark has magical qualities. It was something I did when I want to make a big decision. I daubed ashes in my hair from the fire where I had boiled the bark.

Unwisely, I continued the ritual of the Equilibrium, as the hour assigned for its performance had not passed. I was exhausted, and had eaten only a few mouthfuls at my family's table; the concoction must have had a strong effect on me.

The Equilibrium involves first visualising symbols of energy, as the maga uses ritual to create a spiritual cosmos within her. Pronouncing the godname rhythmically according to specified tempo…regulating the breath…locating sounds within the body…linking sounds with head movements. Her whole body becomes a vehicle of the divine influx. She feels the vibration of the Name, which expands to fill the sphere of the universe.

Then, of course, she must go back by doing everything in reverse, and stomp ten times on the ground, once for each of the operating forces of universe, to return to the physical world.

I didn't get that far.

My mind took off into flights of fancy with figures from the past, words from my reading. There were too many to remember, and they became absorbed into something greater. I began to dance and sing, making up words and tunes as they came to me in the voices. I wonder what I would have sounded like to a passer-by, but at the time I was convinced I made a divine sound.

There was a flat floor of soft soil from the silting of the Euphrates that was comfortable to my sandaled feet, but in my euphoria, I knocked against the rocky walls many times. I must have danced for a long time, a taxing exercise when performed inside a cave, because I was already panting when

I began my ascent up the hill.

The mystical experience is about neutralising the intellect by an assault on the senses; the maga loses her sense of self, and the mind becomes a tabula rasa to permit the intrusion of divine energies. So indeed, had I bombarded my head with images—eagles, arrows, the sun and stars.

The words of my song spun around in a cone of light rising heavenward through the cave ceiling, joining hands with the Elohim in ecstatic unity. My consciousness swirled with the stars, and with each upward turn expanded, until my spirit spread out over the entire world.

'Toward the West, the West', I looked. Were the Elohim so instructing me? It felt so. And it was glorious. I saw a window of light in the night sky and I flew through it like an arrow, finding myself suddenly outside. I ran from the cave like a whirlwind embracing the desert. I knew that surely HaShem intended for me adventure.

For a maiden my age to leave home and family so suddenly and set out across the wilderness was a frightening thing, and at the time I was so confused. It is hard to write, Sisters, that I did the right thing. But I remember the feeling of God's will shining down as if illuminating me, raising the hair on my head. I must have had some of my wits about me, too, since I remembered to grab the Chaldee tablet.

By the time I came to my senses on the hill, the feeling had changed. My stomach was grumbling with hunger, and I was covered in blood and ashes and the dirt of having not slept the night, a layer of grime covering me like a blanket of shame that the world would surely see. I was not running 'toward the West', embracing the power of the universe. I was slinking away in disgrace from the witness of the morning sun.

Besides anger at my family, a fire that has dimmed but never fully extinguished, I remember feeling overwhelmed by the sense of 'naughtiness', a perception of myself with which I was then familiar, accustomed as I was to being berated at home for every chore I had not done. This falls away with age, Sisters.

It has been many years since I berated myself for something that others wished of me. Those of you who are still young, banish such thought from your minds. Decide what it is that you are, and climb that hill.

# Chapter 4
## Exodus

What awakened me back to the earthly world was a strange incident. I was startled to silence when a fox crossed my path and stopped dead still, looking at me with emotionless eyes, perhaps curious at my raving. He stayed ever so tranquil, unafraid. I approached him not; nor did he move his position.

It was only when the sound of people's voices entered my awareness that he scurried off, straight as an arrow toward the scruff. There were hundreds of them, Arabs—a spice caravan camped out on the hill readying for voyage west to the rich cities of the coast.

It was quite dark, and the Evening Star was bright; it must have been late. I had crossed the river but was not wet, so I must have circled the city to the south and crossed by the bridge connecting the two banks.

I do not doubt I looked like a madwoman, my robe and hair wild and dishevelled. I had bloody scratches all over my arms, and the blood dripping down the inside of my leg peeped from below my hemline. Indeed, I probably looked like a ghost from the Underworld.

The people all around me, they were stunned. I still had my prayer veil draped over my head; somehow, I'd managed to hold onto it. So, most of that time they must have seen only my mouth. Still stained red with oak oil, it looked like the colour of old blood, they said. I was even drooling.

I had run up the hill loudly ranting and raving. Not that I

remember. I only know this because suddenly everything was quiet, and it made me realise I had been making a great noise.

The women said I was shouting all the way up the hill, whirling around and tearing at my robe. No one could remember the exact words I spoke, frightened as they were by my appearance and demeanour.

My behaviour was so strange and my words so unusual. They said I spoke in the poesy of a seer, betwixt crazed ranting like a Thracian navi. I spoke in the language of Scripture and the imagery of dreams. Ordinary words were inadequate to express my thoughts; they just didn't seem strong enough.

In my heightened state I spoke, they said, that 'we shall journey across the stars under clouds illuminated by storm and amid the destruction of fire sweeping across human habitation', and 'there will be great upheavals in the lives of men, and eagles shall be beheaded and sprout new heads'. Again and again, I stressed the urgency of journeying 'toward the West, the West'.

There were references to 'Assyrians', I remember hearing myself say it, which made no sense to anyone. It made sense to my Feeling Self, though. Scriptures record the prophets' words, and my eyes read them. Once the Assyrians were the enemy at the gate. Now, it is the Romans, who persecute Jews in a continuance of oppression back to the Assyrians.

It was the Dreaming Self which spake the prophecy. Though I did not yet know the Ossaean doctrines about the Dreaming Self, the Acting Self and the Feeling Self, I understood this. The references to Assyrians and beheaded eagles meant nothing to traveling Nabatu (Nabataean) merchants, but images of stars and a journey West spoke to them of their nomadic lives.

None of the merchants afterward admitted to seeing a fox,

though the spot was not far from where I first encountered them.

There was an impromptu gathering of the men, the leaders of the company, and most of them were urging the natural and proper response to my appearance–to notify the authorities in the city. My sudden arrival was causing some consternation, as the caravan was set to depart on the morrow at dawn. There were evidently several other crises to be dealt with that morning. The group was within earshot, but my senses were heightened. Despite unfamiliarity with their dialect, I heard every word.

'Our contract clearly states the procedure,' one man insisted.

'Our duty is to the host city,' said another. 'If Seleucia is crossed, future watering rights could be under threat.' He appeared to be the boss.

'Persia represents almost half my year's trade,' another commented.

The men all drew several paces away from me. They wouldn't touch me, and steered well away. The women, however, were under the spell of my 'prophecy' and kept intruding upon the discussion. They squealed at their husbands to 'have pity on the child', and took them aside to whisper covert warnings. I might be a powerful witch who would curse their voyage.

'We know not what has happened to her, but look, she's bloodied and bruised from head to toe. We can see that she is in danger, and we surely cannot return her there,' said one woman who seemed to be from the boss-man's family.

'She has begged refuge; listen to what she has to say,' interjected others.

'She is touched by spirits,' said a girl with a gentle face, and

43

she looked me in the eye and smiled.

The men were silent and turned to me, expecting a word.

I let out a wail, 'Do not return me to whence I came, and do not inform the city. The will of God has led me to you.' I said this so forcefully that the company was again stunned, and raised no complaint when, after a few minutes of silence, some of the women at the front timidly put out their hands to take me off to get a new robe.

The women led me to a tent with a bundle of grass tied up and hanging above the entrance, where we would hang a *mezuzah* (a written prayer hung at gates), and a red stripe painted around the inside. They gave me some rags and a bitter black tea with an aroma of cardamom that made my eyes twitch, poured from a narrow brass pitcher with a long arching spout like a hook.

They asked me about my mother, and I cried, but when they asked me about my father, my cries were so fierce I felt my body turning inside out. They brought warm water, and the midwife cleaned a scratch on my leg. Where had that come from? I heard her whisper to the woman assisting her the words 'violence' and 'blood'. Later one of the young boys playing around the tent told me that in the midst of my raving I had complained about my shoulder, but the women could find no wound.

I later came to understand my so-called 'prophecy', if you would call it thus, as presentiments of the war. At the time I understood it even less than I do now, Sisters. It seems, though, that I addressed something in the Feeling Selves of all of them, travellers into the future as we were.

Sisters of Alexandria, do not believe that prophets can foretell the future. Those who see can only see what others may also see—the possibilities that lie in wait, the forces in the balance—they bring these to expression in imagery that stirs us. They present to us the possible deliverance of man, to make us one again with God. If we give strength to the anger and to the hope in our hearts by expressing ourselves in a certain manner, this is good. But the future is what we make it; remember that.

How magnificent it would be to know the mind of God. Oh, to rest against an omnipotent shoulder and let the evils of the world flow where they will, to fall into restful slumber and never to mind about tomorrow's tasks. It would be a comfort. Yet it is a deceit of the Feeling Self. God desires us to make our own world.

I have pondered upon this event in my life, and I have read it differently at different times. The final answer may be that, interpret it how I might, that night was a turning point in my life, and that is all. Things happened the way they happened, and if they hadn't, what happened later wouldn't have happened. At the time I believed that I had received a true prophecy, but that because of my sinfulness it had made me ill. The more I thought that the illness was due to my sinfulness, the more ill I became.

I ate a few mouthfuls of barley and slept all afternoon and night in the tent with the red stripe. In the morning before we departed, I tried to keep out of the men's way, fearful that they might change their minds. I stood on the road heading to Narmalchan and looked back homeward.

From the hilltop, the view of Babylonia stretched beyond, down the luscious Euphrates, her sister Tigris glistening in the distance curving around Seleucia, Ktesiphon and the other towns sprouting in various directions. The farmlands on either side, rich soil from two fertile rivers, swelled with spring crops, barley and sesame. Groves of palm trees lined the banks, from the fruit of which we made bread, wine and honey.

The yellow orange of the early sun flickered on the river. The ancient cities of Akkad and Shinar—Kish, Cuthah, Nippur, Uruk, Lassa—glistened green and gray on the hills, crumbling ziggurats at the summits, strung out like polished jewels on a heavy necklace of jade—where Judah's sons hung harps on willows and refused to sing, where Zion's daughters knelt by the river and wept.

At the time, I was still shaking and delirious; my eyes didn't even see it. But my Dreaming Self must have taken a good look, as the scene returned to my mind's eye many times. I later painted it on a vellum for the Brethren.

There on the cold sandy hill, I turned my face away from this lush land and looked to the West toward the hot sands of the wilderness. I determined in my heart: there is no place in Persia for a girl who loves Wisdom, if even my father will not speak for me. I am indeed too holy for a girl.

At the time, I just wanted to get away. But during the long year travelling across the desert, I realised that I was searching for a place where such holiness is allowed, where they won't force me to be 'a proper maiden'. The caravan was a happy place, and one where my Feeling Self could recover from its wounds, but it was not my true place. I had a different hill to climb.

The Incense Trail had brought this caravan to the Euphrates, bringing frankincense and myrrh from the depths of Arabia. The return journey, carrying silk and spices to Jericho and the

Gaza coast, would take me to a new home.

The demon was upon me. I was familiar with his curse from as early as I can remember, and I struggle to remember my childhood days, so coloured as they were by this darkness. I called him by different names as I grew older, but I think that it was always the same beast.

He would enter me after moments when God had blessed me with extraordinary grace and clarity, though sometimes it was simply that I had been reading a lot or practicing magic too intensely. Cruelly, the divine clarity rarely lasted longer than three days, but the darkness persisted for agonising months, leaving me indelibly wounded each time I reemerged.

As we travelled, I was not yet sensible for many days, sunk in desperate blackness. At night even my dreams were covered in smoke, and I awoke feeling as if I had drunk poison. The black cloud entirely filled my head. I could barely speak, and I would tell the company nothing about my family and why I had run away. Their words were strange to me, and I could only understand some of what was said to me. I didn't return to normal for quite a while. I became very lean.

They gave me nourishment, in bowls of a metallic pottery decorated with curvy script, but I would not eat, and insisted to the women that my body was closed to sustenance. As my bruises and scratches healed, I looked down upon my arms and legs and I could see through the skin to the humours beneath. There I could see the swirling clouds of the demon's influence clogging my veins, blocking any healthy blood.

The only thing I could bear past my lips was the black carda-mom drink, which I came to like and even relish the way it made my eyes twitch. But when they tried to nourish me by giving me camel meat cooked in goat's cheese—it was dried into hard balls they would grind to mix with water—I screamed. I was not skilled enough in their dialect to explain 'camelmeat and milk', so I just pointed to a camel's foot, shaking my head, until one of the women remembered the Jewish laws.

When they gave me a wooden bowl with meat, though they told me it was lamb, I suspected they were trying to feed me onager flesh, and I rudely wasted the meat on the sand. Other items of the caravan diet, like locusts fried in the pan, though not classed as unclean, I considered vile and would not touch.

If I had objected to food cooked over camel dung fires, I should never have tasted hot food. I regret that despite their caring I was distrusting and angry toward the women in their generosity.

There was a girl there who saw that I was troubled and helped me. It was she who had turned the mood of the confrontation, when the men wanted to turn me in to the city authorities, by calling me 'touched'. I believe it was to her that I owed my acceptance in the company.

Her name was Shu'dat. She paid me much heed, and I slowly took my head from the cloud to notice her.

'You appear to be in need of a family,' she said to me. 'Ours is small. We would welcome you.'

She was a few years above my age, born on the road. She travelled with her father Abda, a rich incense trader from Rekem, which the Kittim call Petra, her mother having died many years back. Shu'dat convinced her father to take me into their fire.

'Ours was a lonely tent until you came,' she said sweetly.

Abda gave me the donkey that carries my pack, and inside the blanket under the saddle I tucked my scroll, sealing it away from the sweat of the animal from below and from water from above—though in the wilderness that would be unlikely.

Shu'dat assigned me duties around the tent. The black cloud followed me everywhere, but the daily routine of travel and camp soothed me. I was glad to have chores to do to quiet my mind.

I was in such a sorry state, I barely understood at the time the goodness of Shu'dat. So patiently did she give her love and caring to me during that time when I could not respond, that after I recovered—and it was surely she who had cured me—I did not cease to offer her my affection.

Thus, was I rescued from the dark sin within the heart of my family, as was Yosef saved from the dark well, by travelling merchants with nothing but good in their hearts.

Through Narmalchan and Hatra, as long as we were in Parthian lands, I tried to stay behind the camels whenever we came in contact with townsfolk. I didn't want any questions asked.

We travelled a peaceful land. Pax Romana, they called it, the peace of foreign oppression.

The Nabatu had as much reason to hate the Romans as did anyone else. However, animosity toward other nations—the Greeks (Syrians), the Aegyptians—or other Arabian tribes—the Chaulotaei, Sabaeans and Chaulotaei, and Agraei—was more common in the camp than revolutionary sentiment against Rome or the Seleucid rulers. The lands we crossed, I knew of these peoples from reading. The Nabatu knew them from yearly contact; history, language and literature meant little in the face of 300 thirsty donkeys and camels.

Nabatu merchants in a traveling caravan were very little

burdened by the yoke of the foreigner. To them, Romans were border control. They permitted passage, or rather their local lackeys did, according to rules that never changed. The tax was arduous, but as long as there was profit, and there was, negotiations passed smoothly.

Water rights were the immediate concern; these were managed and controlled at the local level. Once negotiated, however, as long as no one tried to cheat with their weights, the agreements usually remained in place in perpetuity, and harmonious relations continued year after year.

The rest of the company were afraid of me at first, but I soon came to know my companions, especially Shu'dat, sweet Shu'dat, who nursed me through the dark days and pulled me out of my black heart and back into the wide beautiful world. Under her love, I began to recover. I began to give readings, and I felt better if they were useful. To give someone else a little piece of comfort seemed to blow away a piece of the cloud.

They pressed upon me the role of company soothsayer, a job I happily accepted. I might not be able to, nor want to, promise them more fits of prophecy. But I could read their palms, advise them on herbs, and talk to them about what was in their hearts and in their destiny. Now I had supplicants for my 'Hebrew magic' as they called it. My services were well in demand, I can assure you, and they fed me well.

In my new happiness, I put on flesh and regained my health.

The children did tease me. 'Make us a spell, come on', 'Work us some Persian magic'. They were usually satisfied by some cheap sleight of hand trick like pulling a white stone from behind their ears or some words–I used Akkadian–spoken over an object for a charm. Or, by suffixing '*la-ah*' on the end of words, it made them sound magical.

Or I would give them a feather, saying it was from the mythical Varenjina bird. Though they knew it full well to be a sandgrouse, they would at least feign to be impressed. The more sincere supplicant, however, is looking for a transformation in their life, and I always took pains to guide them.

Too afraid of demons was I to talk to the dead, but I used some of the rituals I read about in Babylon. I also knew of the divining arts of the Wise Women of Abel and Dan (early Israelite settlements known for divination); they used the ankle-bones of livestock the way we would use stones.

I analysed dreams, observed the patterns of scattered grain, tossed stones or coins against the sand. I looked at the swelling of incense smoke in the air or oil in water. I am sure I was rarely accurate more than half the time, but the supplicant's embracing of the divine would complete the experience.

I didn't feel that I was very successful in prophesying for foreigners nor interpreting their dreams. Perhaps God spoke through me only to believers, or perhaps I was too unfamiliar with the hearts and minds of those from other faiths. The symbols in their dreams meant different things, and correspondingly, the symbols in my prophecy were alien to them. Or maybe it was because I was still a child and had not yet had proper tutelage.

In any case, my readings were usually on matters of the heart, offering people spiritual uplifting, rather than prophecy, divination or legal matters. I did find, though, that wherever our terms of reference conflicted, they accepted the difference as an exotic detail adding spice to the message. Like the way they had taken to my 'prophecy' about 'the Assyrians', even though the reference meant nothing to them.

I learned more during the voyage. These merchants travelled the world from India to Aegypt, and they all had knowledge of foreign lands. Many of the older women were happy to teach me new lore in exchange for a reading. The more I learned of their lore, the more perceptive became my own readings. Each day I learned more of their dialect.

I have read works of foreign peoples, at least those that have been translated into Hebrew, Aramaic or Greek; curiosity toward other cultures was not new to me. But now, not just from reading, with my ears and with my eyes I learned new things. Daily, my delight in learning about the company and their lives and language was further illuminated by my growing love for Shu'dat.

We took an oath of friendship. 'It's an old Arabian custom,' she said. She, with a sharp stone cut the inside of her hand and mine under the third fingers. Then with a piece of her hem, dipped the cloth in the blood of each, and touched it to seven stones lying about, saying some words I couldn't understand. I copied her actions, pledging myself according to her custom.

Our oaths sworn, we returned to camp in time for supper. The camp ate in groups of thirteen, our tent usually along with the family of Afta and sometimes Yatur. Each party was attended by two musicians. They saw the blood spots on our hems and smiled, and gave us the first bowls.

Although my new friend did not share my Jewish rite, we were able to share discussions of everything else. She advised me on my readings, too, with the knowledge of stars her people knew from the Arabians. I felt that my enjoyment of the caravan life and especially the joy of my friendship with Shu'dat were signs that I was in grace.

We travelled ever so slowly. Many families had young children so numerous we couldn't carry them and they became weary—or rather the parents did. There were no Jews in the company, but after we cleared up from the evening meal, while the other women settled their children to sleep and the older children found wood for the fires, I stepped away from the hubbub of camp at the time appointed for evening prayers. Shu'dat often had duties helping her father with his goods for sale for which I was not needed.

The blood came with every moon now. Whatever happened that night, it made me into a woman. From the depart, I was with the women in the company, helping with the cooking while the young girls fetched the water and served, and I slept with Shu'dat in the maidens' tent.

Israelites and Nabatu are not historical friends, though since the days of Jehu both are vassals to Rome. But differences between our peoples in the past did not harm my standing among the company. There were hindrances of language, but I was accepted.

If any one of them ever thought 'unsociable Jew', 'pampered Persian' or any such, they never spake it in my presence. I was here, living among them, so they could only see me for myself, not for some group I represented.

The daily contact of working together breeds love, you must remember, Sisters, and love banishes hatred. In fact, any misunderstandings that resulted from my being a Hebrew or a Persian were laughed away with teasing amusement or friendly curiosity, not criticism or rejection, though the boys could be bothersome when all in a group. Nevertheless, the difference between us was a constant challenge, a challenge faced by me and not by them, as they were among their own.

As the stadia increased from home, the world became bigger before my eyes, and in a way I could never have found in scrolls and letters. I missed the scholarly seclusion of the archives, but I was astonished to realise how solitary my life had been, or perhaps I was astonished at how social I had now become.

At home, it was me, my father and a silent library full of scrolls. Now, it was me and a whole hill full of noisy people. At home, I never knew people in the way I came to know the caravan company. Foreigners were we, they to me and I to them, yet we saw the same beauties, ate by the same campfires, and slept under the same stars.

At home, I'd spent my days reading the works of Man and listening from behind the shelves to the discussions of scholars. I spent my evenings either in the solitude of my cave, if ever I could, or trying to remain as silent as possible in the company of my family. Here, the discourse around me was constant, all about daily matters—the transport of water, the weather, who was to do what task, who said what to whom—and all in a dialect strange to me.

At home, I was an observer; here, a participant. For the first time I felt myself to be a contributing member of a society. We were dependent upon one another and conscious of a fierce defensive pride in the group as a body. I had a role to play within that body, and being sure of that role made me feel useful.

As you may imagine, I had pangs of homesickness, especially after the way I left, and I sorely missed the smell of scrolls and taxing my mind over the lofty contemplations of scholars. My

Feeling Self longed again and again to hear my father's words calling me his 'apprentice'; but the daily companionable hardships, the beauties and the pleasures of caravan life filled my heart with light.

# Chapter 5
## The lost wisdom

On the road, we had much time in the evenings for story-telling. The men wanted to tell tales of far off lands and wars, and recited the lives of the Nabatu kings and generals and their stories.

They told tales of the beauties we passed by. Every tree or valley had a story to tell. Every copse was the remnant of a grove where ancient people listened to the gods. Each rocky mountaintop was the ruins of an ancient tell, or reminded the storyteller of one.

I loved them all, even when it was a story I knew already, as the teller would give to it his own touch. But one evening Abda embarrassed me by taunting the young men, 'Brothers, you've given us the kings and the wars. Our Hebrew cousin wants to hear tales about the olden days.' He said the words teasingly that he had heard me say so often.

'The olden days, ah-hah', said one of the young men, and took up the challenge.

We were gathered around the fire, the sounds of camels snorting and donkeys braying nearby, men clinking their cups after a meal, and older children, not yet abed, turning their heads up in anticipation of entertainment. There was still light, as there were twelve or thirteen hours of sun during the summer months, and the setting sun shimmered over the vastness of the rapidly cooling Syrian sands around us.

And so, it was against the backdrop of this perfect caravan

scene that I heard the story of the Treasure of the Nabatu:

The Treasure of the Nabatu

Since the days when our city Petra was called Rekem, our people were nomads. Settlement was forbidden, the planting of grain punishable by death, and we kept no slaves. Women were honoured as equal to men, and our ruler called himself not king but friend of the people.

Travelling merchants, we grew rich from the spice trade. We carried on our camels frankincense from the forests of Hadhramaut, with its leaping venomous red serpents, and gold from Sheba to the coast of Gaza, from whence our wares were traded across the Great Green Sea. So rich were we that we sent 1000 talents of frankincense in tribute to Darius the Great King. Every year 10,000 camel-loads of our spice are carried to Rome. There were temples to our god Dushara and his betyls in Alexandria, Rhodes and Puteoli.

We stored our property in tombs made of sandstone and porphyry. And in a secret location up a holy summit with only one approach, climbing steps carved in stone, was a rock–*petra* in the Greek tongue–where we carved a tomb to hold our treasures, our silver, all the rich profits from our trade.

Alexandros coveted the sources of frankincense and myrrh and our treasures, but he never found them, and ruined Gaza in revenge. Once the Greek soldiers found the spot, but we slaughtered every one of them.

For the sake of my love of ancient languages, Abda told me

a further detail to the story. The learned men of Rekem, to obscure the location of their gold from preying fingers, wrote treasure maps in alphabetic codes which neighbouring Aramaeans could not read.

Generals seek for their gold and frankincense, I thought, I would love to see that alphabet.

If characterised by its dearth of water, the treasure of Arabia is its spices, as well as frankincense and myrrh, cassia and cinnamon. Abda told me of these treasures:

'Cassia grows in a lake, and to gather it we cover our bodies and faces with oxen hides. We must be sure to cover our eyes, as around the lake abide screeching creatures like bats which fly at our faces.'

'Cinnamon is comprised of sticks which grow in the country where Bacchus grew up. Birds carry them into the air and make with them their nests, fixing them with mud to sheer rock faces so high men cannot climb. To obtain them we cut up oxen and asses in large pieces and lay them near the rocks. The birds carry them to their nests, but the added weight causes bits of the nests to break off and fall to the ground, from which we extract the cinnamon.'

Abda told me about frankincense and myrrh.

He said, 'Frankincense is born on trees guarded by winged serpents, and to obtain it we must burn torches made of styrax, which the Greeks get from the Phoenicians. Nothing but the smoke from this wood will drive them from the trees, and were it not for styrax, these serpents would invade the whole world.'

'The best frankincense is that from Persia; the yellow is the best kind. That's taken from the third tap. The first taps produce the white kind; it is less fine, but produces a white smoke that carries your prayers to heaven.

'Myrrh, there are three grades. There are two kinds of wild; the best is the one tapped in the summer. If this is adulterated with lentiste resin, you can tell because it sticks to your teeth. But the finest myrrh is stacte, which exudes from the tree naturally without tapping. This can cost up to fifty denarii. In Rome you can get six denarii per pound for frankincense and eleven to sixteen for myrrh. The black spice, pepper, brings forty times its weight in gold.'

I gasped, 'You must go to Rome, Abda. You will become rich.'

'Some do', he said, 'but you must realise the costs involved in the transport. We have to feed our company and our beasts for many moons, then we have to pay for water rights here and there. We pay Temple tax to the priest of Shabwa and taxes to the king of Qataban, and customs at every border. Out of Tadmor, the Romans take a quarter of all proceeds from any camel crossing from Parthia. And in the other direction, the Parthians take a toll. By the time you get to the coast, you've spent between 600 and 700 denarii per camel. Also, demand is all one way. Rome has an insatiable appetite for luxury Oriental imports, but they have little to offer for the outbound—just a bit of wool, linen, glass and metalware.'

Camels, the vehicles of the merchants' wealth, unlike my sweet little donkey, are nasty creatures. Their bodies are formidable, yet they are so stupid they would die of hunger if not led to food. They can last for many days without drinking—up to fifty days in winter—but, thirsty or not, often injure themselves or their drivers in a mad competitive scramble to the watering hole.

59

The Nabatu did not share my dislike of the beasts. The camel was uniquely capable of bearing their heavy packs across the desert; its dry dung supplied cooking fuel in the treeless waste. They made sure to water them every third day, and chanted sweetly to them while they drank. They guided them to their favourite desert plants–*hamd* and *khulla*–and allowed them the pleasure of rolling in the dirt when packs were off.

At one of the campfires, we heard a story from Afta, he who was in charge of our water rights affairs. The Nabatu had another treasure they guarded, a Lost Wisdom of their own:

## The Secret Cistern of the Nabatu

We lived in tents of black sheep's hair, and in the vastness of the Arabian wilderness we never thirsted, as we knew where to find water. The skill of our divining was great, and we of all peoples knew how to make waterproof stucco. Our engineers built shining white cisterns with perfect square corners to hold the water from the winter rains and diverted the might of the Sig River into secret rock channels. We concealed these cisterns underneath rocks leaving signals known only to ourselves and not understood by other peoples, and when in danger we could disappear unseen into our subterranean reservoirs. And so, the Incense Route was ours alone to command. No foreign army could cross the desert unless we came to them with our camels loaded with water skins.

In the days of Augustus Caesar, Aelius Gallus was sent to seize the sources of sap for our spices. But at Hegra, his soldiers became ill on the local water and herbs.

Still did we keep our marvelous dam a secret, and faked our sympathies. 'Ah, yes,' we pretended commiseration. 'Water is always a problem in the desert,' we said.

The men guffawed, though they'd heard the tale a thousand times.

One of the young men was next, with an amusing fable.

There was once an old man who had a donkey, and one day while pasturing the animal in a meadow, the army of Gallus approached.

'Flee with me, quickly,' the old man begged the donkey.

But the donkey stood fast, 'Will the enemy make me carry two packs at once?'

'I don't suppose so,' said the man, so the donkey refused to move.

'What does it matter to me whose servant I am,' the donkey said, 'so long as I carry only one pack at a time?'

I loved the stories round the campfire. Since the days when our ancestors hunted and foraged in skins for their daily sustenance, people have sat like this in the evening, work done, bellies full, telling their stories. They say that it was for our ability to communicate with one another in the hunt that God raised us above the animals. Surely, if He loved us for our communication, it was for our stories. What rose us out of savagery was Wisdom.

I watched as each speaker struggled to utter the choicest words, paint the scene most colourfully, find just the right gesture, in order to tell his story to the throng. I imagined men of long ago before giants walked on earth, with long dark nights to fill, telling their stories with meager language, perhaps creating new words as they struggled to convey meaning, words which were then remembered and fixed in the mouths of the listeners.

I pictured campfires dotting the earth, each spouting forth its own lexicon, creating over millennia the world's myriad tongues. The campfire around which we sat was the descendent of campfires night before night, stretching back to the dawn of man. The stories I heard here had been embellished for generations.

Though terrified by the prospect, I couldn't wait to undertake myself the telling of a story. I, too, had inherited the history of the campfires of my people. I knew stories of my people's past. Now I wanted to tell them to a new campfire, and send the smoke of our entertainments burning into the night and into the future. Now I would become part of the history of the continual creation of the lexicon, part of the history of the campfire.

I wanted to tell my companions the stories I'd heard and told at the well or at the table at home, but I was concerned that it might be too strange for them, that all the references to our God, our forefathers, our Scriptures and customs, our history would be meaningless to them. Would it not be disrespectful, as if to assume that these things would be as important to them?

There are common themes we all thrill to, as we all worship God or gods and we all have the same human desires. An ungrateful son, a jealous husband, warring brothers, a hidden prince, unexpected riches, a fair maiden wronged, a secret revealed. They are universal, and can please the hearts of Nabatu incense traders as well as Jews at a supper table or at a well. I could tell stories that would illustrate these themes. The people would be characters in a story rather than persons of history. Anything peculiarly Jewish could simply be interjected as an exotic detail.

One evening when none of the young men came forward, I stepped up and, struggling with the words, told them the story of the Lost Wisdom of the Magi:

The Lost Wisdom of the Magi

All peoples tell the story of the Great Flood, how in the Age of the Fire when the world was young God flooded all of Eden, saving one man and his family to repopulate the land. We Jews call him Noach, and in my country they call him Atrahasis.

The peoples before the Flood left scarce record. They crafted spears, knives, bows and arrows, and built shelters. Their women wore beads carved from bone drilled so finely the eye could scarcely see the hole. They knew where to find the fruits of the earth—fruit, nut, leaf and root, and could turn them into medicine, poison, intoxicant or material for garment. They knew the secret locations of water, the treatment of wounds and the science of midwifery.

The men observed the tides and the fruits of the sea and hunted the fat of the land. They herded the sheep, the goat and the deer. They hunted the big beasts, the tokens of their savage gods.

Most of the peoples of earth lived little better than the animals they hunted, but the men in great cities—Tantalus, Gadir, Hatussa, Jericho, Aratta and the cities of Asia—taught each other secrets that the beasts knew not. They selected the seed that was strongest on the stalk for bread making and beer. They made the animals bow to them as servants, and they tilled the soil from the mountains to the rivers. They had no kings and no war.

There were priests and priestesses among these who possessed magical knowledge of science, the stars, writing, growing things, breeding animals and smelting metals. They were giants on the earth compared to the miserable generations after the flood. In Albion, they lifted great stones to their gods with their music, and in Keftio they stood on the hilltops with magical rods and brought the rain.

Having watched the stars since the dawn of man, season after season scratching marks on animal bones, they foresaw the turnings of the heavens. They knew of God's intention for the earth. And to the humans who would survive with their livestock in boats and on mountaintops, to scrape a living after the land drained, they left a precious legacy.

On two pillars, one of brick and one of marble, they carved in hieroglyphs more ancient than those used by the Aegyptians or in my country, all the wisdom of the ancients—grammar, rhetoric, logic, arithmetic, geometry, music, architecture and astronomy. Then they buried them, for people to discover one day when we are ready for the knowledge.

The Aegyptians inscribed this knowledge in their Book of the Coming Forth by Day, a copy of which they place between the ankles of their mummified pharaohs. In the seventh generation from the first man, the great prophet Enoch, whom the Aegyptians call Thoth, knew sacred alphabets attaching absolute ideas to signs and numbers by combination, the mathematics of thought, but they were secret; no one ever wrote them down.

It was not the sort of tale they had expected. They had hoped for some girlish tale of star-crossed lovers or princesses. I looked at Shu'dat, and she was smiling broadly. She was not at all surprised.

I struggled with words and pronunciation in adapting to their Safaitic dialect. At first the young boys giggled mercilessly at my accent and the mistakes in my words, but they liked my stories so much that eventually they stopped.

I felt our communication created an entirely new language, not a mutually comprehensible mix of Babylonian Aramaic and Safaitic Arabic-Aramaic, but an Aramaic that Sophia can speak and Nabatu can understand. And in the telling of it, in the words of this new language, the story changed.

As I thought about history within this new, worldwide context, my own understanding changed. In one way, I learned anew from the same old stories, as I sculpted from them the universal lessons from which all people must learn. In another way, the old stories now appeared smaller to me. My land seemed far away, and my people no longer the entire universe they had been, but merely a piece in the complex maze into which I was so adventurously bound. The thought filled me with joy. I kissed Shu'dat and told her about it.

That night, though, I cried for my father.

On further nights around the campfire, they asked for more:

They say that Enoch buried 36,535 scrolls, destined to be found only by the worthy. Some were uncovered by the bearded queen-pharaoh Hatshepsut's mason; he announced, 'Having penetrated all the writings of the divine prophets, I was ignorant of nothing that has happened since the beginning of time.' Possessing secret knowledge can make a man giddy.

It is told that one was found during excavations for the rebuilding of the Great Temple in Jerusalem. In Hebrew, it was called the Book of God's Remembrance. It is thus that the Jews came into possession of great secrets also known to the Aegyptians.

Moshe, our liberator, brought down God's laws from Mount Horeb on two tablets. The first was for his inner circle, and these he dashed before the idolaters of Ba'al. The second set of tablets contained commandments for the people, the ten sacred words.

King Solomon, the great magus of our people, inscribed secret names, in numbers and letters, on seventy-two seals, or Clavicles. He received the knowledge from books carried across the Orient by Avraham.

Telling stories at night gave me a task to keep me from missing my studies and my home, but speaking in front of many people was completely new to me. Speaking in a new language as I was, every day seemed to change me as well.

It changed me, also, in my relationships with people. Who was this girl who was the friend of Shu'dat? I spoke to my new friend in complete harmony and sincerity from a heart full of love, but did the words that came out of my mouth really say what I meant?

Or was I telling a new story? Were the words coming from a new person, one who through new experiences and people was changing? Speaking in a dialect not one's own and knowing other peoples and their lives, there is nothing more exciting. It is also difficult, though, and requires long painful looks in the mirror and friends with patience.

As I learned to concentrate on the stories and the people whom I was addressing rather than on how well I was handling the language or how I felt within myself, I learned to relax and enjoy it. Indeed, in those days I think I understood for first time how it is to communicate with human beings. I told the campfire:

After the Flood, entire tribes of people travelled near and far. The wretched men of these generations retained the more mundane of the survival skills, and continued to till the land, yoke cattle and read the stars. Those who saved their livestock consecrated new boundary stones to face the sunrise, offered sacrifices and continued their husbandry. Noach planted the vine on Mount Sir, and learned viniculture from the people of the Mittani.

The black-haired people said they brought with them

to the Land Between the Rivers agriculture and metal-work and writing. We have found the teachings on tablets from Shinar thousands of years old. Some of the universal symbols—for sun, moon, water—are even older, having been handed down since the mountains were frozen, when men hunted the great beasts.

But most of the ancient wisdom was lost. No longer do we know the sacred measurements for rock crystal, aventurine and amethyst with which the Nubian magi brought the rain. Nor do we remember the harmonies that lifted the great stones; our stonemasons wield no longer the magical Shamir, the stone that splits stone. The most ancient Scriptures record some of the words of the old sacred songs, but we have lost the music. From the time of the scorpion kings of Aegypt the priests of Annu preserved the names in their language of the guardians of the Gates of Heaven and the annals of the coming forth of the dead, but no one remembers the key to their ordering. The principles of statuary, the making of inlaid eyes, the weaving of linen, the fitting of furniture—all was lost. I have read that the ancients could produce light underground without smoke and even turn base metals into gold.

I told the rest of the story later to the women as we bathed in the Tharthar Lake, northwest of Seleucia, from which waters flow into both of the two rivers:

The Daughters of Men

When the world was created, the angels took to wife the daughters of men, for women who lived in those times spake their tongue, and they created kings and queens. It was to their wives that the knowledge of the gods was passed, and through the early years of men, womenkind held it secret.

They who lived after the Flood took their line through the mother. In those days, before the Sun rose in the Twins for the shepherds' festival, there were kingdoms ruled by women warriors. The Carians colonised the lands around the Great Sea with their women sea captains. They knew the precise measure of the earth, and charted their position by the stars and the twelve winds. They sailed even by night, as they knew how to read the north from the Little Bear.

They worshipped the Great Goddess, and the high priestess was her servant. It was she who held the secret keys to science and agriculture. The chosen one of all the maidens, she slept in a golden bed high atop the tower, waiting for the god to come to her at night and so to bless the land for fertile grain. The king was but her consort and reigned only a year before he was burned with the midsummer oak. Sometimes there were two kings who took turns in the queenly chamber, autumn and spring.

Her priestesses sacrificed their chastity to supplicants, and children of the gods, born 'under the old dispensation' at festival time, were raised in the temple and served her worship. Or they sacrificed the babes and slept with the dead bodies, so to assist them in their divinations.

In those days, worship of the gods was not so clean

and well behaved. It was full of death and blood and sex, and unashamed. So, it was at Hebron, where my ancestors danced and sang. The hymns of the Levite singers can still raise hearts, but once there were priestesses who lamented the dying of the barley and made beautiful music unto the Queen of Heaven.

The men in those days bethought themselves chiefs, as they were the hunters; yet did their wives and sisters rule the sustenance of the tribe. The land east of Eden and its four rivers was bountiful. The women gathered the fruit of the land while they sang and tended the young. The men hunted when they needed to. The rest of the time, they sat around carving knives, making arrows and pottery, telling stories by the campfire.

After the Flood the wild game was gone, and the men tamed oxen to till the soil, cursing themselves to the burden of daily toil. It was then that they seized the crown from the woman.

The women rejoiced to hear a tale of their ancient power.

The young men at the campfire were at first shocked at my brazenness, but as they increasingly accepted and approved of my differentness, they eventually admitted to being pleased to see a girl able to stand unabashed in front of the company. 'Our girls just sit around the fire gossiping,' they snickered.

Though I was flattered by the praise for my storytelling, it was not as easy for me as they assumed. There were even a few who actually came to Abda to ask for my hand, which embarrassed me greatly. Whenever he approached me about it, I became upset, and he desisted.

Shu'dat was only a few years older than I, but she was already betrothed. The son of another merchant had spoken to her father. He was quite a few years older than her, but Shu'dat said she 'didn't like any of the boys' her own age. Abda had answered, 'Let me but have my little girl at my lonely hearth for a while longer,' but smiled, knowing Shu'dat's heart, and gave his permission for the man to visit at his pleasure.

'It's not as if he's going to take me away from Father,' said Shu'dat, who told me the story with pride. 'We live in the same camp.' She was very willing for the match.

Yatur often came to share our evening meal or walked with us along the journey. Whenever he was with Shu'dat, she giggled a lot and insisted that I be present with them always. Sometimes he would pay quite a bit of attention to me. Unlike my friend, I was not affected with the giggles, so at first, barring the awkwardness of a foreign dialect, I was able to converse with him freely and easily. I could see Shu'dat's embarrassment for her shyness and even jealousy upon the attention her betrothed paid to her younger friend, jealousy of me who loved her so. This distressed me, yet she continued to insist on my attendance. Then I became tongue-tied with shame, and my words became garbled.

To be in the company of a young man, not a boy like our friends, but a man, goodly of face and deport, a man who is paying avid, flattering attention to you. It is terrifying. And when you think that this man is promised to your dearest friend, it is more terrifying. It feels adulterous. Yet is that feeling not ridiculous? We were simply conversing. I was only responding in order to cover my friend's shyness. Yatur looked to me because he was uncomfortable as well. Why was I exaggerating the situation?

Obsessed by these thoughts, my mind could no longer

concentrate on the topic of discussion. I found myself questioning, do I myself find him pleasing? Yet these thoughts filled me with shame, and I considered taking a purge. Some demon put the question in me, and he must not be heard.

Once Shu'dat and I even had an argument before going to bed, while my ears were still ringing from one of these uncomfortable encounters. The argument was over something silly, and we both knew it.

After our harsh words, I said to her, 'Shu'dat, what am I supposed to do? I have to fill in the gaps in conversation while you finish giggling.'

She burst into laughter, and so did I, but when I began to tell her my feelings about the three-way situation, she told me some things that led me to understand her heart. We fell asleep with our arms resting upon one another.

Shu'dat was pleased indeed with Yatur, and longed to fall into his arms. She feared her own feelings would rush her into womanhood, and she, too, wanted to keep the little girl a while longer. She relished this girlish relationship with me and wanted to enjoy it while she could.

'If the bridegroom is true,' Abda said, 'he will wait.' And so, he did.

After this, things were much better. When the conversations became awkward, I would try to introduce something that would necessarily bring Shu'dat into consideration. Yatur, a good man and truly in love with her, responded immediately, encouraging her participation. So much older than we, I even wondered if perhaps he was entirely aware of our three-way dynamic, but was untroubled, or even flattered by it. I could see that he was flattered by Shu'dat's giggles and shyness, and I do believe he was genuinely happy for her friendship with me.

Shu'dat gradually overcame her giggling as she began to consider the two of us in her conversation as friends rather than as suitor and attendant. I was more pleased with this role.

There was one situation, however, in which I refused to accompany Shu'dat. Of an evening after he was with us at our fire, Yatur would depart for his tent, and Shu'dat would accompany him to the edge of our section, where, if no one was around, he would be allowed to hold her hand, whisper secret things and kiss her on the mouth.

Later in the maidens' tents, even when I was dying to find a corner for my prayers or aching for sleep, she would grab at my sleeve and insist on telling me absolutely everything about these trysts. Before he visited, I had to listen for hours while she worried: 'What shall I wear? What do you think of this necklace? Do these beads go well with this robe? Does it need a belt?'

After he left, it was: 'He said this', then 'I said that', then 'he said that', and 'what do you think about that?'

I had no opinion on the matter whatsoever.

She wanted to know what I thought about each little detail, but I really had no way of knowing what to think at all. It was her romance, not mine. I was happy that she was happy, that was all. But each time, I had to hear it all, every detail. It was rather boring. I'm sure each choice romantic word was very interesting to her. It just wasn't interesting to me.

It was not that I was jealous or had no interest in her happiness, it was simply that I didn't know; it had nothing to do with me. I was an inappropriate authority. 'He called me love tonight. Do you think that means he loves me?'

'I really don't know. Why don't you ask him?'

'Eek, I'd be too bashful.'

I felt again that sense of 'naughtiness'. Why am I so unlike other girls? Even with my darling Shu'dat I can't giggle over girlish joys. Would I ever marry? I determined not, and yet felt 'naughty' for the thought.

Too bashful also was she to discuss wedding plans with Yatur. Shu'dat kept him in suspense, and I could see that he agonised over the unspecified delay. To me, though, she hinted that she desired it before the turn of the year at the latest. She wanted to be with him for the next outbound journey from Arabia, and his clan was due at that point to part ways for half a year from Abda's section of the caravan. They would travel the southern route only, and wouldn't take the route to India.

Many tents were finding the long voyage not so profitable now that Roman ships sailed there and the Sabaei controlled the Red Sea route at Aden. Once married, Yatur would become Abda's heir and so would travel with them.

'If I want to keep Yatur on my stall,' she said, 'that's my closing day.'

Shu'dat pictured that this leg of the journey would be their honeyed moon, and she told me about the wonders she wanted to share with him. 'If only I could share them with you, too, Sophia'. I was with them for the return journey alone, she knew.

I said she could share them with me by the telling, and so she told me about the kingdom of the Nabatu:

Nabatene is about halfway between Aqaba and the Dead Sea. The city Rekem is at the bottom of a long narrow canyon cut into the pink sandstone mountain.

You know how you told me a citron tree will always remind you of your home, as you had one in your courtyard? For me, it's the smell and taste of honey that makes me think of home. It's everywhere, and in everything.

In the country of the Sabaei, it's very fertile. They have myrrh, frankincense, cinnamon, balsamum and calamus. They have so much of everything, they're quite lazy, the Sabaei. They don't even make themselves beds, but sleep in the trees.

They have red snakes there like the ones in Hadramaut, that leap up at you and whose bite is incurable.

In my country there is a great wide plain with wild cattle of every sort—mules, camels, deer, lions, leopards and wolves, and three mountains around it of smooth black sand—the colour of our olives, Sophia—and in those mountains dwell men who are great hunters.

In my country a long time ago, a woman would be married to all her husband's brothers. The brother who was with her would leave his staff at the door, but it was always the eldest who slept with her at night.

I giggled, thinking of Yatur's brothers.

The king had a minister who was one of the Companions, and was called Brother. It was not the son of the king who would succeed, but the first son to be born to any nobleman's wife after the investiture of the king. The king would then adopt the child and raise him as a princely son and heir.

And she told me about the Incense Road.

The Incense Road from Shabwa to Jenysos is divided into sixty-five camel-stops. Each of these possesses secret caverns dug by ancient engineers to trap and guard the winter rains, marked with signs known only to us. Along the route there are also deep trenches dug long ago for travellers to clamber into for shade during the hot hours of the day. No foreign army can cross our land without our permission and without our aid, as there is no water to be found unless one knows the code. At the foot of the Sela Mountains, there are secret caverns where we store our goods.

Some of these stops are markets at which we trade– Marib, Najran, Khaybar. Our towns have tall buildings, with nine floors even, all built of mud. Our temples have capitals carved into elephant heads, painted red and yellow.

In Hegra, where we water our camels, there are hundreds of beautiful stone tombs our ancestors carved out of the red, desert rock. At Khaybar there are orchards of date palms irrigated by our system. There among the dry rocks and sand bloom green leaves and luscious fruit. At Hegra, the gate to the city is a narrow gap between two high rocks that's only one camel wide. It would take our company days to get through that, so we set up market outside at the foot of the red sand-stone cliffs.

In the ruins of Dedan near there, Sophia, there are stone betyls carved in Nabatu and Thamudic, and Dedanit, Minaen, and Lihyanite. In Tayma, there are stones written in Aramaic script a thousand years old.

She knew I would like that.

Chapter 6
Commerce

It was close to 21,000 stadia from Najran in western Arabia to the Nabatu port of Jenysos on the coast. A camel caravan travelling this route usually took about three moons. Ours, the return journey from India and the Land between the Rivers, was longer, almost 50,000 stadia. We camped during the daytime, travelling along the wadis during the night, as the heat of the desert was unbearable, and we traded at every market along the way.

Most of our camps were one day's stops, but at the towns we stayed sometimes weeks.

When we reached the major towns–Mari, Abu Kamal, Uz– the entire company was busy from morning till night. The camels were lodged in caravanserai for a rest, the company occupied in trade with their customers in town. Shu'dat and I had duties at the caravanserai to help with the preparation of food or on Abda's stall at market.

Travelling caravans with grazing animals would usually winter either at Petra or on the coast. On this journey, however, our most important market was Palmyra, the bride of the desert. Cities on important crossroads like this–Damascus, Petra, Palmyra–were rich from caravan trade with East. Palmyra– called Tadmor in their language–marked the crossroads of the two most important trade routes in the world. At Palmyra, the Incense Road we followed met the Silk Road, leading all the way to Chin.

Several of the company had homes or relatives with homes, and once through the administrative ordeal at the city gates, we stayed in one of these, leaving behind the sights, sounds and smells of the caravanserai.

As soon as the camels had been stabled, the preparations for market were already beginning. The gray and brown donkey bags began to shed their blankets as the merchants prepared their goods for display—spices, gold, ivory, pearls, precious stones, and textiles.

My eyes were used to contemplating the treasures of the dead—scrolls, tablets, artifacts—whose value lies in their antiquity and their import to history. Here, blossoming forth from one fire to the next, was the treasure of the living, whose value lies in their beauty and their utility and the price they would fetch at market.

I went too close to one of the donkey bags in my curiosity, and the merchant cast me an evil eye. He was the one back on the hill who had said Persia was half his trade. He didn't want me or any potential competitor coming near to his wares.

And it wasn't just him with this tightfisted approach. The merchants were all jealous of their displays, and the women ran about terrified of their tempers. For so many moons, we had shared the fire and the stars together and eaten together as a tribe. On the morrow, each donkey bag would be in competition with the next.

Despite the merchants' protectiveness, the next day when I had a chance to look at the stalls in the open and the merchants were in more welcoming moods, I found them to be all much the same. As it was the return journey, supplies of frankincense and myrrh had dwindled, and most of the palm-woven baskets lay folded flat back in the corners.

Coming from India, the majority of merchants carried cinnamon–called *qirfa* in their language–and hardened sticks of a medicine and dye called dragon's blood made from the red berries of cinnabar. Most of the other tents had roughly similar wares. Many carried goods made of alabaster or red clay thin-ware pottery with vines, flowers, and birds with bright plumage painted in reds, blues and whites.

Everyone had an assortment of fabrics, beads, spices and foodstuffs. It would be days before the merchants would reveal their choicest items, the unique treasures, and then only to preferred clients.

The prices were fairly standard among all our people, too. Whatever bargains were to be had were among the more universal items. Anything unusual or of particularly fine crafts-manship was priced beyond the fingers of most.

I don't think they had any formal agreement, but the merchants seemed to have an understanding amongst them of what price they could be haggled down to. The bottom offer had to begin at higher than double the original cost simply to cover the expense of traveling half-way across the world. And the price of a commodity was more affected by the local harvest the year before than by the skill of a merchant's selling.

Our particular market was well established, from decades, even centuries, of traveling and trading in this manner. The camp leader's scales and rods were stamped with the approval seals of inspectors of weights and measures and customs officials from India to Gaza, and each merchant in camp calibrated his measures from that. Shu'dat told me she believed they were all scrupulously accurate. Her father, she said, 'will tell you any tale he can conceive about the product, but he would never tip the scales'.

'There is nothing to be gained from dishonesty,' maintained the good Abda, 'cheating only damages the reputation of the merchant and the market.' He said that the merchant's advantage is not in 'giving the customer less than he has bargained for', but in 'persuading him to consider what he has bargained for as amply desirable'.

Of course, I did hear mostly the merchants' side of the question. Understanding Greek, though, I could hear what the customers said to each other wandering through the stands, and without their perceiving themselves overheard, as they thought us all ignorant Arab highwaymen. I looked the complete Arab, anyway, myself, as I had taken to wearing the black headband of the desert nomad to fix my shawl upon my head. Also, I had learned in slipping past the guard at the Antioch Gate how to make myself unnoticed.

Some did seem to suspect the scales; some had even brought their own. But strangely enough, it was the wealthier Greeks, those who could well afford to increase a desert merchant's subsistence, who complained. Their own gain having come through dishonesty, I suppose, they mistrust all others. Suspecting they would be trouble, the merchants sometimes cited them different prices to those they gave the locals. The Arab city folk, coming to market to supplement their daily fare, though they bargained heavily over the prices, accepted the sanctity of the scales. They knew the agreements from ages back, and trusted the crossroads officials' knowledge of numbers and measures as beyond their ken.

Assisting those days on Abda's stall was my only ever

experience of commerce, and I avow that it was enjoyable.

One afternoon we were called upon to serve tea while Abda entertained a preferred customer. He was showing an Etruscan wine amphora—he said it was 600 years old—enclosed by a plug from the cork oak.

The customer, Rabbel, a buyer for a noble family in Damascus, was greatly impressed. The gentleman, if I may call him that, was also attracted by Shu'dat and glanced and smiled at her in an unpleasant way.

Truly, Shu'dat was a beautiful girl, and beginning to grow tall with the confidence of an heiress to a merchant's fortune. For our most important market day, she had put on her best garments, perfumed with smoke from aromatic powders sprinkled on a charcoal brazier, and between the two of us we wore all her jewelry.

She moved with the grace of a young woman who knows herself, wearing a robe of brocade of Araby; and behind her flowed a Damascene gauze silk veil as clear as water. Gold-washed tin coins and carnelians etched with Arabic letters dangled from her forehead; and bells and bracelets tinkled as she walked.

At her neck was a marvelous collar made of lumps of fossil stone the size of medlars, embedded with streaks of gold, raw, unpolished and glittering. These were alternated with smooth cylinders of glass of a smoky opaqueness that counterposed the glitter of the gold. Among the numerous bright, tinkling bracelets on her wrists was a collar of the same design.

'We got this in Minaei. I liked it so much Father let me have it. You know what a softie he is.'

'How could he refuse you, Shu'dat? If I were in his place, I would give you anything.'

Her eyelids were painted shiny green with crushed malachite, and when she smiled her whole body gleamed like a basket of jewels in the vibrant colours of her array.

She had dressed me for the occasion, too. If ever I admired an item of her possession, she would urge me to borrow it. I was not as tall as she, but 'robes can always be tied tighter at the waist', she said. That day I wore a borrowed robe of Indian cotton printed with a design of birds, and a belt of Indian silk blue as the sky. She bade me put on a necklace, made of small tubes of green glass. We had both perfumed our hair with sandalwood incense.

The man had started by making improper comments toward Shu'dat. 'The lovely daughter has grown up fine,' he began. Abda and Shu'dat thanked him politely, but he would not stop. 'What do you think of this old pot, pretty? Do you want me to buy it?' His unpleasantness escalated until he suggested to her, 'Would the lovely daughter like to keep a man company afterward, perhaps?'

When the customer wasn't looking, Abda gave Shu'dat a gesture. She gratefully retired, and I finished the serving, when I heard the pig of a man say to Abda, 'Never mind the Etruscan pot, what a price I would give for the daughter!'

Abda left me in the far corner ready to serve when called upon, a position from which I was able to observe the proceedings.

While they haggled, I looked at the amphora. The scene portrayed was of a banquet, in detailed black painting on red pottery. Men and women sat, as equals, enjoying the revelry. The Etruscans took their names from the mother, I remembered. And here were Shu'dat and I, submissively serving tea and exposing ourselves to improper behaviour.

The sale occupied the entire afternoon, during the course of which I served the customer with every fancy condiment and fine wine we had. Abda and the man discussed everything but the amphora—news from Damascus, the latest scandal in Rome, the season's most renowned gladiator in the circuses.

In Rome, the emperor castrated his boy slave Sporus and married him, complete with dowry and bridal veil, 'imitating the lamentations of a maiden being deflowered' during the ceremony, said Rabbel, hitting Abda aggressively on the elbow. 'He treated him as wife, called him Sabina, and paraded him through the Street of the Images showering him with kisses. Someone commented it would be well for the world if the madman's father Domitius had had that kind of wife.'

Though I enjoyed the picture of the emperor and his 'wife' parading through Rome, I found Rabbel's sniggering disgusting, as well as his attempts to bully Abda into the world of his manly arrogance. But Abda had the merchant's knack of never saying anything to offend. He skillfully skirted around the customer's offensiveness, always seeming to agree with whatever vile statement was on the table, yet never actually doing so.

'Surely we are used to the excesses of our rulers,' Abda suggested amicably. 'It's no worse than with Gaius. He made his horse a consul and sired a child by his own sister.'

Behind the doorway where she sat, I whispered to Shu'dat, 'and wanted the Jews in Jerusalem to worship him as a god'. She sweetly gestured her outrage on my behalf.

Caesar had discovered a plot to assassinate him by supporters of the Roman orator Piso, and there had been many executions.

His revenge went to obsessive extremes; he forced numerous innocents to kill themselves, including the popular general of Asia, Corbulo. 'Many commanders in the provinces are plotting revolution', Rabbel believed.

No price for the amphora in question was mentioned for a very long time, Abda merely making vague suggestions that it would be extraordinarily costly. Instead, another object was produced, a pipe made of bone, and much was made of this object, with much discussion of price.

In the end, the man bought both; he paid 2,000 sestertii and ten denarii, a sum comfortably higher than what Abda had first asked for the amphora. The amount represented over half of Abda's entire intake from the market. He had paid a high price for the thing and had had this particular customer in mind as a potential buyer. Abda said to us, 'It is risky to place too much expectation on the high end of the market, but the proceeds make one bold.' He said, 'Rabbel always buys from me. I'll have to look for a really good piece to buy in for him in Gaza.'

Even in commerce the laws of courtesy apply. I thought, if only they applied to men's behaviour toward women.

Pleased with the day's takings, Abda gave Shu'dat and me each a silver denarius, which we gleefully spent on treasures, I on a red silk underscarf for my head, she on a wooden bracelet. I left Shu'dat to the haggling, as she had the skill of practice.

She arranged the underscarf for me under my headband between my shawl and the tresses over my brow—and I slid the bracelet onto her wrist. It was of olivewood from Adiabene carved with vine leaves, and made a dull click against the white bone one she already wore, which Abda said had been her mother's.

'Maybe it was cut from the vines planted there by Noach after the Flood', I said.

'There was I concerned only with the price, while you, Sophia, are still thinking about the olden days,' she teased.

There were enough bronze coins left over that Shu'dat also bought a dowry bag, 'to drape over the camel at my wedding', she said. It had embroidered pockets at the tip, with cowrie shells that tinkled as it shook, and tiny little mirrors.

We abided a full moon in Palmyra, and they were the most exciting days of my life. Shu'dat and I helped on the stall, explored the market, ate exciting foods, and had conversations with a myriad of folk. The entire world was there, it seemed. We walked everywhere, when it was safe or we could find accompaniment, hand-in-hand like sisters.

Never had I seen such wonders—and so many. The heavenly scents of cinnamon, cassia, iris and frankincense seduced customers to stay longer enjoying the luxury, also keeping off insects and protecting the crowd from human odour in the heat.

In the fabrics market, we saw Sidonian red wool and woolens dyed purple by women from the island town of Kition with a stain they extract from shellfish (the manufacture emits such a stink, the old stories say, it killed off all their men). Abda bought us skeins of wool from Colossae woven with strands of purple with which to sew winter tunics.

As we explored other corners of the market, we saw eggshell-thin pottery from Keftio; Phoenician glass coloured blue with copper from Badakshan; rich brown amber from the rowan thickets of Sarmatia; necklaces of lustrous white fisheyes from Dilmun, which the Greeks call Tylos; obsidian black as the inside of the Holy of Holies from the Aru islands; nephrite jade from Yarkand and Khotan. We watched Syrian jugglers; we gorged on juicy dates from Jericho and tasted nutmeg from the Indies.

Music wafted in and out of the alleys from under tent flaps where rich men were entertained by dancers. Shu'dat and I found a crack in the seams of one and took turns watching.

The music was calming, rolling up and down with no beginning and no ending—it made me think of lounging in the shade of a citron tree sipping cool pomegranate juice. We couldn't see far enough in to espy the instruments.

The dancer quite shamelessly revealed broad areas of her body; plump chunks of it jiggled as she shook her hips, around which looped a silk scarf sewn with hundreds of tiny disks of tin pressed into coins. The coins tinkled pleasantly as she whirled in syncopation with the jiggling of the corpulent flesh of her belly. Above a huge expanse of nakedness, her breasts were precariously contained by a silk jacket covered in jewels and tin coins. Her elbows, knees and ankles were bare as babies' and flaunted their nudity at every turn. The only part of her that was decently covered was her hair.

Like the music, her dance had no beginning and no ending; she shook from side to side and twirled round and round, jiggling and tinkling, in constant motion. She bent and turned her body in ways I have never seen, moving with such skill and suppleness, her dance so practiced she seemed to perform each difficult feat with ease. I almost forgot the shock of her lewdness in the appreciation of her art. I am certain her gentleman customer was of a different mind, but we caught no glimpse of him, as the guard shooed us away.

I dragged Shu'dat and Yatur to the antiquities market, where a trader showed us a Kushite spear handle plated in electrum—a mix of gold and silver more precious than either, inlaid with pieces of blue glass and carved with seven enigmatic letters. The man said they meant 'stand fast', the invocation of the warrior. We saw pieces of bronze salvaged from the Colossus of Rhodes, or so the man said.

In Palmyra, many of the men visited brothels. Abda may have been among them, though I did not discuss it with Shu'dat. Some of the tents were even within our caravan.

In Palmyra, just like everywhere in the Empire, the Temple of Baal was adorned by statues of the emperor and his family.

As in most cities of the East, there was a large Jewish community, as the people of Palmyra are the sons and daughters of Israelites who fled the devastation of Samaria under Sennacherib and Hebrew mercenaries from Persian Aegypt.

I did not seek them out. There was too great a chance there might have been gossip from Seleucia about runaway daughters. But I was curious, and I tried to follow them when I saw them at market, without being noticed, to listen in upon their conversation.

There was one who by the attitudes of those in his retinue, I was certain was someone of high rank, a priest, as it turned out—a Pharisee, I could tell by his long tzitzit. His retinue fawned and fastidiously manoeuvred so that none of the merchants touched his great person.

'What did you negotiate?' his eminence was asking a retainer as he exited one of the tents.

'He wouldn't let it go for less than 400 denarii, even for you, *Chaver* (Friend).'

'*Ben kelev*, Bey'a!' he exclaimed. 'I could buy a slave for that!'

'Son of a dog,' I translated for Shu'dat. Such words from the mouth of a holy priest of God!

'This one knows you're the son of Ishaq the priest,' Bey'a returned. 'He may have put his price up.'

'The fraudster! I must find something, though. My brothers will all be there, and I can't be outdone by their gifts while I'm in these robes.'

'Don't worry. We can find something both worthy of your rank and within the reach of your purse.'

'At the same time, Caecilian will be dining with us. It wouldn't do to outdo his gift.'

'The decurion?'

'Yes, she wrote that he'd accepted.'

'Hmm, tricky to strike just the right tone.'

The priest seemed to be searching for a birthday gift for his mother, who was throwing a party.

'What is the lady's taste?' said Bey'a.

'She's quite interested in statuary at the moment, as she's just put in a *paradis* (pleasure garden) at the villa.'

'Well, we should have plenty to choose from there. Let's try the antiquities market back that way.'

A priest indulging in Greek idols! And sharing table fellowship with Roman soldiers!

I heard the last pieces of their conversation.

'It's not just the cost of the bauble that worries me. The transport of it to Apamea will be fraught. No matter how I equip myself, we'll be ripe pickings for bandits.'

'The Damascus road, then, along the King's Highway?'

'Might as well take the shortest route, the Homs road

through the mountains. Either way, we go through bandits. Jews are targets for anyone these days.'

Rich Jews lived in constant fear, caught between the wrath of the Romans, the envy of the settlers and the revenge of the People of the Land.

'Perhaps it would be best to dress as Greeks on the road,' Bey'a then suggested as they wound their way past our stalls and out of our hearing.

I was tempted to get Shu'dat to tell him about Abda's wares, but that would have brought the men too close for comfort, and, in any case, it was unthinkable for an unmarried girl to address a stranger. The antiquities market was on the other side of the agora, too far for two girls to go without escort, so I had to leave to my imagination the picture of this rich Pharisee buying a 'bauble' like Abda's Etruscan banquet vase.

After we left Palmyra, there was a parting among our company. Tax collectors and soldiers came to tax us, and then those tents bound for the coastal markets of Berytus took the Damascus road to the west; our sector of the caravan headed south.

We abided a week in Pella while the hot winds from Arabia passed, then passed over the mountains and crossed the Jabbok River into Peraea, heading for Jericho. It was lusher here, as we left behind the desert of Syria and its sparce buckthorn shrubs now to see oak and olive trees and palm plantations.

Past Amathus, we crossed the Jordan River into Judaea, entering Roman Palestine, and the green mountains gave way to arid monotonous horizons. Between the Jordan and Jericho, the land was barren and low lying; Jericho to Jerusalem is rocky desert.

Jericho sits atop a treeless mountain range stretching all the way to Scythopolis, near a spring that nurtures balsam, cypress, ben-nut and honey bees. So fair was the climate that townsfolk dressed in linen while the rest of Judaea is under snow.

Jericho, where the first men experimented with husbandry, attempting to tame the leopard and the gazelle. Men at Jericho had built fabulous walls of strong bricks of clay tempered with crushed bone and shell, to shield them from the Great Flood, the walls that were felled by the power of Joshua's magic. I saw them, the preserved north side. I saw Herod's Royal Palace; it was burnt during the war. Now, atop the ruins and the Lost Wisdom of almost 10,000 years, sits a thriving city surrounded by lush farms.

Naturally, there were Jews in Jericho, but as I had matched my dress to those around me, I managed quite easily not to attract attention.

At Jericho, there was a further parting of the company, as many were bound for Jerusalem. Our sector continued southward along the wadi Arugot to buy copper and to the Sea of Death to buy bitumen, then to cut south of the mountains toward Beersheba bound for the Nabatu port of Jenysos to winter on the coast.

From the fertile Jezreel Valley where the Herodians had their winter estates, we passed Herod's groves. Balsam and date palms unbroken for a hundred stadia. Once cleared to pass, it took us a full day to walk by them, a long one.

The great Solomon had only a temple and a little citadel. King Herod had palaces at Herodium, Strato's Tower and Jerusalem; and estates in Batanaea, Gaulinitis, Trachonitis, Lydda, Azotus, Jamnia, Peraea and Idumaea. The best of our land given him by Rome, he fortified fortresses, where he kept dungeons for enemies of state and the occasional prophet.

As we entered the land of my forefathers, I entertained the troupe with stories about King Herod:

The kings of Judaea and the Romans win their empires by war and accord their domains by marriage, parcelling out our people and our lands as dowries and wedding presents. All over Palestine there are new towns which Herod and his progeny built with riches taken from our lands and named after wives and sisters of the Caesars. Herod's sons and daughters married for empire. His grandsons are the client kings of Chalcis, Commagene, and Nabatene; his granddaughters married into the alabarchy of Alexandria, and into the royalty of Cyprus, Lybia, Cappadocia, Emesa, and even Rome.

Nor do the priests of the Lord in Jerusalem marry for love. The Holy of Holies is ruled as well by the politics of marriage and war.

Herod served the Romans, backing each horse in just the right order. When he became king, he conducted a bloody purge of the Hasmonean priesthood. More Edomite than Israelite, this King of the Jews erected temples to Tiberius, statues to Augustus and looted the sacred tomb of David and Solomon to build his Greek city of Qesarya.

His army were not Jews, they were mercenaries paid with his wealth from our lands. There was hardly a Jew in Herod's court, so enamoured was he of the company of Greeks. His priests allowed a gymnasium to be built right next to the Temple, and shortened evening prayers in defiance of the heavens so they could watch the games.

When he died, Herod's land came to be taxed under a census. But to number is to tax, and we owe the tax of our offerings only to God. We shall not be numbered.

The people of Galilee revolted. Their leader was Judas of Gamala (Judas the Galilean), a messiah to the rebellious, the true king of the Jews. The revolt was crushed, and the Roman prefect seized the sacred vestments of the High Priest so they could choose their own lackey. Idumaea—I pointed to the road ahead of us where our caravan headed—became part of Roman Judaea.

When Herod died, he left enough unmurdered sons to form three factions, and they connived and schemed. The days of the Pax Romana were not to last.

I heard the Jericho Jews whisper, Sicarii, the Daggermen, had sprung up again in Jerusalem, mingling with festival crowds and stabbing aristocratic opponents with their short-curved knives. From their master Judas, they learned a passion for liberty. They thought little of death, only that they may call no man master.

Others would lead the Many into the countryside promising miraculous signs of deliverance, living on the charity of pious donations, also thereby bypassing the tax collectors, and the Romans would send cavalry to cut the mob to pieces. The procurators hunted them down and crucified many of them. The rich folk called them bandits because they refused to pay tithes and, away from their fields, had to steal to eat.

I told Shu'dat, 'When I heard the priest in Palmyra say that Jews are targets for anyone these days, I thought he was referring to the usual stuff—circumcision, dietary laws.'

'No, no. There's unrest in the whole Empire,' she said. 'It's not just you Jews. In Rome rules one cretin after another, and our taxes pay for them to sit in luxury.'

That was probably the most revolutionary thing Shu'dat ever said in my hearing. As for me, however, with each new piece of information our travels gleaned, my world grew larger. In Jericho, I'd heard much about the Zealots, and a few people had made incendiary speeches. I liked what I heard. When I told Shu'dat about the Zealots, I called them 'we'.

I think that was more surprising to me than to her, though. She seems to have been under the impression that all Jews are innately rebellious. Despite our differences, she liked me for mine. Although I was younger than her, she considered me to be a strong person. I wish I had that opinion about myself.

It was politic for the Kittim—as we called the foreign soldiers—to seek secrecy in their cruel repression, and the seizure of Zealots by night was common practice. Thus, were we never wrest from the foreigner's yoke, even in our sleep. They used the Rich among the Jews as their agents.

When they couldn't find a man they looked for, they would keep his wife and children in chains. When they found him, unless rich, he was sent for torture. They turned all our words around. They called the campaign Summer Rain, and by this pleasant-sounding banner they hoped to crush our spirit with terror. Their onslaught of destruction against the beautiful stone walls of Jerusalem they called Iron Wall. Our government, they wouldn't even recognise as legal. They granted no vote to the People of the Land.

The new procurator Albinus allowed families to buy prisoners' freedom with bribes, so the people simply took up a collection, and all the heroes were out. So much was happening in the world that my parents had not seen fit to discuss with me.

As we progressed down the Wilderness Road, we met people coming from the south, from Idumaea, and heard their tales.

These people were not plagued by soldiers. The Romans had been quiet for years. They complained loudly, though, about 'priests'. These were the very same priests, of course, whom they invited regularly, with proper hospitality, to perform their seasonal ceremonies. The harmonious cycle of agriculture depended on the ceremonies; but they resented the control, and they resented the tithe. The priests also dominated the leather trade, one of the main industries of the region. There was a feeling in the towns and in the countryside, 'We must turn to these priests to fulfill our duties to God and bless our crops, but they do not lead us righteously.'

As in Galilee and Samaria in the days of Yonathan the High Priest, to this land had come priests from Jerusalem to forcibly circumcise the Edomite peasants. Memories like that die hard.

The local priests of the Judaean villages, too, rural Levites, had no power. Hypocrites like the rich Pharisee at Palmyra replaced the Levites who had looked after the people.

The Hasmonean priesthood in the Temple had taken from them the collection of tithes and first fruits, and they were now dependent for their sustenance on stipends from Jerusalem. Some of them were starving.

The high priests in Jerusalem, the rulers of Palestinian

Jewry, were traditionally chosen from among six influential families. No longer was righteousness the qualification for the post. Since Jason won the priestly robes and ephod from Antiochus Epiphanes with a bribe heavier than that of his brother Menelaus, the position had fallen to the highest bidder.

The *corban*, the Temple tithe, a half shekel or two drachmas paid by Jews all across the Diaspora, funded lavish lifestyles for these priests, and it was not spent on administrations to the poor. Instead, the poor were told they were 'reaping the corner of the field, cheating on their due offering to God', if they could not give the best of the beasts, the best of the oil, the best of the wine and the grain. The first fruits of all the land went to the priests.

The priests' friends, the moneychangers, changed our Roman coin to shekels, so not to allow purchase with unclean money of animals for sacrifice to the Lord, and the moneychangers took their cut as well.

In recent years there had been mass refusals of payment of the first fruits offerings, and Flaccus the Governor of Asia tried to stop tithes of Temple Tax from his province, causing trouble between the Greeks and the Jews. The High Priest Ananus had sent armed soldiers at harvest time to seize the tithes from the threshing floors. Memories like that were fresh.

'Taxes, Sophia, taxes,' Shu'dat said. 'Whether you're a merchant or a peasant, you pay the penalty, and the penalty is gold.'

'What would it be like, Shu'dat,' I wondered, 'if we could travel anywhere we liked and didn't have to pay at the border?'

She paused for a moment and looked at the fire. So confident was she of her position, it was difficult for her to imagine a different world.

'If we could travel anywhere we liked, I would want you to be with me and Yatur next year in Arabia.'

She said it many times.

On the road or in camp, Shu'dat and I, unless engaged in separate chores, were always together. We finished each other's sentences, giggled at the same things; around the fire in the evening we held each other's hands; at night in the maidens' tent our bedrolls lay side by side. The children, especially the boys of around twelve and thirteen years, teased us for being 'tribads'. They had not an idea what it meant, I'm sure. There were no women lovers in our camp, at least none who let others know. The boys just knew that it was something to say to tease women who loved one another.

When they saw Shu'dat and Yatur together, they teased as well, saying, 'When's the wedding?', 'When's the baby?', 'Why don't you kiss her?' and such like. But it was not so vicious. Marriage and babies are what the elders ordain, what love is supposed to be. Other kinds of love are more difficult to understand, and frighten those with small minds.

I said to the boys once, 'It was for love that God raised us from the animals,' but this only sent them into further gales of giggles. Ever after, when they teased Shu'dat and I for 'loving' each other, we simply refused to smile and replied, 'you speak truth'.

The happiness of my friendship with Shu'dat was deeply stained by the knowledge that we were to part company, and every few days, she would entreat me afresh to stay with the caravan.

'My father's stall is prosperous enough to dower the both of us,' she said, 'we need you.' No princess on earth would offer such to a mere friend.

She pleaded with me to 'accept the attentions of one of these fine merchant boys...' I started to frown as I usually did at such suggestions, when she added, 'or two.' And I joined her in giggling, as we both knew to whom she referred–Garm'alib and Taim'alib, twins. 'Even when Yatur and I are married, Sophia, we can remain friends just like this.'

It pained me all the more hearing her pleas, as I suffered from the same desire. How I longed to keep hold of Shu'dat forever. Had only she been able to read, my later dwellings would have been piled with letters written, not knowing where or how to send. I've written so many of these letters in my mind, I think some of them have ended up on these pages, as I write to you, Sisters, what my Feeling Self has yearned to speak.

Tears flowed from my eyes when I described to her my intent. 'The people I seek are learned priests who possess great and secret knowledge. It was for this that I left my home and family.' It was difficult to speak with Shu'dat about my scholarly dreams, as she shared them not.

'What's the use of making scratches on some old skin that could have been used for clothing?' she complained. 'They'll never win you a chariot race or a war.'

'These are only earthly glories. Words are to the glory of God,' I replied.

There was nothing she loved more than me. She loved Yatur, of course, but it was true; her marriage to him would not have come between us. My love, however, would part us. It grieved me as much as it did her.

'You must teach me to read, since you love it so much', she

said in her pain.

'I must,' I promised, but never did.

The farther we moved away from Syria, the closer came my parting from Shu'dat, and I welcomed the clear desert air for my prayers. One is always closer to God in the wilderness, where in the quiet of the hot sun or the night stars one can feel the divine breath on the cheek, as the hustle and hassle of human life seems small in the vastness of God's wonder.

Past Jericho, we entered Judaea. We travelled south past the fortresses of Hyrcania, Herodium and Secacah.

West of Ein Gedi, we parted. On the night before I left the caravan, Shu'dat and I both cried so desperately that the women said she must remain behind, and it was Abda and Yatur's parents who accompanied me to the Salt Sea. I gave Shu'dat my red silk underscarf from Palmyra. 'Wear it at your wedding,' I begged her. I would be replacing it with the grey headband of the Ossaean Novice. Where I was going, I would not be allowed personal possessions.

She was the best friend I ever had.

## Chapter 7
## The Yachad

We parted at the forking of the Maraba Road. The merchants were in a hurry to reach the rich markets of Jerusalem.

On a high plain surrounded by palm trees, with a view from the top from the mouth of the Jordan to Ras Feshka, we espied Mizpeh Ein Gedi, the stone-built huts of the Yachad, clustered around a well. Here above the noxious fumes of the pale, dull blue Sea of Death, fresh springs flowed down from the high cliffs of Judaea, channelled through waterways dug by ancient engineers. Springing from underneath the dry, dry desert, they watered neat rows of date palms and huge fig trees. As we climbed toward the settlement from the hot sand, the abundance of green was cooling to the eye and the air filled the chest with freshness.

To the southeast of the camp, at the foot of Tel Goren's citadel lay the town of Ein Gedi, where they nowadays traded bitumen from the Sea to Aegypt for mummification and water-proofing boats.

It is called the Sea of Death because nothing will grow here. It was here that the Lord wreaked vengeance on the unrighteous of Sodom and Gomorrah; the soil remains poisoned with the tar and brimstone from antiquity.

We were welcomed into the compound, and at the sound of the click of the gate closing behind us I was overcome with tears. Abda consoled me, and while Yatur's parents rested separately, we were ushered in to see the Overseer.

The moment introductions were accomplished, however, before the Overseer had even finished waving in refreshment, Abda blurted out: 'Sir, this girl is like a daughter to me. She has given great comfort to our company, and has worked wonders for those in need and spoken prophecies for our wellbeing. We wish with all our hearts not to lose her, but she desires to reside with you and learn your teaching.'

He was perhaps excessive in emotion upon parting with one who had become an adopted daughter, but I was mortified to hear my little fortune-telling described as 'wonders' and my mad ravings as 'prophecies' in front of such a holy man. Perhaps it was a question of lexicon, and he did not intend such a great word. I would have swooned if he had mentioned my interest in magic.

I was certain that this Abba Ahissa wouldn't approve of my using holy songs with heathens, especially not being of the priesthood and being a girl, much less my use of magical incantations of ancient godnames.

As my guardian, it was certainly Abda's place to make my introduction, but to have revealed my suit so abruptly! I had intended first to suggest that my family had sent me for tutelage, and I had gone as far as to forge a letter purporting to be from my father, outlining our ancestry and begging the community to accept me as a novice.

I was torn by the shame of being praised in the midst of intending such deceit. I was very glad later that I had not given this letter to the priest, as it is one of their rules to never hide anything from members of the Brethren. Nor do they heed genealogies; what was valued here was one's zeal for righteousness and charity.

'Sir, your recommendation is well received,' the priest said to the merchant, 'and I assure you, my child,' he said turning to me, 'we welcome all supplicants. The Yachad turns away none who are Jew born and bred.'

He was an elderly man with a long white beard, rather stern in his words but with a kind smile. He wore a white head-band. He noticed my discomfort. 'Speak, child. Tell us of these wonders.'

'One cannot deem it a wonder simply to listen to what is in people's hearts. Sometimes HaShem speaks and I am listening.'

'To listen is holy, my child. Your guardian says you wish to learn. And what would you study?'

'The Holy Scriptures and the Wisdom of the Ancients.' I worried that my eyes red from crying made me look ill-suited for a scholar.

Abda looked bewildered. I think he had expected that my connection to the man was familial.

'Our rule is strict,' responded the priest. 'We haven't much time outside farming and prayers for reading and copying.'

'According to your instruction, Abba.' I touched the hem of his cloak.

'I applaud your obedience. Nevertheless... study of the Law is not seemly for a woman... of course.'

I had expected him to say this, but I took heart when he added, 'of course'. It was as if he were reciting a rule with which he himself did not agree. Furthermore, his voice raised slightly as he said it, as if we were sharing a joke. I remained silent, looking down but smiling just a little.

He smiled back, 'Our door is open to all Jews and proselytes, especially those who wish to follow the Way. It is only out of interest that I would know your mind.'

'And I gladly reveal it,' I said.

'Have you a particular interest?'

'Yes, Abba. And I have a gift, as well.' Abda had already presented the priests with gifts from the caravan, spices, fruit and a skein of beautiful blue silk, insisting on including my little donkey, which Abba Ahissa set aside for the Poor. Now I was the one blurting things out.

Abda was spellbound as I pulled out the Chaldee fragment. I had once shown Shu'dat my shard, but she wasn't very interested. Abda's eyes seemed to see a maga producing a starry amulet.

The priest examined the alien cuneiform letters. 'It's beautiful, but I cannot read it.'

'I can read a few words, Abba. It is Old Amorite, written in Shinar script, the language of our forefather Avraham.' I tried to pronounce it in their dialect.

'It is rare to find a maiden so learned.'

'I studied it with my father in the royal archives in Parthia.'

'Is that where this fragment comes from?'

'Yes, Abba, with the compliments of my family.' I blushed with the sin of my lie, but fortunately he was looking at the fragment.

The tablet would be my gift to the order—my dowry, I thought; the study would be my issue.

'A goodly gift, my child. We thank you, and we will offer it secure keeping, but this artefact is yours. You are our gift, the gift that the Lord has sent to our community. You are come to us, and we welcome you,' he said.

After our tearful goodbyes, Abda and Yatur's parents returned on the road back to the caravan, and I was ushered in to the Inspector. In every city in the Diaspora, there is an Ossaean who welcomes visitors and takes charge of the *tzedakah* box, for charity collections, which is hidden secret from the Roman tax collectors. At the Yachad, every visitor or novice passed first by the Inspector.

I swapped my camel hide sandals for ones made of sheepskin tanned with pomegranate. He took my earth coloured woolen robe and gave me a white tunic made of flax and a spade for covering my feet. 'Bodily eliminations must be buried from view,' he said, 'so as not to offend the sight of the Lord.'

During the evening meal, as my status was undecided, I did not sit with the general congregation nor certainly not with the priests and initiates. I sat in table fellowship with the outsiders. These were people who wished to abide with the Yachad but did not follow the Way. They were called Joiners. They all wore red headbands.

I sat next to a Greek girl from Qesarya named Alexia. On her other side was her bosom friend, a brown-skinned Cyrenian named Philyra. I knew I would like girls who were friends with foreigners. I had further cause to like Alexia, for the reason which had brought her to the Yachad. She had fled the recent anti-Jewish riot in Herod's city. There were many refugees from anti-Jewish violence in camp, but they were all Jews; Alexia was Greek. She was disturbed to see her Jewish neighbours killed, and it led her to the Jewish houses to offer support. There she had heard about the Way and came to yearn for the Kingdom of God.

The riot was over a property dispute concerning land

bordering a synagogue. The Greek owner erected structures, and young Jews tried to hinder the work. A prominent Jew gave Florus a bribe of eight talents to sort the matter in their favour, but the procurator had pocketed the money and done nothing.

Gessius Florus was Procurator of Judaea, winning his post by knowing the right people in Rome, of course. His wife was friends with the Empress Poppaea Sabina. But he was not popular, an arrogant man who lost no opportunity to advance his own fortune through bribery and extortion.

The following day, there was a disturbance in front of the synagogue where Jews came to Shabbat worship. A Greek mob was waiting for them, the property owners of Qesarya, the citizens, the attendees of the circuses.

One of them sacrificed some birds on an upturned chamberpot.

'You know why this made them mad,' she said.

'Scriptures prescribe this as a magical cure for leprosy,' Philyra added. She was a Jew born and bred, so she knew our holy books.

'They were trying to cast a plague on our people,' I said. 'You may not know the works of Manetho...'

They didn't.

'Manetho's history of Aegypt says that our Lawgiver was named Osarseph and led a band of lepers.'

This silly dispute over a wall had erupted in a massacre. There was fighting, and the cavalry came. Florus' men turned on the Jews, slaughtering many.

Jews 'would kill each other over a word', said the Greeks. They considered this a slur because they do not understand the power of the word. The Kittim rule with force; we rule with

Wisdom—that is the rule of the Law.

Philyra said her people had come from an island which had fallen into the ocean.

'The whole island?'

'Yes, long ago, before there were Greeks.'

Before there were Greeks..., I mused, before one people ruled another by force...it must have been a golden age.

After the meal, Abba Ahissa continued my interview, examining the Chaldee fragment.

'It is a Babylonian prayer to Attis,' I told him.

'What is this magic? 7, 14, it makes no sense.'

'It is a bad translation, by someone who transcribed it and did not understand the old language.'

'And you know the language of Avraham?'

'I know some words, Abba, but some of the words are missing here, you see, rendering the existing words incomprehensible.'

'So, you have translated it correctly?'

'No, Abba, I can make sense but only a piece of it, but one day maybe I shall know the whole. Perhaps with the help of your Sages...'

He challenged me, 'Our holy community has little use for Persian hocus-pocus. Why should we concern ourselves with foreign gods when we follow the one true God?'

I stood my ground. 'I believe this work could be interpreted another way, to render a key to the Kingdom of God. I believe it contains ancient Wisdom that is lost from our scriptures.'

'Our elders would frown upon works of ancient idolatry.'

'I would be no blasphemer.'

I thought of the secret practices back home in my cave, which I had hidden so fastidiously from my father. Perhaps I

106

was sinful to always believe that God intended me for the work to which I was drawn. I admit that I've struggled to achieve the obedience my masters so wanted me to learn.

At the time, my submission reassured him. 'We have few documents from those days, and few translations of this wedge-writing. And it would be useful for scholarly purposes to know about our ancestors,' he mused. 'I will consult the Council. We have very strict rules…, of course.'

I smiled again at 'of course'. 'Your discipline is my joy, Abba,' I said, again kissing his hem. And so began my tutelage with the Yachad.

I slept in the corner of Abba Ahissa's upper room that night. My place in the community would be decided by the Council of Twelve on the morrow. The heavy smell of charcoal smoke drifting up through the floorboards and through the skylight in the roof above me, I could hear the elderly couple below conversing pleasantly between them as I drifted to sleep. The talk was surely about me, but they sounded welcoming.

I awoke after a deep sleep and helped the Mother in the garden in the afternoon during study time while the men met.

When the Father returned home, he nodded to his wife with a smile, the affirmative to a question that hung in the air. She beamed a smile in return, and they both turned their smiles upon me.

'The council welcomes you into the Novitiate,' said Abba Ahissa.

Either he had told them only part of my story, or they had not reacted to it with the disapproval he had intimated. He left me with an understanding. 'The Brethren study all peoples' works, as all wisdom comes from the same place', but I must obey the Law. If I did anything against the order or unseemly for a woman, he would follow the rule of the Council.

Nor was that the end of my good fortune. The elderly couple went even further in their welcome of me.

The priest's wife, whose name, as God has willed, was the same as my own mother's, Sherah, continued, 'Sophia, you are of an age for the maidens' huts, but we would invite you, if it should be your will, to abide with us.'

'Our son abides at the Nazirite camp in Mird, you see,' said the Father, 'and we have no daughter.'

'Our hearts yearn for such a gentle companion,' said she, 'and my old hands need an assistant around the house.' Although my scratches and bruises from the hill in Babylon had healed many moons past, and the black demon I had fought had long been bound by the love of Shu'dat and her caravan life, the Mother seemed to know there was a problem. 'Whatever is your pain, child,' she said with kind words I never heard from my own grandmother, 'we pray that we may help you soothe it.'

I was overwhelmed and leant my forehead tearfully to their hems. Ima Sherah comforted me with a shawl, and said, 'I think you might still want for a mother, dear.'

She was right. I had fled my parents, but I was still a child. My Feeling Self yearned for a mother and a father as my Acting Self yearned for a teacher. Yet my tears of happiness were also tears of grief and shame. My father had taught me well, but in leaving had I betrayed him? No, I thought, he had betrayed me.

And my mother? My mother loved me well, as well as she might, first being ill and then with her arms and belly full of sons. Should I not be censured for so readily transferring my love to the Father and his wife? Should I beg God's forgiveness for my sinful ungrateful thoughts? The happiness of the years that followed convinced me that I was not in fault. I had all the comfort I needed in the space above Ima Sherah's fire.

There was a ceremony where I was given the grey headband of Novice, and Abba Ahissa adopted me as daughter according to the rules of the Yachad. The priest who spoke the words didn't seem to mind using my Greek name. It was considered an auspicious name for a female scholar. The Yachad name for Sophia/Wisdom was Epinoia, the First Thought, as evil exists only in the face of man's ignorance, but no one was going to name somebody that.

In fact, there was little assistance for which Ima Sherah needed my hands around the house. Meals were prepared and consumed communally, as was the washing of wool and linen. I was given duties along with the other women, but they were not taxing.

Neither did the Father's comments about the suitability of scholarship for a woman prove to be a problem. Women, as well as men, were allowed plenty of time for prayer and study. One of the physics was a Mother; she knew much knowledge and healing. There was another of the Mothers, Ima Miryam, who gave me much wisdom.

Word spread through the camp about the Chaldee tablet, though my exotic interest seemed less strange in this encampment of scholars. The learned men of the Council said that the tablet was my 'talisman', and that I should keep it. The Yachad would safeguard it in the archives, but I should consider it mine own.

At the time, I wondered if they had disdained or repudiated my document, or belittled my interest in the fragment as the silly fancy of a child. Later Ima Miryam told me, 'an object like that, which seems to you and only you to be more important than other objects, this is a sign that it is an object of power for you. As for the text, we can always make copies. Other scholars are free to study your document, as the archivist will safely store it, but it may be your especial interest that best nurtures the knowledge it offers.'

Dwellings and communal buildings at the Yachad were without ornament, as truth is the origin of simplicity, and our garments were simple—a woolen cloak in the winter and a linen mantle in summer. Our days were the suns and moons of pious farmers. We used no oil upon our skins as did the priests of Jerusalem—it was considered a defilement. We bathed thrice daily in pure living waters, and we changed not our clothes nor sandals until they were worn thin from work.

Before the rising of the sun, we were not allowed to speak of profane matters. We rose in the darkness solemnly, dressed in white linen and processed to a holy well to perform ablutions and Shacharit (morning prayers) at sunrise. Then we travailed in the fields, and at the fifth hour, after purifying our bodies again we broke our fast in silence at tables separated by rank. We ate no meat nor anything costly, one bowl filled with only one type of food, mostly bread seasoned with salt and hyssop, and drank no wine but clear springwater. After Noon Contemplations, we travailed again.

Working in the fields was also a religious ritual, as we see with our eyes and feel with our hands the goodness of God infusing the earth with its richness. Prayers were said at each stage of agriculture, and we rejoiced in the Lord's bounty on our table. Never was the weather a reason not to work the fields.

The Ossaeans were said to work miracles with fruit, vegetable and vine, and I learned their earth magic and the planting and harvesting rites. As we worked, those knowledgeable in such matters would teach us the secrets of the plants.

Each plant had its own sacred number, cosmic vibrations to which its growth responded, and those with most dissimilar qualities—according to the soils they favour, the humours in the air, or the pests that plague them—were planted furthest apart. In the fields of the Yachad, the principles of *kashrut* (dietary laws) were strictly applied. Each crop was prohibited from mixing with its neighbours by stone walls and tall hedgerows.

Much of this knowledge was a result of scholarship, but a lot of it was simply long experience with farming. The Yachad had been cultivating in the wilderness since the days of Yannai. They had learned to enrich the sandy soil with seaweed from the Sea of Death, washed clean from its salt and tar, and to protect crops from crawling things by planting the Persian Insect Flower.

Once morning work in the fields was done, and there were many hands for that, then it was time for study and prayer. For those following the Way, as now I was separated from the Joiners, afternoons until the tenth hour were devoted to study and prayer, different grades of initiate speaking their prayers at different hours. The study was organised in grades like the prayers, with certain teachers called Maskilim (Sages) and craftsmen giving instruction at certain hours. As well as teaching, the Sages were responsible for keeping demons away from the Yachad.

After breaking fast, all but the Kedoshim—the saints and elders—joined those in the fields until supper. Those women with cooking duties finished slightly earlier. Ma'ariv (evening prayers) was said at sunset, after which we would partake of the goodness of the fields, which we also ate in ritual cleanliness. Sometimes there were guests at supper at the table of the Joiners.

In the evening, those who qualified attended nightly meetings for Scripture study with the priests.

Nor was the life of an ascetic always quiet and sober, for God loves beauty and the arts. We played the flute; we sang psalms and hymns to the heavens in every meter and melody known on earth. We clapped our hands and danced in the desert, the women following a 'Miryam' and the men following a 'Moshe'. After the evening meal we sang hymns called *zemirot*, in choirs divided antiphonally into men and women, using hands and feet to keep our accompaniment.

It was not a requirement, but most took up a musical instrument. I began to play the tabla, the resonant drumbeats reminding me of the rhythms of sacred songs. I did a bit of painting, but the only one that was any good, I thought, was the one of Babylonia viewed from the hills.

## Chapter 8
## The demon in the black cloud

I had yearned for the holy life, but it was the anticipation of the Yachad's store of ancient knowledge that had sped my feet across the stadia. I was quick to inquire about the Yachad's archives and offer my services.

'Archives—it is irregular, a girl working among the boys,' Ima Sherah argued. 'You should rather be apprenticed to one of the Mothers.'

Abba Ahissa said, 'Wife, you see the child is longing to touch sacred scrolls again, and it is not a sinful desire, but a desire to serve the Lord. It is not for us to defy it.'

They both smiled at me, and it was agreed.

The archivist Shaphan accepted me among his apprentices, and I soon divided my afternoons between prayers, lessons, fields and working there. The beloved treasure of a community of scholars, the scrolls were well looked after in the desert. But I had learned a few extra things in the big city, and in my youthful zeal, I itched to impart what I considered my superior knowledge. The archivist, however, did not appreciate my presumption.

My biggest disappointment was my lack of access to works of foreign Wisdom. There were Hebrew, Aramaic, and Greek scripts, but none in the ancient languages.

I repeated to Sofer (Scribe) Shaphan what Abba Ahissa had said on our first meeting, commenting somewhat antagonistically, 'I had understood the Yachad was open to foreign works.'

'We are open to them,' the archivist responded, raising an eyebrow, 'but we do not expend our labours on them at the wrong time.'

'What does this mean, the wrong time?' I said, and asked permission myself to be allowed to copy foreign books. The Sofer flatly refused me. 'After your initiation is passed,' he said.

I complained of this to Abba Ahissa, but he said, 'We have works here in our hut; you may practice your writing at home.'

Day after day, I came home burning with anger, but I continued to hope for the fruition of my studies under Sofer Shaphan.

Being a girl, I had to sit at a separate table from the boys, which added to my frustration, but really, I was used to this kind of isolation. What I could not support was the isolation from learning.

Outside the archives I managed to speak to some of the boys about their studies, and of course other brothers came in from time to time with inquiries about which they were willing to discuss.

Several brothers were passionants of the wisdom of the Orient, more acquainted with Zoroastrian writings than this girl from Persia, the roots of the Ossaean teaching having come from Assyria. The Yachad was the righteous remnant, true to the law before the days of Yannai. Queen Shlomtzion had given the Tzadikkim certain minor fortresses for protection, the old Hasmonean fortress of Secacah and the Yachad at Ein Gedi among them. The Diggers of the Well had made the desert bloom for more than five generations.

Some brothers studied lost arts like the secret letters of the Gaulish Druids, which they struck in code upon their shins or noses to converse across rivers. So, on islands of the Great

Green Sea do priests speak with their fingers. Brother Yosi taught me some of the shin language. It was very comical when one substituted the nose.

In time I discovered that there were shelves way up high in the archives stocking the most ancient of Ossaean scriptures, tablets and scrolls in Chaldee, Akkadian and Aegyptian glyphs, with secret knowledge of sacred geometry and wisdom of the stars. The Brethren marked the fields in advanced geometry passed down from the land of Goshen. The Aegyptians who taught them knew the sacred rules from the long measuring of their floods. In Idumaea, they knew the names of constellations and letters since before the days of Job.

These were the treasures possessed by the Yachad which I was not allowed to touch. These were what Shaphan denied me because it was 'not the right time'. This Wisdom had been handed down to the Kedoshim from Avraham, preserved by the prophets of Mount Carmel, and I was not allowed to read it.

These treasures were kept in cabinets under lock and key, and the keys were firmly in the hands of Sofer Shaphan. Certain that my calling to the Wisdom of the Chaldees necessarily drew me to these cabinets, I outright asked permission to read them.

He forbade me, 'These are for the higher orders.'

'Master, I am drawn to this work through God's grace. I have been commanded,' I pleaded. 'It is in search of this Wisdom that I left my home to seek admission to the Yachad.'

'Your admission is granted, Novice,' he said strictly, 'and there will be the time for you to pursue your search, but you must not hasten. There is much you must learn first. I regret if you suffer with impatience, but it is not for you to decide where you are commanded.'

I went red in the face and could not reply, and bristled for many days, wondering over his meaning by the comment 'suffer with impatience'. Indeed, at the archives, I only studied what he commanded, and it seemed as if all that ever was was books of rules.

So, I learned the rules.

> No engaging in commerce with the uncircumcised, for 'the righteous may not trade with the Sons of the Pit'.

> No spitting on the ground, for there were those who were jealous of Ossaean magic and 'would steal our emissions for evil sorcery'. Spitting in Assembly was a penance of thirty days.

The rules regarding purity were especially strict:

> 'The holy water of the *mikva'ot* (ritual pools) must originate from a source untouched by the unrighteous'.

...as were the rules about comportment within the community:

> 'Respect the privacy of Brethren in prayer, for it is when one is by oneself that one is in the presence of God'.

> 'Whoever has interrupted his companion whilst speaking must do penance for ten days'.

> 'Whoever has borne false witness against his brother shall not partake of holy meals for six months'.

I conducted my studies with permitted books in between duties at the archives, but Sofer Shaphan upbraided me for it whenever he could think of a menial job for me to do. With his knowledge, he could certainly have helped me in my studies and my prayers, but he never did. The only words he ever spared me were of lists that I should write or dusting I should do. In the earlier period, I had even made a cutting remark, commenting petulantly that 'I wouldn't know whether the Yachad had anything to teach me, as I haven't been allowed to learn anything yet'.

He may have taken it as I intended it, but he deflected me, explaining that 'in our order, we study different things at different ranks'.

I already knew that. I was complaining that the disciple was dissatisfied with the master.

After several moons, I had ceased to propose any Babylonian reforms; I just did what I was told.

I sought guidance from Abba Ahissa my adopted father.

'It is not for you to decide the work HaShem requires of you,' he rebuked me, 'for everyone shall know his appointed position in the community of God. And none shall be exalted above his allotted place. You made yourself an enemy by lacking humility. You should have listened to what your master had to teach.'

'But he hasn't taught me anything.'

'He has given you the teaching, but you have not listened. Your ears and heart must be open first.'

Ima Sherah agreed with him, 'Your anger is closing you. Anger is like the sin of idolatry, as you are denying that God is in His power in the world.'

'Obey the three principles,' the Father reminded me, 'love of God, love of righteousness, love of man. You cannot love the knowledge before you love the teacher who possesses it.'

My transgression was not merely toward the archivist, Abba Ahissa said. In my childish shouting, I had closed my ears and heart to hearing God's wishes. 'This is why your work has not found you grace.'

He was right. I had two problems, my unhappy relations with the archivist and my unhappiness in my duties.

'I would counsel you to go to Sofer Shaphan and beg forgiveness, and pray to the Lord to open your heart,' said the Father.

I know it was the obvious thing, but at the time, his counsel was against my own heart. Should that nasty man, so devoted to boring lists, so seemingly unenthused by the ecstasy of knowledge, have the right to say what is God's will for me? Any more than my uncle should have?

I prayed devoutly all night and stayed long in the *mikveh* on the morrow, but that afternoon I did not go to the library. I could not bear the thought of seeing Sofer Shaphan. Abba Ahissa went in my place, bidding me wait at home. When he returned, he called me in again.

'Sophia, my dear, Shaphan is not averse to forgiving the over-enthusiasm of your youth. He maintains your work has much improved, and he is willing to have you there. He questions most honestly, though, if you will find grace in the work.'

That I should not find grace in a library—it was shocking to me. Both my background and my Acting Self pulled me to scrolls and tablets. Was I not born and bred to the service of an archivist? The Yachad had no stipulation against women scholars, so why should I be rejected?

The Rabbi kept me at home while we discussed it over many evenings. Every time I saw the face of Sofer Shaphan in my mind, my Feeling Self filled with utter unhappiness. Should it be true that he came to do by me differently, could I do by him differently?

In the end it was Abba Ahissa who went to him. As my adopted father, he told Shaphan he believed I was too young for the work, adding that the Mothers wondered if it was the right environment for me 'in with the boys'. The archivist granted to release me from my apprenticeship.

'Your heart is still closed, Sophia,' Abba Ahissa told me. 'Find some other duties for a while. There are many ways to serve God. The doors to the library may open again if HaShem so wills.'

Yet, I was devastated. Techniques for the care and copying of documents were the greatest skills I possessed; could I not offer these to God? It was work that I both knew and loved, yet I had failed. Again, I had made myself an enemy, through no deliberate evil but through my lack of understanding and selfishness.

All the verbal arrows of my family on that horrible night came back to haunt me. I couldn't imagine ever working under the archivist again, I dreaded even seeing the man; I couldn't even bring myself ever again to read at the archives. For many weeks, I suspended my studies and fell again under the curse of the black cloud.

In the end though, it must have been God's will, as it was thus that I came to be apprenticed to Ima Miryam. She cared for me in my illness, and she most verily worked magic upon me.

My adoptive parents could make no sense of my exaggerated melancholy. My hearing again heightened, I overheard Ima Sherah berating her husband on my account.

'Husband, you judged her as a priest, but you are more than that to her. You accepted God's gift of this child to us, and now you must be a father to her.' She spoke more softly after that, but I could hear the two of them talking about my troubles back home, how I was 'sensitive'.

'Is it a demon?' I heard her ask. He responded in the negative, but I couldn't hear the rest.

After that, he spoke many times comfortingly to me, assuring me that I'd done nothing wicked.

I asked him, too, 'Abba, is it a demon that pursues me?'

'My dear,' he replied, 'I do not think so. It is only that you are young. You expect too much of yourself. You have lessons to learn, but so do we all. Think not that at my age I know everything that must be known. Surely, I have much to learn about being a father, as I see I have so upset you.'

'No, no, Abba,' I protested, 'the fault is mine.'

'Learning from our mistakes is what HaShem requires from us, but you, girl, take it too far,' said Abba Ahissa. I did manage to laugh, but such was my dejection at the time, the remark only made me feel worse that I had so over-reacted to my new father's counsel.

'Perhaps it is exorcism she needs,' I heard Ima Sherah whisper on occasion. He disagreed, but gave his permission to seek guidance from Ima Miryam.

Ima Sherah went to Ima Miryam to ask for the performance of an exorcism. I couldn't wait that long; the pain in my head was so acute; I was dangling on the precipice of Sheol (hell). After all, I knew the exorcism rites myself. I smeared spittle on my forehead, and repeated the formula, over and over, minute after minute, as if the words could form a net to hold me back from the cliff edge.

Declare thy name, and speak only thy name.
I, Sophia, order you to be gone, be gone, be gone,
depart from my days and depart from my dreams.
Depart, I implore you, and never return.

Desperate, I knocked my head over and over against the floor,
as I boiled up a basin of the nine-leaved hellebore; it was said
to have cured the madness of the daughters of Proteus.

Ima Sherah found my basin of hellebore, and suddenly all
the Mothers were worried about me. She escorted me to Ima
Miryam's hut, but I was so taken by the cloud I was unable
even to greet her with politeness.

'She really troubled us when we saw the nine-leaved hellebore,' Ima Sherah told her. 'This is some demon that follows
her from Babylon.'

'That is not a potion to meddle with, Novice,' Ima Miryam
replied, 'especially in your state. It can cause madness as well
as cure. Calm yourself, now.'

The original recipe included mare's blood. I suppose she
really would have cautioned me if I'd tried to use that.

The demon spoke in my ear, 'You've never fit into any family,
not at home, and not here; all you cause is trouble. You never
have good relations with elders. No one could ever love you,
because you don't love them. Think you're a scholar? Think
you're a lover of God? Your heart is nothing but selfishness.'
The evil words poured forth with my tears.

Ima Miryam listened and listened. It seems there was some
word she was waiting for, something I did or some words I

said, because when that moment came, her eyes opened wide, and grasping my elbow she said quietly, 'Stop, I command you to stop.'

The room was suddenly as silent as on that hillside with the fox. I looked in her eyes, fully expecting a demon to burst forth from my chest and nothing less. My heart beat hard, and I heard her every word intensely. Her eyes softened.

'It is not a demon whom I command, but you, Sophia.' She was silent for a long time, I, the chided pupil, pondering her meaning. Then she explained. 'There is no fault in you, Novice, but laziness. Laziness,' and she tapped the floor with her staff; tap—I stand accused. 'Stop,' she tapped, tap—and I am released.

With that one word, 'stop', the descent into Sheol did simply that; it stopped. My Feeling Self paused at the edge of the cliff, regained balance and took a breath, and I was suddenly able to notice things around me. The air in the hut was fresh with the smell of herbs; the cauldron boiled on the hearth. It was time enough for me grasp the branch she held out for my rescue.

'You give the demon too much power. He is nothing', said Ima Miryam. 'Look, there is your black cloud.' She waved her staff in the air and made a noise, 'Fhoo', as if blowing the cloud away like a tiny puff of smoke. It was a brilliant image.

She counseled me not to neglect my invocations, morning, noon and night, and to speak the words 'I command you to stop'.

'You don't need an exorcism,' she said. This practice needn't even require a special time of day, I could simply say those words silently in my head, and bid the wicked words begone any moment they arose. Every morning in the mikveh, I must pledge, 'today I will command the words to stop'.

'Remember that you are good. Just a little lazy, as are we all,' she said. 'If you ever forget to love yourself, do this for me. When the evil thoughts come, you will not be alone. I will be there to remind you.'

It was the most comforting thing anyone had ever said to me.

Before I left, she added, 'as, of course, will be your Chaldee maga'. She knew the secrets of my Feeling Self. I must have confessed my arcane pursuits in the course of my ravings. I actually giggled.

When I arrived home, Abba Ahissa and Ima Sherah both embraced me; they could see the change.

The heaviest yield of citrons was in the autumn; and in the grove after prayers, though I daily told him to 'stop', the demon was still upon me for some time. I contended with him in between the fruit trees as he cast his threatening shade in the space where the Lord lights not my soul upon the earth. In those days I called him by the name of Abaddon, the king of the locust demons.

With the lengthening of the hours, his stature did increase, and I was ever more powerless, neither to bind him nor to cast him out. I felt him manifested in every trick of the light and felt locusts on my skin at every breeze. The works supervisors knew not of my struggle, of course, and did not comment on my morbid contemplation.

When I returned to her on my first free afternoon after the harvest, Ima Miryam saw the turmoil in my face.

'Sophia, you jump at nothing but your own fear. It is nothing. Seek not to banish the demon, but to bind him. You have the power to do this because you are his master. Stand in the morning and see how he decreases, as God shines in his power upon the loveliness of the day. That is the one side.' Tap. She tapped the wall on the eastern side with her staff. 'What you see in the evening is nothing but the reflection of your own power. On the other side,' Tap, and she tapped the western side, 'It is not the demon increasing, it is you.

As God has dominion over the day, he gave us our angels to guard the gates of night. So do not shrink from the shade, love it, embrace it, welcome it back into your bosom. The goodness of God is both light and dark.'

On further occasions, Ima Miryam further lifted me. She told me tales of the universe, not that she knew the workings of the stars, she simply knew how to tell a story. As I listened, I felt as if I were flying in the sky. I thought, how small am I, yet how intricately connected to every other small piece in God's vastness.

After I had been visiting Ima Miryam for several weeks, she remarked, 'where is the black cloud now, then?'

I happily admitted I had not thought about it since the day she told me the story of the universe. 'Fhoo', I said, waving my hand in the air.

'Do not slacken in your invocations. The angels will give you the power,' she said.

It seems easy. But I do slacken.

Abba Ahissa and the Elders approved of the new arrangement. The cloud was gone. I had found an Elder with whom I did have good relations. I became Ima Miryam's disciple with enthusiasm.

Ima Miryam held a staff, though she was not aged, being of years that could still bear a child if such were her destiny. She did not walk with it. She was quite young for a Mother, and the picture of health. Every step she took was with a slight bound, and she never seemed to tire. She was always moving, she never sat still. She loved the saying of Shammai: 'Speak little, do much'. When she smiled, you wondered if she were mocking you. When she spoke, she always put on a performance, using the staff as percussion.

The thatch of the walls surrounding her in her hut gave a yellow hue to her hands and bony cheeks under her blue headband that reminded me of my mother under the citron tree. Her skin was always very dry.

In her easy approach, she drew me to her. My ear was so opened to her, I practically memorised her every word. I think I knew her for my master the moment I starting noticing who was around me during my black days. At first, I felt that whatever I had learned in Babylon would be welcome in her chambers. I felt a trust for her such as I had felt for Shu'dat and for my father, especially after she pulled me away from the demon.

I basked in the radiance of Ima Miryam's holiness. For a few weeks I was still distressed about the archives, but each time evil thoughts entered my head, Ima Miryam's face appeared before my mind's eye, and I continued my chores. Just a little laziness is all, I told myself, I'll say prayers this afternoon. 'I command you to stop, Fhoo!' I snapped at the nothing demon. I felt safe from the black cloud for months and months.

While ever assuring me, as did everyone else too, that my feelings about what happened should not keep me from the archives, Ima Miryam consoled me.

'You need not go yourself. I can obtain works for you, and Abba Nehuniyyah, the Sage who teaches you Tanakh may provide you with materials.'

It was kind of her, and indeed she kept me busy with scrolls and papyri. But they were always the ones she assigned, it seemed, never the ones I desired.

To my protestations of desire to read the ancient works, she would say, 'This Wisdom will be opened to you, Novice. Do not hasten. There is an order by which you must learn, Sophia. Do not struggle against the discipline, for in following the Way is true freedom. It is this lesson that Shaphan tried to teach you.'

Perhaps I had indeed learned something of humility from my chastening, as I had not mentioned the subject of magic to Ima Miryam. It was she who asked me. In the days of the dark cloud, it would not have occurred to me anyway. She was obviously a woman of power–the Saints seemed to acknowledge this, and she wore the blue headband of Master. Some of the Novices called her Miryam Maga. Surely, she would take me for a child or a charlatan. Yet, I was warmed by the way she approached me.

'I hear you know some tricks. Teach me what you know; I'll teach you what I know. You shall be my apprentice, and the apprentice shall also teach the master.'

I said the only trick I knew was how to listen to people, tell them what they wanted to hear, and pray to God.

She said, 'I shall have little to teach you, then. You have already grasped the heart of it.'

I said I couldn't believe she would accept me 'after seeing me in such a state'.

'That has passed, as God wills,' she said.

'I also owe thanks to you, Ima,' I said.

The Council permitted my study of Ossaean magic, learning Ima Miryam's 'tricks'. 'They know the difference between sorcery and divine magic,' she said, 'but there's no need to invite censure.'

Abba Ahissa would discuss with me, though always with a bit of a twinkle in his old eyes, as if secretly amused by my silly notions. He did often warn me against blasphemy, but I had no fear. I was righteous in my magician's quest for God.

'Great magic can be a mistranslation of greater mysteries,' I impertinently told him.

'But perhaps it is too focused on the stars and nature rather than God,' he mused. 'It is dangerous for Man to try to touch God.'

'No,' I said. I dared it because I believed it. 'God wants us to touch Him. Magic builds a fully developed person; it builds the personal power of the maga, and He is pleased.'

He kissed me on the brow, and directed me to speak about it to Ima Miryam.

She loved hearing of my flights of fantasy regarding the Chaldee maga, but often when I told her about one of my 'tricks', she would say something like, 'Leave that one, child; you're not ready.' I told her about a Nabatu spell for power I'd learned from the caravan women involving eating the liver of wild game.

She merely retorted, 'Flesh is banned to us.'

I continued to feel a desperate anxiety, but I think she was right. My strange experience in the cave was a warning that I should not practice magic without tutelage.

Yet still I argued, 'Why do others get to decide when I am ready? Is it not a matter of choice, my choice?'

'No,' she said, 'it is because your masters can see further than you can. When you are ready, the choice will be yours, but you must listen to guidance to know when you are ready.'

'Do not rush so along the path, Sophia,' she counselled. 'Give yourself time. It is not wisdom to be in such a hurry to learn everything. The hour for everything is ordained in heaven. Learn each step well, or the ladder may fail you.'

It is good counsel, but I doubt if I have lived it.

Duly chastened, I succumbed to the Ossaean programme, and eventually I became more patient. For all that first year of noviceship, I never even looked at, much less studied, my Chaldee tablet, the gift I had given to the Yachad, which Abba Ahissa had assured me was still essentially mine. What would have been the point? I had no materials to use in such a study, no references. There were lexicons; these were not secret knowledge. But I had already consulted these in Babylon, so there was nothing new I could add to my understanding.

There was plenty to learn, anyway. Everything Ima Miryam taught me was wonderful, and filled up all the time I wasn't in the fields or in prayer. There was much to learn in Tanakh–Scripture classes–as well. Chaldee study could wait for the future.

# Chapter 9
## The best disciple

I ma Miryam already had two disciples.

The elder disciple was named Tsuiyah. She had been raised in Sekhem (Egyptian healing rite), blessed from birth in the Way, and she wore a bluegreen headband. She resided at Ein Qaneh, another camp, but she came for lessons to ours now and then. Though she was not far above me in age, she did not become my friend. My heart so longed for an older sister like Shu'dat had been to me, but Sister Tsuiyah was ever cold.

I felt she considered my Novice status a contamination that would rub off onto her if she should ever approach me. Every rebuff injured me twice. First, because the senior disciple rejected me, second because of the sharp contrast with the warmth of Shu'dat's love which I so missed.

I pictured in my mind's eye Shu'dat in all her Arabian finery at her marriage. The year had turned, she would be departed by now across the Arabian desert with Yatur by her side. How I would love to have seen my beloved friend under her bridal canopy, all the riches of the Orient adorning her camel procession and the smile of a woman's happiness on her beautiful face. But instead of soothing me with such a happy image, it grieved me to remember days when relations with an older sister were so full of love.

I asked Tsuiyah to tell me about Sekhem, and she replied curtly, as I should have known she would, 'we are not permitted to reveal the mysteries to one whose time has not come.'

I, for my part, thought—well may she know the mysteries of Eliyahu, but what does she know of Chaldee or the history of Shinar?' So, we studied together, but not side by side, each on opposite sides of the Mother.

Ima Miryam was not concerned. 'You may learn together without liking,' she told me.

The junior disciple was a darling girl of about eight years named Imme. Imme was distressed by our conflict. Tsuiyah had been with the Mother when the girl arrived, and they were familiar to each other. Imme's sisterly joy at seeing her senior again was tempered by the friction between the two of us.

From whomever of the Brethren I sought guidance, I would hear more about my lack of humility, and I tired of hearing it. To me it seemed the problem resulted rather from Tsuiyah's lack of humility. So, I stayed quiet about it, and tried to concentrate on my studies.

Imme was one of the many orphans of the persecutions taken into the camp, adopted by Ima Miryam as I had been by Abba Ahissa, and permitted to enter as full Novice due to her gracious disposition. So, for ceremonies and when she could be persuaded to trouble herself with it, she wore the grey headband as I did.

Despite her tender years, she had already learned much from Ima Miryam, especially about herbs and flowers. Too small for the fields, she tended the hortus and courtyard gardens with the Mother in the mornings, with help from the physics and their apprentices when they were not indisposed, and played with others of her age in the afternoons.

She was fond of making me an infusion from pure pool water when I arrived in the afternoon. She would pick just a certain combination of herbs and flowers, 'guessing my mood', she said, as I sat down. I don't know whether she guessed right, but I always felt refreshed as we began our lessons.

Imme showed me the secrets of the hortus and the qualities of flowers. The balsam flower, she showed me, has 'three of those and five of those', she gently picked off the petals with fat little fingers to show me the tiny parts on the interior, 'and five of those that become the fruit. Beans are similar, but no other flower is exactly like that.'

She taught me so much, yet it was never a lesson, but rather an exuberant game. They were little adventures where she would reveal to me the wonders of the earth, as if they were treasures she had buried just for me to discover.

She taught me the ingredients for her simples, referring to every flower and herb as 'this one' or 'that one'. 'The one with the hairy stems'. 'Beware the stems on this one, the hairs stick into the skin'. 'Some of this one for sore eyes when you read too much, Sophia; and a tea of that one to stop the overflow of blood when you have the woman's bleeding—put in enough to make the water as brown as palm bark. 'That one when it's painful passing water'.

So disinclined was she to tell me the names, one would think she didn't know them. If Ima Miryam were present, however, she would tap her staff to make the girl speak the names of the magical plants—'mugwort', 'periwinkle', 'meadowsweet'. On the urging of Ima Miryam's tapping, she was more often than not quite able to produce them promptly.

'When you speak the name of it, you claim its power,' Ima Miryam taught us. But even without the naming, the concoctions seemed to draw curative abilities from Imme's bubbling

131

affection and energy. The transfer of power seemed to work the other way around.

When the black cloud was upon me, Imme brought me tea of geranium, lavender, rosemary and orange blossom, though indeed it may have been her cheerful attention that lifted my spirits as much as the sweet aromas. One sixth day she brought me a bowl of strawberries saying, 'the Mothers worry that you have not desired to marry.'

I happily ate her berries, but explained, 'Imme, many men and women choose not to marry, especially in these Last of Days.'

'You mean because the world is soon to end?'

'That's right.'

I did not make her sad by so saying, as we all believed this to be a joyful expectation.

She had a quietness of speech that was hypnotising. Though often over-energetic when lessons were going on, when she herself spoke, it began with a tinkle and ended with a whisper. The softness of her words made you listen, and as the end of her utterance lilted upward, she would look glistening into your eyes and smile the most angelic smile. As if she were about to say, 'I'm going to tell you a delightful secret, just you.' One wanted her ever to say more, as if by hearing more of the story you could be transported into her halo of sweetness.

No matter their rank, if any brethren rebuffed her, I would make bold to say something, something like 'she only wanted to let you know that she has made a tea for you'. If I incurred rebuke, at least the pain would be lessened for her, as it would be we two disciples together. A few times I had to do penance for ten days for 'speaking before one of higher rank', but in my heart I did not repent. Nor do I believe HaShem held me at fault.

In gratitude for the herbal lore Imme taught me, I taught her Greek, as she was keen to learn it. She particularly wanted to write the letters, so we mostly did that.

For her, it was not the power of letters to name the communications of the hearts of men in our yearning for Wisdom, from across lands and throughout time–that was what fascinated me. For Imme, it was the letters themselves and the dances they make, their forms, differences and correspondences.

Ima Miryam smiled, 'And so the apprentices teach each other. God's wisdom increases.'

There were times when other Novices and Sisters would come for lessons, too. When it was a group of us, Imme would be calmer, and we could listen in peace. She told me that in group lessons, when her mind felt the urge to wander, she would wile her energy trying to guess each pupil's mood. She had the knack of sitting beside just the one who would be most cheered by her bright little countenance.

Ima Miryam's staff was made of almondwood, straight as straight, polished and treated with bitumen from the Salt Sea so it would never rot. At the head of it, strapped into a hessian weave, was a shiny black stone, shaped like a large egg, around which she would wrap her fingers. She used this aid not for support, but for punctuation. When she wished to draw a comparison, tap went the staff to the left, and tap to the right.

'Anemones–tertian fever; Black briony–scrofula; Oil of osier bark–stiffness of the limbs'–there was a left-right tap for each pair. 'Cochicine–for gout; Sweet cicely–for warts'.

It did not do to sit near her when she was teaching, which she would always do standing, though we were allowed to sit. Imme was even allowed to run around or be distracted by other things, as children are wont to be. It reminded me of my brothers' cacophony and disturbed me. Soon or later, though, tap would go the staff in front of whatever had attracted the girl's attention.

'Bitumen in wine, Imme?'—tap—'watery elimination'.

Much knowledge has fixed to my mind and jumps to the tip of my tongue for learning by the staff. When I banish my demon, I see the wave of the staff and hear Ima Miryam's voice 'Fhoo'. It is as if my Feeling Self and my Acting Self are working together. My ear hears the tap of the staff, and my memory retains the words. The Mother said it was because the rhythm connects with the Dreaming Self.

Such things stick in the mind:

> The secret names of the sun—tap—girls?
> Orjares, and Tomas.
> The four names of the moon?—tap—
> Asonja, Ebla, Benase, and Erae.

When a conclusion had been reached, and she wished to hear discussion or questions from the pupils, Ima Miryam would stand the staff directly in front of her, both hands resting calmly on the black stone.

The staff was an ancient thing, handed down from mother to daughter, maga to maga. Its antiquity and its symbol of the continuity of teaching spanning the generations gave it much power. Until her death, no one but the Mother was allowed to touch it. As Ima Miryam was a bridesmaid of God and would not have a daughter of her own flesh, the Staff of Matriarchs was promised to Imme.

'She has a gift,' the Mother told me. 'And as she is orphaned, the Yachad will always be her home. She will continue the Way after me, as will you.'

I did not dispute her, nor on account of Imme's gift, nor on account of her choice of heir to the school. Though distracting at times, Imme truly shone with adorable goodness. With the wisdom of maturity, the piety of the Yachad lifestyle, and Ima Miryam's guidance, surely, she would one day be a Kadosh (Saint) of great holiness.

It was thoughtful of the Mother to put it to me thus, so as not to engender envy. Nevertheless, though I was not honest enough to admit it, I think I coveted the precious object. Not that I regretted the joining of my goods to the Ebionim; I had nothing to give up. Only my little tablet fragment, and that was best preserved in the Yachad archive, anyway; nor was my bedroll nor saddlebag the place for an antique piece of clay.

Yet my wicked heart yearned to possess such a magical object, a talisman held in the hands of ancient matriarchs, and my eyes lingered especially upon that shiny black stone, of which Ima Miryam's whirling fingers so rarely allowed a glimpse. Seductive was the desire to be the best disciple, the most famous pupil, the favoured daughter, the chosen one.

That night I went to bed thinking of my father and all the shiny things Shu'dat and I had seen in the Palmyra market, and had covetous dreams.

Once Imme saw me eying the Staff of Matriarchs when it was standing in the corner out of Ima Miryam's hand. So skillful was she always at guessing my mood, she utterly shamed me, without having the slightest intention of doing so.

'When Mother goes to the ones who sleep, I'll say you can hold it whenever you like.'

This shocked me, as I had not hitherto acknowledged even to myself that I was envious. I, the devoted disciple, rankling against the Mother's word? I, the celibate Ossaean Novice, desirous of a worldly bauble? And darling Imme, surely, I could harbour no uncharitable thoughts toward such an angel?

I blushed and giggled, caught out, 'You'll do nothing of the sort, sweet creature.' And I kissed her cheek. 'The Staff of Matriarchs is Ima Miryam's talisman, and when you are Mother it will be your own. No one can take it or borrow it from you.'

'Yes,' she replied thoughtfully, 'Mother says magic is special for each maga.'

'The ancient writers in Babylon said it as well. Anyway, perhaps I shall have my own talisman.'

'Yes. We shall look for one for you.' She nodded, and we both stood taller as we held hands and went to help Ima Miryam with whatever it was.

I gave thanks to God that Ima Miryam in her straight-forwardness and Imme in her sweetness had freed me from covetous and prideful thoughts, and I slept well that night.

One afternoon Imme saw me crying, and learning that I was grieving for my father, sat with me and listened, passing me the cloth. Soon she also began to unburden her own grief about her parents. She was so young, the memory of it was not clear before her, and she was not really able to put the story into words. But she cried the entirety of it into those tears, and when finished, popped back up to finish the day with the brightness of a squirrel in the morning.

'Not me,' I told her. 'I'm all moans and tears like a thirsty camel mourning for her young. Crying always make me exhausted and ashamed of myself.' I considered that the tears were connected to the demon and that it was my own sinfulness that had brought about whatever was the problem in question.

That was not how she saw it. 'It is not the tears that are bad. It's what caused the tears to come. Tears wash away the hurt.'

She was right, I thought. Tears can wash away pain. But what about guilt? What about the realisation, just too late, that you have done something wrong? What about the pain of knowing you have sinned?

'Repentance is what washes that pain away,' was Ima Miryam's answer, accompanied by a tap on the second letter of the word 'RePENtance'. 'And what redeems the soul is'—tap—'works. The girl speaks truly, Sophia. They are as water dripping onto a stone. However tiny each drop may feel, together they are a force that can wear away a mountain.'

'What about the tears that come from injustice?' I said. 'Things that hurt you but you cannot change.' *A proper maiden, a proper maiden* echoed in my ears like the braying of crows.

'The first thing to do is to put the blame where the blame belongs,' she instructed. 'Women have a tendency to blame themselves for injustices done to them. And weak people have a tendency to blame the victim.' She clasped two hands around the black stone of her staff and looked at me, inviting me to say something, but I was silent.

'Belial and the Sons of Darkness can be defeated, but the pain of injustice can never really be healed,' she said. I knew it to be true. Because I never took the steps, the hurt remained

137

rooted within my breast.

'Do not begrudge your tears; they heal you. Instead, pour them out as a sin offering to God. Come the morning, perform an act of loving kindness or bravery.'

It was wise advice, and it stood me well in later years during the war.

After she had so well consoled me, that night I consoled Imme as she went to bed. Though her tears had washed her clean from grief, no one had truly explained to the girl just why her parents were murdered. I did not myself know, and nor did Ima Miryam. Imme knew that her parents' demise was part of the birthpangs of the End of Times, but she couldn't understand it. As we become older, we may come to understand these worldly events, but only because we have accepted evil and sinful things—greed, vice, blood and sin—as truth.

'Why do people want to have war, Sophia? The Kittim soldiers are so strong and they have big weapons. If people fight, they will get killed.'

'That may be true, Imme,' I said, 'but there are some things worth dying for. We men and women are small compared to the greatness of God. The things that are sacred to God are worth defending, even with our lives.'

We talked about that for a bit, but she started to get distressed again, and it was becoming so late Ima Miryam was giving me the eye to say the child needed her sleep.

We had imparted to each other a piece of our pain. Surely, it is a comfort to feel that one is not alone. And as Imme maintained, a good flood of tears from time to time clears the soul. In the end, though, it is in looking to larger things that we gain consolation and hope.

I told her I would sing her a song to soothe her into dreaming. The Dreaming Self is most receptive to heavenly energies just upon waking and just before sleep, and in song.

I stroked her hair. 'Take shallow breaths and you will be calmed.'

It was an old song about the New Jerusalem.

> Of righteous government there will be no end,
> the wolf will not threaten the lamb, nor will the leopard
> threaten the kid,
> the desert shall rejoice and blossom as the rose,
> the parched ground will become a pool,
> the trees shall clap their hands,
> and the nations will be drawn to the light of God.

As her eyes began to droop, she asked, 'Sister, what it will be like when Moshiach comes?'

'I don't know, Imme, but surely it will be better than this.'

I saw her the following day, and she recounted to me a dream she had seen. She was with her parents at the Yachad, and all the courtyards were full of roses, 'red ones and white ones'. The walls were glowing with light. But there was something happening in the direction of Jerusalem, and she was very afraid of it, but her parents refused to notice.

I told her she had surely seen a prophecy and urged her to go to Ima Miryam or one of the dreamreaders about it. I regret that I was occupied with something and did not go with her. I don't know whether she did.

I studied Greek and the Law, as did we all. I also learned bits of knowledge about herbs and medicaments, numbers, the stars. In our women's secrecy, Ima Miryam taught me about magic, medicinal roots and the magical properties of stones.

I mixed dried plums, crushed flaxseed and senna pods from Alexandria on the morning of the sixth day to induce elimination before sunset so as not to defile the Lord's day on the Sabbath. I learned to mix an aromatic red mead for a miscarriage and to catch the afterbirth in new wool from the first shearing of the season. I learned to save the first blood of a virgin as a libation for the hortus.

And we learned how to curse. For this purpose was it that we journeyed to an ancient terebinth grove for a lesson on the properties of trees.

Imme and I accompanied Ima Miryam, and there were three other girls and their master Ima Symacho, and two more Sisters. Ima Symacho was from Adiabene, and the two mothers—Hebrew and Kardouchoi—had been fast friends since their Novice days.

All but Imme, we women fasted, and bided the night in a holy cave. We all wore our whites, left our hair uncombed and our nails unpared, and drank nothing but pure water. All alone were we, without guard nor attendant, but we faced no danger among those ancient boughs. No man would have profaned our sanctuary.

It was in the eighth month, hot with the full of summer, and the kerm-oak was in bloom. We left the cave early enough to reach the deep forest before the hour of Mercury, as this was the hour for making a maga's staff and wand. One of Ima Symacho's disciples had passed her seventh-year initiation and donned the blue headband, and it was time for her to have her own instruments of power.

'Your staff should be made of oak, almond, cane or rose-wood, a wand of cedar,' Ima Miryam instructed, 'both of virgin wood, cut by a single stroke.'

She showed the girl, Sister Enishbai—we must now to call her Ima Enishbai—how to inscribe them. We were all respectfully silent as she wrote upon them in ink mixed with a drop of blood from a male gosling:

> *Agla VN JHVH* along the length of the oaken staff,
> and *YHVH Adonay Agla Craton* along the length of
> the cedar wand.

Ima Miryam drew in the undergrowth with the tip of the Staff of Matriarchs the five pentacles of Mercury. The Mothers, Miryam, Symacho and Enishbai intoned:

> 'Bless and consecrate this wand and this staff, that they
> may obtain the virtue...'

The day was devoted to learning the Wisdom of the trees, and we walked, Ima Enishbai with her new wand in her sleeve and staff in her hand, a path trodden by Ossaeans since the Diggers of the Well.

In the woods Imme had plenty of opportunity to run around, so she was calmer and more attentive than was usual. A Novice so young would not as a rule leave camp, but the knowledge fell within the purview of Imme's gift; indeed, she seemed as full of wisdom on the subject as the Mother, and she bubbled over with joy at the chance to impart her enthusiasm to me and the other girls.

At each tree, the Mother imparted the information that

Wisdom would have known, shaking a branch with a tap of her staff; and the young disciple added bits–infusions to be made, magic tricks–little things she thought would please us. This dual instruction–a combination of Wisdom and Love– taught me well my lesson that day.

Before the little sprite could get carried away with telling me every detail of the simples to be made from each leaf or bark, Ima Miryam cautioned her. 'We come to learn the magic of the Grove, Imme. Leave the physics' remedies till later.'

The answer to Ima Miryam's first drill was, as usual, known by everyone but me. She put the question to Imme. 'The girdle of the trees, Imme, in their ordered ranks.'

She counted them off on her little fingers as Ima Miryam rested her two hands on the black stone of her staff:

> First in flower is Almond
> next to ripen Hawthorn
> spring rain brings the Terebinth
> the drying of floods the Vine

The trees followed in season, and each had its letter, forming in their sequence a calendar alphabet. Tree-magic was one of the secrets of our order.

> willow, hawthorn, kerm-oak, terebinth, almond, vine, guelder rose, reed

The eighth month stood for *tav*, for example, the blossoming kerm-oak, twin to *elah*, the terebinth, to whose grove we came in pilgrimage. These letters had the numerical values of 11 and 12.

142

The vowels, which must not be written, are: silver fir, furze, heather, white popular, and yew. These represented the intercalary month.

Ima Miryam taught us:

> The woods suitable for sacrifices:
>
> cypress, bay, almond, fir, pine, cedar, savin (juniper), fig, olive, myrrh, laurel, aspalathus
>
> Make cradles of oak, as the forest, too, is newly born.
>
> Rest not under nut trees with nine-leaved branches, as there congregate demons.
>
> When hawthorn flowers, wear no new clothes, nor comb your hair.

Ima Symacho said to me, 'Remember the seasons, Sophia, as they are important in shapeshifting.' The Mothers had decided that shapeshifting was my gift. 'Later you must learn the guardians of the letters, and the seasons will give you a clue to the remembering of them.'

We reached the clearing the centre of the grove, the most sacred spot, and there was no more tapping of the staff or shaking of boughs. Imme was told she could run around the outside while we entered the circle. We filed in silently, treading softly upon centuries of leaf fall and moss. The trees around, ancient terebinths, gnarled and irregularly formed, were dripping with age.

All around the circle, to the tips of the aged, drooping

branches were tied hundreds and thousands of papyri and strips of linen, enscribed with prayers in inks of various shades. Some fronds were so laden that their strips scraped the ground, and the lower halves were red with soil and greenish-black with moss. The ones at eye level, I could see some of the words. Whether from the celibate camps or the mixed ones, Sisters usually wished for good health and Mothers for good health for their children.

Ima Miryam rested her staff upright, her hands covering the black stone, and spoke softly. 'Sisters, we have entered the Sacred Grove. Here, we are no longer the people we were before we began our fast. We are in a place apart. Here, we are fully merged with the infinite history of the earth and her magic.

'Before the beginning of the earth, Death was already in existence. And Death begot of itself seven male demons—Jealousy, Wrath, Tears, Sighing, Suffering, Lamentation, Weeping—and seven female demons—Wrath, Pain, Lust, Sighing, Curse, Bitterness, Quarrel. These demons mixed with each other and begat forty-nine genderless demons.

'Long ago in the mother of this grove, Michal, priestess of Hebron, learned the power to bind these demons. Solomon, the great magus, bade his artisans construct magical bottles to encapture them, and he devised formulae for the matriarch's binding spells.'

This was the other reason for our outing. We had a spell to cast.

'We come to the Sacred Grove to lay a maga's curse,' she said, 'upon Ananus ben Ananus, the Tzaddik (Sadducee) slave. In corruption his Herodian priests pervert the order of the heavens in the house of God. In treachery the Wicked Priest murdered the Just One (James the Just), who was Bulwark of Jerusalem. In violence the Sons of Ananus invade at harvest time the threshing floors of Asia.'

For seven moons I had lived in a great company, but isolated by desert from the rest of the world. For seven more I had lived the life of a pious recluse, mostly learning rules that only applied inside our walls. Now in this secret of all secret, isolated places, the outside world suddenly violated our sacred circle. We were involved with happenings in the holy city to our west; we were even trying to magically change them.

Without appearing to have moved at all, Ima Miryam produced from her sleeve a tiny glass vial. One moment she was speaking, her two hands curled still and firm around the black stone head of her staff, in the next, she was holding upright before our eyes a magical bottle, her other hand still firmly clutching the staff. The procedure was utterly motionless. Her sleeve didn't even flutter.

We were enthralled. Was this one of the very bottles with which King Solomon encaptured the demons? Even Ima Symacho—who would certainly have seen this object before, maybe even this ritual—was white with awe.

It was approaching sunset, and the sun had fallen below the canopy of the trees. At the instant we perceived Ima Miryam's hand holding the bottle, we noticed the clearing suddenly became brighter than it had been for the hour previous. The sun filtered through the trunks of the old trees, and the new light enabled us to see the vial sharply, though it was tiny. It was of green glass; ancient it must have been if indeed crafted by Solomon; the interior was bluer. Ima Miryam's fingers covered just enough of the top that we couldn't see how it was stoppered.

We watched in the new light as she passed the vial to the east, south, west and north, four times in succession as she recited the formula.

> I, Miryam, adjure you, ye angels who are appointed over destroying all the sons of the flesh, that you anni-hilate this Ananus ben Ananus, on this twelfth hour on this twelfth of the eighth month.

I regret, for the sake of you Sisters who might wish to hear more of the Lost Wisdom of the Magi, that I did not write it down at the time; it was very long. But I remember quite well the final phrase:

> Son of Darkness, by the curse of Abaddon we curse ye, curse ye, curse ye, even unto the depth of the Great Abyss into deepest Sheol, into which we shall cast, hurl and bind ye!

We stood in silence, Ima Miryam utterly motionless, as the sun dipped below the horizon, and the scene changed before our eyes. A final shaft of sunlight illuminated the glass of the bottle like a burst of lightning, keeping it bright before us.

Now the bottle shone purple, and above it, above Ima Miryam's fingers, the light began to turn pink, as if a mist were escaping from the vial. Or as if the wax plugging the cork were melting into the air, transmuting into that ghostly colour. All our awareness was concentrated on the vial, the pink mist and Ima Miryam's arm. If the birds sang, I didn't hear them. If a squirrel moved from bough to bough, my eye didn't take it in.

My Master had the forty-nine demons at her command! How could I fear the locust king, when I was under the protection of such a maga? The moment seemed to last forever, but when it was over, it was over. The instant the last ray of sun disappeared, the vial reverted to its original appearance, green glass with a bluish interior, as if the pink mist had been suddenly stoppered.

Ima Symacho, acting as supplicant, handed her a strip of lead about the length of a finger, and she pulled out from her sleeve a *sicarius* (short curved knife). Each of us wrote one letter of Ananus' name backwards, three times, each in turn writing a letter, and she buried it at the foot of the largest terebinth, as we chanted 'Amen, Amen, Selah'.

Ima Miryam stamped her staff ten times to finish the ritual and return to the earthly world, and we were allowed to attach our prayers to the terebinth stems. In those days, I was still praying for better relations with Sister Tsuiyah.

When we returned to the Yachad, the welcome we received seemed loud, almost profane.

In the course of events, we would see, and I will recount it to you, Sisters, that the maga's curse did prove binding.

I certainly cherished my apprenticeship with Ima Miryam. I questioned, though, if I were really suited to the study. Her teaching was all about activity. She was always moving–tapping her staff to demonstrate things with an energy that connected to her Wisdom. Disconcerted as I may have myself been by the distractions of Imme's jittering and the tap-tapping of the Mother's staff, it suited her, and it suited the subjects of her discourse. My nature is, I think, more of one of solitude and studying things intently from close, close up.

Indeed, though the mysteries and the lore of the Mothers

drew me like a nail to a magnet, and I loved Imme to adoration, I had difficulty enjoying lessons filled with such distraction and physical activity. I looked forward to the quiet seclusion behind the screen in prayer, the Torah readings on Shabbat. The Shabbat readings after the main rite were divided by rank, so I was separated from the pre-Novice little ones, and I relished the hours of quite recitation.

And I learned shapeshifting, which the Mothers all avowed was my gift. Though Ima Miryam knew well the secrets of the grove, she, with her gift of action, was too robust to be a shapeshifter.

I liked the secretness of shapeshifting, and I already had a knack for it from my practice getting past the guard at the Antioch Gate. Ima Miryam granted surprisingly easily that I was ready for tutelage with Ima Symacho.

None of the Hebrew Mothers had the gift. Ima Symacho said it was magic from her own country, magic of the fish-goddess Inanna-Nanë. She was from Adiabene, which she called in her language Hadahban, of noble birth, they said, a convert from childhood to our religion and our order. She was versed in Arabic magic as well as Hebrew and Aegyptian, which once past my initiation I would be allowed to study.

She knew Ossaean shapeshifting, too, and taught me to contemplate the three ages of the Lawgiver—the darkness of ignorance in bondage, the clarity of the desert where false values slip away, and the final hope of the Promised Land.

Each time of the year, each hour had its dedicated angel and corresponding vibration; shapeshifting was the practice of attuning the mind to these vibrations. Our exercises were conducted in the woods around camp. 'Nature magic is easier to conjure away from the habitations of Man,' she said.

'The first stage is about abandoning the self to the forces of nature, clear the mind to focus on the seasons of the goddess,' Ima Symacho taught me. 'You must lock up the Feeling Self, and don't allow it to speak. You are not a creature upon the earth, you are merged with the earth, flowing upon waves of wind, water and sand. You are no longer Sophia, you are nature, you are the air, you have no form. When you are among others, you are not an element within the crowd, you are merged with the crowd. There is nothing about your form that exposes your identity.'

This was the state of *devekut*, being dedicated to God.

She often quoted a saying of Hillel: 'Appear neither naked nor clothed, neither sitting nor standing, neither laughing nor weeping.' It was about achieving the equanimity of devekut.

'The second stage is about harnessing the seasons and over-taking their power.' she taught me. 'When you are Aryeh the Lion, you are stronger than Samson, and your power brings the ripening. When you are Gedi the Goat, you are the warm, nurturing rays of summer. As Nachash the Serpent, the instructor, you slither your influence through the back corners of winter. As Dagim the Fish you slide through the cracks in the melting ice.'

'And when I am the Fox?' I asked.

'When you are the Fox, you become the sneaky accomplisher of your own designs.'

She would drill me, 'How would you draw into your soul the properties of the Fox, its nature, its cause, its influence?'

But instead of tapping with a staff like Ima Miryam, she facilitated my learning by holding my eyes with hers, unwavering, until the passage of long moments quietened the activity of the world and my Acting Self, and I could listen to the waves of wisdom within.

I answered, 'I would think upon the Thought of the Fox until it became one with Mind, listen to the Name until it became one with Voice and look at the Reflection until it became one with Reason.'

If that sounds easy to you, Sisters, you are wiser magae than I.

There was indeed more to it than simply managing to slip past the guard, but part of it was just a case of learning a new lexicon, and Ima Symacho was right—learning the trees and their seasons helped me remember.

'By using the spirits of nature, you can make yourself invisible to those who do not see. By attuning, with every fiber of your being, to the vibrations of the heavens, your being becomes as the air around you.'

She taught me the names of the spirits to harness, the ministers of Alniras. But if ever I wrote anything down, I must be sure to use the correct pen, ink and paper for the day and hour; naturally she bade me learn them as well by rote:

Cheros, Mayton, Metagir, Ebiros, Dionedis, Ugemenos, Abadem, Periberim, Trangialem, Transidem, Succantos, Abeloy, Bored, Belamia, Castormy, Detel

When I was shapeshifting with Ima Symacho, we were in a different place from the Yachad, away from Idumaea, from the world of man—it was the same as the magical place we entered in the terebinth grove, but secret—only us two. It was as if we were invisible.

I delighted also in the lessons I was permitted to attend on Tanakh, which were always taught by one of the Fathers, usually Abba Nehuniyyah. Giving lessons on Scripture to women was something the Pharisees and Tzaddikim would never do.

I was only allowed to sit the Fathers' lessons if there were other virgin Novices, of which there were none near my age in our camp, but in the caves and tents around the area and in other camps, there were Sisters, Novices and some Mothers who would come. The Sages would also travel camp to camp to give lessons and readings.

The Yachad followed the word of the Lawgiver in all things, and to blaspheme his name was death. But the Kedoshim, the senior priests, said the Tanakh of the Temple priests was as false as their calendar. The true Law had been handed down orally from Moshe to his initiates, an inner circle. The books they used in the Temple were a false Torah brought to Jerusalem by Ezra the Scribe, along with his beastly sacrifices.

Abba Nehuniyyah taught us, from the secret books of Moshe, that in all existing things there is an Active Cause and a Passive Subject, the Active Cause being the intellect of the universe and the Passive Subject being the kingdom of man. So is the world passive and immobile until endowed with life by the intellect.

'When bad things happen, it is never by chance,' he said. 'It is always a consequence of one's own works. The ultimate goal of the righteous is to work out what is wrong and right, using the Torah as guide.'

I was not the only new arrival to the wilderness. There came a constant stream of refugees from Galilee to Idumaea, escapees from massacres and riots, victims of banditry, survivors of treachery and broken agreements, runaway slaves and those whose masters or patrons had taken advantage of the lawlessness of the times to tear up contracts. From the charity boxes, the Ossaeans also liberated captives, and scores of emancipated slaves chose to abide in our camps, many becoming proselytes. Orphans also were readily accepted.

The Yachad welcomed all Jews and proselytes into the rules and rituals of the first year. All travellers were offered hospitality for three days and three nights. There were separate camps also for the Joiners. They were mostly Diaspora Jews like me and People of the Land, but there were some foreigners, and they brought news from other nations.

Throughout that whole year we were much distracted from our prayers, as messengers came often from Jerusalem. The Fathers grumbled about 'the constant intrusions', but I consumed each piece of news as if in hunger.

There had been a great fire in Rome, three entire districts utterly destroyed. The mad emperor Nero had blamed the fire on one of the Jewish sects in the city, the Notzrim, a sub-branch of the Pharisees who also looked to the Kingdom of God, and there was a terrific persecution of Jews. Some were covered with the skins of wild beasts and thrown to wild dogs; others were sent to the mines or crucified. Now Caesar had expelled all Jews from Rome. This created a flood of refugees, and there had been many troubles. Hot-headed young men in Jerusalem were arguing for war.

In the cesspool of Rome, the Mother of Whores and every obscenity, senators gorged themselves on rich food and vomited so they could consume yet more, and spent their evenings in orgies at the baths, as the people turned more and more to the worship of foreign idols. It was said there were 30,000 gods in Rome.

Amid this world of iniquity, there were those who turned to the True God. The promise of God for a Shabbat day of rest was a gift to the People of the Land, and the dietary restrictions simply made good sense. A Jew working for a Jewish landlord was permitted to eat freely of the master's crop. A Jew could not take interest—abomination of abominations—from a Jew, so by the simple act of circumcision, one could negate interest on a loan. Everyone who wasn't rich was in debt, so it was a big incentive. The People of the Land yearned for the justice of the Law.

And it was not only the Poor of the world. Nero's wife Poppaea Sabina, his nephew Onkelos, and his freedman Epaphroditus vowed to the righteousness of the Law. From slave to nobleman, the promise of justice between men and love of one's neighbour spoke to the depths of people's hearts. And then there was the promise of the Messiah.

Zealots were in weekly, sometimes daily contact with the Yachad. We shared the messenger's jubilation when Mattathias, son of Ananus' brother Theophilus, became High Priest, the first to be elected by the priests and not appointed by Roman soldiers or Herods.

The Zealot messenger cried, 'The Kittim tried to bring their idols into the Temple of the Lord and laid their profane hands upon our sacred tithes. We resisted. Now a priest of Melchizedek wears the High Priest's ephod. The New Jerusalem begins today.'

The ascension of the Order of Melchizedek was a mutiny

against the hierarchy of the Temple. The Notzrim had hitherto held the post of Bulwark, but High Priest was a colossal advance for the Ebionim, which we called our movement to feed and to unite the Poor.

The victory of Mattathias marked the elevation of the Peace Party faction of the Ebionim in the city. The defeat of the two Yeshus (Yeshua b. Damneus and Yeshua b. Gamla, penultimate High Priests) marked the fall from dominance of the Pharisees and the Gamalielites of the house of Hillel, but I haven't come yet to that point in my history.

During the Feast of Unleavened Bread, celebrated on the first evening of Pesach according to the Temple calendar, Cestius Gallus, governor of Syria, was in Jerusalem, and thousands of Jews gathered to complain against Florus. An enormous delegation from the Yachad went up, including Ima Miryam, most of the other Masters and all Sisters and Brothers who were able.

I was under vows at the time and could not myself go. I had to hear about it from Sister Tsuiyah after my vow was complete.

'Florus sat just next to Gallus,' she said, 'laughing. He pretended the Jews had been the authors of the disturbance. Gallus had no more than a word with him before he departed for Antioch.'

# Chapter 10
## Mem

When the Lord's light had shone upon me for a full year, I was sealed into the new covenant, the rite of Mem, and could now bathe in the purest of the holy waters, though I was still not allowed at holy meals. I swapped my grey headband for the green one of Seeker.

Now I would be required to take a Hebrew name, which would be inscribed on a white stone, my token of membership in the holy community. I had never asked myself what 'matriarch's name' my mother would have given me had she been able; I hadn't wanted to. But as a magician, I knew how important was the name, and I prayed for a favourable reading.

I dreamt of a garden, a woman under a tree. There was a man, but he was off in the distance somewhere, not visible.

I sat at Ima Miryam's feet for interpretation.

'The woman receives the bounty before the man has entered the paradis?' she said. 'Given to you, woman, is the first fruit of knowledge. Chava, Eve the First Woman, sends you this guidance.' She explained:

> Eating the fruit of the tree of knowledge was not the sin of woman. It was our greatest deed, as knowing good and evil is what gives us power. The maga partakes of the substance of God, and she becomes one with the Elohim. The knowledge of one's own ignorance instils the heart with the fear of God, and therein lies Wisdom.

'In Aegypt, they say that it was Eve who breathed life into Adam,' she said.

'And that after Abel, she bore offspring with the seven authorities and their angels,' I said, which made her laugh.

Later I marveled that she knew not that my brother's name was Adam–Adam, of whom I had been so jealous. And like my dream remembered it, though he had sought my attention, he was as one invisible, so often did I ignore him.

When I was a babe, I belonged to my mother and she to me, but when I attended my father in the archives, I gave Mother over to Adam and the brothers that followed, and my father was my companion. Adam, it means 'red earth'. When he was born, I left the red earth of home and mother to reach for the blue sky of Wisdom.

During the day in the man's world of the archives, I could forget the burning of jealousy and longing for my mother. The new world opening up for me of studies and holy pursuits filled the ache of my heart. The more important my father became to me and the more immersed was I in his world, the more I left behind by mother and the life of womenfolk. For my sin, Adonai, I believe I turned from her in revenge.

I also ignored my brothers, and Adam especially wanted my companionship. After the family meal in the evening, when I would help Grandmother and the freedwoman tidy away the implements and Mother was quietening the little ones to bed, Adam had the habit of pulling at my hem, wanting to play. How often must his earliest memories have been marked by a rejection? I was ever anxious to finish the chore quickly and get away from Grandmother's scolding voice; the only other thing on my mind was to find some quiet corner of the noisy house, there to use the last minutes of the lamp for reading, or if it were still light, to escape to my cave. The brother who loved and needed me was not in my thoughts.

On one occasion, my rebuff was so uncharitable that the boy started crying, and said, 'What's more important? Plates or Adam?'

I saw my error. 'Adam, of course, darling,' said I as I threw my arms around his little neck.

On that occasion, Grandmother nodded for me to leave the washing and go to him. But on a hundred other evenings, I did not go.

That night I cried for my brothers. My brothers, part of me considered them noisy creatures, part of me loved them as my blood. Surely, they were all of them lovely little boys, but they had never been part of my life–at least not the life that happened inside my head. O Adonai, forgive me, since I have not seen them again since, that I did not make a better sister for them then. If I displeased Him as a sister to my brothers, I prayed, now as a woman, I will enter this new family as Eve, newly born and newly named.

To my sisters at the bathing, I told this story:

The first man on the earth was named Adam. Eve was not the first woman, though. Adam had a first one–the dark maid, Lilitu the Huntress, who refused to be ruled by him and made him to lie beneath her in her bed with the goat-demons where the owl nests. She was all three–mother, daughter and maga–and from her womb delivered slithering serpents and eyeless ones.

The Almighty One sent three angels to bind

157

her–Senoy, Sansenoy and Semangelof–and the demoness flew away on her owl wings, leaving the world of men behind. In my country, mothers place amulets of protection against Lilitu in their newborn babes' crib, and they sing a song that tells of her binding:

Vanquished and trampled down are the bewitching women.

Vanquished on earth and vanquished in heaven.

Vanquished are their constellations and stars.

Bound are the works of their hands.

Ima Miryam told the women of the Lost Wisdom of the Goddess:

Before the rule of man, the People of the Land worshipped the goddess. Her names were Inanna, Ninhursag, Ashtoreth, Ishtar, Allat, Anatha, Mylitta, Cybele, Anaïtis, Dindymeme, Aphrodite, Venus.

The world was divided into the three phases of the goddess–Lion, Goat, and Serpent–birth, marriage and death.

But when the Almighty One bound the Queen and her Angels, so on earth did Man wrench power from their mothers. As above, so below.

All over our land and the lands between the rivers, fathers took their sons to war and awarded them land and slaves. Men inventoried the spoils of victory, and priests ran the government. Women were left with only our magic. The secrets we held that they never knew, they could not take those from us, but to them, in their madness for acquisition, of what use were mysteries? What was lacking could simply be taken.

Woman's magic fell into the mists of the past, ritual marriage rites forgotten, the year king's burning first delayed, then cancelled by a surrogate. No longer did the trumpet blows of Malchuyot announce a new king every autumn. Our God demanded no such price for his favour, for he desireth steadfast love not burnt offering.

Men began to sacrifice a scapegoat for the king. They crucified them within a stone circle on a T-shaped cross of terabinth wood, to give them immortality.

From every high hill, Judah worshipped sky gods and imitated the practices of nations with golden idols, the Queen and her Angels banished to the woods, and the stones they erected to her ensnared in the bog.

When the tail of the Lion entered the summer solstice, the Lord of Heaven dethroned the Queen, and the Goddess ruled no more. We stopped listening to her voice, and the heavens also closed; we could no longer hear His voice either.

Holy women, who once were queens and high priestesses and ruled a world without slavery and war, once held the power of that secret knowledge. Now we can go no further towards the throne of HaShem than the Court of Women, and hardworking wives have no time for the magic of the matriarchs.

We left something behind of the Lost Wisdom when we demoted the goddess. We lost love and mystery. Humankind then sang in tune with the birds and the wind; now we only listen to the Law. We are become so rational that our hearts hear nothing but the words that repeat in our heads.

The knowledge of the goddess has disappeared with a whisper into the sacred forests, now all ploughed over for fields.

Another Mother spoke up. She, too, had a story to tell about women and the goddess. I smiled with excitement, as it was Ima Symacho, who schooled me in shapeshifting and with whom I had visited the terebinth grove. In the previous week, when I sat at her feet, she'd told me that, as a woman, I possessed strong magic. 'It is woman,' she said, 'who is keeper of the mysteries.' The wise Mothers were beginning to teach me the secrets of the Sisters of Zadok, treasures of knowledge passed from woman to woman since the time of the serpents. Sitting at their feet, soon I, too, would know them.

With the sacred waters of the pool cooling our bodies, we heard the story of the Fall of British Magic:

> The queen of the Iceni tried to counter the Kittim with British magic. The sacred laws of their goddess ordained hunting of the hare to be forbidden on all but May Eve, the transgressor's penalty was to be struck with weakness. Queen Boudicca let loose hares during the battle in hopes the Romans would strike at them and lose courage. But the goddess heard not their prayers. The victorious Second Legion Augusta sacrificed to Jupiter and Mithras.
>
> They were glad to get an influx of slaves for the

market. They hadn't had any fresh meat since the Battle of the Weser River (against the German tribes of Arminius).

They controlled the world from Cyrene to the Danube, but Queen Boudicca had shaken them in their arrogance. Her warriors had crushed the Ninth Legion Hispania and burned Londinium and Verulamium. The Romans wrote that there were more women in the ranks of warriors than men. Her story gave heart, and warning, to tribes and kingdoms across the empire.

Later I played with Imme, pretending that Ima Symacho was Boudicca—she fit our image of a foreign queen—and we were her daughters. I would lead the Iceni, and Imme would lead the Trinovantes. Girls played war games as much as boys in those days. With the boys, it was about fighting and swordplay. The girls' play was more about intrigue—learning each other's secret watchwords or capturing and rescuing each other's princesses in towers.

The time for my initiation was approaching, and I needed to select a name. One's Mem name was usually determined from the stars, where our destinies are recorded by the Lord of Heaven. My own star, from my birthdate 21 Kislev in the Year 3809, rises fifteen degrees in Kasshat the Archer, the sun my Lord two degrees in Aryeh the Lion, and my goddess twenty degrees in the Archer.

I told this to the astrologer, a disciple of Abba Liliukh's, but when I recounted to him my dream and what Ima Miryam had said, he said, 'By all means, you shall have Chava as your Mem name. A true prophecy is more formidable than an astrological calculation.'

He read my palm and my stars, and said, 'You have eight parts of Light and only one part of Darkness. This part, though, is very big.'

Readings never tell you anything new, do they?

My marriage partner was also ordained by the stars, he said, though I told him I was pledged to follow my master Ima Miryam in celibacy. He said, 'that may be your desire at the moment, but the stars say otherwise. Your husband is not of the Way; and you will know him over a pool of blood.'

'In that case I should make sure to avoid meeting him, for the sake of both my purity and my safety.' I considered it witty, but he did not smile.

He handed the name to me on a white stone written in Hebrew letters, and I kept it in my sleeve to be used on admission to prayer meetings. This stone would identify me as an initiate in a gathering of Ossaeans anywhere in the Diaspora.

I wasn't much fond of the name, though. Perhaps it is a sinful desire that hangs onto the name my father gave me, the power that was my old self. Chava just didn't take hold, though oft when Ima Miryam scolded me for thinking my studies more important than my chores or my duties in the field, she would call me 'Chava Sophia'. In any case, nobody stopped calling me Sophia. My new name was only ever used upon admission to mysteries. Some Mem names stuck and others didn't; and most people were called by nicknames, regardless, like 'Curly' or 'Elbows'.

I took Mem at Shavuot when the ceremonies of the Covenant Renewal took place. The Overseer presented me to the Many, who cast their white stones to accept me. When I heard the words 'and she shall establish her steps to walk perfectly in all the ways of God', a shiver ran up my back, and my hair tingled. It was the magic I had been hoping for.

All religious and community matters in Jerusalem, and to an extent those in the wider world of Diaspora Jewry, were determined by the Sanhedrin–Tzaddikim–yet they were lackeys of Rome. The last thing on earth they wanted was the liberation of the Jews. Scriptures they know, and they are skilled at quoting them to their advantage. Yet no more could a shaft of wheat (camel was a mistranslation) pass through the eye of a needle than could one of these enter Paradise.

Their families–the six high priestly clans–enjoyed favourable patronage under the Herods, and even in these troubled times, they defended it with treachery against the people. Law and order was their top priority; commerce came second; God came last, and the people never.

The Ossaeans' charity system bypassed their economic system. We collected donations for the Ebionim, and two days per month, the bursars distributed money and food. It was what our *corban* (Temple tax) should be used for, instead of funding lavish dinners with sinners, especially now when salvation is on the horizon.

Most of the people simply wanted peace with Rome, but many followed the Way, and many supported the works of the Ebionim. Other sects, the Notzrim, even the Pharisees, joined us in this work, for it was written: *If you pour yourself out for the hungry, then shall your light rise in the darkness.*

The arrangement was little threat to the Romans; it served as a bonus to the bread and circuses they gave the people from their own loot-purses. It was, however, at variance with the

Sanhedrin and the Herodian priests, as it took offerings from their hands.

We also refused to pay the sin tax, as we will not commit sins against the soul. Instead we donated that tax to the collection boxes. When Ossaeans of the Way were raised in Mem, we sold all our property and gave everything to the Ebionim.

The government of the camps was conducted at an Assembly convening once a week. Like everything else at the Yachad, this was organised by hierarchy. The Saints and Elders, all men, of course, Fathers like Abba Ahissa, Abba Nehuniyyah and others, those who wore white headbands, sat in the Assembly Hall, while those with blue headbands, the rest of the Fathers and Mothers, men and women separated by a reed screen, sat in an adjoining room.

Outside were Brothers and Sisters and further out from them the Novices and Joiners. Thus, discussions in the hall were relayed outward to the decreasing ranks like buckets of water quenching a fire. We didn't get to hear every word, but because some heard some things and others heard others, we generally got the gist of whatever happened and who had put forward what opinion.

Broadly speaking, barring internal matters of justice or administration, on the agenda of every Assembly was the question of how to bring about our Redemption. The sects in our religion had different positions, and our sect, the Ossaeans, was further split by different positions. During these days, the positions did not yet have names. People didn't yet sew stripes into the inside of their sleeves to proclaim their partisanship. People didn't say 'I'm a member of this faction' or 'I support that strategy'; they just argued.

Eventually, every issue–whether it was taxes or cooking pots or smoke from holy candles–became connected to the question of the war. Those against war used words like 'righteous' and 'heaven', while those in favour talked in terms of 'Fifties and Hundreds' and 'garrisons'.

Soon these positions became entrenched, and there was a physical separation of the Yachad. Those of the Peace Party remained at Ein Gedi or the other camps, and those of the War Party encamped at Secacah (Qumran) to prepare for the Day of the Lord. The fortress was the stronghold of the Kanaim, militant followers of the Way.

This is how I became a Zealot.

The first question was–What was righteous and what was not? Should one follow the food laws of Leviticus 2 or Isaiah 7? What about the sealing of Gentiles and Diaspora Jews? Was circumcision an absolute requirement?

Hillel the Nasi (Prince) had said that the most important laws in the Torah were two: Love thy God and Love thy Neighbour, the essential balance between man and God and between man and man. These were called the law of *chesed* (lovingkindness) and the law of *tzedakah* (charity). 'The rest is no more than *midrash* (interpretation),' he said.

As for chesed–Love thy God, the sects had different interpretations.

The Saints of some sects said it was faith that brought a man to eternal life. The key to salvation was found in fully and honestly trusting and believing in God. The Brethren said, as Yochanan (John the Baptist) had preached, that faith is empty without works.

We are called Ossaeans because we are Doers of Torah

*mitzvot* (acts of faith). The law is no temporary nor voluntary requirement. It is not only principles of faith that call one to righteousness, but actions. True righteousness comes only through strict obedience to the rule of Wisdom and Justice, obedience to every jot and tittle of the Law. Our covenant with God sets right our balance within the permanence of the universe. Circumcision, the mark of this covenant and the sign of our worship, is not an optional extra. Dietary laws were the means by which we purified our bodies.

Ima Miryam said that in order to love God I must embrace the black cloud that falls upon me, love it even, with the indulgence of a fond parent. She insisted this was the interpretation of chesed. How could I love that which I feel to be evil within me, since I had been used to thinking of it as demon-borne? To love God, I must first truly love myself, even the bit of me that is of Darkness.

For those who believed faith is only justified by works, these days when thousands were giving up their possessions and leaving their lands to go into the wilderness to await the Coming of the Lord, the interpretation of works came to apply more and more to support for the war, the practical ways by which to feed the Poor and arm the militias.

As for tzedakah, Love thy Neighbour, there were as many disputes. Did it mean–Love that Greek who is your neighbour? Or Kill that Greek because he killed your neighbour? Did it mean–Love thy neighbour even if he is thine enemy? The Shammaites said it meant–'Love thy neighbour and hate thine enemy; in righteousness shalt thou judge thy neighbour.' Hillelites said, 'Love all men, even thine enemies.' Under the rule of the Kittim, that was a lot to ask.

The Pharisees say that tzedakah is the principal of the two laws, and they strive to 'be holy as the Lord God is Holy'. Yet they wanted nothing to do with the unlearned People of the Land. The Tzaddikim wanted to take monies from the collection boxes to pay for beasts to bloody the Temple altar-stones—the Rich robbing from the Poor.

The second question was that of war. Could we bring about the Kingdom of God on Earth simply by praying and eating the right things? Or do we have to confront the Kittim, the Sons of Belial, with righteous swords?

Then, if war was desirable or even inevitable, how should we go about strengthening our hand?

Must we widen our garrisons by accommodating to smooth things, loosening the requirements for Greek, Cyrenian and Aegyptian Jews, thereby increasing numbers to join us? Most of the Joiners were understandably for this position.

To the looseners, to make our dream of the Jubilee appealing to a wider crowd, we should even include Gentiles and rich people in the movement. We should even allow the uncircum-cised to sacrifice in the Temple.

Or rather should we tighten the walls, become ever stricter in our zeal for the Law and our persecution of transgressors? Gamaliel the Elder said, 'Gentiles have impure motive, and incur the penalty of Gehenna. Idolaters have no share in the World to Come.'

The Sicarii threatened to kill anyone they caught reading the Torah who refused to be circumcised, and the lawless in the countryside used forced circumcision as a weapon of terror. 'The Greeks and the People of the Land should obey the Law even if they lie in darkness and don't know it,' they said, 'or else they bring down the wrath of God on us all.'

'What about whores and sinners and bandits?' I asked Ima Miryam.

I told her about the lewd dancer in Palmyra. Could such a sinner be saved? And her rich customer? Perhaps he leaves his wife at home, covered head to toe in black clothing and purple bruises, while he indulges the sins of his body with fleshy harlots.

'It is their choice if they enter the Kingdom. Every human being ever born has the choice to be the most righteous ever, or the most evil. Such sinners revel in their transgressions,' she said. 'Happily, do they break the law, even the most fundamental law of chesed. For they love the gratification of their Acting Selves more than they love God. Can the Kingdom of God embrace those who are not Children of God? They who have not signed the covenant and paid the price shall not inherit the reward.'

Most Fathers of the Yachad were proponents of sharpening the resistance–heeding the right strategy, following the true messiah, the correct prophecies.

Abba Ahissa and most of the Saints and Elders followed this path. Sister Tsuiyah claimed to wear these stripes, but I suspect that she just liked obeying rules. She wanted only to please those older or higher in rank than herself. In all the years I knew her, she never once had to do a penance.

Many of the Fathers abstained from either militancy or capitulation, anticipating a peaceful ascension, a miracle of faith–like when the Israelites triumphed over the Aegyptians or when Cyrus the king returned us from Captivity. Our task was to prepare for the End of Days, they maintained, and wait for God to indicate when the time is come. We came to call this position 'sitting on the wall'. It is not a neutral position; it implies consent. We were taught to 'not stand idly by our neighbour'. I believe this can sometimes require taking up the sword.

More people in those days could wait no longer for the Lord. Although she became increasingly in favour of war, Ima Miryam was of this school. They argued for hastening liberation. Many Fathers preached against this, saying that to seek to hasten the End was to rebel against God's spirit. However, she said, 'The Day is ordained by the heavens, but we can hasten the hand of God, bring it on more swiftly by our own works. The impulse from below brings forth an impulse from above.'

We were tired of waiting for magicians. We yearned for freedom, and so many visionaries told us we could have it, the Many were whipped into a frenzy. A magical hastening of the hand of God would not be enough. 'God will power our hand,' they said, 'but we must strike the first blow.'

Ima Miryam also believed in broadening, the conversion of non-Jews, and deepening, the winning over of Diaspora Jews to the Way.

But what of the Rich? Widening the net to include the wealthy? Their money would be of great use for the sustenance of the Poor and the maintenance of fighters. Or were they, themselves, the enemy?

As for the conversion of the Rich, she said, 'they have generously donated to the collection boxes.'

Then there were the bandits. They donated mainly to themselves.

There were those who carried hastening even further, saying

the Day was coming so soon, we needed to prepare ourselves in an instant. The magic of Mem and Sekhem should be transmitted now, right away, so when the king arrived, we would be ready to inherit the Kingdom of God on Earth.

There were powerful magicians in those days, and the people were eager to flock to them. I myself had previously been against this, believing that the Lost Wisdom was the secret of the chosen few, and I had been terrified of false prophecy, as my demon of the black cloud attests. How many times had we been led into failure?

# Chapter 11
## Debating the Day

Normally, only those of Elder rank or above would participate actively in the discussion at Assembly, but during
this period, the decorum at Assembly began to break down.
Mothers and Fathers, still shy of shouting in at the doorway,
started throwing into the hall in the direction of the top bench
ostraca written with their own opinions.

One Assembly was so momentous we ever after referred to
it as 'That Assembly'. The Assembly had been called to debate
the question of sending funds to Yochanan, an Ossaean who
was mustering troops and fortifying the stronghold at Thamna.

The coffers of the Ebionim were overflowing. The Day of
our Redemption drawing nigh, so many, who, due to being
tied to the fields, could not do the work, were happy to donate.
Yochanan was preparing for our fight, and he was even of our
order. I had thought the Saints would immediately vote in
favour, but the Peace faction was still strong, and the sitters
on the wall loved to drag out arguments so that nothing got
decided.

Though most of our Sages did not want to fight the Romans,
the Yachad adopted a policy of steadfastness. Though we did
not join the militias, we refused cooperation with the Kittim.
We would not be moved from our strongholds, and even when
tortured, we would give no information to the soldiers.

From outside, we heard shouting.

I can't remember who it was, but it was one of the Inspectors, not Abba Ahissa. He had shouted, 'The collection boxes are for feeding the Poor. That's it!'

The ostraca flew so furiously that a few of the Saints were wounded on the shin!

Then, we heard more shouting and a shuffling of feet.

'What's happening? What's happening?' we urged.

'Fathers have stormed the meeting and pulled that Inspector and some of the Elders from their seats,' those closest to the door reported.

'Who? Who?' we wanted to know.

After all these years, Sisters, I can't remember them all, but one of them was Abba Liliukh.

From the outer circles around the building we heard a thud and a shuffling of feet.

'What's happening?' we cried.

'It's the women–the Mothers and even Sisters–they've pushed over the reed screen and stormed the meeting,' the green head-banders reported.

Sisters! Who normally wouldn't have even been allowed inside the building!

The holy men in Assembly expected us women to be silent on the subject of war, but quite often in matters concerning the collection boxes, Mothers were consulted, as it was the women who conducted most of the work of the Ebionim. At That Assembly, the two issues coincided. The Mothers were determined to be heard.

I was even more excited to hear that the group was led by my Master, Ima Miryam. We heard a bang and a shout of 'Now!', and the green headbanders said, 'She's produced a flash of blue lightning and a puff of smoke.'

It was one of her favourite tricks. She employed it to illustrate the need for quickly overturning old ways of thinking in order to facilitate action. And so it was for that purpose here.

'What did she say?' we cried.

'She said, "Enough of this sitting on the wall. The Kingdom of God is NOW!",' they said.

Never had I been so proud of my Master, and I would have gone about camp with a big smile for days had it not been that the fallout from That Assembly was so catastrophic.

During the night, in secret, six men from among those who had been dragged from their seats and their families ran off to Jerusalem to join the Pharisees!

Unfortunately for the needful militias, their number included the Inspector who had shouted 'That's it'. He had a key to the doorlock on the Treasury, and absconded with funds from the collection boxes, some third of our funds at the time. They had been intercepted by some of the Kingdom-is-Now faction—though not Ima Miryam, who had told them her work was to continue teaching the Wisdom of Eliyahu—but they didn't try to stop them. Instead, after a tussle over the boxes, they themselves took the remainder of the funds.

Half they sent to Yochanan at Thamna, with three fighting men and their families. The rest they sent to the Kanaim at Secacah with four fighting men and families, and among them were Anna, a Seeker I was friendly with, and her husband Uzziel. We heard that during the day several from the celibate camps had joined them along the way.

After That Assembly, some Sisters and I were tasked with the cleaning of the hall. We had to read the strewn ostraca, because any containing sacred words, letters or numbers could not be discarded and would have to be stored in the *genizah* (storage facility for sacred works). The matters were so serious, but really, we had such a laugh.

Here were some of them:

> 'I know that you, Father Aleph are from Lydda and you, Father Bet–I can't remember the names–are from Jaffa, both towns defended by the stronghold at Thamna. Will you leave your own hometowns undefended?' Here was someone for whom steadfastness was not enough.

> 'We must put on our full armour, thus to take a stand against the devil's schemes.' 'The Sons of Light shall rise up against the army of Belial, who violate the covenant.' These were also from the War faction.

> 'God gives to each his portion, the judgement of the ungodly, the glorious portion of the elect.' This must have been from a sharpener.

> 'You're trying to exhort money by threats.' From the sitting on the wall faction.

> 'Even the vessels of the house of the Lord did Cyrus the king bring forth'. Here was a magical hastener.

> 'It is written, the hand of God will strike only after we've engaged for six battles. Who can tell, whether here or at Thamna?' A magical hastener, who nevertheless was for war and was for donating to Yochanan.

My favourite was 'Standing in the middle of the road, you are hit by either the carrot cart coming in or the bread cart going out. What difference?' Obviously, someone who wanted us to get off the wall.

The camp did not quieten for many weeks. There was also new friction in our school.

Sweet little Imme was upset and cried, 'Everyone is fighting!'

Tsuiyah, on the other hand, naturally disapproved of any rule-breaking.

'What seized the Mother?' she said. 'Violating Assembly like that?'

'Somebody needed to shake up those tired old men,' I replied.

'Tired old men! You call the Saints of Eliyahu tired old men! You need to do a penance, Sister Sophia.'

The friction continued at the well. Like everywhere else in the world, the fetching and carrying of water at the Yachad was done by the girls. It was a chore I had dreaded back home, where the talk was about nothing but which boys you fancied or the correct cooking of lentils, but here it was a hive of excitement.

We discussed everything from That Assembly to the coming of the King Messiah to our works with the Ebionim. Everything that was debated by the men was also debated by the women at the well.

Because everything else was organized by rank, the well was also the only place I ever met with Joiners like Alexia and Philyra. Philyra now wore the grey headband of Novice, and she was accepted at some of the lessons I also was sitting.

I asked Alexia, pointing to her forehead, 'Why still the red?'

She said, 'I don't mind giving up sausage, but 613 mitzvot!

Sister, it's too much.'

'But you don't have to be circumcised. What's the stumbling block?'

'My brother is also a Joiner, Barak, here in camp. You've met him? No? I couldn't leave him behind,' she said.

In Ima Miryam's hut, Tsuiyah was often minded to keep a civil tongue toward me, but at the well she would lash out, drawing pleasure when the older girls agreed with her.

I was telling the girls that like my Master I was a hastener–I wanted to take action now–and certainly a deepener–I wanted to welcome Diaspora Jews–but also a broadener–in favour of recruiting new combatants through the conversion of non-Jews like Alexia–for that my year of happiness with the Nabatu had taught me to love foreigners.

One of the girls said, 'Sister Sophia, birds must stick to their kind. Eagles fly with eagles; crows nest with crows.'

'We are neither eagles nor crows,' I said, 'because we know how to love. We bind it around our neck and write it on a tablet of our heart.'

'You'll surely not smear your neck with bacon fat?' said Tsuiyah disdainfully.

She shunned the Joiners at the well as if the uncircumcision of their brothers poisoned the skin on their hands.

'For us, of course, but for them, eschewing pork should not be a necessity,' I said.

'You would allow them to eat pork?' she spluttered.

'If it's butchered humanely, and it doesn't make them ill, it's their business what they eat,' I said.

'So, you would sit with people eating food sacrificed to idols?' she huffed.

'No, I wouldn't sit in table fellowship. I keep all the mitzvot myself. But they could have their own table. As long as they will fight the Kittim,' I said.

'Their own table? In our sacred hall? Are you mad?' she cried, storming off, sloshing her bucket in anger.

I said to the girls, 'The ones I would not have in our sacred hall are the Rich. They are the Sons of Belial, the dinner-mates of the Kittim.'

For a while then, whenever Tsuiyah arrived and I was in Ima Miryam's hut, she would leave, and when I arrived and she was there, I would leave. She called me 'apostate' and 'bacon-lover' and 'piggy', and I also, was unkind, saying, 'All you care about is rules. You always claim it's for some lofty principle, but really, you're just a horrible person. It's not just foreigners; you hate everybody.'

I complained to Ima Miryam, 'She's always sweet smiles with you, Mother, but out of your sight she's a rabid dog.'

'Unfortunately for you, dear, rudeness is not against the rules. Personal affinity is not regulated by the Sages. You must each learn the lessons afforded therein.'

'She is a glob of snot. That's the only thing I've learned,' I said, but was scolded.

'I can see that you've learned that you don't need to base your opinion of yourself on the opinions of others,' said the Mother.

On the contrary, I think it is a lesson I never learned.

'What has she learned, then?' I whined.

'That's not your concern,' she admonished me.

Poor Imme was even more upset by this situation than I, and after each incident, she would cry.

I assured her, 'Sister Tsuiyah and I may not sit side by side,

177

but I shall always be Ima Miryam's disciple, and when you are Mother, I'll be yours.'

She found this amusing, and thus I was able to console her.

Surprisingly, I felt better quite soon after. No longer had I to strive for Tsuiyah's approval, and I enjoyed sitting instruction free from her judgeful eye.

The Yachad was strict, but there were communities that would welcome people like Alexia's brother. Sha'ul, a Cilician, had founded synagogues in Galatia, Thessalonica, Corinth and Rome comprised entirely of converted pagans. Broadening with him also involved loosening, being less strict on matters of the Law.

'Slaves, obey your earthly masters with fear and trembling,' he wrote. The slaves I know wouldn't like to hear that.

Sha'ul told his Joiners in Rome that to love thy neighbour was to pay taxes to Caesar. 'Pay your taxes to Rome,' he said; the authorities are God's servants. Even my unrebellious Shu'dat wouldn't like that. He couldn't have gotten away with preaching so in Jerusalem, where his talk of justification by faith alone caused a riot.

'Since faith alone is necessary for salvation, one is free from the moral obligations of the Law,' he preached. You can understand why the Zealots didn't like to hear that.

Sha'ul was a member of the royal family, a Herodian, that company of Belial.

There were members of the king's family who pretended to be on the side of the Kingdom of God. They, too, had a plan for the liberation of the Jews. Herod divided his chief priests into the orders of Avraham—himself in Jerusalem, Yitzhak in the East, and Ya'akov in West and Rome, building allies among

178

the nations by swapping marriage contracts according to the balance of forces. Avraham, Yitzhak and Ya'akov.

A triarchy like Rome—a convenient number, just the number of remaining Herodian princes to whom Caesar had distributed our land. Herod's vision involved getting rulers of the Nations to circumcise in order to marry his daughters. We called this deepening, looking to Jews in the Diaspora for support.

The Herodians had called Antipater the Anointed One—he traced his line to Judah through Caleb son of Jephunneh—until his father Herod killed him. Now, of course, Herod Agrippa was king, and Roman generals appointed the High Priests.

That was the Year of the Four Emperors, and while the New Jerusalem enjoyed the sovereignty of Jewish rule and the expectation of the Kingdom of God on Earth, Rome was in such turmoil that the rumour spread easily that Nero had not in fact committed suicide but had fled to Persia, from whence he would come to overthrow Vitellius.

The Herodians cherished the prophecy of Daniel that promised that the wound would heal. This meant that the emperor Nero—I tell you this; they actually thought that madman was the Messiah—would rise again from the dead and come from the East to reconquer Jerusalem.

One man from the isle of Kithnos near Patmos tried to turn this myth to his advantage, pretending to all and sundry that he was the risen emperor.

Sha'ul had been a heretic-hunter, one of the persecutors of followers of the Way; he was himself responsible for the execution of one of the seven deacons of the Notzrim. But a priest named Ananias convinced him that the Baptism of the Holy Spirit was a better strategy. Faith in a dead saviour could pull the salvation-hungry Jews away from their works of war.

He claimed Yeshua the Notzri (Jesus the Nazorean) as the risen one, and on this basis appointed himself apostle, never even having received Sekhem.

Being a Herodian by birth and by nature, his vision was the same as Agrippa's—to build a great Jewish Empire across the Diaspora, by marriage or patronage or religious conversion, in readiness for the Day of the Lord—coming any moment now—when the righteous would be granted eternal life.

Five times the Sanhedrin lashed him for heresy, and every time he came to Jerusalem, he caused a riot. The Sicarii issued a permanent ruling against him, and were under Nazirite vow to kill him on sight.

Sha'ul brought the fornicating daughters of Herod and uncircumcised Kings of the Nations into the Temple to worship in the Inner Court, where it is forbidden for foreigners to tread. The Levites in white, disciples of High Priest Mattathias, wanted to kill him.

The Yachad at Ein Gedi and our associated camps feared Agrippa more than Rome. But more than Herod or Rome we hated the Herodian priests, and we hated their Greek influence in the Temple. In Jerusalem, the corrupt Tzaddikim in the Temple were in the pay of the Romans, bribing their way into the priesthood with all its revenues just like their predecessors did with the Maqabim. Only with the Restoration of the True Temple, with a true Zadokite heir of Aharon as High Priest could order return to the universe.

The Saints therefore foretold the day when a kingly messiah of David and a priestly messiah of Aharon would lead Israel triumphant over seventeen nations. It was predicted by magi all over the world that a saviour would come during these days, and we watched daily for the Coming of the Prince. The sheep can only wander aimlessly without the guidance of the shepherd.

Like many Jewish sects, we looked to a prince of the line of David to liberate us from the foreign yoke; anyone could see that what we needed was another giant-killer.

There are Jews from that tribe in Seleucia today with their own versions of the registries. The Yachad were in possession of secret genealogies, and we safeguarded the messianic lines. But unlike other sects, we cherished prophecies concerning a third messiah, the prophet.

The Teacher of Righteousness, the Mebaqqer (Overseer) of all the Ossaeans, so holy we Novices were prohibited neither to touch his person nor speak his name and whose person we would probably never even see, was the prophet. He dwelt in Damascus.

So, according to the Saints of the Yachad, the prophet had already risen. We awaited a priest and king.

'When all three are assembled,' Abba Liliukh would say, 'prophet, priest and king will together reign.'

One of the old Fathers from Mird, I can't remember his name, spoke to us of the End of Days: 'Witness the convulsions in the air and among nations! The Serpent has ceded its seat to the Double Fish, and the stars converge in the heavens. The Day of the Lord is nigh, when the Prince of the Congregation will rise up to smite the Sons of Seth. The Temple will be rebuilt anew, our fortunes restored, the king in his rightful place and a priest of Zadok in the Sanctuary. On that day we will see the New Jerusalem.'

The commanders at Secacah would have said, 'and the Sons of Light will defeat the Sons of Darkness'.

He continued, 'In the days of Abraham things were not as they are now. The men of Ur were pushed into the isolation of a nomadic life by the greed of Shinar.

'Today we live differently. Look around the land, settlement and civilisation as far as the eye can see, from Palestine to Alexandria. The contrast in forces which once were carefully kept in balance are now irrectifiably confused, tossed and turned in a whirlwind of violence and social turmoil. The forces of violence are winning. We need a new goal now, a new star.'

I asked Ima Sherah what he meant.

'He spoke of Moshiach, child. The one whom the stars foretell, the one who is to deliver us.'

Magi all over the world had read the stars and seen. Draco the Dragon was passing into a new age, Dagim the Double Fish, the bread and wine of Dionysus. A new millennium was beginning. When shepherds held their festival at the spring equinox, the Sun rises in the Fish, and now Šabbetai (Saturn) and Tzedeq (Jupiter) join her. A great world leader was foretold. We Jews had been spurred to war by these prophecies for generations.

This is what we had learned from Abba Liliukh, who taught us the stars. A fifth kingdom was coming (after the Assyrians, Medes, Persians and Greeks), and this would be a Jewish one, ruled by a messiah with divine powers.

At home, I asked Abba Ahissa about it.

When Ya'akov the Just was detained in the Temple, it is said, High Priest Ananus asked him, 'Oh Just One, whom we all are obliged to trust, announce unto us what is the gate of salvation.'

'The Just One was a Nazirite, holy from his mother's womb,' said Abba Ahissa. 'He took no drink nor flesh nor razor to his head, and wore only white linen. So devout was he in his prayers for the people that his knees were as hard as those of a camel.'

The Wicked Priest knew that the salvation of Israel rested on two pillars–a son of David on the Throne of Solomon, the pillar of Boaz; and a son of Zadok as Melchizedek priest, the pillar of Jachin–but he had vowed never to reveal the secrets of the Way, and refused to explain to the Son of Darkness the Twin Pillar paradigm. That midrash called for the removal of Roman rule and their puppets the Sons of Ananus.

It was on Yom Kippur in the year Ananus was High Priest (62 CE), the Wicked Priest under Ima Miryam's curse. The lower priesthood had won the right to wear white linen, the garments of the Way, in the Temple, and Ya'akov had won the position of Oblias–Bulwark of the City–so he would officiate on the Day of Atonement. His father had so served once on a day when the High Priest was unclean.

Thus, it was that Ya'akov the Just wore the High Priest's ephod that one day and entered the Holy of Holies in the black robes of a Nazirite high priest. He chose the day according to the Jubilee calendar.

Ananus ben Ananus challenged him and took him up on the tower. People had gathered in the Outer Court and in front of the Temple steps for the blessing and the sprinkling of the ashes of red heifer, and they were shouting from below 'Hosanna, son of David, deliver us.' Ananus entreated Ya'akov to use his influence to calm the crowd.

'Instead, he rose majestically on the pinnacle,' Abba Ahissa told me, 'and all below, it is told, heard his voice: 'You Poor, the time of your redemption is here. You shall see the Son of Man seated on the right hand of the Power, and coming with the clouds of heaven.'

This is what we have all been waiting for, so his speech did little to cool the fervour of the crowd below.

'They went wild and started up the mount,' Abba Ahissa said. 'Ananus in his fury had Ya'akov seized, stoned and thrown over the parapet to his death.'

From the pinnacle Ya'akov prayed, 'Father, forgive them, for they know not what they do.' But the people forgave them not, and there was an uprising in the city. By law, whatever crime he was accused of, he should have had the right of trial by the Sanhedrin; that much was given his brother. The principal men complained to the procurator and demanded Ananus' removal from office.

The evils that seduce Israel, preached Ya'akov and the Rechabites, are the three nets of Belial—fornication, pollution and riches. The New Jerusalem would not be for kings who marry their nieces and women who divorce their husbands at every turn in the politics of the land. They are the heirs to their fornication. Or for Herodian priests who stole tithes from the lower priests in the countryside and with their riches covered the face of the Temple porch in gold trays.

It was not for these corrupt lackeys of Rome the riches of the Temple of God. In their zeal to please their masters, they daily pollute the sanctuary with offerings on behalf of Gentiles— the error of Balaam—when they offer sacrifices for Caesar. The diversion of sacred monies to building Pilate's aqueduct, the ensigns, the moneychangers, they were all direct violations of the stipulation against accommodation to foreigners.

We have always looked for messiahs. We had Apollonius of Tyana, Hezekiah the bandit chief, Benjamin the Aegyptian and the shepherd king Athrongaeus. There were desert healers, Onias the Circle Drawer who brought the rain in Galilee and Hanina ben Dosa north of Nazareth. In the Idumaean countryside, there was a bandit messiah named Tholomaeus.

In Samaria of our days they followed a great magus, Simon of Gitta. The Kutim (Samaritans) looked to the line of Yosef, tracing their heritage through Ephraim and Manasseh. Their aim was the restoration of the Temple on Mount Gerizim and the northern kingdom of Israel.

Simon studied magic under Thrasymedes and Yochanan the Rechabite, called the Baptist because he conducted mass Mem ceremonies on the banks of the Jordan. This was a seditious act against the Sanhedrin, as the collection boxes thus bypassed the Temple taxes and moneychangers. There were other baptisers, too—Bannus and Tosephtha.

You didn't have to be King of the Jews to be a messiah. Throughout Palestine, Peraea and Syria there was one on every hilltop, and every faction had its champion. It was easy for each group to have its own scriptures proving this or that; there was a lot of competition. There were scriptural and genealogical references to be found for any serious contender. The Restoration, involving one or more messiahs, descended either from David, the Maqabim (Maccabees), the Herods or Judas the Galilean, was the desire of every revolutionary Jew. But finding the right champion from the genealogies—there were so many of them—depended on which faction you supported.

The genealogical rolls at the Temple had been burned under

Herod the Great, so now all the factions squabbled over whose was the true list. The rabbis had gathered together almost 500 passages from the Scriptures that, notwithstanding apparent contradictions, they averred were prophetic of the coming Messiah. There were 900 camel-loads of commentary on the lists in Chronicles.

One day that winter we had a visitor, a soothsayer, and I asked permission to have him read my Chaldee tablet.

Sofer Shaphan was asked to send my tablet over to the unclean chambers, and they asked the soothsayer to read the fragment. Of course, he didn't know the script, but he laid his hand upon it to feel the magical forces.

Women were not allowed in, but the Brothers told me that he said, 'apocalypse, unbearable oppression, needless sacrifice, confusion, impotence'.

I wondered if he had read the room and its occupants or the clay, but in either case it was an ill portent.

# Chapter 12
## Jubilee

Abba Liliukh instructed us in star-gazing. He was named after the prophet Eliyahu, who one thousand years ago with the prophetess Lalaitha had founded our order at Mount Carmel.

Abba Liliukh lived in a cave, outside of which was hung a small bone plaque with holes and pegs which he moved each day to mark the movements of the seasons.

Inside, there was a magical machine, the prized possession of the Kedoshim, that tested the calculations made according to the sacred calendars. This device evidently consisted of revolving metal balls representing four of the main stars in the heavens–Sun, Moon, Earth, and Morning Star–which spun around according to their actual workings, but only Abba Liliukh and his apprentices were allowed to see it.

Nevertheless, Abba Liliukh showed us how the planets moved as we looked at the skies at night. There can surely be nothing more pleasurable than sitting out on a cool night watching the stars, feeling the enormity, permanence and motion of God's universe. I could still show you how to find the head of the Serpent and how to locate the rising of the sun, but I remember little else.

I commented to Sister Tsuiyah, 'When I need to know the time of the sunrise, I'll simply go to the astronomers' cave and ask them.' To which she frowned disapprovingly and completed the calculations on her knot belt with conspicuous ease.

What stayed in my mind from those lessons was the power of the prophecies promised by the stars in our days. The Wheel of the Four Winds circling within the Wheel of the Twelve Beasts, everything in Ezekiel, it was all considered to foretell the Day of the Lord.

There was an urgency. The stars predicted that now was the time. There wouldn't be another fortuity like this for a thousand years. Someone had to come up with the right program, the right messiah, the right date on the calendar.

Abba Liliukh's lessons were the best attended of all the lectures at the Yachad; Fathers, Mothers, Brothers and Sisters came from camps all around and even from the fortress of Secacah, and many of these came despite being as baffled by the mathematics as I was. Everyone felt the excitement.

The ancient magic teaches us that an orderly movement of affairs in the nations of men is reflected by order in the heavens. And it is in the workings of the heavens that God makes known His will. As above, so below.

The timing of God's rule on earth is ordained by the stars. But exactly how that order was ordained was open to debate.

The Brethren said that ours was the true calendar from the creation of the world, which God gave to the Lawgiver from the mount, the Lost Wisdom written down by Enoch when the lands of Eden were flooded. The Enochics used twelve months of thirty, with four extra days, which they learned from the land of Sheba.

Our Jubilee calendar, which we have straight from the hand of Eliyahu, reveals that the Herodians profane the Temple by sacrificing on the wrong days. The priests, in their corruption, follow the moon, and their cycle of priestly service is out of sync with the order of the heavens. The Temple of Jerusalem was supposed to maintain the order of creation, and here during these the End of Times, correct ritual was more essential than ever.

Under the old system, when new moon appeared, all over the countryside fires were lit on the hilltops. Now the division of months was decided by the Beth Din (Court of Justice) in Jerusalem and verified by witnesses, a process naturally open to disagreement.

After the passing of years, when error compounds such that the lambs are still too young and the chickens too small for Pesach, they add an intercalation, an extra month Adar Sheini between the spring months of Adar and Nisan.

Our Jubilee calendar follows the sun.

The year begins at the vernal equinox, but always on a fourth day, the day God created the heavenly bodies. Thus, the Pesach meal would be taken always on the fourth day, Fifteenth of Nisan. Yom Kippur falls always on a sixth day; Sukkot on a fourth day; Shavuot on a first day. Thus, the universe moves in perfect numerical harmony.

A year has four seasons of thirteen weeks. Every seventh year is a Shmitta Year (Sabbatical Year), and to every seventy sevens was added forty-nine days, and this period was called a Jubilee Year, beginning on Yom Kippur. At this time all debts would be cancelled, slaves freed and all land returned to its former owners. Our intercalary month would be the beginning of the Kingdom of God on Earth.

The Yachad sent no beasts to the corrupt Temple in Jerusalem. Nor did we make sin offerings, though we did send our first fruits at Shavuot. We observed our own holy days and collected

189

our own holy taxes.

We awaited the Day of the Lord, which, the Saints said, was to be found in the correct astrological interpretation of the prophecies of Daniel and secret books of Enoch.

According to the Greek system, history was divided into Great Years of 4000 years. Enoch had written the world would end in Year 4900, eighty years after the Temple was restored, creating a new Israel that would spread a millennium of peace over the entire world. Daniel had foretold of seventy weeks of signs, a week of years or 490 years from the rebuilding of the Temple to the Day of the Lord, the day of our deliverance.

On this day, the Mount of Olives would split in two and the sun turn black, and from the Heavens would come the Power of God on the clouds of Heaven to wreak His wrath upon the Sons of Darkness. The Kingdom of God would rule on earth, and all the world would stream into Jerusalem to worship the Lord.

We calculated one hundred years between Adam and the Exodus, added to the forty generations in Genesis between Adam and Noach—that would be two thirds of the Great Year. There were seventy weeks of years between the rule of Cyrus and that of Herod. Herod's coronation was Year 3900 from Creation, and he had rebuilt the Temple in Year 3920. So, the New Age was to begin in Year 4000.

The exact year depended on where you chose as your starting point and which calendar you used, but all over the world everyone agreed it was coming soon.

Did the rebuilding of the Temple date from when the decree permitting it was issued or when construction began? There were decrees authorising building repairs by Cyrus in Year 1291 or 1292, by Darius in 1272 and by Artaxerxes in 1211. If you dated from the time construction originally began, 521 years had already passed. Added to the seventy years of the Babylonian Captivity and the seventy-nine years between the first Return and the edict to rebuild, we were already off by 250 years. And did construction date from the beginning of work or completion? Herod had begun remodelling the Temple in Year 771, but the masons were only just completing it now.

Some of the Scriptures, too, were so old by this time that their interpretation was uncertain. Laws contradicted each other and didn't address obvious things, and references in the prophecies had been forgotten. The very obscurity of the works meant they could accommodate confusions.

As each messiah failed to fulfill the prophecies, the prophets had to consult the calendars again, as the whole seventy weeks of Daniel had to be recalculated. This was usually accomplished by shortening the rule of the kingdom of Persia.

That's been going on since the Maqabim. Each time the Restoration fails to happen, somebody ends up crucified, and crowds massacred. Then the Doctors of Law rush around trying to find another prophecy to be fulfilled, another messiah whose particulars matched, revising their dates to make the numbers fit. The patriarchs keep getting older and older.

The Jubilee calendar had predicted the Restoration in the days of Yochanan Hyrcanus the second; another expectation for the last year of Marcus Antonius Felix's procuratorship was unfulfilled. Yochanan the Baptist had expected the Restoration in Year 3781; it hadn't happened. His revised dates of eight and ten years afterward also failed. Sha'ul of Tarsus blamed the failed Restoration on the Ossaeans, yet the date the Christians picked, four years after that, was equally off-target. High priest Yonathan ben Ananus lost power after only one year when his predictions did not come true. According to revised calculations, the Temple should have been restored in 3797. The most recent update was for last year, and nothing happened then, either.

The signs in the heavens disappointed, as well. 1 Elul 3758 (Aug 12, 3 BCE) there was a conjunction of the Morningstar and Tzedeq (Jupiter); 15 Tammuz 3759 (June 17, 2 BCE) it was the Eveningstar. Thrice that year Tzedeq rose in conjunction with the King star (Regulus in Leo). On 21 Elul 3754 (Sept 15, 7 BCE) Šabbetai (Saturn) and Tzedeq rose with the two fishes. Not a cloud of heaven in sight.

Perhaps the heavens were so disrupted that the old formulas wouldn't work anymore on earth. The Elders said that at the End of Days, a new kind of king would be revealed to us. We waited for the moment, consulting all the prophecies.

Hope deferred makes the heart sick, and our hearts have been made sick over and over again. In the face of constant defeat and disappointment and oppression spanning the centuries, there were only two possibilities: either reconsult the calendars or blame it on demons.

Reading the skies was the job of the astronomers, and Sisters were not encouraged. We were expected, however, to learn the meaning of augurers' pronouncements, and Abba Liliukh was always the one who taught the Novices. Aside from Abba Nehuniyyah, he was my favourite of all the Fathers at the Yachad, and this was primarily because of something he did at the first lecture I attended.

The lesson had been on calendar questions and the correct

dating of festivals.

After the lecture, he produced a wax tablet with a chart of dates for special days during the year, the Vernal Equinox, Sukkot, the cutting of the barley sheaf. These days would fall upon different dates according to the Babylonian calendar of the Pharisees used in the Temple, the Macedonian calendar brought east by Alexandros (Alexander the Great) or the calendar of the Kutim, who fixed an intercalary month whenever it suited them.

The date varied according to whether the new moon was first observed before or after the Vernal Equinox, bearing in mind that Hebrews reckoned the day from sunrise, while Mesopotamia counted from sunset, and the heritage of Alexandros throughout Syria marked the New Year from the autumn.

No wonder our land was in such disorder; we couldn't even agree on the date.

There were four columns of dates and some of the spaces were left blank; the exercise was to compute these dates according to our Jubilee calendar. The Novices were instructed to copy the chart onto our own wax tablets, filling in the blank spaces. It was a simple case of computation, a question of adding thirty days every nineteen years on the Babylonian dates and referring to a second chart listing the years when the new moon of the Vernal Equinox was sighted.

As a Babylonian Jew, I was accustomed to the Pharisee reckoning, and I had never seen the Jubilee calendar. The other Novices, even the ones who had come from outside the Yachad and had not used this calendar all their lives, were at least familiar with it. Abba Liliukh watched them springing to complete the exercise with ease while I held back, and he stopped us for a moment.

'Before HaShem revealed the secrets of the skies to Enoch, who read the stars?' It was an easy question, so it was put to the younger Novices.

'The magi, the people of Shinar, the Aegyptians, the sons of Avraham, the Chaldees,' they responded.

'That is correct,' said the Father, and he took a second blank wax tablet and set it before us, carving on it a new column. 'The Aegyptians used a system reading from the heliacal rising of the Dog star, the Chaldees read from the moon. Each month had thirty days and the year 360 days. Add a column, and compute the days according to the Chaldees.'

It was a calculation that I had performed many times in my own scribblings, involving subtracting the intercalations. The Father noted now on my face the same affinity for the exercise as the others, and he smiled at me. With this kind gesture, Abba Liliukh enabled me to participate with the same level of enthusiasm as the others without drawing their attention to my relative ignorance.

It was the first time since arriving at the Yachad that one of the masters had shown respect for the knowledge I brought with me from Babylon. Even Ima Miryam, who spoke so clearly to my heart, seemed ever quick to disregard any wisdom I had gleaned from outside the tutelage of the Yachad.

Afterward, I asked him if he knew cuneiform, and he said, no, only translations, but these he said he would procure for me to read. Thus, I gained access to works from the archives that Sofer Shaphan would never have permitted to one of lowly Mem rank.

After two years with the Yachad, I took the Twelve Vows, and was admitted into the holy waters, and I began my study of the inner mysteries.

The Sons of Zadok knew secrets from the Book of God's Remembrance, rituals by which to reach the three stages of consciousness. These were called the omnipotence of God and Man, Divine Love, and Holy Breath. On learning these, I began to include some exercises in Holy Breath in my readings, of which, contrary to my concern during my original interview with Abba Ahissa, the Fathers did not in the slightest disapprove.

I mastered the ritual for transferring energy that is the starting point of all Ossaean magic. This is a technique which children of the Yachad, those who follow the Way, learn from a very early age. I could produce the same effect as the experience I'd had on the hill outside Babylon, when I'd felt like my imperishable soul was hovering above the entire universe. Now, however, I knew the tricks to protect myself from evil influences, and I feared not that I would fail to return to the earthly world.

Mothers, whether or not your children follow the Way, teach them this, as it calms the soul. The inner lives of young children are so turbulent.

The ritual consists of concentrating attention upon an object and melting your soul into the being of that object. When your Dreaming Self and the object have become truly united, let it go, and your soul will float away from it. This must be easy, without effort, lest the intentions of the Acting Self intrude. This is when the magic happens. Suddenly, you will hear the birds singing, the cauldron boiling, or a fox will appear from

195

nowhere, and you will know that HaShem has spoken.

I learned the vibrations of the various metals and crystals and techniques for rising in prayer to the first, second and third heavens, the secret names of the Watchmen, and the signs to watch for at the gates. I learned the secret names of God up to the Seventy-two Letters. I learned the True Names of the angels, and on which days and at which times of day to invoke them. The seven earthly powers, we invoke in the morning, the seven cosmic powers in the evening. There were seventy-two angels who guarded the Names of God, and 72 is the number of their invocation—*hayah hoveh ve-yihyeh*.

The Names were all in foreign tongues—some in old Kanaan, some in Assyrian, some in Akkadian, and some in a form of Aegyptian I knew not—for it was believed that their power could best be seized in their own tongue.

I learned the names of the seven evil angels, the angels of darkness, a secret possessed only by our order. I can pass on to you this treasure, Sisters. They are:

Samael, Za'afiel, Za'amiel, Ragziel, Qasfiel, 'Abriel and Meshulhiel

In my Mem rites of the previous year, I had pledged to preserve the secret names and never reveal these things outside our order, but that doesn't matter, now. They no longer hold power on the earth, and the Ossaeans are no more.

Though I desperately feared the demon inside my head, the Mothers taught me to reject the Jewish fear of the demonic arts. God's kingdom is a maelstrom of competing forces—angels and demons, light and darkness, God and his Holy Spirit, sunrise and sunset, summer and winter, male and female, marriage and celibacy. Demonic forces are only evil if not balanced by heavenly forces.

The best way to deal with demons is to ignore them. They live on attention and get their power from winning the battle with the magician. Refusing to do battle unseats them. As Ima Miryam taught me, I can keep them at bay by simply instructing them to 'Fhoo,' begone. Ossaean healers strove to so strengthen the angels that the demons would starve from lack of sustenance.

I later experienced an Ossaean exorcism—in fact I was the supplicant. I shall write of it, and it was very different from those practiced elsewhere. Where a countryside priest would curse the demon concerned, if even he knew the name, which was rare, an Ossaean exorcist would praise and invoke the angel seated opposite that demon in the heavenly realm. Each force in the world has its counterforce, with man in the middle, and it is in balancing these forces that we live a righteous life. Other tricks could also be used, like speaking the demon's name backwards or in code.

I would not learn these techniques until I'd studied for seven years, when I would learn the pathways up to the eighth heaven—Muzaloth—and the secrets of drawing a circle to create rain, the ninth heaven—Kuchavim—and how to predict heavenly events, and the tenth heaven—Aravoth—where I would see the face of God. At this stage in Ossaean tutelage, I would learn how to raise people from the dead by reciting the 216-Letter Name of God. And I still desired to solve the mystery of the Chaldee tablet.

I asked Abba Ahissa about the True Name.

'Since the death of Simeon the Just, the Name is no longer spoken in the Temple,' he said. The high priests now are all unworthy.

'For the Four-Letter Name, which Moshe passed on to Aharon, they substituted the Twelve-Letter Name, which they taught to priests, and the Forty-two-Letter Name or the Seventy-two-Letter Name, which they taught to the righteous. After the Exile, there was no one left who remembered the pronunciations.'

And the True Name of God vanished with the Lost Wisdom, I thought.

On the matter of prophecy, I received much guidance, as I was among masters. Every time I had a dream, true or false, I had a score of Fathers and Mothers to assist me in interpretation and prayer.

There was a formal programme of instruction in prophecy, as the Ossaeans had been renowned for this for centuries. We learned to use the Four-Letter Name to tune our inner light to the will of God, attaining the spiritual state of *devekut*, and detach from the fantasy of the present.

We would attend prophecy lessons on a hill outside the gates, where the magi had erected star-gazers. Yet each Father differed slightly in his midrash.

'That is reasonable,' said Abba Nehuniyyah, 'as each seeker may learn in a different order. The teacher must know the path of the student before he can guide him on it.'

'Abba, sometimes there is a contradiction between something the Torah says and something we know from the study of earthly matters—alchemy, science. What are we supposed to do?' I asked.

'The Law is true, and science is the study of truth, so we need a resolution,' he answered with conviction. 'Perhaps we are not understanding the books properly, and we must seek good teachers. It's also possible that the science is not final, that it will eventually be understood differently.'

He told me that coming to the Yachad was a sign that I had learned the first step in prophecy—Man's Obligation in the World.

'You have a strong desire to glorify the Lord. The second step—Monitoring One's Actions—you have begun to learn.'

I reflected that he was right. Over the two years, I had become more disciplined. I'd concentrated on the lessons I was given, and I'd learned them.

'Now that you are initiated, your destiny will be clearer to you, and you'll have more freedom to follow your heart,' Abba Nehuniyyah assured me. 'You won't have any problem with the next two steps—Being Honest to Oneself and Protection from Desire. The step you will have difficulty with, Sophia, is the fifth one—Purifying One's Thoughts. You leap so all over the place, your angels have nowhere to rest. Your head is so full of noise, they cannot advise you.'

For a moment, I wondered if he and Ima Miryam had gossiped about me, he seemed so well to know the weakness of my inner soul, and I reddened. I think not, though. It was a talent of the Kedoshim to easily weigh men.

In either case, he was correct. Though I mastered his other lessons, I never grasped that one. My head remains a mess, leaping like a gazelle between angels and demons. Years with the Brethren, men and women so worthy of my respect, taught me humility. The war taught me all about hating Belial. It was the noise in my head that kept me from holiness. Perhaps that is why it was not my destiny to become a Kadosh (saint). But here, again, I jump forward in time.

Abba Nehuniyyah's teachings were also useful in shapeshifting, as Ima Symacho pointed out. 'The twelve works of the soul are also the works of the maga,' she said.

Abba Nehuniyyah had taught us that the twelve works—fasting, study, meditation, prayer, submission, service, solitude, simplicity, worship, guidance, confession and celebration—corresponded to the signs of the months.

'The unruly Bull's work is study; the powerful Lion's is submission; the silent Fishes are for celebration,' said Ima Symacho. 'Balancing the contradictions of the powers is what enables you to seize them.'

Around that time, I became acquainted with Abba Ahissa's son, who visited our camp from time to time when he was not under vows, and with his parents' encouragement he introduced me to a brother, whom he said had scholarly interests akin to mine. Brother Guryon had passed his three-year initiation and was already sharing the holy meals. To work closely with Ossaean scholars was what had brought me across the desert, though I suspected the rabbi and his wife had other hopes for the introduction. So Guryon was invited to our hearth and allowed to study with me.

I was beginning to accept that at the Yachad, knowledge was to be gained only by patience and convincing a master that one was ready. Guryon, however, was willing to speak. So, I asked him about Sekhem.

'I know you cannot reveal any mysteries, I said. I just want to know something about it, how you felt about it. Did it change your life?'

'There's nothing wrong with conveying to a Seeker my feelings about the experience,' he said.

'Yes, that's the knowledge I seek. The words and rituals are only important, in the end, because of the magical effect they produce. I want to know about the magic.'

He had taken Sekhem near the Jordan River, where Rechabites had held dawn bathings since the days of Eliyahu. They had even passed their seven days of seclusion there at the bank of the brook.

'We took the holy waters at Karem beyond the Jordan, where Eliyahu ascended to heaven,' he said, 'just like in the days of the Baptist.' With Guryon were ten or twenty other Seekers, even some of whom had been Gentile Joiners, circumcised proselytes. 'The Brook of Kerith is the purest of waters, and the tradition of history makes it even holier.'

'Yes, I know what you mean', I said. 'I have seen stones of power. The magic of the holy ones sinks into the rock, feeding those who come after with its power. In a trance, one can see light coming from them.'

The rite had impressed him, of course, but it seems he was most impressed to discover the regard that the villagers in the area held toward the Ossaean priests.

'You know, many of them still pay their Temple Tax to the Yachad and not Jerusalem,' he informed me.

That must date from the days of Simeon the Just. Even Alexandros, at whose feet the kings of Persia and all of Asia prostrated themselves in awe, bowed to that Ossaean prophet.

The uplifted initiates had carried back with them baskets of oranges, lemons, quinces and pomegranates, gifts of the villagers from their orchards to feed the Poor.

Brother Guryon taught me the names of Chaldee Angels, and we studied ancient scripts. Together we translated a few of the words in my tablet, but even at that we were nowhere nearer a full rendition.

He was very tall, which I have always considered an attractive trait in a man, and from many years toiling in the fields, he had huge, muscular arms, stained dark as kerm oil. I did find him goodly of face and demeanor. But I was uncomfortable being teased by the other girls on his behalf, and I did not like the suggestive prodding of Ima Sherah.

I came to have deep feelings for Guryon, though still more as a fellow scholar and friend than as a potential sweetheart. It was because I had so schooled myself to feel in a certain way. Like I felt for my father. Or rather like the scholar-to-scholar part of my relations with my father. The thought of Guryon touching me, as a man, would be as frightening as if my father had. *As my uncle had*, my Dreaming Self said, but my Acting Self heard it not. I didn't allow myself to think about it. Whenever Guryon said something approaching intimacy, I avoided him for a few weeks.

There were strange conflicts between us regarding the subject of our study. He seemed to approach the translation of the tablet or the study of angels as a linguistic exercise, and was satisfied if we only solved pieces of the puzzle. Translating five words instead of four, that was his goal, not solving the equation and divining the True and ancient Name.

And more important to him than translating five words for the glory of God was translating five words when I had only translated four. That's how it seemed to me. Knowledge which came from my hand or mouth was something against which he wanted to compete, rather than to absorb into his own lexicon. And he was disapproving of magic. This made me even warier of him.

I learned a lot from him; yet after being with him, I felt exhausted like a warrior after a battle. He would often seem to be disagreeing with me on points where, in fact, he agreed with me perfectly, and the only point of difference was that it had come first from my mouth.

One day he said to me, 'You seem to think that the Chaldees invented God, Sister Sophia. HaShem was there from the beginning of the universe.'

'Of course. What are you saying?'

'If you seek the most ancient name, should you not be looking to the tongues of the most ancient peoples? Have you read Aegyptiaca?'

'Yes. Manetho writes that the Aegyptians ruled for thousands of years, thirty dynasties of pharaohs, Ethiops and queens among the first of them.'

As I said the word 'queens' he actually snorted, I heard it. He said, 'The Brethren have safeguarded the secret name of the Aegyptians.'

We had learned it; that name is Auwen.

Guryon continued, 'The Kanaanites also, you remember, came from there, at the source of the Nile, before they planted their vines all across the lands around the Sea. But before them were more ancient ones. The Chaldees, where do you think they came from?'

I suspected that Brother Guryon's desire was to catch me in ignorance and thus belittle me; I hope my eyes did not betray me above my veil. I tried to show only enthusiasm.

'The kingdom of Kush.'

'The heritage of Ham', he said, as if correcting me. But I so loved the subject of our discourse that I forgot to be annoyed with him.

'Yes. They were the first of men. It is said they are the most powerful, most just, most beautiful of the human race, and God was said to be most beloved of the scent of their sacrifices.'

'I saw once a sample of their script,' I said. I reached for a wax tablet and reproduced the seven Meroïtic symbols I'd seen on the Kushite spear handle at Palmyra. 'The merchant said it means 'stand fast', but I don't know what was the sound of the word, nor which letters are which, which are the vowels.'

The vowels were of special interest, as they were the secret letters. It was likely that the secret of the Name of God was in the vowels.

'Brother, we must learn about this language,' I said. 'You must ask among your brothers to procure for us documents. Will you?'

He promised, but didn't.

I complained about it to Ima Symacho, 'I wonder if there is any reason to study with the Brother; he seems so fearful of my learning anything.'

'It's not that, dear,' she said to me. 'He wishes to rule you. It is his way of loving you.'

'It is no kind of love that I want.'

'I can see that. And yet he may win you. But you don't have to limit your studies to suit him. There are others you can go to. Have you discovered any of the wisdom of Kush from your own researches?'

'Abba Nehuniyyah says their New Year was 11th of Av, our midsummer, as they lived on the southern side of the earth, and their Great Year began 481 years before ours.'

'And could Nehunniyah tell you anything about their tongue?'

'He said he read once that it had nineteen consonants and four vowels.'

What was the most ancient secret name of God in the language of the most ancient of men? Though I sought it all my life, I never learned it. Nevertheless, Ima Symacho taught me a magical recipe from their traditions.

'I have no gift for ancient languages, but I can teach you a bit of magic from our dark-skinned ancestors. I can see that it is right for you to know it. It is a recipe to make fire from powder without torch nor candle.'

Indeed, I could go to others for knowledge; I could go to her. 'Please teach me,' I said.

Together we entrapped a rock rabbit and kept it for a while, feeding it well. We collected its waters for three days, then let the poor thing go. She showed me how to dry the urine in the sun until it became powder, making sure to keep it clean from evil influences in the air.

'Now it is time to see the fire,' she said.

She began to hum a monotonous tone, no words, as she gathered the dry, powdered urine in a flat stone bowl, and beckoned me up a hill, holding the bowl before her ceremoniously. The sun was setting behind her shawl, its shadow casting her face black as Kush.

She stood at the top of the hill, still humming, and placed the bowl on the ground. She began the ritual, and her shape shifted before me, pulling me back in time, into a time of magic more ancient than Aegypt.

My Dreaming Self saw an ancient Kushite priestess, a queen, longer ago than my Chaldee maga, to whom perhaps she had imparted her lore through the ages. A woman from the other side of the earth, and from so far off a time that her name could not be known by human memory. Perhaps she was from so long ago that she had no language and communicated with her gods only by humming.

The Kushite maga beckoned me to move back, and I obeyed as one bewitched. The sky was quite dark now, and I could see only her eyes in her shaded face. She motioned me to regard the bowl.

Then she took from her sleeve two flints and swung her arms round striking them together. She herself leapt back in a swirl of dark robes, as a spark hit the bowl, and the tiny pile of powder exploded like a miniature volcano.

It was the greatest magic I had seen since the terebinth grove.

And yet my relations with Brother Guryon did not improve.

That was the year we saw the great shooting star in the sky. We didn't even need the stargazers. There was a comet, and a bright star shaped like a sword hanging over Jerusalem that turned every way in the sky. This phenomenon lasted for almost a year. So many of the Brethren and People of the Land came to the Yachad, there was a semi-permanent camp outside the astronomers' cave, waiting for imminent announcement of something either fantastic or aweful.

That was also the year (66 CE) King Tiridates and the three princes of Parthia visited Rome, accompanied by their magi, after the truce at Rhandeia, to worship Nero as the risen Son of God. They had seen the star all the way from the Pontus.

The sign itself was disconcerting enough, but my discussion with Brother Guryon when we first saw it was troubling to me. It was on the day they celebrated the Feast of Unleavened Bread in Jerusalem.

There had been heavenly works in the Holy City, too, Guryon told me. 'On Pesach, at the sixth hour of the night, the great bronze Corinthian Gates opened of themselves, and at the ninth hour a light shone around the altar in the Sanctuary, a light that lasted for a half an hour.'

'Yes, we heard this from the messenger, but wasn't that the wrong day?' I said. How could it be a true sign if it was on the wrong day? The priests of the Yachad had waved the first barley sheaf three days earlier, according to the Jubilee calendar.

'It was on Pesach of the TEMPLE calendar,' he said forcefully, as if correcting me. He continued, 'and when the priests sacrificed, a heifer brought forth a lamb right there in the Inner Court.'

Imme, who was bouncing around the hill in front of us, popped up, 'That's impossible. Heifers have calves, not lambs.'

I nodded, 'And they cannot give birth. The priests look after them for three years before sacrifice to make sure they remain pure.'

Guryon insisted, 'It was seen by thousands of people.'

'What do these signs mean, Brother? Is that up there the star foretold by Balaam? The star come out of Jacob?' I said. 'Surely that is the Sword of the Lord. Look around this hill, all this joy and expectation, yet still some of the Fathers see prophecies of destruction. They say the bronze gates opening foretells letting enemies into the city.'

He remarked, 'When a comet passes through the Hunter it heralds the end of the age, they say, that from Judaea would go forth men destined to rule the world.'

'That one, did it pass through the Hunter?' I asked.

He sniped, 'I don't know. YOU'RE the one who's studying star-gazing.'

There we were, with hundreds of people around us, witnessing the astronomical event of the millennium, the heavens illuminated before our eyes with the power of God, and Brother Guryon's concern was in showing himself above me!

A few days after that, there was an even greater sign. Just before sunset, chariots and troops of soldiers in armour were seen running about among the clouds, surrounding the cities.

On Shavuot, according to the TEMPLE calendar, as Brother Guryon would have said, fifty days after the signs at Pesach, the priests entering for evening rites were interrupted by a quaking of the earth, accompanied by the voice of a heavenly multitude saying, 'We are departing from here'.

'God has abandoned the Temple,' the terrified priests cried. Many of them fled across the Jordan, terrified by the signs and the prophecies.

As above, so below.

It was Year 3826, the prophets calculated, from Adam.

# Chapter 13
## Ebionim

I ma Miryam, in her teaching filled with activity, was a proponent of the Works faction, as was I, despite my bookish nature. She was much occupied with the Yachad's works among the Poor and the People of the Land. Indeed, a far greater proportion of her effort was spent in collecting and distribution of alms than in teaching. There had been a time when the Yachad were isolated desert hermits. But now things were moving quickly. She drew me into this activity with her enthusiasm.

'HaShem will save us only when we act to save ourselves,' she explained. 'We must win the people of our own land to the rule of the Law before we can win the Nations. The End of Days is now.'

She said this with a calm joyousness that I could not feel. 'The time is now' drummed in my heart as well, but my Feeling Self heard it as 'Time is running out'. I felt a sense of desperation—we must hurry, we must hurry—but no joy.

Ima Miryam was clear as crystal in her purpose and focused on the work at hand. Me, I was constantly blocked by a tension in my gut and in my shoulders from my Feeling Self telling me to hurry, hurry, hurry.

'Keep your spirit calm and your hands busy,' she said. 'The hour for everything is ordained in heaven.'

I recalled her counsel against hurrying the seeking of knowledge. 'It would not be wise,' she'd said, 'to teach the principles of architecture to Imme. They would mean nothing to her. It is not that we are keeping secrets from her. We are only safeguarding the pleasure that she would have should she choose to learn them when she is ready.'

The remembered image of eight-year-old Imme wearing a mason's apron as she bounced around the hortus made me giggle.

'There is a time and place for works as well as knowledge,' she said.

There had been troubles between the sects, and not only the Pharisees and Tzaddikim.

The Notzrim were taking up a collection. Simon Cephas, one of their three 'pillars', was in prison, about to be executed by King Herod of Chalcis. Cephas had been the leader of the sect before Yeshua the Just—then they were called Barjonim, the Sons of Yonah—and some said he was the grandson of Judas the Galilean. A letter from their Inspector in Qesarya circulated among the followers of the Way as far as Rome, urging for a delegation to plead for the prisoner.

The Inspector appealed to our sect's common abhorrence of beastly sacrifice in the Temple, but then slighted our steadfastness, accusing us of 'not yet resisting to the point of shedding your blood'.

It was an unfair slight. Furthermore, our support or not of this campaign was not a question of zeal; it was a question of either policy or resources.

An Ossaean would neither give alms nor shed blood in support of Sha'ul, that Spouter of Lies, but a Son of Yonah was a different matter. So, it would have been a tough decision in terms of policy; it was the question of resources that decided it.

The women at the well had heard only snippets of the debate in Assembly, but we had our own discussions. As it was a question of Ebionim funds, distribution of which was under the purview of the Mothers, the women would be directly consulted.

Since my taking the Twelve Vows, Sister Tsuiyah was nicer to me, but I was too, too pleased of it. I would tense my jaws upon encountering her, and on receiving her friendliness I would heave an audible sigh.

Imme once told me, 'You are yourself without her, Sister Sophia. You can be yourself with her, too.' As usual the little tyke was an example to her elders.

Tsuiyah was certain the Saints would not support the campaign, yet she resented the implied slanders upon our order. 'It's scandalous to claim we are cowardly in our works. The Ossaeans were the first of the sects to support the Maqabim. Whenever it's a question of defense of the Law we have always gladly resisted to the point of death.'

'And after all the good works of the Brethren,' I agreed. 'It won't be the false accusation that decides the matter, though.'

'True. We just can't afford the funds. The collection boxes were already exhausted once by the delegation to Nero to free the Temple Wall sages then again by the splitters of That Assembly. And now we may have a war to fund.'

She referred to a wall ten Zealots had built on the upper-most building of the western portico of the royal palace of the Hasmoneans in Jerusalem, where King Agrippa had built himself a large banquet room where he dined with his Greek friends on meat sacrificed to idols, from which, in their profane entertainment they looked down upon our sacred rites.

Our Galilean commander Yosef, as a young priest, was among that delegation to Rome sent to defend the Zealots, and quite struck the fancy of the Empress Poppaea. Nero had released the prisoners and granted that the wall could remain.

'If we do not contribute funds, we must at least send a letter of support,' Tsuiyah continued. 'It was Cephas's works against the impiety of the king's household that gave heart to the Temple Wall martyrs in the first place.'

'Simon Cephas is assuredly a hero of the Ebionim,' I concurred.

Cephas's Barjonim had also had a role in the strike against Caligula's statue. In the days of the procurator Fadus, Cephas's Assembly hosted a great gathering to denounce King Agrippa the son of Aristobulus, saying that Herod's family should be barred from worship in the Temple. When word got to the king in Qesarya, he invited the sage to visit and inspect his premises for righteousness. There, Cephas baptised some among the king's household into the Way.

'Has he friends in the Temple? You know they've threatened to tear it down,' another girl said.

'The Gamalielites? To a certain extent. Did you hear what the Nasi (Gamaliel II) said?' she said.

'About destroying the Temple?'

'Cleansing was the word, not destroying. He said if it was a human project, it would fail, but if it is of God, none would be able to stop them,' said Tsuiyah.

'That's just sitting on the wall,' I said. 'Won't we be doing that if the Assembly doesn't support the delegation?'

Some of the other girls were muttering about 'defending heretics', but I believed, as did many, that allies must be united

212

when our objectives are agreed.

Someone repeated an old ruling of that Tzaddik slave Caiaphas, 'It is better to have one man die for the people than to have the whole nation destroyed.'

I said, 'That is too cruel. But surely, Sisters, these days a delegation to Rome is too costly for the sake of one man.'

During the discussion Ima Symacho had joined us at the well. I dutifully stood up to let her sit on one of the rocks.

'It is indeed a question of cost,' she pointed out, 'Tiridates' delegation to Nero took nine months, and each day cost 200,000 denarii a head.'

Another Sister said, 'With the blood of the martyrs of Rome less than one year old, and with all the refugees from the persecutions, we have bigger problems.'

Tsuiyah agreed, 'Our collection boxes are for the Ebionim and for the support of the militias.'

I also reluctantly agreed. The collection boxes had more important things to fund than trips to Rome. The Assembly evidently agreed with us women and voted against a delegation.

Ima Miryam noted the decreased frostiness between me and Sister Tsuiyah, and she was certainly happy to see the particular friendship between me and Imme.

'You do well with the girl, Sophia.'

'Anyone would do well with her; she is an angel. Also, Ima, I had younger brothers—too many of them. It is nice to have a younger sister.'

'I avow that you enjoy young folk,' she insisted. 'How would you like to work with young girls in the villages? There is an urgent need to teach the Way among the children of Godfearers. Younger Sisters can help, as the little ones are less afraid of you, and your knowledge of Greek will be valuable.'

As she spoke, I thought of my brothers. I, enjoy young folk, my Master says? I rarely remember enjoying my brothers—Adam, I can count my good memories on one hand. Maybe I was no good with boys, but could I be a good sister to girls? Perhaps this was a path I needed to take in penitence. Adam and Yonah, Mikha'el, and Ya'akov, my mind pictures you in one big noisy blur. If I can give my service to another, will you absolve me? In the great balance at the End of Days, perhaps I will have earned forgiveness.

'We don't have much time,' Ima Miryam was saying, 'the Day is coming.'

'Ima, I barely know the Way myself. How am I to proselytise?'

'Don't worry about that. These children have a good teacher, and their parents are devout. Your role would be not so much to teach, but just to be an older friend for them, help them with their Hebrew, that sort of thing.'

I was convinced. Speaking to foreigners was no shock to me after my sojourn with the Nabatu, and I looked forward to learning about life among the Greeks.

'Yes, I will.'

Ima Miryam was pleased at my uncharacteristic obedience.

Those on high evidently approved, as the next day she told me she had put my name forward.

'I have heard from Nehuniyyah that you know your Scripture. The girls are reading Jewish history at the moment; they may have many questions. But if they ask you a question you don't know the answer to, just say, 'I don't know'. They can always ask their teacher.'

The Ossaeans travelled near and far teaching, collecting

214

donations and distributing substance from the charity boxes—instruction, worship, and charity.

It was the only time we ever bore arms, as travel necessarily risked intrusion from bandits, though I never needed weapons. Shapeshifting always seemed to serve me as long as travelling parties were small. In a larger group, such as the one that went into Ein Gedi, numbers made it safe.

In each community there were seven men called the Good Brotherhood who were in charge of the distribution. Naturally, though, the women did a lot of the work. The Sisters and Mothers of the Yachad went down with the regular group to Ein Gedi every market day.

Desert areas are bleak and yellow. But the mountains there are dotted with caves, and some of them have hidden pools fed by waterfalls where you can bathe or drink. The valley around Wadi David bursts into green.

To get to where our friends lived, who would escort us, we had to walk along a part of the coast, stepping past foul smelly rock holes filled with brine and strange devilish substances growing in them—one hole glowed cabbage green with them, another blood-red. The Sea was the brightest of blue in the full sun, bluer than the sky; I remember Abda said it changed colour three times a day, reflecting the sun's rays in varying tints.

The sea also periodically spat up refuse from Sodom and Gomorrah, and huge lumps of black asphalt resembling headless bulls would collect on top. 'Annually, it floats to the surface,' Abda said, 'and they foreknow the season twenty days before by a foul smell, which tarnishes silver and gold.'

'It sticks to the boat until loosened with a woman's menstrual blood and urine,' he'd told me.

From the town of Ein Gedi, some of the men and women of the Ebionim escorted us down the Wilderness Road in the direction of the fortress of Masada, veering back down toward the village of Qiryat 'Aravaya. It was along this road that my little pupils lived.

I was assigned to three Greek girls, two sisters–Calantha and Clio–and their cousin–Cynthia, of eight, nine and ten years. Their parents were generous sponsors of the Ebionim.

Though I only spent about an hour with the girls before their minds wandered and they ran off to play in the fountain, there and back, the journey took most of a day. Jealous of time taken from my studies, I began by visiting only once a moon. Soon though, I realised that any bond we formed and every phrase learnt, the girls would forget it after a week or two, so I started going every market day.

The little sisters' parents were Alexandros and Ianthe, whose forefathers had settled here among the descendants of Lot during the days of Alexandros the king of Macedon. Alexandros and Ianthe spoke nor read not a word of Hebrew themselves, but being 'not blessed by sons' as Alexandros said, he was 'determined for his daughters to read the word of God'. Ianthe had converted to Judaism in her youth, and he, when he met her, was 'as smitten by her faith as by her beauty', he told me. 'Eight days after I heard the Word, I was circumcised,' he said proudly as he curled his arm around his wife's waist.

'It is true,' his devoted wife confided, 'my husband is as pure and true to the Law as any born Jew.'

And I can tell you, Sisters, over the many market days I travelled down to Ein Gedi, I found this to be true.

So overjoyed were they for my assistance in their daughters' education, for which the Yachad took no fee, every time I visited, they insisted that I must stay for the evening meal, which Cynthia's parents would sometimes share. The Inspector had approved the rules of their table, and the folk with whom we came had plenty of permissible invitations, so I was pleased to accept.

He being a prosperous merchant, the house was grand. Two columned corridors of irregular width with a long narrow courtyard in between, and along the walls murals painted of landscape scenes. The fountain was located in the wider of the corridors where the chairs were brought for supper.

Not only was I pleased to sit in table fellowship with Greeks, though only a girl, I, recognised as 'the teacher', was accorded the place of honour. It was a respect no one but my father had ever accorded me.

Ianthe sat with her husband, and the girls and their cousin, too, and they are just as naughty at supper as were my brothers, I can tell you, though they went off to play in the fountain after eating.

Both parents seemed to enjoy having the girls at meal, and whenever one of them responded to the scholarly guest intelligently, they beamed smiles upon the child. It was contagious. Contrary to my attitude back home, where I would gladly have stuffed my brothers' noisy mouths with balls of wool, I found myself beaming, too, at the children's raucous participation.

The girls' knowledge of things in their foreigners' world about which I knew nothing proved interesting information for me as well. I longed to introduce them to Imme, as they were of the same age. They had in common both their boisterousness and their youthful wisdom. But she was not permitted to leave the camp.

Though Ianthe set out the plates at the beginning, the food was served by their servant, a Jew named Melissa.

'She is not a slave,' Ianthe assured me. 'She is paid well, has all the holidays, and we follow all the laws.'

'I am certain that is so,' I said. A wife of twenty years my senior, to look to me for justification? I felt embarrassed. 'Good wife, you are a guide to me in your righteousness,' I said.

Indeed, the Jewish servant was not as those I am accustomed to. I learned absolutely nothing about the identity, life or family of Melissa. I attempted it, too, but was blocked every time. As the company discussed things over dinner, however, Melissa, as she refreshed our cups or cleared away our plates, would participate freely in the discussion. It was the strangest thing I have ever seen.

No personal issues were broached in front of the servant, matters about the children or the family, but as we discussed the wider issues of the day and even the deepest questions of philosophy, Melissa's opinions were listened to with equal attention as to the master's. If the servant was in the kitchen when something interesting was said, Ianthe would yell, 'Melissa, Alexandros just said…what do you think?' and she would pop her head out to respond.

Perhaps the Kingdom of God is not one where there are masters and servants, but if masters and servants are finding common discussion, something must be changing.

Alexandros was a merchant; he had some dealings with the Nabatu, though he told me he knew not Abda's caravan. His business was with the Aegyptians, for he was an exporter of the bitumen harvested by the Idumaeans; and his table was rich.

Knowing our Nazirite tendencies, there was never any meat on the table when I was invited, but Ianthe managed to bring to her table every other delicacy south-eastern Palestine had to offer. While adhering to the confines of my order, I dined so well at Qiryat 'Aravaya that the subsequent night at the Yachad I could barely eat a crust of bread with the other Seekers.

Having paid no fee for the Ossaean tutelage, Ianthe never failed to load a donkey heavy with fruit and other luxuries to take back 'for the Poor', she said. I asked her to favour me by including rolls of papyrus for the archives; Alexandros had a never-ending supply from the Aegyptians.

Once, Ianthe said she wished I would instruct the girls in matters of the Law.

'Madam, I'm only an Ossaean Seeker. And, though I am not yet a woman and mother myself, I think your daughters' hearts are true. You have their instruction, and in their grace, they will hear it truly.' She appreciated the compliment, and it was truthfully meant.

And so, having found a loving elderly family with Abba Ahissa and Ima Sherah, I found a loving younger family among Godfearing foreigners at the house of Alexandros.

Of course, I bathed before reentering the holy compound, but I did not feel defiled.

That would change.

The girls were full of questions about the meaning of things, and they were reading about Jewish rites, so I happily sat down with them to puzzle over the text.

They were reading it in Greek, but the father was anxious I should teach them Hebrew, so I composed the lesson by taking the phrases from the text and teaching them the matching phrases in Hebrew. Not always something they could use in their daily lives, perhaps, but they enjoyed it.

The girls, even little Cynthia, were fond of drawing images, so I taught them little phrases in Hebrew, easy ones, and they would draw pictures on squares of Alexandros' papyrus to illustrate the concepts. They enjoyed this immensely. I would say:

'I am eating mutton. I am not eating pork.'

'We are harvesting the barley. They are harvesting the grapes.'

'These herbs are bitter. Those herbs are not bitter.'

'Today is Pesach, Father is reclining.'

'Today is Sukkot. The priest is binding the *etrog*, *lulav*, *hadass* and *aravah* (the Four Species: citron fruit, date palm frond, myrtle boughs and willow branches).'

I would review the girls by showing them the pieces of papyrus, one after one, while they repeated the phrases. I sometimes wondered whether they were not learning the pictures rather than the words, but I was overjoyed at one meal, when Calantha, as Melissa served her some nutroast, turned to me and said in Hebrew, 'I am not eating mutton.'

I looked at Alexandros and Ianthe, and we all beamed.

'Sophia, why do people say that Jews are mutilators?' little Cynthia asked me once.

Both her cousins and I giggled at the big word.

'Cutting the foreskin is a symbol of cutting the foreskin of our hearts, thereby we open ourselves to God's mysteries. Some are circumcised when they are eight days old, for some it is when they first begin to follow the Way.'

'Our father was circumcised,' said Cynthia.

'That's right. It's like the seal your father uses in his business.

Circumcision is God's seal upon the flesh and upon the heart.'

'Our mother, too?'

'She too, abides by the Law. She covers her hair and keeps the Sabbath holy. She cooks you lawful food, does she not? And obeys the *mitzvot* of the Law?'

'Yes.'

'And she loves you, and instructs you in the good and right manner of things?'

'Yes.'

'Then she follows the Way.' I was proselytising, after all.

'Why do they say Jews hate people?' was Clio's question. 'You don't hate people, do you, Sophia?'

'Of course not, especially not you,' I smiled, and tugged her sleeve. 'I think it is because our ways are not like theirs, our purity laws separate us from those who do not follow them. Yet we cling with pride to our traditions and our God even unto death.'

Calantha argued, 'The soldiers want us to be like everyone else.'

I agreed, 'Yes, they want us to be all good servants in the big household of Rome.'

It was she, the eldest, who unveiled the most obscene slander. 'Why do they say Jews sacrifice humans?'

'Calantha, that's ridiculous. Where have you girls been hearing these things? Do you believe them?'

They all said, 'No.'

'Then do not listen to them,' I said.

That spring, Ima Miryam and I celebrated Purim at Qiryat 'Aravaya, a festival not celebrated by Ossaeans, but we joined with other Jews and proselytes like the girls' family in the parade. Ianthe and her sister Cynthia's mother helped us make orange pastries filled with poppy seed and distribute them to the Poor. We feasted together at Qiryat 'Aravaya, and Imme was allowed to come.

The wives and grandmothers from every household had each brought a dish, and the huge table was laden. Many plates held Bardawil sea bream or Kinneret (Sea of Galilee) carp; there was bread of various colours and grains; herbed olive oil and *tzir* (salty fish liquid from salting fish) to dip the bread in and *hiliq* (a fish sauce cheaper than garum) and mustard-honey to sauce the food. Other foods had been flavoured with dill, cumin or black nigella. There was *miqpah* (lentil) stew with garlic and cabbage, figs and dates, various foraged salad vegetables and eggs gathered from different wild birds. There were also plates of locusts, which I did not eat. As many in the company strictly followed the dietary laws, we had no meat, and only the men drank wine.

I might have been right that Imme would befriend the girls had it not been for language differences. Though perfectly keen to learn Greek letters when sitting with me in Ima Miryam's hut, Imme was shy to speak the language, and knew too few words, anyway.

The girls on their part looked upon learning Hebrew as a fun game, and whatever words they learned, they quickly forgot. It had not occurred to them that they might speak this exotic language with other children. At supper, Imme clung close to Ima Miryam, and the girls clung close to their mothers.

# Chapter 14
## The lion's den

I had been with the Yachad for almost three years, and was preparing to receive Sekhem. In the middle of the barley harvest, the arrival of a market boy from Jerusalem drew us from the fields back to camp. He had an urgent warning for our community.

The boy was in the household of a Jewish merchant, a certain dealer in scrolls, maps and documents, who came upon a parchment with evidence against our Yachad. The merchant, with an idea of its worth, both for gold and for malice, intended to take it to the Sanhedrin.

The Yachad have a code to conceal our writings; only we knew the key. Agrippa's spies were everywhere, you see. Just to give you an example—it is of no danger now—for Herod, we write 'the red man of Edom'; for Pharisees we write 'seekers of smooth things'; Jerusalem is 'the lion's den'; and 'Kittim' means the Romans and all their Greeks. Or we used gematria code, substituting the numerical value of the letters for names, especially for those who were targeted for assassination; Emperor Gaius, Caligula, for example, was 616; Nero, Neron Kesar, was 666.

It seems the parchment the merchant had acquired contained a list of this code concerning our commentaries on calendar matters. Such a document should never have been enscribed. A rendition of the code would empower the Romans to prosecute us for seditious literature.

The boy, a Jew himself, had understood some of the interest in the parchment and knew of the Yachad in the wilderness. He spoke not to the master, but did speak with his friend, a slave of the household.

We owe probably our lives to this slave, a Greek named Athanasios, who was the merchant's scribe. He had contrived to spill an entire flask of ink, making it appear an accident, completely obliterating all the words on the parchment. Enraged, the master had whipped him severely. Thinking only that he had been deprived of a worthy sale, the master seemed not to suspect intrigue, so the boy was able to run here to warn us.

It happened that Abba Ahissa was Overseer of our camp that moon—the office rotated among the Elders in cycles of twelve. He said, 'This could put us all in danger, not only our documents, but our lives. The Sanhedrin will hear of this. If they can interpret the prophecies concerning our calendar, the days on which it would be propitious to rally the people...'

Ima Sherah concurred, 'it would be evidence enough to put our Saints in prison, at the least.'

He immediately convened an Assembly of the Saints and Elders, with the special inclusion of Sofer Shaphan, the issue of documents being under his purview.

As usual, we waited excitedly outside the Assembly Hall to hear the announcement. There were two. The first was: 'We shall send all our works to safekeeping at Secacah.'

As the Saints and Elders exited the building, Sofer Shaphan emerged, and he headed straight toward where I was standing with the other girls. All the painful memory of my bad behavior and the shame of Shaphan's rebukes flooded into my mind, and blood rushed to my scalp.

Is this some new rebuke? I thought. Does he know that Abba Lilyukh gives me documents to read? What is his opinion of magic? Would he disapprove to know of the womanly secrets shared in Ima Miryam's hut or the shapeshifting in the Idumaean woods? For a brief moment, the black cloud filled my eyes and I lost sight, so that by the time I regained my senses, he was upon me.

'Sofer,' I said trembling.

'Sister Sophia, the care of precious documents is in your blood, and I know you to be a lover of the Wisdom of the Brethren.'

He noticed? He knew me?

'I have put you forward for the team supervising the loading of our works. We will not have long, no time to select only the potentially offensive works. We must hurry.'

I was speechless, but accepted the assignment by touching his hem.

I later asked Abba Ahissa if he had put the Sofer up to it.

He replied, 'No, daughter, it is your own gifts and your own works that have earned you this respect.'

The second announcement was: 'We are in debt to this slave. We shall send our healers to tend his wounds.'

Ossaean healing was more excellent than that in general use in the cities, and our Therapeutae were sent for from all around the Sea, for not only did the Brethren possess simples for healing bodies. The holiness of our emanations cured people of diseases of the mind–appetite, fear, grief, and covetousness, and other vices.

The Alexandrian Therapeutae, our brethren in Aegypt, were

famous throughout the land. They knew the power of nature; the powers also of the body, its fluids, and their effects, and how the soul operated upon the body; the manner of composition and dissolution of the sins of anger and covet. Healing was about looking for the reasons for the illness rather than the causes.

They taught that all disease was caused by deviation from the Law, as it is when we deviate from the Law that we allow the Feeling Self to erect its selfish barriers between ourselves and God.

The Ossaean skill of absorbing energy from the forces of nature to use in healing was not for Seekers; it would be another four years before these secrets would be revealed to me, although some inner mysteries I would learn after Sekhem in a few moons.

I wish I had sat more often at the feet of the Ossaean medics. The knowledge would have been of use to me during the war. Nevertheless, I already knew herbs, and my magic was soothing. I had learned many things from Ima Miryam. It was she who put me forward for the work.

I knew the physic. Ima Miryam had sent me many times to assist her and sing prayers at her healings. It was not only the Yachad who relied upon Ima Devorah for healing. Villagers and Godfearers from many *parsa'ot* (10 parsa'ot = an average day's walk) came for her care. So, she was to return to the desert as soon as the slave's condition permitted. She would assess the wounds and instruct me; I would remain to visit with daily ministrations until the cure was complete, abiding with Ossaean brethren there.

While Ima Devorah hurriedly prepared the medicaments, I

assisted the supervision of the packing up of the scrolls. While heartbroken to see our works depart from our hands, yet we knew the urgency of our danger. Furthermore, we knew not what care the slave was getting while this time was passing, and it was a day's march to the city.

So, while our men were sent northward to Secacah with donkeys piled high with saddlebags full of scrolls, a delegation was despatched quickly west to Jerusalem, and the physic and I went up with them.

Imme gave me three bags of her famous concoctions. They were differentiated by flowers or herbs tied around the necks. 'This one is for pain, this one for sleep, and this one to cleanse the blood,' she said.

'I won't have you there with me to judge the patient's mood,' I said, and kissed her.

She noted wisely, 'The boy says he is barely in this world. He will be in no mood at all.'

The day after we had departed, servants of the Sanhedrin with their officers and their bailiffs apparently came to examine our works, searching for evidence of sedition against Caesar. They found nothing but inventories in Aramaic of our store-houses and records of our donations to the Poor. They had come looking for a band of rebels conspiring to revolt, and found nothing but pious desert farmers.

With the aid of the Kanaim our secret documents were safely cached in caves near Secacah.

We ascended to the Holy City through the Gate of the Ossaeans.

The city was densely crowded, more so even than I had expected. Thousands of workers had been brought in to complete the rebuilding of Herod's Temple, now they were out of work and lacked pay, yet they refused to go back to their homes in Galilee and Judaea, and sprawled about menacingly.

I saw for the first time the astonishing Temple of God. The building is the most beautiful in all the world, and yet my Ossaean heart abhors the vile sacrifices; the offering of the lips for judgement is better than flesh offerings. I prefer the clean sacrifice of one's soul in prayer to all this blood.

Also do I abhor the priests, the Tzaddikim slaves. There they sit, priests and Levites, they make sure they get the best bits. After everyone else is finished, the sacred portion is theirs for their own consumption. Thus, in their corruption blood continues to pour on this Mount.

There was a grand Roman forum and theatre in Jerusalem which patriotic Jews, especially Ossaeans, shunned. The aristocracy, the high priests and the Kittim, lived in the Upper City near the Temple high above the stink of ordinary folk. The priests even had a bridge from their residences to the Temple to avoid any contact with *hoi polloi*.

In the new quarter past the Sheep Gate, we passed by rich houses in yellow stone with wide gardens of poppies, lavender, saffron, oleander and cypress. We could smell the lavender over the garden walls and the saffron and other spices emerging from kitchens where sweating slaves and servants cooked for their betters.

But Oh, the Temple, the size of it, the beauty of its architecture—it was justly renowned.

We arrived at dusk and were quickly smuggled into the slaves' quarters. The other slaves had tended him as best they could, but he was in terrible shape. They had removed his bloodied clothing—he wore the tunic of a freedman, so he must have been of value to his master—and dressed him waist-down in a loincloth. His back was a mess of bloody wounds, and his arms, still blotched with ink, were striated with lashes having attempted to deflect the whip. The slaves had tried to clean them, but they had not done it properly.

Ima Devorah was in charge, and I attended her. The patient was breathing but uttering nothing but groans. With difficulty we dispensed a cold tea containing medicaments into his mouth to provide him with liquid and give him surcease from the pain. As I sang, the physic gave it another cleansing, and demonstrated to me the manner of getting into every corner and anointing the raw flesh with medicaments to keep out the evil vapours in the air.

After the second day Ima Devorah returned to the Yachad, and thereafter, every day at dusk I visited Athanasios, to wash and anoint his wounds, feed him and change his bandages.

Jerusalem has never been the great city of which we dream. It has always been under the hand the foreigner. But we still dream it. The Aegyptians, Assyrians, Babylonians and Persians dealt with subjugated Palestinian petty kingdoms by cutting off the head of the snake, taking the king or prince home hostage along with the priests, nobles and skilled artisans, and deporting them elsewhere in the empire, while at home some empire-friendly lackey was appointed client king.

Many of the deported were forced to labour building pyramids, roads, aqueducts, or taken as soldiers into Aegypt. Some were later returned and given land and positions. When Alexandros conquered Persia, he came, too, with his Seleucid Greeks.

The Romans had ruled our land for seven generations, and they had been invited. The Herodians had caused so much trouble in all their squabbling, Pompey was asked, invited in fact, to invade.

All Jewish kings since have swapped favour between this power or that, while they taxed the people and dragged us into wars fought brother to brother. Thus, throughout history have we been ruled by Jews whom we had not anointed, our land bought, bartered or conquered by foreigners who cared only for our dates and our olive harvest. Lucius Aelius Lamia never once set foot in Syria during the entire ten years he was governor there; that's the kind of people they were.

It is true, Jerusalem was once wrenched from the hands of the Seleucids under the Maqabim, who created the Hasmonean dynasty, but even then, Jerusalem wasn't fighting for herself. The sovereignty of our people hung in the balance, but the matter at hand was ever: whose vassal shall we be—the Seleucids of Antioch or the Ptolemies in Alexandria?

The Greeks who came with Alexandros took our cities generations ago, and before him were Aegypt, Persia, Babylon. As they conquered, they brought home slaves, mixing them with slaves from other wars, until they could only speak with one another in the language of the master. Everywhere one went in Jerusalem, people were speaking Greek.

So not only in Tabariyya (Tiberias) and Qesarya, even in the Holy City, Jews were basically Greeks not only in speech but in spirit. Here in our Israelite cities, Jewish settlers, though we had wealth, only had right of residence. These Greco-Syrians were the citizens, and soldiers responded to their call. Greeks in my mind were those people in a society advantaged by the conquerors. It was a strange thing to see a Greek a slave.

We stayed in the household of the Inspector for Ossaeans, who—imagine my bad luck—turned out to be distant cousins to my mother in Seleucia.

They were village Ossaeans, not strict followers of the Way but involved in the works with the Ebionim. No one flinched when I declined the meat. There were prepared for our coming, and there were plentiful dishes from which to choose.

I had thought no one in Jerusalem would have heard of the ignominious departure of one girl in faraway Babylon, but after three years and more, news had passed between the communities, and they had heard the story of the runaway.

How many Jews are named Sophia, after all? I could hardly deny that it was I. How I regretted I hadn't identified myself from the first by my Mem name. But even had they not recognised the name, my youth, gender, and Persian accent alone might have betrayed me.

'They are circulating near and far copies of this portrait of you, which is actually a very good likeness,' the mother said.

It really had not occurred to me that this would happen. I had run far away from home to the wilderness. The chance that I would meet someone who had contact with my family at home—it had not crossed my mind.

I stuttered, 'It is indeed a good likeness.'

They waited as I took a breath. 'There were circumstances... My parents may not know of it.' I lowered my eyes.

'Nor us, dear?' said the mother.

'Forgive me, Mother.' The shock of having my shame reappear unexpectedly before me brought tears to my eyes. The mother glanced quickly at the father, a look that said, 'we've seen these situations before'.

He said, 'Never mind, Cousin Sophia. You are welcome here, and you may guard your secret as you wish. May we not, though, inform Babylon that you are safe and well?'

'Oh yes, if you please. I have been mindful to write to my father. Upon your next convoy, may I include a letter?'

'Certainly. They'll be coming from all the Nations for Sukkot. We shall contact the Babylonian contingent then.'

I left with them a letter, telling my parents I was well and apologising for causing them grief. As it happened, they had more to tell the community in Babylonia than of the discovery of their runaway daughter.

The third day, I fed Athanasios porridge. Ima Devorah had shown me how to treat his wounds impersonally, as a physic, but it was the first time I had ever touched a man's body other than my father's, and I felt shy of it. His skin, the parts not scarred with whip marks, was lighter than mine. I was conscious that he was 'a foreigner' and felt more shy.

He was still unable to sit up, so I fed him as he lay face down on the bench. As he bent up to the spoon, I could see a bit more of his face. He had a nasty healed scar across his brow.

The new wounds were less raw and bloody, but if anything, uglier even than on the first day. He could speak, but in respect for his pain, I spoke little to him. I was accompanied by my cousin Yitzhak—his mother was a timid woman and feared to trek across town to associate with slaves—and the market boy Menelaus. We all remained as quiet as possible. The master was now in residence, they said, so the slaves all came in and out on tiptoe, trying not to betray our presence.

The patient did say to me, 'What is that song you sing?'

'Prayers to God for your recovery'.

Only later did we learn that he knew Aramaic. I spoke to him in the Koine Greek taught me by my father.

'Why would your God care for me?'

'God cares for all who are righteous.'

I sensed that he was not pleased with my singing, but I defused him by the compliment. He said nothing more then, but the following day he requested that I no longer sing prayers for him.

'I am grateful for your care, but I have no need for your prayers.'

At this, it was I who was defused.

I was anxious, seeing his continuing discomfort, to use some of my magical knowledge in his treatment, but was frightened to suggest it, given his surliness. I could not do so without his permission and participation. The supplicant must play an active role. Finally, I dared.

'As well as healing,' I ventured, 'I also know some magic. I know a ritual for keeping out infection?'

He started, practically barking at me, 'No magic. Only your anointments.'

I remained motionless for few seconds, until he said, 'I'm sorry. I do not believe in superstitious things.'

I softened, and he continued, 'It is your knowledge of medicaments that has healed me, not some hocus-pocus.'

The expression of gratitude was small consolation. I remained chastened and did not speak much for the rest of that visit.

By the fifth day, though movement was painful, he was able to feed himself. The treating of his wounds was still agony for him, but after the bandage was finished, while I packed up to leave, I perceived he was able to converse, and sit up when helped.

It was not right that I, a virgin, did speak first, and it is forbidden to hold familiar intercourse with Gentiles, but the fact that he was a slave and I freeborn emboldened me, as well as my desire to show gratitude to him on behalf of my Community. In these troubled times, so many of the old conventions were already changing. By this time, we had learned that he spoke Aramaic.

I had two questions of urgency.

'Why did you risk this suffering on our behalf?'

'Your people are enemies of the slavemasters and the priests who run the city.'

'That is true.'

'Then we are on the same side. But I am only one slave against the might of Rome. This was one thing I could do.'

My other question was: 'Why did your master punish you thus? To whip you so sorely for simply ruining a sale? It cannot be defended.'

'It wasn't just the sale,' he explained. 'Though I tried to make it look like an accident and admitted nothing, Master suspected me of some conspiracy.'

'For our sake you have greatly suffered and endangered yourself,' I said.

Yitzhak was greatly impressed. He said, 'We are deeply in your debt' and touched the hem of the slave's loincloth. I'd never seen anyone do that to a slave. But as I came to learn, Yitzhak was not one for respecting the divisions in society created by our rulers.

'If you fight Rome,' the slave said, 'you will repay me.'

My cousin Shulamith, Yitzhak's sister, was near my age, and once recovered from the shame of my confessions, I was happy to befriend her, though we disagreed much.

She had split with her family to take the Mem of the Notzrim, that new and peculiar superstition. They followed one of those desert messiahs—the one who threw over the money-changers in the Bazaars. Shulamith's mother had witnessed it.

Yeshua had led an insurrection in Jerusalem, but his life had ended in crucifixion. The spirit of revolution had not yet spread from the villages to the cities.

He was recruited by the Barjonim, the Sons of Yonah—heirs to the zealous spirit of Judas the Galilean—and they'd backed his claim to the throne. Along with some Rechabite converts they formed their own faction. From the Mount of Olives, he preached to the People of the Land and organised them into Fifties and Hundreds, rallying them to the ancient banner of the Notzrim.

They said he was the saviour promised to us. They called him the Notzri in memory of Yeshua ben Pandera, who lived at the time of Yannai and had been hung on Pesach Eve for sorcery, and his followers invoked the name of Yeshua the Notzri in their incantations.

This had caused a schism among the wider Ebionim works, as most of the supporters of the Baptist went over to them after he was beheaded.

All who followed the Sons of Abiud in that branch of the Davidic line, Ya'akov the Just's faction, had joined the Notzrim.

'The Yachad do not support their loose interpretation of the Law,' Abba Ahissa had explained to me. And there were other differences between our sects, he said.

'They believe that the brother Yeshua was the Messiah, the veritable incarnation of Yeshua HaNotzri, and this they claimed after the man's death, if you can believe it, and after all his prophecies had failed. The king's ascension to the Throne of Solomon is to happen in the afterlife, and so it has already happened, they say. These skewed beliefs will pollute the Jewish people and keep us from salvation.'

We weren't waiting for a messiah, Shulamith said. The messiah had already arrived. Thus, we didn't need freedom from Rome and we didn't need to cleanse the Temple. We could create our own little world where we would be safe.

It was soon after the protest over Pilate's aqueduct. Our Brethren were leaders in that revolt as well. Our Scriptures hold that when the source of a liquid stream is pure and the lower vessel is not, then the impurity 'up-jumps' into the upper vessel. Pilate's aqueduct went right through a graveyard. We couldn't have the righteous in Jerusalem bathing in unclean waters.

There was an uprising led by some messiah in Tirathana near Mount Gerizim in Samaria at the time (35 CE) as well. It was probably Simon Magus, a disciple of Yochanan. They believed they were to uncover some precious artefacts buried there by Moshe. The procurator, Pontius Pilate, crushed this movement so violently, he lost his seat over it.

After the incident at the Bazaars the Romans arrested Yeshua and crucified him.

According to Shulamith, however, Yeshua's crucifixion wasn't the failure of the prophecies; it was the announcement of our victory. 'The aeon of the evil angels is over,' she said. 'Our Lord has brought all the spirit powers under his control.'

I could not see any signs of this victory having happened.

And I remember saying almost exactly those words.

After I had returned from mikveh after treating the slave, my cousin bounded up and took me eagerly by the hand. She invited me to attend with her one of their sect's ceremonies.

The prayers were to continue over the night and the morrow in three hourly intervals, marking key events in the day of their leader's death. I went along to the first one, which celebrated the final meal he had with his followers.

At the second ceremony I had heard that the congregation practice a sacred kiss. This 'love feast' sounded scandalous to me. Though Shulamith insisted, 'It is quite pure and holy, I promise you.'

In the synagogues of the Spouter of Lies, I heard, ordinary men and women, too, perform the sacred miracles of bread and wine, and uncircumcised Gentiles and people who have not even undergone instruction receive Mem, 'turning water into wine'–they call it.

And they eat pieces of the Messiah as a dead god–they actually call the wine 'the blood'. The idea of the magus giving people enchanted food–parts of his body–to induce love comes from the Sidonians. To me, even more awful than the idea of blood sacrifice was the idea that the blood of the sacrifice should be drunk.

I greatly enjoyed partaking in her ritual, different to what I'm accustomed to, and I found the devotees and proselytes, all the rabble of Jerusalem, to be good and true. New sects like this were springing up all over the land; everyone was looking for a saviour.

In those days people believed that at the End of Times martyrs would be raised bodily from the grave like the bones of Ezekiel and given new arms to usher in the New Kingdom. The 'resurrection of the righteous' was as big a topic of debate at the time as circumcision.

The Pharisees believed in the resurrection; Tzaddikim did not. Ossaeans said it was all a question of fate. Naturally, the Zealots were keen to swell their forces with supernatural aid.

The point was, Shulamith claimed, that he rose from the dead.

There were new messiahs now, living ones, and there were a number of them, too. Why did Shulamith need a dead one?

'Yehoachim was cut off by the prophet Jeremiah,' I accused. 'You know the line of Nathan was disqualified.'

'That was a long time ago, Sophia,' she retorted easily. 'People aren't looking for the Son of David, now. They're looking for the Saviour of the World.'

Her response startled me. I had to agree; by that time, I cared nothing for genealogies. The taste of our power was upon me.

I continued, 'The real question is whether or not people will follow the line of Yehoachim, and after his death at that.'

'That is not the real question. The real question is—Has the Kingdom of God arrived? You will see, Sophia,' she said.

Abba Ahissa had told me the story:

The religious wing of the Sanhedrin charged Yeshua with necromancy and blasphemy—they said he'd raised his brother-in-law from the dead, and when they arrested him, he was practicing mysteries with a naked young man.

Yeshua's disciple hadn't actually been dead, of course, when he raised him; he had simply spent three days lying in darkness in a cave. It is always easier to hear God's voice when all other influences on your senses are repressed, and when you listen for nothing but that for an extended period of time, you can hear more.

The ritual he was performing with the young man they called 'enshroudment' which did not survive the War. Ossaeans also held rebirthing rituals in caves, performed on the initiate's seventh year. It is a practice Moshe learned in Aegypt from the Bee kings of Goshen.

The ceremony denotes initiation into a second stage, the first stage of which is Mem. The corn dies and comes back to life. Baptism is a purification; this ceremony represents a sacrifice.

The political wing of the Sanhedrin wanted him for causing a riot among the moneychangers and for claiming to be the Messiah. The Romans wanted him for sedition against Caesar and disrupting the commerce of Empire at the Bazaars. The moneychangers wanted him for reparations. And the Herodians weren't too happy to hear him called King of the Jews.

He was all alone when the cohort came for him. Even the Sicarii turned on him in the end.

Eleazar and all his seven Maqabim brothers died a good death willingly and generously. But what kind of messiah leads a failed revolution and then dies a coward?

I could not argue along these lines frankly with Shulamith, as her eyes were like stars. She seemed to find comfort in the idea of the nobility of sacrifice. It was a viewpoint held by many at the Yachad as well, and it did not please me. What is the value of sacrifice if you do not win?

## Chapter 15
## Florus

Florus' high-handed treatment of the Qesaryan troubles had not ended with the suppression of the riot. The priests and prominent Jews who had taken the rolls of Law to Narbata sent a delegation to him in Sebaste to complain, but he instead imprisoned them and demanded seventeen talents from the Temple Treasury in retribution.

No trip across town could avoid crowds of people listening to speeches by the Zealots. They were led by Eleazar ben Simon, and he gathered to him many hot-headed men.

The aristocrats were almost as hot-headed, and they did their best to take the best porticoes for their audiences, so I also heard the situation from their point of view. It was Thebutis, one of the high priests, whose daughter-in-law I later came to know:

> Since the prefect took the holy vestments of the Altar and profaned the High Priest's robes, they have sought to come between us and the rightful worship of God. Pontius Pilate rose the standards of the emperor in this Holy City, and raided the sacred monies of the Lord for his aqueduct. Mad Caligula almost put a statue of Zeus in the Temple.

When I came the sixth day, the slave Athanasios was sitting up and feeding himself, the fire of his pain abated, and he

240

regarded me for the first time. Ossaean whites were for pure quarters only; I was wearing the rough brown wool robe of a Jewish maiden from the countryside. Of my face, of course, he could only see the eyes, but unused as I was to the regard of young men, I blushed, though hopefully, he could not see it beneath the veil.

While I bandaged his back and arms, I could not help but to study him. The danger had passed as his wounds healed, and I was able to notice other things. Swarthy of face, but not muscular in build—his tasks as a clerk did not require physical strength. His arms seemed thin and white as I compared them to Guryon's. He had a strength, though, bred of suffering, I thought, or perhaps of the pride one feels from learning.

I could not stop my Feeling Self from thinking, 'not a handsome face, not at all'. I could now see that the scar across his brow reached all the way down to his chin, pulling at one side of his mouth to ugly effect. Inadvertently, my hand reached out and almost touched the scar, my fingers still smeared with unguent. At once, I felt a flash of shame and pulled back.

This wound was at least eight years old. If my hand had not required to heal, why had it reached thus? Was this not licentious behavior for a maiden? I was being too familiar with this slave, who was not of my people. I was his physic and he my patient.

Yitzhak came to my aid, 'a previous thrashing?'

Had he seen my discomfort? Athanasios offered, 'It is no longer painful.'

'Except to the heart?' I sighed in relief, grateful for his good manners.

'Yes, the remembrance of it still fills me with rage.'

I was so moved by his suffering and sacrifice that I imagined this early scar must have also been from some noble act of defiance. 'It is an abomination that a man should enslave another man, let alone to whip him like a beast. I share your anger.' I told him.

'Yes,' he said as I packed up my medical bag, 'I believe that you do.'

As he recovered, Athanasios became less surly, and as long as I did not mention religion or magic, was happier to talk. He told us about his duties for the merchant, and I told the company about my emigration from Babylon and about my refuge with the Ossaeans. He soon forgot the rules of a slave's conversation: only speak when spoken to; only say what is necessary; never question; never trust anyone; never reveal oneself.

Yitzhak, mindful of his role as chaperone, participated avidly in these discussions. He warmed to the patient immediately. With a man's heart, perhaps, he was less frightened by the slave's bluntness. He was well pleased with Athanasios and not at all shy about seeming too familiar, and our discourse thereafter became ever more pleasant.

Loathe to pronounce the sibilant at the beginning of Athanasios' name, Yitzhak joked around with his tongue, as if following Athanasios' tutelage. He called him Tasios, and so I began to do as well. At first, I feared the proud foreigner would take offence at our twisting of his language and his name, but he seemed to like it. Later he told me, 'No one has ever given me a name out of affection.'

Athanasios and Yitzhak found common conversation in the events of the day, and I learned much about the political

242

situation in Jerusalem.

We discussed philosophy, the history of far off places and languages of their peoples, the Romans' civil war. More than anything, we talked, in hushed tones, about freedom.

'Our scriptures tell us of an abode beyond the ocean in the home of the North wind at the End of Days,' I said.

He made a sour face. 'What do your scriptures tell you about today?'

After that, I started to ask myself the same question. Perhaps Shulamith was right about the Kingdom of God. It was not a day to be yearned for after death. It was a call to arms. As Ima Miryam often said, the Kingdom of God is now.

I told them the fable of the donkey and the old man, and though Athanasios enjoyed it, he said it was not true.

'I would have any other master but Rome,' he said, 'and I would take as master any who will fight Rome.' Though he himself was in thrall to a Jew, yet he would strike a blow to ease our chains. He said they are linked to the chains that bound him.

Yitzhak said, 'Not to slight your sentiment, but our goal is for a righteous government under holy Law; it is the dream of Jews.'

'A revolution of the Jews alone won't work,' Athanasios responded. 'Rome is too big.'

'Well, there is the empire of the Jewish Diaspora to look to,' said Yitzhak. 'Rome is only as big as the world she keeps in bondage.'

'Neither to slight your brethren, Yitzhak, but what support have you seen from the other provinces so far?'

It was true. The exilarchs in Alexandria and Babylon were

as pro-Rome as the Herodians.

We could hardly avoid talking about the situation in the city. Whatever opinions one held, it was the topic of conversation in every household and on every street. Jerusalem was in an uproar over Florus.

He had not rescinded his demand for seventeen talents. That was 102,000 denarii, a sum enough to feed 560 families of eight for a year. These monies were to employ the masons out of work from completion of Herod's Temple. Florus gave no further justification than that the tribute was 'for Caesar's needs'. He was mustering a force to march on the city.

I was discussing with Shulamith, while we kneaded dough for bread, the circumstances of my leaving Babylon when the whole business began.

The story her family had heard was that after having a kind of fit at the evening meal, I'd had an argument with my uncle, and had not been heard from since. At the mention of my uncle, I felt a lump form in the pit of my stomach.

'He convinced my father to make me marry.'

'We heard the tumult was over the question of your studies,' said Shulamith.

'Well, yes, he said to be a book lover was improper for a maiden.'

Improper maiden. I blinked as I said it. My Feeling Self heard the words in my uncle's voice. I felt my hand wanting to beat at my robe. I had flour patches from my fingers to my armpits, one big sticky one right on that spot–that spot–on my shoulder.

She continued, 'and you fell on the step.'

Fell on the step? Then I remembered it, the flash of a memory of scraping my leg brought an accompanied thudding ache deep in my belly.

So blinded am I by my tears, I don't see Uncle until he is upon me. He accosts me in the alley beside the house, grabbing me by the elbow. That face, that look of triumph. At last he was getting his way in our family, and he had convinced my parents to let him wield the whip. At last he would quench his jealousy and disrupt our comfortable world. He says horrible, horrible things.

'Bridesmaid of the Lord, are you? Who are you to say what is or isn't God's will?' he says.

'No man for you but Itamar, say you? What is he then to you?' he says.

'Itamar will miss his little girlfriend now,' he says.

'Farmers not good enough for you scholars, are we? Itamar loves his exalted position, doesn't he? He would be nothing but a penniless philosopher were it not for the wealth of my father's lands,' he says. 'Your pride needs a knocking, girl. Or who will marry such a harridan?'

I listen, stunned, as he rages, as he says the most horrible thing of all. He puts his hand on my shoulder and presses my arm heavily.

He says, 'I should teach you to be a proper maiden.'

Even worse, then, his words turn to honey, poisoned honey. I had not wished to give them power by remembering them. *A proper maiden, a proper maiden* rings in my ears as with his other hand he reaches for my thigh.

I had never told anyone. I'd not even acknowledged it to myself. My Feeling Self had buried it somewhere beyond memory. During all that time on the caravan trail, I never even told Shu'dat, intimate as we were.

During all that period when she so selflessly cared for me, I blocked it, and everything else from home, from my mind. I replaced certain words and phrases with substitutes, as if by never repeating the word itself, I could strike out the memory from all of my senses.

When an unwelcome picture presented itself to me, I would turn around in a circle and beat against my robe, to make myself stop thinking it. For years I forgot even what my uncle looked like, and I never again in the rest of my life attempted the Equilibrium.

Now with several years between Uncle and me, I was ready to speak my heart to Shulamith as we cleaned up from our baking. But I had no time to do so. The tiny flash inside my head reverberated outward with a bang.

The noise outside was Zealots going house to house, their womenfolk banging on pans to attract a crowd. 'Poor Florus, poor Florus', they cried as they passed a basket around collecting coppers. 'Spare some shekels for Florus. Poor Florus is destitute of possessions, so miserable he's taking profits from God.'

Ossaeans carry no coins, but I ran out and threw in a loaf of bread wrapped in palm leaves, and would have joined the gathering raucous throng had Shulamith not pulled my elbow.

'Cousin, don't give alms to those Zealots. We pay our taxes and our first fruits.'

'And so, you shouldn't. Look how the high priests use it.'

'Our Lord said, render unto Caesar that which is Caesar's; render unto God that which is God's.'

'It's different now, Shulamith. We have rendered unto God,

and look, Caesar robs it from us. Look around us. These are momentous times.'

'This Zealot business about expelling foreigners from the Temple isn't momentous, it's dangerous, and it will bring down the wrath of Caesar and the king. We must rely on the king to argue on our behalf. Don't you realise there are two more cohorts waiting to march from Qesarya?' she frowned. 'How long do you think these terrorists can get away with this?'

'At least the Zealots really give it to the Poor.' It was a spiteful comment, and I deserved her rebuke.

'That is an evil lie. Our charity boxes are for the Ebionim as well as yours.'

'Your Saints have been using donations to live the high life, traveling around making speeches and dining with Pharisees and Greeks.'

'That is also a lie.'

'What about Ananias and Saphira, your proselytes? They were Saints, weren't they? They'd taken vows of Sekhem.'

'Enshroudment, we call it.'

'Well, it means giving everything you own to the Ebionim, doesn't it? But the Barjonim caught them holding back from God.'

'The rebuke was more severe than the crime. And I wasn't a believer then, I hadn't been born yet.' She began to cry under my reproach, and I regretted myself.

'You are right. I'm sorry; I burden you with my frustrations.'

'Anyway, it is difficult for people to sell everything they have and give it all to the Poor,' she argued.

'It's only the Rich that seem to have a problem with it. You know what they say—No more can a shaft of wheat pass through the eye of a needle than can a rich man enter the Kingdom of Heaven,' I said.

'Strictly speaking, Cousin,' she said, 'a shaft of wheat CAN pass through a needle, with a bit of difficulty, if you polish it well. The Rich can be worthy if they are righteous and charitable. The Queen of Adiabene fed the Poor of Jerusalem with her riches during the famine of Claudius.'

'The Poor bless her for it. But do you say that a queen may purchase her way into the Kingdom? Is the Word of God for sale? One of her relatives hasn't even been circumcised, and he's reading the Holy Torah.'

'Through our Lord, we can all enter the gates of heaven. Queen Helena was reckoned righteous by her works,' she said.

'Or her riches. In the end you can't trust people like that, Shulamith. Your Sha'ul is Herod's foster brother. What kind of friend is he to Jews?'

'Abba Sha'ul is no teacher of mine. Stop tarring me with the same brush.'

'Well, what are your teachers doing now? What happened to Cephas's garrisons?'

'The Saints are bringing in the Fifties and the Hundreds from Asia to Aegypt and Cyprus, Sophia.'

'Well I don't see them. You're as much a hastener as I am, Shulamith, but you seem to think your collection boxes alone will work the magic.'

'The funds are used to spread the goodnews to the Fifties and the Hundreds,' she argued.

'Where's the good news? I don't see it. Foreigners steal from our Holy Temple, and soldiers walk our streets.'

'The good news is that even among the Gentiles the righteous are Sharers in the Kingdom of God.'

'The bad news is that if their faith is not accompanied by works, their coins are worth nothing.'

'I don't think you're a Hassid, Cousin,' she said. 'You're one of those Zealots.'

At my cousins' house that night, I heard the story of my family's grief over my leaving. My father had become very lean and quiet, speaking to no one; my mother bewailed the loss of her 'only daughter'. Only now that I am gone does she notice me, I thought. So many times and in so many ways had everyone asked me what happened that night that I finally spoke of it to my cousin, though I begged her not to reveal my guilty secret to her parents.

'Do not people say that if there is worry in your heart you should speak it?' she consoled me. 'Now, you have done so, you have spoken it to a friend. Sophia, you have to remember that your uncle is the guilty one, not you,' she said. 'You must redress the balance, blame the hand that struck the blow and not the bruise. Forgiveness is very important,' she said, 'but before forgiveness comes the forgiveness of oneself, and that begins with placing the blame where it belongs. You torment yourself searching for a reason why you drew your uncle's wrath upon yourself, yet it is not your character nor your behaviour that is in sin.'

My Acting Self knew this, of course, but my Feeling Self could not keep abreast. Every time I contemplated that night, the skin under my hair prickled as if no amount of bathing could cleanse my shame.

She urged me to unburden my soul to my parents. 'You need not only to mind your own self, Sophia. You have a duty, here, to do the right thing and to protect others. You must tell your family. You know, with these people,' she said, 'it is never just once.' I promised her I would write to my father and tell him the whole story, to send home with the Babylonian caravans after Yom Kippur.

Athanasios was well; and we had said our farewells. His further care could be met by the slaves around him, as the wounds were clean, and I had left medicaments with them. As I left this time, Athanasios placed a piece of papyrus in my hand, with writing in Greek letters on the front and back. I was pleased to see him well enough to have been writing, and he had a good hand, if I am any judge of Greek. Yitzhak rolled his eyes at me, but I ignored him.

I was intending to join the next group heading in the direction of the Salt Sea when momentous events intervened to prolong my stay. I was returning to my cousins' house from Noon Contemplations, and people were rushing toward the walls.

Florus was marching up to Jerusalem, come with his horsemen to steal from God.

I grabbed Shulamith as she ran up to greet me, and we rushed up the nearest steps to watch from atop the wall.

They marched through the gates, and invaded the Court of Women. There were only about a thousand of them, but the vengeful army of the Kittim is a fearful sight.

Florus stormed into the Temple Treasury, and purloined his seventeen talents from our sacred tithes.

'The Abomination of Desolation,' someone wailed.

It was unbearable, the worst insult ever to our Holy Temple. Pompey, the first of the Roman conquerors, had profaned the

Holy of Holies, but he had not dared to touch any of the sacred things, even the monies.

I couldn't stop myself from taking a moment to read Athanasios' papyrus.

On the front it said:

> There is no such thing as justice in the abstract; it is merely a compact between men. (Epicurus)

And on the back, it said:

> Man is the measure of all things. (Protagoras)

I did not agree with either of his references, which is probably why he selected them. I heard my Feeling Self say 'cantankerous slave'.

Florus set up his forces in the Upper Market and began crucifying the 'Poor Florus' Zealots. First, he had defiled the Temple of God by robbing the sacred Treasure, now he was executing men who had done nothing more than make jokes in the street. It was the worst of a wicked procurator's outrages. Crucifying someone for making a joke was even more indefensible than lashing someone for spilling a jar of ink.

People swarmed into the square like bees after an attack to their hive, and we were pulled along with them. Some were remonstrating piteously with the soldiers—didn't they realise that this or that loved one on a cross was actually one of the principal men, and of the Peace Party at that? Others were pushing past the men trying to pull their loved ones off crosses.

There was an upper story of rooms in the side buildings, and people were cramming into them to get a better view.

Shulamith and I managed to duck into the back of a shop and climb up to one of them, the storage room of that shop.

The soldiers began to kill and plunder, and Florus gave them leave. The more they killed, the more people swarmed into the square and into the buildings on three sides of the square. It was mayhem.

Many Jews were killed. It was not only Zealots who were crushed, but members of the aristocracy, even Jews who were Roman citizens of equestrian rank. Florus' men didn't know Zealot from Pharisee. We Jews all look the same, do we not? The soldiers were scarcely going to bother looking inside our sleeves. The very people who had argued most fiercely for bowing our heads to the foreigner lost their heads to his sword.

King Agrippa's sister Berenice was in the Holy City at the time, performing a Nazirite vow, and supplicated herself before the Roman procurator from the roof of the Hasmonean Palace which overlooked the square. Yet they did not desist. I remembered Ima Symacho's words about the waning of women's magic. The princess stood barefoot and shaven-headed in supplication, but all the holiness of her Nazirite chastity did not sway the wicked Roman's hand.

I was pulled from the upper storage room by some matrons who were tending the wounded, and I returned not to my cousins' for many days. So, having only the day before finished my nursing of the courageous slave, I had my first experience nursing courageous Zealots. Shulamith volunteered as well, complaining, 'Did I not tell you they wouldn't get away with it? And now we are all paying the forfeit.'

The matrons had set up a make-shift clinic in a disused section of a house near the Jaffa Gate, and a group of volunteers were bringing in the wounded. Abba Jairus, who was in charge, was an Ossaean Therapeut from Alexandria.

I knew no medicine other than whatever herbal remedies Imme had taught me and what I'd gleaned from Ima Devorah, but Jairus was glad to have a fellow sectarian.

'At times like these,' he said, 'anyone with schooling must be a Therapeut.'

Below the market as well, crowds were clustering, denouncing Florus and calling for a delegation to Rome. Now it was not just Zealots who were rebelling. The whole city was up in arms. There was fighting in the streets for three days.

The aristocracy, though their brothers' and rich friends' blood was as thick in the market as the Zealots', thicker even, still they pleaded with the people for peace.

Two Roman cohorts were on the march from Qesarya. 'We must greet them in penitence,' the Peace Party wailed. But their voices were drowned out by the shouts of anger as the rebel forces swelled; day after day, more people rallied in the Upper Market. Yitzhak and his father were with them.

As the two cohorts, a reinforcement of another thousand men, marched in from Qesarya, the priests led a delegation of supplication to greet them. They wore all the holy vestments and carried the holy vessels, and were accompanied by harpers and singers. Their garments were rent, their heads covered in dust, as they fell down before the soldiers.

The rebels and the people watched from the walls as the soldiers marched in. There was no respite in the clinic from the 'Poor Florus' riot, and the flow of wounded did not stop. Shulamith and I were occupied with the wounded, but we heard about it from Yitzhak. He wore even then the stripes of the War Party. From the ramparts he and his father watched the Peace delegation confront the Romans.

'There they were, meek in submission. It was almost as if they were offering the holy vessels of the house of God to the centurions in tribute. And instead of accepting the supplicant crowd, Florus's forces attacked! Some groups began to curse the Kittim, but the soldiers clubbed them. It looked as if one half of the crowd had bowed to the soldiers and the other half had attacked them. No one on the wall could make sense of it. One advancing and one retreating, the two halves of the crowd ran into each other and were utterly trampled at the gate.'

Had the soldiers not seen the penitent nature of the crowd? Or had the priests' delegation, or some of them, upon seeing their brothers so treated, changed their minds, and in an instant switched from penitence to militancy?

After this second outrage, the whole city revolted. A few thousand fighting pilgrims became tens of thousands of enraged Zealots. Shulamith and I were sleeping at the clinic as it was unsafe to cross town. During our waking hours the bodies came streaming in. Their relatives could hardly recognise them for burial.

The fresh cohorts broke through, and advanced through Bezetha toward the fortress of Antonia. Florus led his men to join them, but the anger of the people was too great.

'We came down from the walls and lined up on the rooves pelting the Kittim with stones,' said Yitzhak. 'The two cohorts retreated in defeat back to the palace, as we cheered from the rooftops. They have longswords, arrows, lances, siege engines, and horses. Yet we defeated them with slings and stones.'

The Zealots, fearing the Romans might recapture the Antonia

Fortress, destroyed the colonnade linking it to the Temple, but they need not have done. Florus' defeat was complete. He left a single pitiful cohort, 500 men, who remained in the palace under house arrest during the revolutionary days after.

The defeat of Florus marked the end of the hand of the foreigner in the Jerusalem. From 20,000 stadia across the Great Green Sea, the Beast Nero—may his name be obliterated—heard our battledrums. We had declared war on Rome.

The leaders of the Ebionim movement had set up a refectory not far from the clinic which was run by Joanna the widow of Herod's man Chuza. She was a follower of Shulamith's sect, and she had funded the works of the Just Ones with her own riches. Rich men, benefactors of the Ebionim, pledged their wealth to feed the city.

We had finally gotten a respite at the clinic, and Shulamith and I were enjoying a meal courtesy of the collection boxes. Yitzhak brought us the news there: 'The Zealot priests have abolished sacrifices on behalf of foreigners. The Temple Captain has abolished the daily sacrifices for Caesar.'

The last time the sacrifices were cancelled was during the riot following the execution of the Temple Eagle martyrs.

Here is the priests' story: Some man in the city had a friend named Kamtza and an enemy named Bar Kamtza, and his servant mistakenly brought a dinner invitation to the wrong one. The man was angry when Bar Kamtza showed up, though the unwelcome guest offered to pay for his meal. The host threw him out.

Bar Kamtza, to get revenge, went to the Kittim and said, 'Why don't you let me bring a sacrifice from Caesar to the Temple? The priests will like that.'

He, desiring to provoke the Zealots to revolt, blemished the beast by putting a mark on its upper lip and took it to the priests. Of course, the Shammaites rejected it.

'People will say that blemished animals are offered on the altar', said Zechariah ben Abkulus, and they put Bar Kamtza to death.

'We gathered all the Levites in white and stood next to the marker stone at the Inner Court,' said Yitzhak, 'and proclaimed, "On this stone is writ that for a foreigner to enter beyond this mark is instant death. The red men of Edom and his fornicators shall no longer pass this mark, or they will feel the point of our knives".'

The king and his family were banned from worshipping at the Temple. This declaration effectively banned the king from his own capital city.

Shulamith was as terrified as I was elated. 'The Temple Captain is one of the sons of Ananus; he's gone against his own father.'

'On their whispers a curse!' exclaimed Yitzhak.

I said, 'The forces of righteousness are against him. Eleazar is under pressure from the pilgrims and the Levites.'

'He cited Ya'akov the Just among his references, you know,' Yitzhak said, looking at Shulamith.

I said, 'As the Oblias preached, the Herodian priests have for too long corrupted the Temple with things sacrificed to idols. Now it is purified; the Temple is restored to the Law.'

'No, it's the Temple Captain who is breaking the Law,' Shulamith said. 'Sacrifices for the emperor have been legal for sixty years, since Pompey.'

'According to the law of the Kittim, not the law of God.'

'But Sophia, you know how this will look to the Romans. They'll say the conquered are giving laws to the conquerors.'

'Sure, it is essentially a cancellation of tribute to Rome. It is time for it,' said Yitzhak.

I added, 'Haven't we seen the signs that our liberation is coming?'

She remained fearful, 'How can you say that? Florus is gone, but another will come. They will crush us in their fury.'

Rioting continued in the streets between the people and the pilgrims who supported the Zealots in the lower priesthood and the principal men who supported the Herodians. They occupied the Upper City with the Roman cohort to back them, pushing leading Pharisees before the Bronze Gate to plead for peace.

On hearing the news, King Agrippa rushed to Jerusalem from Alexandria, after meeting with the tribune from Gallus in Javneh, where he received a delegation from the principal men wanting peace.

Bringing the envoy with him to Jerusalem, the king called a meeting in the gymnasium to plead for peace. If he wanted to address zealous Jews, he had chosen the wrong venue. The stricter Ossaeans would never set foot in one of those abominations; but Yitzhak was there.

The king pleaded with the crowd that Florus was to blame, not Rome. 'We must pay the tribute to Caesar, or the Romans will make an example of us to other nations and seek reprisals on Jewish colonies in other cities. Why don't we behave ourselves like the other colonies? Rome is so powerful,' he argued.

Princess Berenice, still under vows, watched from the roof

of the Hasmonean Palace.

'Only in Palestine are we so troublesome they deploy soldiers on the streets. And we are the only client nation not required to send our men into the legions. We should appreciate the special treatment we've received. The dream of Jewish freedom was dead long ago,' the king said; 'we must embrace the modern world of Empire and commerce. 200,000 people in the great cities of the Empire would die were it not for the emperor's stipend of grain. Today, the princes of Parthia send their sons as hostage. Even the noble Athenians are content to be slaves of Caesar.'

Then Agrippa argued that Florus should be obeyed until a replacement arrives. That was when the crowd began hurling stones.

'The king was so poorly received,' Yitzhak said, 'he had to flee the stadium!' The Roman cohorts were defeated, the king stoned by the crowds.

The roads safe once again, I returned home to the Yachad; but I was changed.

# Chapter 16
## Accused

As it is forbidden to accept gifts from foreigners, I gave Athanasios' script to Sofer Shaphan for the Yachad archives, by way of Abba Nehuniyyah. He reportedly said, 'The writings of Greeks, it's only the sound of words.'

Ima Sherah teased me for 'mixing medicine with pleasure'. She said to her husband, 'It's no foul air she's contracted in the city, but a sweet one.'

I assured her than my conduct had been maidenly. But no one was of a mind to scold me after the news I brought. Jerusalem the Holy was, for the first time since the Maqabim, in the hands of the Jews.

Daily we longed for more news from the Holy City, and we were not disappointed. It seemed every other night there were guests at supper.

The Pharisees, in hysterics after the insurgents' brilliant victory against Florus, held a meeting in front of the Bronze Gate to condemn the Zealots. Ananus ben Ananus, the Temple Captain's father, the leader of the Herodian faction who were in the majority, the object of our curse from the terebinth grove, had addressed the crowd.

The Herodians wanted state sacrifice and the imperial cult immediately restored. 'Look at the Temple,' Ananus said, 'It is glittering with gifts from foreigners.' The victory of the Maqabim and the feats of our forefathers was the stuff of storytellers. In the real world, taking on the might of Rome was utter folly.

They despatched delegations: Simon ben Ananus went to Florus; and Sha'ul, Antipas and Costobarus went to Agrippa, as they were of the king's kindred.

We girls heard all the news almost as soon as it happened. If I was in the fields, I heard it immediately upon reentering camp.

'A conspirator was murdered,' Sister Tsuiyah informed me. 'Someone found a letter on him implicating some royals and took them to the Sons of Dorcas. The Galilean general Yochanan of Gush Halav brought a band of Kutim Sicarii up to Jerusalem.'

His father had been a disciple of the Baptist.

'They've executed three men from the king's family– Antipas the Temple Treasurer, and Levias and Sophas, sons of Raguel,' she reported. 'They were sentenced by the Zealots, but the Sicarii beat them to it, snuck into prison and cut their throats.'

'How did they do it? A gatekeeper or guard is more likely to keep the locks tight for Ananus than to turn the keys for a Kut (Samaritan).'

'They had the letter as proof. They claim these men had secret communication with the Romans.' The letter could have been just what the anti-royalists were waiting for to make their move.

'The Kutim?' I wondered. Were we now seeing the uniting of the sects of the Ebionim? I hoped that the Kutim would consider the enemy of their enemy to be their friend.

'Is this a sign of forces of the Ebionim at work? Are the Kutim looking to the Kingdom?' I said.

'It may not be the same kingdom,' said Sister Tsuiyah. 'The letter will be the official reason. But I think it's old wounds, Sister Sophia. Now they have evened the score for the years of strife.'

After these executions, the Zealots deposed the High Priest Mattathias and restored the seat of Aharon, drawing by lots, as was the ritual in the days of the twelve generations. They appointed Pinchas ben Shmuel, a stonemason. During the investiture the priests from the six families wailed, 'he is not even the son of a high priest.' But Pinchas was more lawful and purer, eighty-third since Aharon in the line of Eniachim.

The stonecutter was completely unknown to the works of the priesthood and could barely read, but the Zealots emboldened him. 'Your righteous ancestor Pinchas in his zeal for God averted pollution from the camp of the Israelites. So was the everlasting priesthood conveyed upon his seed.'

'We have won our victory,' they said. Pinchas had but to follow instructions. 'The words for the rituals you may find in books. If you have the heart, God will send you the spirit.'

The democratic appointment of Pinchas the Just represented the fall of the high priestly families, their corrupt rite and their unjust rule. Anything tainted with the stain of Herod or Rome was now profane.

As the Zealot priests celebrated Shabbat at the Temple, the remaining Roman soldiers surrendered to Eleazar ben Simon and were put to death. Jerusalem, under revolutionary government, awaited the vengeance of Rome.

Even out in the wilderness, there was much excitement. All the old questions now seemed to have new answers.

What is the New Jerusalem to be? What shall we do with our treasure? Who will be king?

And there was fear, too. In the spring a larger force was sure to come. How would we fill our bellies and safeguard our fields and homes while our men are off fighting?

In this heightened period, when everything was happening, and the whole world was opening up before us, I was about to enter confinement before taking the vows of Sekhem. I prepared for my retreat. I would join the camp at Mar Saba, the camp of the celibate and pregnant Sisters of Zadok, in preparation for the ceremony. We women went there for five days every month at the time of our impurity. I would fast for thirty days and shave my hair as a symbol of my celibate vow.

The hair is a symbol of maidenhood; in ancient days brides would tie their hair with oak leaves upon marriage. After Sekhem, I would observe the same laws of purity as the priests and Levites, for I would be eating the holy meal at the community table.

It would be only for one moon, but I would grieve for separation from Abba Ahissa's family and Ima Miryam. I would miss star-gazing and the studies with Guryon. I would grieve even more to be removed from the revolutionary excitement. In the celibate camp we would be cut off from the world and would not receive news from Jerusalem.

Were it not for the strength with which my Feeling Self held these selfish and rebellious thoughts, I would have relished the cloistered life of a celibate. I had once discussed with Ima Sherah the possibility of a permanent transfer to Mar Saba after my seventh-year initiation, though I cried when I suggested it.

Ima Devorah, a married woman and so a suitable escort, attended me as I paid a visit to the household of Guryon to pay my respects before entering confinement. She waited at the door, conversing with his mother and sisters, while I called for him in the forecourt. I intended to make a gift to him of my parchment copy of the Chaldean spell, as I would be occupied with women's rites. I knew the strange letters by heart, anyway, even though its meaning was far from read.

I knew from Abba Ahissa that he had asked for my hand in marriage, but my answer had always been the same. Still, I could see that he was in some distress upon our meeting, as was I, I must admit. As I recounted to him how much I had appreciated our studies and my feelings about entering confinement, a tear came to his eye and I was moved.

'Sister Sophia, you know that I have asked for you. Will you not reconsider your decision?'

'I'm sorry, Brother Guryon. I have taken a vow. My life and maidenhood are dedicated to the Lord.'

We progressed into exactly the same argument about virginity and marriage that I used to have with my uncle, only Guryon was gentle and loving, not attacking. Every argument—'the Lord wants Israel's seed to grow strong, our mothers and sisters knew their duty'—this time though, was accompanied by protestations of love. His eyes, full of love and desire, were beautiful in their ferocity.

Marriage would not make me to renounce my vow to God; his sisters would help me with the women's work I so despised; I could continue with forever with my studies and 'instruct our children in my piety'. This picture of myself—Guryon's little possession and under his word, surrounded by his sisters in a world of female industriousness—appalled me, yet he blindly continued offering it to me as a betrothal gift of great treasure.

Guryon's expression of feeling threw me into confusion, as truly, I did find him pleasing. I was stirred, and cannot deny that I admired his manliness. But I was at once ashamed of the feeling.

I would admit to you, Sisters, that my daily intimate contact with the slave and my cousin Yitzhak had been an experience to which I was not accustomed. I had been for almost a moon in the heart of wickedness, in the city with all its foreigners and its men. I had daily touched the bodies of wounded Zealots.

I felt suddenly afraid, and my conversation became less and less sensible. I was terrified of the feelings he was expressing and of the feelings springing up in my own breast. I extended the parchment towards him, a gesture of finality, holding it with both my hands, a signal that upon the bestowing of my parting gift our meeting would be finished, and also a physical protection for myself against terrifying sentiments.

With his right hand, he grasped the parchment firmly and spoke with authority.

'Sophia, I want you to be my wife. My love is so strong that it must be the will of God.' As he said the last three words 'will of God' he put his left hand on my shoulder and caressed me earnestly. On my shoulder, right there, on the same place...

'Who are you to say what is or isn't God's will?' I heard myself shout.

The face of my uncle appeared before my eyes, with that look of anger and hatred, and the words I had remembered, 'teach you to be a proper maiden', echoed in my ears. My shoulder burned like fire, and I started screaming, but my ears could not hear it. The entire household ran into the forecourt, but I was running out, the physic behind me trying to keep up, running back to camp.

I was in a state of madness, and the women could get little sense from me. I ate nothing, and my Feeling Self in its crazed state buzzed inside my head all night long. I called for 'my father, the only man God has allowed for me', but when Abba Ahissa was summoned, I did not want him.

I cried about 'my shoulder, the burning, the blood'. I kept repeating, 'blood, blood', though they assured me I was not bleeding. 'I'll show you the blood,' I screamed, 'it is drowned by my tears.' And I scratched my face with a fingernail. So did the prophets of Ba'al cut each other with knives to bring the rain. It was straight from the scroll I had been reading before that night.

I recited the Nazirite vow over and over—'I shall drink no vinegar of wine, nor liquor of grapes, no razor shall come upon my head'—and when unrestrained spun round and round tearing at my skirt. So many times they asked me, 'What happened, child?' I replied in bits and pieces from the back of my mind, including even phrases in Chaldee and quotations from the Tanakh in Hebrew.

I said things that seemed to make more sense to them: 'God has told me what it is to be a woman', 'never can I return home where I'm not loved'. I also said things like 'he touched me where it is not allowed' and 'he cannot force me to marry' and 'Ashmedai (Asmodeus, the demon of lust) took his hand'.

I heard the physic say, 'she was alone with him for but a few moments.'

Naturally, the women thought what had occurred was that Guryon had touched me. But was the touch 'endearing or innocent'? I heard them debate. Though I screamed like a witch, the midwives examined me and announced, 'she is undefiled'. Nevertheless, reports of my ravings led the men to accuse Guryon of impropriety. The group which had been bound for Mar Saba on the morrow was delayed for my sake.

A priest skilled in exorcism was called from Mird, summoned by Abba Ahissa.

He burned the heart and liver of a Letos fish in sulfur brimstone, and seven times washed my mouth and head with the most sacred of the waters, but he was unable to name my demon. He held his hand over my head and recited from a large scroll, 'I sound the majesty of His beauty to confound and terrify the spirits of destroying angels, demons and the Lilitu', and I rocked back and forth to the rhythm of the words. I would let no man touch me, so he was attended by a woman, another Sherah, who knew much about affairs between men and women.

The exorcism calmed me, and I did feel some of the vapours leaving, but it was Sister Sherah who began to make sense from me. Instead of asking me big questions like 'what happened?', she asked me only small questions: 'where were you standing?', 'what was written on the parchment?', 'at what hour did you arrive?'

As I began to become more sensible, the Sister helped me to figure out what happened and why I was so crazed by it.

'It is grievous that men are weak,' she consoled me, 'or perhaps, they are not sensitive enough to our weakness. Now, it is time for you to forgive.' I heard her say to the exorcist, 'It was an earthly demon that caused this madness, and not Ahmedai.'

By the time I could speak sensibly, I realised the trouble I had caused. The initiates had departed without me for Mar Saba, the story of my behaviour had spread throughout all three of the main Ossaean camps, and the men had isolated Guryon on the charge of violating a sister.

Of course, he denied it, and throughout my three days of madness had demanded to be allowed to see me and beg my forgiveness for his forwardness. But the men, thinking some abuse had transpired, would not allow it. They had gone as far as to call for a trial on the morrow, 'now that I was well enough to testify'.

I hate to think upon how he, in his innocence, not to mention in his affection for me, must have felt to be unjustly accused. Acknowledging my own feelings of affection for him, I felt ever more guilty to have placed him under suspicion.

By that time, it was I who was begging to see Guryon to beg his forgiveness, and I who was isolated and not allowed to do so. I cried and cried and begged everyone to forget the whole thing.

Sherah, the exorcist's assistant, said to them, 'She remembers an abuse from the past. The Brother is guilty only of professing love.' The exorcist told the Council, 'It is a demon of this earth who torments her, not one from Gehenna.'

But the Court of Inquiry had already been summoned, four priests and six Levites.

I had to remain in an antechamber while they sat in the Assembly Hall hearing the accusations. Presumably, I couldn't hear their words, but as usual, the demon spake them in my ears with exaggerated horror. Surely, they were discussing my every sin, condemning me.

As the wronged party, Guryon was supposed to make the accusation against me, but this he refused to do. Though the judges may have in their hearts admired him for this, they nevertheless had to punish him for disobedience. As well as hurting him so unjustly, I caused him to incur this punishment.

By the time I walked into the hall, I could barely see. They questioned me fully, and I answered truthful and trembling with shame about all the matters that previously I had only spoken of to Shulamith.

I told everyone about the upsetting night I left Babylon, and there in the Assembly Hall before all those men, I even told about my uncle. It was the most painful thing I ever experienced in my life, Sisters, more painful than that traumatic family meal, more than seeing men die in the war, almost more even than seeing Jerusalem burn.

I cried and cried, 'I never meant to accuse Brother Guryon of anything. I'm sorry. I'm so sorry.'

But the Overseer ruled, 'Your intentions are for the Lord to judge, Sister. We sit to rule upon your deeds.'

The judges ruled a *gezerah* (prohibition): 'The judges accept your testimony, and perceive that the true guilty party in this matter was your uncle. Yet it is not those events that happened in Babylon upon which we sit. We are called to adjudge your accusation, and we have found you to be false to our code.'

I never accused him, I thought. But I was not allowed to appeal.

The Levite who brought me the news tried to console me. 'This means that although they feel obliged to punish you, just to uphold the rules, they won't do it in earnest. The maximum banishment period is only six months, anyway, and they never uphold that unless the accusation was malicious in intent. No one believes you guilty of that, Daughter.'

Nevertheless, the earth disappeared beneath my feet. It was bad enough that I had so falsely treated Guryon and that all the camps now knew of the evil spirit that bewitches me, a secret known only by God, my adopted parents and Ima Miryam. I had never even told my father. It was bad enough that the court of inquiry had to hear my entire shameful story.

I well knew what the punishment was. Had I not spent many months in Sofer Shaphan's archives learning the rules of the order?

Had Guryon truly violated me, his punishment would have been to be hung on a tree. But I had accused him falsely, though not intending to. For this, the punishment was banishment from holy meals. The vote had fallen—all white stones for yes, I had accused him falsely, no black. They had to vote so; I was indeed guilty of the crime.

Guryon had not harmed me, he had only awakened the memory of an earlier experience my Feeling Self could not forget. My uncle had not harmed me either, though he had intended it. My betrothed would have found me undefiled.

In my heightened state from intense studying and terror of his words and actions, all the images and memories associated with that night formed a jumble in my head. The blood on my leg was not because my uncle had harmed me; it was merely a cruel and confusing coincidence that the moon called me to womanhood on that same night. My Feeling Self had seized upon that imagery to express my injury.

I was crying as if my heart was made of tears, and the women were not allowed to give me comfort. When she got a chance, one of the Sisters whispered, 'They almost always relent after a while. In your case, it will be fine. Go to the women's camp and take a vow. Come back after a few weeks, and they'll welcome you back.' She kindly added, 'It's not your fault. You had an evil spirit.'

No, I thought, this evil spirit must be cast to the wilderness, banished. I could never show my face here again.

Finally, Ima Miryam was allowed to see me. Yet she came to scold, not to console.

'Chava Sophia, do not amplify this; you know you are wont. You begged forgiveness of Guryon, and he gave it even before it was asked. The Council ruled as our precepts ordain, so you must abide by the prohibition, but it is only for six months. You will have to put on a grey headband and eat with the Novices for a while, nothing more.'

But it was already too late; the smoke was filling my body, and I could hardly hear her words.

Sister Tsuiyah, as my senior, was allowed to see me, as she was in camp. I was not happy to see her, but to my surprise, she seemed genuinely distraught at what was happening to me.

'Sister Sophia, Brother Guryon is fine. Don't make too much of this,' she comforted me.

It was Sister Tsuiyah who brought me my 'talisman' the Chaldee tablet. When she could see I was determined to banish myself, she actually shed a tear, and said, 'HaShem shine His light upon you then, Sister,' and embraced me with a warmth I had never before felt from her.

At this last moment, my prayers of all those months, my supplication at the terebinth grove, was answered. My moment of adversity had broken the wall between us of coldness and competition. It was the one thought that lifted my heart as I set off from the Yachad in disgrace.

Imme was not allowed to see me, and so concerned was I with myself, the thought of the girl had not entered my thoughts. This must have been distressing to the sweet thing, though she may have understood more about the situation than I thought.

When I went to pick up my bedroll, there was a hawthorn twig, broken not cut, resting where my head would have been. The Sisters would have thought nothing but that it must have blown in with the wind. But remembering our lesson in the terebinth grove, I knew it was a message from Imme. Hawthorn, it cleanses the Feeling Self of negativity and stimulates forgiveness. But who was forgiving me now? Even Ima Miryam to whom I turn for spiritual strength was one of my accusers.

Later, I understood better Imme's message. Again, I was bowing to the fear of my own shadow, some danger that existed only in the spirit world, not one that could harm me during the day. I kept the twig and rolled it up in the bedroll as I gathered my effects.

Years later, I sent to Ima Miryam, begging her to let Imme know—it did protect me. I carved it into a wand small enough to keep in the bottom of my sleeve, and I used it in my readings to charm supplicants' dreams. Many of them believe that the hawthorn wand has power and they would gasp at the object as I flourished it. I smiled to think of Ima Miryam tap tapping her almondwood staff and Imme innocently offering me use of the magical object, and my response that one day I would have a talisman of my own.

'Does the wand really hold these powers?' they would ask, and I would respond, 'The Dreaming Self faces dangers the Acting Self never sees. If the one can stand firm against hostile spirits, the other will be invincible.'

It wasn't really true. The war showed me how easily the

271

life of a man can be extinguished, however firm his spirit. Nevertheless, it was good for supplicants to hear it.

By that time, I was walking away. I had on my traveling clothes and took with me only my bedroll, my white Mem stone, my Chaldee tablet, a parcel of barleybread wrapped in some of my writings, and a jar of water.

As I left the camp, I could barely see the road, I was crying so desolately. Guryon watched me leave, nothing in his eyes but sadness. Could he see in my eyes my regret? I don't know. Could he see—I have wronged you. I am sorry? I don't know what he did see, but his eyes conveyed no hate nor even anger, only confusion and hurt. It pained me further to see him so meek.

I walked away, for the second time a refugee, this time not up into the wooded hills above the Euphrates, but into the heat of the Judaean wilderness. Again, in a crazed state I was leaving my home.

I had learned wonders with the Brethren. The holy life of the Way was where my heart belonged, but my heart had betrayed me. How utterly wretched I was to have disobeyed their righteous teachings, and my sin against Guryon was great. I would purge my spirit by dedicating my life to war.

Though I had no prophecy, dream nor divine guidance, again also, I knew where I was bound. I headed northward, down from the high cliffs of the Yachad camp, down to Secacah, the fortress of the Kanaim, my ears popping as I pondered my destiny. A woman cannot be a warrior, but I can cook with the meager goodness God provides for desert dwellers, and soldiers are always in need of a healer.

# Chapter 17
## Secacah

Secacah was just west of the border to Peraea, within the lands of King Agrippa, and the king's troops would soon be on the march. It was some 200 stadia, possibly a day's march north from Ein Gedi, but I stopped the night near Tekoa within sight of Herod's fortress (Herodion) to rest my feet. As a girl travelling alone, I tried to stick to the wadis, but when I had to use the road, it was empty. By that time, anyway, I was skilled enough at shapeshifting to risk any road without attracting attention.

Strangely, there is no need to cover one's face or arms when travelling along the Sea of Sodom. Though the sun is hot, the air is thick and protects the skin. There is much need, however, to protect the nose. The stinking yellow residues of Gomorrah bubble up through the mud. My fox is the red one of the desert, though, and her nose is less keen.

As I became the Fox, I crafted my designs. As I became the Desert Viper, I aimed my poison at the Sons of Darkness. As I became the Yellow Scorpion, I sharpened my sting.

By the time I arrived at the gate, my tears were dry, and I was ready for battle.

When I identified myself at the gate, I found that my reputation was known before me. It was not my behavior toward Guryon that had preceded me, however, it was my knack with magic. Zealots welcomed all who bore a hatred for Rome and for the Herodians. I told them I had come to fulfill a holy call to battle. They had the same Calling, and so understood it.

They called me Sophia Maga, and when we received news from Jerusalem, the militiamen would ask me for readings. The news was exciting, and my prophecies were mostly of hope, of victory.

On admittance to the fortress, the priests and generals in command there seemed more concerned with my state of purity that with my reasons for leaving the Brethren. The warriors of the Kanaim remained in a continual state of Nazirite purity, ready at any moment for the Day of Vengeance. On that day would the King Messiah call the garrisons of the righteous—the Sons of Light—to battle, joining with the Ebionim to rise against the Kittim, whom they called the Sons of Darkness.

The Kanaim were a military sect, most of Ossaean training and not far from the Brethren in their pious zeal—Zealots who strictly observed the cycle of rituals, a lifestyle not popular with everyone. These soldiers, however, spent their afternoons in military training rather than prayer.

Like the Yachad, these holy Zealots had nothing to do with the Herodian priests in Jerusalem and paid taxes neither to Herod nor Caesar.

The same debates took place at Secacah over the import of the days and the stars. We still timed our prayers and I timed my conjurings by the Jubilee calendar, but among the company were represented many factions—Pharisees, Tzaddikim, even some Kutim. There were even foreigners who joined our camp. All four calendars were consulted.

I met again Anna and Uzziel, who had previously defected here after That Assembly, but I lived with the unmarried girls, and there were few of us. Some of the militiamen had wives and families, but there were hundreds of men to feed. With so few women's hands, our communal meal was a bigger task than at the Yachad. But the scarcity of female company led me to treasure it more. At Secacah, I actually came to love women's work.

Orders were to remain and defend the fortress, but many men, whenever fighting broke out, left the fields to join the battle, and we had to make up their work. Furthermore, at every rumour of a new messiah, a sign in the heavens or confirmation of a prophecy, we would lay down shovels and hoes and swarm to the hills to listen to the preaching.

Apsalom, the general in command, told us, 'Feed our militias now, and cease your waiting for the Day. If it tarries, wait for it, for it will surely come.'

The commanders were afraid the Messiah would come just at the moment when all the fighters had run off following the latest rumour. Commander Apsalom said, 'Though you should hear the Messiah is just around the corner, do not desert your posts.'

The militiamen did not starve. Not only did we have our own fields and olive grove, from time to time would come delegations from other parts of the land bringing us alms. Peasants whose families would starve if they left their lands were throwing every coin they could into the collection boxes of the Ebionim.

The compound of Secacah contained also a metalworks and pottery. In more peaceful times, these had contributed to the commerce of the region. Now they were used to supply the works of the garrisons.

Though both Ossaeans and Kanaim strove for the removal of Roman rule and their puppets, Secacah expected one messiah, of the lines of Aharon and Israel combined, a priest-king whose title was Melchizedek, the Prince of Righteousness. He would lead the heavenly hosts in a cosmic battle against the forces of darkness, when heaven and earth unite in the Kingdom to yield the judge.

I was glad to become reacquainted with Anna and Uzziel, who, happily, did not ask me any questions. They assumed it was haste for the Kingdom that spurred my feet northward.

Uzziel was friendly with Mattai, who with his wife Justa and his three children were in camp, and I was glad to make another friend.

Justa was a Kut, and theirs was not a matching that enjoyed much peace in our land. Mattai and Justa were from Ginea in Samaria, and had long defended their love from the prejudices of tribal hatred, but with three children now, the struggle had tired in them. The children were no longer safe in Samaria due to violence between their peoples, which, along with Zealot desires for the Day, brought them to Secacah.

I requested to be on the same rota as Anna and Justa for kitchen duty, and we enjoyed many discussions while cleaning up the pots and dishes.

Secacah was, if anything, stricter on food laws than the Yachad, as we were to be ready at any moment to receive the King. My white stone entitled me to the holy food and drink of the camp, but even I was scolded from time to time by Lysia, the woman in charge of the cooking rota. She scolded Justa more harshly, and Anna and I tried to instruct her before Lysia's eyes could catch her in an infringement.

'Not that cloth, Justa,' we would point out. 'Those are dishes for the top table and Commander Apsalom.'

'What?'

'You just used that cloth to dry the plates of the Tens and the Fifties.'

'What's wrong with that? They are equally wet.'

'They may be equally wet, dear,' we would school her, 'but they're not equally pure.'

'Why not?'

'Uncleanliness travels upward as well as downward, remember?'

'That's crazy,' she would complain. 'It's still just water. Water washes away any uncleanness, surely?'

Her mind differed from ours also on the subject of our victory. She believed that the Restoration would take place on Mount Gerizim.

'That was the location of the Temple of Solomon,' she maintained.

Though many disputed this, I did not. By this time, I realised that it was not the past that mattered but the future.

She pictured the Day of the Lord as a final apocalypse. 'We will all die together, and thus be reborn together.' She quoted the prophet Ezekiel: 'On that day he will open our graves and bring us up from them, bring us back to the land of Israel.'

'Of course, the resurrection of the righteous,' I argued. 'Yet we are only judged righteous by our works. Our dry bones will not speak for us.'

There were some in camp who went further than this, wanting war but not wanting victory, expecting suffering and defeat to bring about a magical outcome. It was a belief beloved by the early magi, but the idea did not please me. It was almost the reverse of the Brethren's dream of miraculous ascension.

Anna teased, 'Our Sophia Maga is not a magical hastener, you see.'

I protested, 'I do pray that we can move His hand. I just think we have to act for ourselves.'

Nevertheless, Justa thought that the Kutim's and the Jews' Day of Glory were the same and that the two peoples needed to unite. This was the policy of Simon Magus, and this I agreed with.

'Judah's stick of wood and Ephraim's stick of wood must come together in our hand,' she said.

I said, 'But why only our two nations? Isn't it prophesied that all the nations will come together? That's how Rome became strong; so, must we to fight against Rome.'

I had been at Secacah for something over a moon when one of the Ossaean brothers in camp spoke to me in the fields. He was preparing to travel to the Yachad at Ein Gedi on route to a Nazirite confinement, and asked if I wanted to travel with his company.

'We need you here, but I believe you really desire to return. It's been forty days, they'll take you back now,' he said. I cringed to learn that he knew my sin. 'The statute calls for six months at the strictest, but really, Sister Sophia, in practice it's hardly ever more than a few weeks. What happens is, you come back, and everyone is so happy to see you they forget why you left in the first place.'

'Furthermore, they know that you are not guilty,' he added. The Elders in Damascus, a higher authority, had rebuked the Yachad for a miscarriage of justice in my case, he told me, citing a statute book with an amendment to the Levitical admonition against approaching one's mother's sister. They included the phrase 'or your niece'. 'If the same thing happened again,' he said, 'you would not even have been punished.'

I blushed to think of the Saints in Damascus discussing my shame. I told him, 'Thank you, Brother, but though they may forget, I may not.' However, I did think of Abba Ahissa and his wife, and I sent with him a letter beseeching unity of heart, though our lives be thus separated. And a letter to Ima Miryam begging her not to separate me from her wisdom.

When I received a reply, it was from my adopted mother. It seemed that war fever was upon the Yachad as well.

'The pious ones say we are come to the End of Times, which only the righteous shall survive, as we are the Heirs of the New Covenant of Chesed,' she wrote. 'They say God's victory will be in heaven. Some Brethren are lost in prayer, for which soldiers in the vicinity torture and humiliate them. But some have turned to the earthly battle. The prophet wrote of this time as two times and a half.'

Daniel had thus prophesied of the time before the commencement of the End of Days. The period of time was just right since the death of the Just One. The final battle was about to begin.

With their young men drifting from the fields to stronghold upon stronghold, the countryside was starving. The Mothers and those Brethren who hadn't joined militias were organising food for the fighting men. The Ebionim charity boxes were open to any Jew with a sword or a stave in his hand, and with letters of introduction from the Zealots, militiamen took away with them a few days' supplies.

Ima Sherah pledged me their love, echoing the Yachad's assurance that all was forgiven. 'Guryon offers his complete understanding and absolution,' she wrote. 'He is courting a young Novice. He bears you no ill.'

I was happy to hear that, but I would not go back. The days of holiness and study were passed; now I thought only of war. I was a Zealot now.

My conscience was sufficiently eased by these events that I decided finally to bear my soul to my family in Seleucia. If the End of Days was upon us, absolution was imperative. I could not see in the New Kingdom with the guilty story on my conscience. I wrote a letter to Babylon, which I addressed to my father, telling them what had happened that night with my uncle. It was a very long one.

Months later, a delegation coming up for Sukkot brought a reply, which my Jerusalem cousins sent on to me. It was in my father's hand; the women of the household of course could not write, but in it I could hear not a single personal word. Every line seemed to have been dictated by Mother, Aunt or Grandmother. And instead of being angry at my uncle, they were angry at me.

After many assurances about how much they apparently missed me and how much they wanted me to come home, I heard Mother's voice. 'The scene you described, Daughter, must surely have been from your imagination. It cannot have been as you said. You know you clouded your head so constantly with religious silliness, Sophia, and you were ever a naughty girl, always reading and studying instead of helping with the chores.'

You knew it was not as I said, Mother? Were the birds in the bushes your witness? Which was it, Mother? Nothing happened, and I imagined it? Or something happened that I well deserved for being so naughty?

'Aunt says,' he wrote, 'that as you grew older and ceased to be your father's baby girl, perhaps you came to harbour unnatural feelings. In any case, Uncle denies it, and as she told your mother, 'Wives believe their husbands'.'

Can you believe that? My uncle, the bane of my childhood, who tore me at the age of fourteen from my family? With his fat belly and his evil hands? The very idea that my eye could look upon him with unnatural feelings! So, wives believe husbands, and sisters believe brothers. But nobody believes daughters? Which was it, Aunt? Nothing happened? Or something happened that was all my doing, wicked Jezebel that I am?

'And Grandmother says,' he wrote, 'that the betrothal had not yet been official, so the contract with Huna's father would still have stood.'

Grandmother's position, I gathered, was that either way, as I was still *intacta*, it would not have meant cancellation of the contract with Huna's father. Which was it, Grandmother? Nothing happened? Or something happened that fell short enough from violation of my virginity that my in-laws could not legally reject me?

Perhaps they were trying so desperately to find their own truth to the story, any perjury was granted. And why only one, when three different lies would do? Even now, even for me, even when confronted with just how grave had been Uncle's interference, my father could not find his own voice to speak up for me.

Further, my mother and grandmother seemed more concerned about my zealotry than my honour, taking my hatred of Roman rule as a personal affront to the family. A torrent of condemnation flowed from the little I had written of the revolutionary mood in Palestine. Imagine what they would have written if I had told them about Florus, the Kanaim and everything.

'You are so young, you'll get yourself into trouble mixing with dangerous people,' he wrote my mother's words. Having been so ill as a young wife, she was terrified of anyone taking risk.

'We have always obeyed the Law,' I read Grandmother's voice, 'our family has been Persian since Nebuchadnezzar. We hold lands and respected positions in Mesopotamia. Your father is an official in the government, Sophia. Will you join hands with those who take arms against such a government? What concern is it of yours if Judaea rises in revolt? A Jewish kingdom will never happen, Sophia. Remember what happened to Anilai and Asinai.'

She referred to a tale she told me of when she was a young bride. Two brothers of the Babylonian exilarch had raised troops and defeated the Parthians. The independent Jewish kingdom of Nehardea lasted but seven years before a counter-coup brought the old guard back to power. People always remember the defeats, never the victories.

So much was happening by then, I didn't have the time nor the desire to reply to the letter, and as far as I was concerned, any group of Jews travelling east, carrying letters or no, was going in the wrong direction. We needed every hand aimed westward toward Jerusalem for the battle to come. I let the matter lie, shoved the entire story of my childhood back under the mat, which is just where they wanted it.

I never spoke to my parents again, and I know not even if they still lived after the war.

I did remember Grandmother's lesson of Anilai and Asinai,

though. I remembered: expect the counter-coup. As Abda used to say, 'When the camel's nose has entered your tent, the foot is already on the way.'

Herod Agrippa, King of the Jews, on reception of the delegation from Ananus, did not go straight to Rome to insist on Florus' immediate removal and a reprieve of the seventeen talents. He did not take up the sword to liberate us from our foe or to avenge us of these injustices. He did not do any of the things we would have hoped for from our king. He sent an army against the people.

It was the season of the olive harvest, and everyone was in the grove, smaller women and children up in the trees picking and the men and older women below gathering the fruit into baskets.

We could see someone arrive at the southern end of the grove, not from Jerusalem in the west.

We rather suspected something momentous, as that morning the Teacher of Righteousness had arrived at the fortress from Mount Carmel. Shortly after that, the younger of the Kanaim left in a big hurry bearing arms, and the Teacher of Righteousness remained in consultation with Commander Apsalom. All day long we'd been waiting for news, saying 'what's happening?' 'has the war started?' 'has Florus come back?'

My friend Anna was with me in the tree. I said to her, 'A messenger, certainly. But he's not come from the lion's den (Jerusalem).'

'Looks like he's come from the south,' she said, 'from Ein Gedi or Masada.'

'Who would send a messenger from Masada? The fortress

of the red man of Edom (Herod)?'

Men were gathering around the man, and women and children were climbing down from the trees in excitement.

They started singing, but we couldn't hear it yet. The first tree picked it up, then the next, and by the time the singing reached our tree, the entire grove was in song. '*melekh hamoshiach, melekh hamoshiach…*' (King Messiah)

Anna and I had reached the ground, and we embraced each other, saying in one voice '*hamelekh!*' (the king). We joined the song as everyone in the grove crowded around the messenger.

His news trickled back to us at the back of the crowd. 'The Sicarii have taken Masada, killing the Roman garrison.' 'He's seized the king's armoury.' 'The king has arrived.' 'Menachem, son of the Galilean, prince of Judah.' 'The Day of the Lord is upon us.'

Despite everything we had been told, there was little work done the rest of that day. The men brought out wine, and we all drank three cups. The king and his Sicarii were marching northward. In a few hours they'd be here at our fortress. Everyone who did not have a specific job to do sat at the gates waiting and singing.

Menachem was grandson of Judas the Galilean and royal prince of the line of Pelatiah. He led the Sicarii Sons of the Galilean faction. He was backed by the Ossaean leadership in Damascus, and the Doctors of Law saw him in all the prophecies.

The Sicarii armed the Edomite peasants with the king's own weapons, and they joined Menachem's growing army, heading in force back north along the Wilderness Road toward Secacah. They were so numerous we had to set up a separate camp to accommodate them.

Menachem was dressed in kerm-scarlet robes, a golden band encircling his brow. Above his head flew embroidered banners, some emblazoned with the lion of Judah, some with the harp of David. The People of the Land strew beneath his feet palm fronds, poppy petals and lavender. We Kanaim greeted him rapturously, with trumpets, flutes and cymbals and banners according to our rule. We played the eight-stringed harp, crying, 'oyoyoyoyoy' and sang, 'Who is like you, among the mighty…'

Our king had come.

Menachem the Comforter, the Star, whom we later called The Suffering Servant, Menachem the Messiah—and he was to dine in table fellowship here, with the Kanaim—the upper orders, of course, no one below the rank of Father or General would attend. But the lowliest of Zealots like me still absorbed all the excitement of the preparations, and we were all there at the gates to cheer his arrival. I saw him, with my own eyes. Moshiach.

The previous evening, his generals had sat in table fellowship with the Saints at the Yachad.

The story of the banquet proceedings filtered down quite accurately to the girls, as we all understood the importance of the event. The priests on the periphery and the women in the kitchen told the young men in the outer court what they saw, and they reported it around camp almost word for word.

The prince entered at the head of the congregation, dressed all in black, as the Ossaean priests in white assembled before him, and then followed the captains of the thousands, sitting each according to their rank.

The Teacher of Righteousness himself served the prince the

first fruits of bread and new wine, as he ranked higher even than Moshiach. He blessed first the bread and then the wine, and then the Prince extended his hand to the bread. The Teacher of Righteousness then anointed his brow and feet with olive oil flavoured with myrrh, cinnamon, kaneh bosum (cannabis) and cassia.

It was the ceremony of kingship.

The king had been anointed and shared table fellowship with the prophet. Priests of the Ebionim had purified the Temple. The Day of the Lord was upon us; and it was not a day too soon. The Romans were coming.

On the Feast of the Woodcarrying, the day for firewood to be brought in, Agrippa invaded Jerusalem.

Zealots occupied the Temple, the cohort of Florus' Kittim had been barricaded at Herod's Palace at the Jaffa Gate for a month. Eleazar ben Ananus, Temple Captain, forbade the back-stabbing royalists from coming up with their wood offerings. There was a huge influx of pilgrims up for Tu b'Av (15th of Av, marking the beginning of the grape harvest), among them Zealots and Sicarii, strengthening the anti-royalists' hand.

Eleazar ben Simon bravely led the Zealots against the Agrippa's forces.

The king had not come via the Jericho road, so we needed not to maintain full defense of the fortress. Secacah sent the city all the garrisons of the Kanaim under Commander Apsalom, and leading the Thousands was Menachem Prince of Judah. Among them was the husband of my new friend, Anna. It was the season of the Burning of the Fields, and we women had to take over the work.

I was starved from my years at the Yachad for company of my

own age, and Anna was only a summer short of my years. We were so amenable one to the other that we did most everything else together as well. Uzziel and Anna were newly wed, and when not militarily engaged, he was with us as often as possible.

Shu'dat and I had been a friendship of differences; Anna and I shared so many things. I could speak to her about much that I had hitherto guarded tightly inside my bosom. A married woman, she was not shy to hear the story of my uncle and of Guryon; I could speak of it, now. I even spoke to her a bit about the demon in the black cloud, something of which I had never spoken to anyone but Abba Ahissa and Ima Miryam, unless you would count exorcists.

Anna and her young husband Uzziel both looked to the Kingdom of God, and I was glad to have company with whom I could share my thoughts about the world. Everything was in a state of flux and confusion, and there were questions, new questions, about everything.

At Secacah, prayer, ritual and Scripture were, if anything, more zealously followed than at the Yachad; but contrary to the contemplative, studious atmosphere of the Ossaean retreat, here was constant talking, arguing, discussing and transmitting of news. As we cut vegetables, we discussed the marital affairs of King Agrippa's kindred. As we burned the old grainstalks, we debated upon the strength and strategy of Eleazar ben Simon. In the evenings we heard lectures on the history of the Roman Empire.

Meanwhile, we were never short of messiahs. The Gerasene Simon bar Giora ravaged the Idumaean countryside, gathering thousands, supported even by some of the prominent men in the cities.

Though the garrisons of the Kanaim spoke excitedly of him, the Saints at the Yachad and in Damascus disputed Simon's qualifications.

'Granted, he's no royal prince,' said Anna.

Uzziel said, 'What do we care for their genealogies and their scholarly interpretations? We've lost patience with the Doctors of Law and their calendars. We're looking for a king who will lead us to victory.'

As Shulamith had said, of what matter is the Son of David now?

Anna added, 'The rumour is also that he's tall, strong and good looking.' We giggled, and Uzziel pulled her sleeve in play jealousy.

Justa reminded us of the other Simon, of Gitta, the Kutim's hope.

'If only the two Simons would join their forces,' I said.

Bar Giora's followers called him king, yet this king saw further than those who had come before. 'The Kingdom of God is not only for Jews,' he said, 'slaves as well must be free.' Slaves were running away from their masters to join him. I found myself wondering what Athanasios would have to say.

The counter-coup came for Jerusalem as it had done for Anilai and Asinai. King Agrippa attacked Jerusalem, his own city, with his troops and 2000 horse, and on his side, hating the Zealots more than they hated Florus, more than they hated the Kittim, were the high priests and nobles, the property owners, the tax collectors, the bailiffs.

Our garrisons joined the defense of Jerusalem, and Uzziel and Mattai were with them. The entire population of the fortress, along with many people from the land around, thronged to the rooves to see them off. So many squeezed on top of the tower that one child fell off and broke his leg.

He was wearing the kerm-scarlet, his progress accompanied by trumpets and singers. Menachem the King, riding off to conquer Jerusalem. Like Simon Maqabi, off to cleanse the Temple, he was on the back of an onager colt—triumphant, humble and riding on an ass.

'The Prince entered the city through the Golden Gate, from the East, shining and glorious like the rising sun. And we marched behind him, the Fifties and the Hundreds,' Uzziel told us on their return.

Menachem's lavishly equipped army and royal robes were impressive, and his reputation was further augmented as 'the companion of the holy ones' on report of his endorsement by the Teacher of Righteousness.

'Rapturous crowds proclaimed him king,' said Uzziel, 'laying palms at his feet, shouting 'Hosanna, Immanuel'.'

Once again, a son of David sat upon the Throne of Solomon.

Uzziel continued the tale, 'The Sicarii raised their curved knives and were followed by the myriad ranks of the Ebionim; they forced their way into the Temple and joined with the Zealot priests. Everyone in the city lauded Menachem as King. We swarmed the Upper City and its rich estates, forcing the royalists out, and burned down the house of Ananus in the Upper Tyropoean Valley, and the palaces of Agrippa and Berenice.'

'Thus, did we have our wood for the offering,' we shouted.

'Our next target was the record office, where we cancelled in the holy fire of revolt all the debtors' letters of credit.'

'If they will not give us our Jubilee,' we shouted, 'we shall take it for ourselves.'

With the triumphal entry of Menachem, everything changed.

Eleazar's lot—they hated the Romans and the Herods, but more than them, they hated the Sicarii. The burning of the record office and cancellation of debts was too much for them. To liberate Herod's debtors was one thing; to liberate their own was another. They needed Menachem to defeat Agrippa, but they didn't want to overturn the rule of property.

Hillel the Nasi wouldn't call him Messiah. What they really wanted was to recreate Hasmonean rule; they reached no higher than to put a different high priestly family in power. The New Jerusalem was more than that.

Eleazar and his men fought for seven days with stones and slings. The Roman guards had all been slain, and the royalists were besieged inside Herod's Palace.

The Cilician Sha'ul acted as go-between, taking messages from the Herodians to the king camped outside the city. Philip ben Jacimus, commander of Agrippa's guard, was one of his disciples.

The Tzaddik chief priests, the Pharisees and the Herodians sent for Gallus. History was repeating. Again, the Jews invited the Romans to invade.

The next day, there was a mass pogrom against Jews in Qesarya—'collective punishment' they called it. In Qesarya, Scythopolis, Ptolomais, first Jews wreaked their vengeance, then Greeks wreaked further vengeance.

On the First of Tishri 3827, according to the Temple calendar, Agrippa sought terms. But he did not realise how great was the people's victory. Our victory would usher in a Year of Jubilees, freedom for slaves and bondsmen, redistribution of land for the Ebionim. We offered no terms. We wanted nothing less than the Kingdom of God on Earth.

For an anointed king to have attacked his own people—this was a breach of everything we value. The shock of it united thousands who had previously not supported the rebellion.

'How different is Herod Agrippa from Judas Maqabi,' said Uzziel, 'who fought bloody battle after bloody battle to win our freedom. How can we bow our heads to this foreigner, who is on his knees before every insignificant general, procurator or tribune the Kittim send up? His grandfather called himself Magnus, he thought himself so glorious, yet even that fornicating Edomite usurper in all his power was a whining sycophant of Rome.'

'After this, Jews will never again bow to a Herod,' I said.

'The garrison of the Kittim, now terrifically outnumbered, retreated to the towers, where we cornered them. We took Antonia Fortress and slew them all, apart from the commander Metililus, who was circumcised by the Sicarii. No longer will foreigners watch with their weapons while we offer sacrifices to God,' said Uzziel.

Agrippa and his troops were driven out of the city.

After Uzziel and the garrisons returned to Secacah, we heard daily from messengers from the city.

The treachery of the royalists had to be rooted out at the base, and Prince Menachem scoured the city. He found that Tzaddik slave, Ananus ben Nedebai, who had once been High Priest, and his brother Hezekiah hiding in an aqueduct and had them beheaded and thrown from the north wall.

The Peace Party seized the Upper City, and the War Party the Lower City and Temple, in a two-week stand-off.

'We still face an enemy within,' Uzziel commented. 'We of the Prince are allied with the Sicarii and Zealots in steadfastness, but we are still opposed by the accommodators under the Sons of Ananus.'

The royalists were soundly defeated, but it was more than that. The Wicked Priest and the Herodians had revealed their true colours for all to see. The Many said, 'The Sanhedrin and the priests are two-faced; they'll betray us to the enemy the first chance they get. They are in control, but they are not friends of the people.'

In speeches, many of which we heard reported word for word, they praised the New Jerusalem and swore allegiance to Jewish freedom. Look inside their sleeves, however, and you'd see the stripes of a royalist. Ever mindful of their property and the crumbs from the table of Empire they enjoyed at the expense of the People of the Land, they wanted nothing more than for Agrippa to return in greater force and rob the Temple again for tribute to Rome.

As a Galilean bandit, Menachem caused their noses to constrict. As King of the Jews, he was a threat to their power. They would rather a pig sat on the Throne of Solomon than Menachem of Judah.

Eleazar ben Ananus tried to turn the Many against him. 'Why should we free ourselves of one king only to bow down to another?' Eleazar said.

We were not yet united in confidence. The victories over Florus and Agrippa were only the beginning, we knew, of more challenging battles to come. Jerusalem was in confusion, and in times like this, people turn to the leaders they have always turned to.

# Chapter 18
## Beth-horon

It was the season of Planting, but there was little industry in the fields.

In Jerusalem the Pharisees were still the dominant force among the moderates, and they met with the high priests to survey their position. Eleazar ben Simon and the Zealots had control of Temple Mount; there was nothing the moderates could do but support the revolt. They kept one hand tied behind their backs, though. Among them was Josef ben Mattathiya, a Pharisee from a Hasmonean priestly family.

Still triumphant, Menachem went up to the Temple in full armour to worship in state with his Sicarii, among them a garrison from Secacah led by commander Apsalom. Uzziel's garrison was not with them–fortunately, as it turned out.

Menachem was still wearing the royal regalia, and Eleazar ben Ananus coveted those robes. On the Temple steps he and the people he had deceived attacked the glorious prince. In treachery they pierced the king.

A few of the Sicarii escaped and fled to Masada, including Eleazar ben Jair, Menachem's cousin. Menachem himself escaped only as far as Ophel Hill; there they took him, tortured and slew him and his sons, along with others including our righteous commander Apsalom. The prophecies had promised that the Pierced Messiah would recover; alas, Menachem did not. One more messiah departed the battlefield.

Menachem the Star, tortured and slain; it was too dreadful.

The King Messiah come among us, yet before our glory was won, to be cut down in treachery. All our years of yearning, crying 'How long, oh Lord, how long?' into the wind. And no sooner does he appear than he disappears again, our hope and longing dashed against the ground.

In my opinion, Sisters, this was the beginning of our down-fall—the day the Messiah was slain, and not by the Kittim but by the Jews. The agony of our situation was too great to bear. We had built the New Jerusalem, yet the reality was far from the heaven on earth we'd sung about. The city was still riddled with back-stabbers and people who wanted to open the gates to the Romans at the first opportunity. Forgetting the rule of righteousness eradicated the very reason why we were fighting for it.

In the Nations of the Empire, there was an eruption of vengeance against the new freedom of the Jews. In every Greek city they rose up against the Jews among them. The Greek citizens of Qesarya slew or drove out every Jew in the city. Refugees flooded into Secacah and the camps of the Yachad.

But we were no longer a meek and marginal force. Jews rose up all over Syria and Judaea and in revenge attacked Greek villages. Our militiamen captured the fortresses of Cypros and Machaerus.

Greeks continued to kill even other Greeks—the Judaisers—those who were proselytes to the Way. In one city only, Scythopolis, the Jews protected their Greek neighbours from the Jewish mob, and the Greek mob decimated them for it.

This marked a monumental cross on the hill of the works of the Ebionim, Sisters. As Jews and Greeks fought each other in reciprocal vengeance, the interpretation of 'Love thy Neighbour as thyself' became 'Attack thy Neighbour as he has attacked thee'. The righteous said it was only lawful to kill in proportionality—only the exact number of Greeks should die as the number of Jews they slew—but nobody was counting; and never could our violent works have equalled theirs.

As Greeks and Jews purged each other's neighbourhoods of the foreigner, the arguments at the wells, at the marketplaces or at supper tables changed. There was no more middle ground, each group clung to their own in protection from the other. Arguments for and against war divided every city. If you were a Jew you were a rebel, if you were a Greek you were an appeaser. It didn't take much for Greeks to be motivated to murderous thoughts.

There had always been disagreements about religion. Now differences in ideas about revolution were causing peoples to fight against each other instead of waging war against the common enemy. Greeks against Jews, Jews against Kutim, Jews against other Jews.

We listened to the roll—Scythopolis, Askelon, Ptolemais, Tyre, Hippos and Gadara—cities only; the names of the dead would be reported later. My mind noted the colonies omitted from slaughter. Only in Antioch, Gerasa, Sidon, and Apamea did they spare those that dwelt with them and would not endure to kill any of the Jews.

I thought of the priest in Palmyra with the bauble for his mother in her paradis at Apamea. A picture came to my mind of the lady enjoying her birthday party in peace, surrounded by unbroken garden statuary of naked Greeks. From my stomach emitted a twisted laugh.

It was not the moment for levity, so I suppressed it, and

it erupted instead on my face as a grimace. People looked at me strangely. I pondered the irony of the garden in Apamea with its Greek statues, pristine and safe all in rows on their platforms, while our brothers lay broken and dead, and my grimace twisted further into a sob.

If the tide had not already turned with the murder of Menachem, the pogroms marked a sea change in the revolt. Rich Jews in their fine houses and villas who might otherwise have yearned for salvation sold their lands and goods, but not to give to the Ebionim. They pulled up stakes and moved to Syria, Decapolis, and Alexandria, or beyond the Jordan.

The last letter I received from Ima Sherah informed me that the trips of Ossaean Sisters into Ein Gedi on market day had ceased, and the Joiners of the Yachad had all run away.

I thought of the divine grace that shone upon me during my caravan days, that came I knew from the love I shared with Shu'dat and all her tribe. Persian Jew and Nabatu, we loved one another. I don't know whether we would have shared the same ideas about revolution. I didn't think of revolution myself, then. I wondered whether the caravan would have heard news of our revolt. Would they be on our side? If I could send a messenger to Shu'dat, would she bring Yatur and all his brothers to our aid, join their camels to the Fifties and the Hundreds?

'The Kittim can't have their Pax Romana with all this turmoil between peoples,' I said to Uzziel. 'The land is out of control. They'll have no choice but to send the legions, and we will not be ready.'

He argued that we had time. 'Nero's on holiday for an entire year, doing the rounds of the four Gentile Games. So vain is he for applause, he employs 5000 aristocratic hangers-on as an advance cheering section for his performances.'

'But he has generals, Uzziel. You yourself told me that the emperor has appointed Vespasian to march against us. We cannot be lax in our preparations.'

During the months of Gathering, the nationalists in Galilee revolted. Our troops there were commanded by Yosef ben Mattityahu. The news we desert dwellers received from anywhere north of Jerusalem was scant, but the news from Galilee was eagerly awaited.

Even when we had no witness at the event, after two or three days, news began to trickle south. Army hangers-on are keen to boast of what they've seen to everyone around as they dawdle behind the action.

By the time we heard the story, so many people had heard it from so many people, you didn't know what to believe. One day we heard one hundred were killed; the next day the figure would be 5000. Rulers and leaders of soldiers have their own tales to defend, so it's doubtful even whether historians years from now will know the real truth. Only those in command of soldiers and taxes can tell history as it happens.

But it is we the Ebionim who make history with our works. They are only the figureheads. We may leave our enemies to make their own versions. Among ourselves, Sisters, we must speak the truth.

Cestius Gallus was on the march from Antioch with the Twelfth Fulminata, one of the Syrian legions, along with horse and archers from King Agrippa and the client kings of Commagene and Emesa, Herodians by birth or marriage.

I propose to you, Sisters, that sometime around then, there must have been a secret, treacherous meeting of Herodian kings and heretic preachers. I admit, such a gathering was never reported to the Romans or anyone else. Indeed, I have no evidence for it; it is only a guess. They must have conspired.

In Armenia, Tiridates had been overthrown and Tigranes installed as king. The Romans had been defeated by the Parthians at Rhandeia. In Qesarya, Greeks and Jews were rioting over citizenship rights. In Judaea and Idumaea, rich Tzaddikim priests invaded the threshing floors to seize taxes for the Temple but were stoned by the people. It could have been as early as then.

But whether or not such a meeting took place, I can name for you the guilty parties.

At the head couch reclines General Vespasian—may his bones rot. He takes his orders from whatever cretin currently sits under the eagle in Rome. He has been graciously offered the seat of honour by the sycophant Agrippa son of Agrippa son of Herod, king of the Jews. The Pharisee Yochanan ben Zakkai is with them, representing the people. They are served by fleshy harlots meat in unclean vessels from animals sacrificed to idols.

Says Vespasian to Yochanan, 'If there is a jar of honey round which a serpent is wound, would you break the jar to get rid of the serpent?'

Ah, general, you simply don't understand us Jews. Rabban Yochanan is silent, but later the rabbis said he should have responded, 'No, we take a pair of tongs and grip the snake and kill it, leaving the jar intact.'

Snickering at them are the corrupt priests and the panoply of Herodians across the Diaspora, desiring the conflict to be resolved one way or another. It matters not which way, as long as they retain their riches.

These snickerers I accuse for treachery against the Jews and betrayal of our dreams of liberation: Agrippa's brother Herod king of Chalcis, who beheaded Theudas and Simon Cephas; other kings of the Nations, Herodians by marriage, Diaspora rulers who joined him in war, including Antiochus of Commagene, Sampsigeramus of Emesa, Cotys of Lesser Armenia and Polemo of Pontus; the Alexandrian alabarch Demetrius and his wife Agrippa's sister Mariamne, who was an apostate to the Law; Agrippa's sister Berenice—the greatest fornicator of all—who married Marcus Julius Alexander, the alabarch's son, then married her uncle the king of Chalcis before living in incest with her own brother and then slithering onto the adulterous bed of our destroyer Titus; the procurator Felix, whose divorced his wife to marry Herodian princess Drusilla; Tiberius Alexander, procurator after Fadus; Herodias, Agrippa's sister whose marriage to Herod Antipas had incited the beheading of the Baptist and war with the Arab king; Philip of Jacimus, general of Agrippa's guard, who turned his soldiers upon our people; the priests who invited Gallus into the city.

These Jews here named I implicate in the betrayal of our Jewish Kingdom. Were an Ossaean permitted to wager or to swear an oath, I would do so. If I had Ima Miryam's magic vial, I would use it to invoke all the demons. If I knew the location of their banqueting hall, I would torch it.

They did not rejoice with the Many the coming Kingdom of God. They did not give of their gold to the collection boxes to equip the Fifties and the Hundreds. They did not feed the starving Poor of Jerusalem, fighting for our freedom. They did not support our glorious revolution.

No, while we toiled, they ogled naked youths in their

*gymnasia*. They donned their togas and reclined next to Caesar, enjoying luxuries paid for by our tribute, dining on meat sacrificed to beastly gods. When the battle lines formed, they scurried over to the other side.

I accuse here people whom I am certain are Sons and Daughters of Darkness. I would come to accuse those who considered themselves not our enemies, but who betrayed us by collaboration that they dressed up in the language of peace.

Chief among these will be Sha'ul and his brother Costobarus, representatives of the Herodians. They petitioned Nero in Corinth, laying the blame on Florus, but in the act of doing so, they brought down the wrath of Rome upon the people. It was from their petition that Nero commissioned Vespasian to ride against us.

I told the story of the serpent and the honey jar to Anna and she said, 'What would you have replied, Sophia?'

I said, 'The bees made the honey. Let them decide.'

The population was swelled with pilgrims come up to keep the Feast of Sukkot when Gallus first attacked Jerusalem. Townsfolk had erected on the rooves their Sukkot booths of myrtle, palm and olive branches. The Greek townspeople tried to open the gates of the city, but the War Party bombarded the soldiers from the wall. Though it was Shabbat, yet they did not spare their works.

Insurgent forces were growing daily, and they slew hundreds of soldiers. Eleazar ben Simon's Zealots pursued them to Beth-horon, forty-five stadia from Jerusalem, when Simon bar Giora ambushed the attachment from behind.

In open country, they remained in formation, but as the terrain grew steeper, it provided a perfect opportunity for ambush. As the soldiers trudged through the pass in their heavy armour, they were waiting targets for our shot-slingers and javelinmen from the caves and crags overhanging.

When the formation bogged down in the narrow passages, militiamen ambushed them from above and penned them in, showering them with darts so relentlessly they had to abandon their stone-throwers and siege engines and all their baggage. Gallus was pressed back to Beth-horon, shedding Roman armoury for our men gleefully to seize.

The Romans lost 5300 men and 480 horse, and Simon's men seized all their weapons, baggage and animals. They even took the eagle standards. The rebels pursued them all the way to Antipatris, then marched back up to Jerusalem singing hymns of victory.

Marching alongside Simon's runaway slaves and Edomite peasants were two princes from the royal family of Adiabene, Monobazus and Kenedaios, proselytes to the Way. Perhaps they were kin to Ima Symacho? Adiabene Jews had supported the Hasmoneans against the Seleucids, the only Jews in the Diaspora who did so.

Simon was also supported by Silas called the Babylonian, a prince of the Tobiads from the exilarchy, and Niger of Peraea. Silas and Niger were disciples of Sha'ul, which caused a bit of controversy in camp, but the commanders said, 'As long as they fight on the side of righteousness'.

This was a high point for us, Eleazar and Bar Giora fighting together, princes of the Nations joining in.

Suddenly, perhaps fearful that the seasonal rains would cut off his supply lines, having lost all his baggage at Beth-horon, Gallus turned around and retreated to Gabaon, abandoning the conquest of the city. It seemed a miracle. We felt we had won our victory.

A force twice the size of that which had crushed the Iceni, and our men had defeated them. This was the biggest Jewish victory in 200 years, an incredible triumph, and news spread quickly all over the Levant. Surely this was the final sign from God that the Day was coming now. The whole world was turned upside down. Of all the questions we had been debating, the most important one had always been—Can we win? Beth-horon gave us the answer. The cycle of the heavens had come full circle; our final triumph was nigh.

This final act of insurgence committed us to war.

By this time, almost all of us at Secacah, whether or not we supported Simon bar Giora as king or Eleazar ben Simon or Niger the Peraean, were anxious to join the Fifties and the Hundreds in the city. The miracle of Gallus' retreat was certain to be short-lived. Vespasian would come.

Uzziel said, 'The commanders still urge defending the strongholds, but the militiamen talk of marching up in force.' We only waited for the right day.

'The Herodians despite themselves are caught up in the elation,' messengers reported. 'They've had to come over to the War Party.'

The people had chosen a new government in a mass meeting in the Temple. And, as is natural, they chose for the posts people everyone already knew, high priests and nobles. Ananus ben Ananus was *strategoi* (military governor), and would lead the government. He had been removed from the high priesthood for executing Ya'akov the Just and provoking an insurrection in Samaria. But they needed him now. He appointed as High

Priest Yeshua ben Gamala.

This was the next stage of the revolution. The moderates among the existing rulers' class took charge of the government, so as not to leave it for more rebellious hands.

After his official report of the elections, the messenger to Secacah commented, 'Eleazar ben Simon is in possession of the booty from Gallus and still holds Temple Mount, so he has to be listened to, but he received no post, nor did the hero of Beth-horon Simon bar Giora.

'And while Jerusalem forms its new government, many leading citizens are sending money to Yochanan of Gush Halav in Galilee. Now, Yochanan has formed his own party in opposition to Josef.' Pharisees never held much authority in Galilee.

The focus of the revolution shifted to Galilee. Rebels took Tzippori (Sepphoris), Gabara, Gush Halav (Gischala) and Tabariyya (Tiberias), and throughout the autumn and winter, Galilee remained in rebel hands.

Wild with excitement upon our victories at Beth-horon and in Galilee, Niger the Peraean crowned himself king. He and his band of Peraeans burnt down the Royal Palaces at Jericho and Betharamptha and other fine houses, gathering much booty.

Our commanders relied on the collection boxes and our own agriculture and had no need to support revolutionary banditry, but many of the Kanaim sympathised. 'We'd rather be fighting than looting, but we'd rather be looting the houses of our enemies than sitting here waiting.' So many men were itching to join Niger that the commanders who now filled Apsalom's seat had to argue strongly that we must stay to defend the fortress.

As for the diadem on the head of Niger, Uzziel said, 'As long as he wins.'

Then with Silas the Babylonian and Yochanan the Ossaean of Thamna, Niger marched on Askelon. There they were ambushed by the Romans. Yochanan's and Silas's forces were wiped out, but Niger survived by hiding in a cave.

His men searched for him in lamentation, and after three days, he reappeared before them. This miracle filled the Jews with unexpected joy. Out in the desert, support for Niger grew. 'Here is the resurrection of the righteous,' we said. 'Niger the Risen One, Messiah. On the third day, he rises again from the dead to arms on earth, according to the prophecy.'

In Idumaea some of Herod's veterans had revolted and fought the king's men; and we'd sent a garrison. But the militiamen were unsatisfied, eager for bigger battles. They complained. 'We need to send an entire force, not just a small contingent. If we stick so jealously to our own carcasses, they'll keep picking us off like flies. The fight is in Galilee. What are we doing sitting on the wall in Idumaea?'

Secacah was in charge of the defense of Peraea and the Jordan crossing. Apsalom had commanded—and his policy was still adhered to—that we join our works only to battles occurring in Peraea, Idumaea, the Salt Sea region, and Decapolis if the fight reached that far. However far the generosity of the collection boxes stretched, we could not absent the fields for long.

At any point the legions could march upon any fortress or stronghold. We didn't have enough forces to man and fortify them all. But our commanders only had to say the word to bring more garrisons from Alexandria, Syria, Cyrene or from across Mesopotamia. So, we thought.

# Chapter 19
## Zion

It was the season of Nourishing. The lecherous quail had migrated from the south, the oak was in leaf and the anemones tinged with the red of Tammuz' sacrifice.

Jews had held Jerusalem for five moons.

In ancient times it was said we were free from invasion during the month of Daisios—our month of Sivan—between the rising of the Pleiades and the Threshing. But come the anemones, popping up red between the stones, we must to prepare for armies.

The Roman army was on the move. Vespasian and the Fifteenth Legion marched to Ptolomais, from whence he sent a garrison against Yosef in Galilee, and Titus—may his bones rot—sailed to Alexandria from whence he marched the Fifth and Tenth Legions.

The Romans demanded contingents from all vassal kingdoms in the region. Agrippa called in the kings of the Nations, many his relatives by marriage, those Sons and Daughters of Darkness; and his army along with other client king allies, as well as Malchus, the king of Arabia, was in Antioch, the capital of Syria.

Ananus and the new government prepared to be besieged.

There was one who was a Messiah to the Galileans, Jesus bar Sapphias. We in Idumaea and Judaea had little time to build our hopes and prayers upon him. His period of glory was too short and ended too tragically. He led the rebellious of the

Galileans against the forces of Josef, but was opposed by the collaborating citizens of his own town Tabariyya. At Joppa, defenders led by Jesus bar Sapphias were lying in ambush in their boats on the Sea of Genneseret when hit by an evil gale. They were crushed against the rocks and picked off by the Kittim as they straggled to shore.

The Galileans' call for reinforcements went out. Delegations arrived with letters and first-hand accounts. There were pleas from Gush Halav, Gamala, Mount Tabor. From Galilee came the cry–Defend the Freedom of Zion.

Anna said, 'Shall we not rally all our forces and fight them in one place?'

Uzziel agreed, 'The Kittim move as one force and strike a big blow with their war machines.'

Mattai agreed also, 'We fight like a swarm of little ants, hoping to kill the elephant by millions of tiny bites. But it takes more than one hill of ants to bring down an elephant.'

An Assembly was held to discuss immediately sending the largest delegation of fighters we could muster to Galilee, to come up from behind the Romans at Yodfat and lift the siege. The commanders, though, said no, by the time we got there it would be too late, and the Kittim would pick us off on the retreat.

'We can only fight them battle by battle. Without the Roman's armoury, our strength lies only in the knowledge of our own terrain, wadis where we can travel unseen, caves where we can hide away, mountain crags from where we can sling stones. Our duty is to till the land, to fortify the strongholds.'

I could see why they argued thus, as it seemed every messenger brought worse news than the one before. It is easier to rally the people if we are winning.

Many Kanaim said the important stronghold is Jerusalem, which was my belief, as that was the seat of our new government. The final battle would have to be there. If I had not known before that my destiny aimed me once again toward the holy city, Sisters, I determined it then. In Jerusalem, we were winning. Twice I asked and was refused permission from the commanders to join delegations westward.

The commanders still said, 'We are a new nation, and we must defend our territory. A land is protected by its fortresses; we will defend the strongholds.' Secacah was strategically located to guard the road from Machaerus to Jerusalem; we could not leave that route unprotected. So, we tended our fields and waited for news.

It was Justa's opinion that the commanders refused to send reinforcements because of old wounds in history. Galilee was filled with Samaritans, she said. 'The commanders are saying they've never supported the Jews' struggles. There's too much bad blood.' She said when Galilean Jews passed through Samaria on their way up to festivals, Kutim regularly taunted the pilgrims with stones. They would mock them with huge bonfires in the night so they'd think it was dawn.

'It was in our town that the trouble started about the pilgrim,' she told me.

Samaritans killed a Galilean Jew on the road up to a feast in Jerusalem, and the procurator refused to address the incident. The bandit Eleazar ben Dinai led Jews into Samaritan villages and massacred many. After that the troubles between Galilean Jews and Samaritans went on.

'It ended in four crucifixions, didn't it?' I remembered.

'Yes. Of the Samaritans.'

'In Qesarya the Greeks had bribed Nero's secretary to annul the equal rights of food distribution to widows and orphans; that started it,' Justa told us. 'At Beth-horon along the public road, Stephen, a Samaritan Greek servant of Caesar...'

'and one of those who distributed to the widows of the Ebionim,' I added.

'...yes, he was stoned to death by the Shammaites. The procurator sent soldiers around the villages in collective punishment.'

'That was only going to fan the flames.'

'Yes, and since then the Shammaite persecution has spread to Phoenicia, Cyprus and Antioch.'

'The Kittim have done everything to fan the flames of hatred, you know,' I pointed out. 'Jerusalem exploded after that soldier exposed his backside to worshippers at the Temple.'

'At Lydda, too,' she said. 'A soldier tore up one of the rolls of Law and threw it into a cooking fire.'

The protest had only calmed down when Cumanus had the soldier executed.

The revolt in Galilee was on the wane when we received a letter written by the military commander of Galilee himself. It was a copy of one sent to Ananus in Jerusalem and was making the rounds of the fortresses. The letter was sent from Tabariyya, but we knew that since writing it, Josef had fled to Yodfat (Jotapata), where the rebels were besieged. We had received that news already from the Zealot command at Tzippori.

Josef used language intent to terrify, pleading with the commanders in Jerusalem to sue for terms. 'We cannot fight the Romans in Galilee if you do not send reinforcements,' he wrote. The letter exaggerated the might of Romans. I had seen Florus' men; I knew what a cohort looked like. Yes, they were mighty, but they were not invincible.

Josef's letter threw the camp into confusion. Many would have rushed off to Galilee had we not already had news that the siege at Yodfat was not progressing well.

I was sad at this point, and much sadder later, as it turned out, to lose Mattai and Justa. They came to us with all their children in tow.

'My eldest Amram has been suffering abuse from the other boys,' Justa complained. 'It has served to strengthen his sense of himself as a Samaritan, and we are following his lead. We're going back to Ginea.'

Mattai showed me the inside of his sleeve, where I recognised the stripes of Simon of Gitta.

'I never thought this of you, Mattai,' I said in my shock. 'You never mentioned it before this.'

'Samaria also has seen the signs in the skies,' he said. 'Simon is rallying the Fifties and the Hundreds to Mount Gerizim.'

'You must urge him to correspondence with Eleazar and the other leaders,' I said.

Anna and Uzziel also urged them. 'We must join our sticks of wood together if we are to resist the battering rams of the Kittim,' Uzziel said.

Nevertheless, they were decided. 'We've already missed the barley harvest. If we go now, there will be time to bring in the grapes,' said Justa.

After they departed, I asked Uzziel, 'Do you think Simon of Gitta will win?'

He said solemnly, 'Samaria is weaker than Galilee, and

Galilee is losing.'

Vespasian, bored with the siege of Yodfat, dispatched the Fifth Legion to Mount Gerizim and crushed them in a flash. I hope that Justa and her family were not with them.

Messengers arrived from Tzippori during the vine harvest. Yodfat had fallen. They had held out for forty-seven days. While we wailed, the travelers were allowed to bathe and partake of food. It was a sorrowful crowd that gathered outside the Assembly Hall to hear their story.

As we listened to the exploits of the Galileans, the young men wanted to cheer for our brave soldiers, but it was an uncomfortable feeling. By the time we heard the tale, we already knew of the tragic defeat, and most of us felt that tears were more appropriate than cheers.

With so much bad news coming from Galilee, we developed a custom. At the point in the story where a brave exploit was commended, though we knew the story had ended in tears, the men had to constrain their desire to cheer, they would instead express their patriotism by shouting sternly, 'vengeance upon the transgressors', and they would punctuate the recital at certain emotional points with outbursts of 'vengeance' or 'transgressors'.

There was an amusing story in this sad tale, as the people of Yodfat, when they had run out of oil to pour down, had defended against the Romans' attack by dropping wet fenugreek below their feet.

The men of Yodfat taunted the Kittim as they slipped on the wet mess and slid into the valley, shouting 'Throw away your lances and your arrows, for we will defeat you with salad.'

'Fenugreek', one of the children whispered in my ear,

310

giggling quietly, and I remembered Imme with her love of words. I shushed the girl, but you can hardly expect a child to sit solemnly for soldiers' talk. Many children were fussing, as all their mothers' and guardians' attention was on the messengers.

After the defeat at Yodfat, in every town and at every fortress—Tzippori, Tabariyya—the people were divided between the aristocrats, who wanted peace, and the rebels, who wanted war. The townsfolk followed the aristocrats; at the moment the Zealots lost control of the battle, they intended open the gates to the Kittim. Every town was in a state of civil war, and as soon as the soldiers marched the other way, they turned on each other.

Insurgents in the area surrendered. Gush Halav, Mount Tabor and Gamala were in our hands, all other fortresses and towns fell to the legions.

During the month of summer fruit, the Romans captured Josef, intending to use him as interpreter in Jerusalem. A messenger from Galilee reported: 'The Many are infuriated by the commander's surrender, the coward, the traitor. He probably did some secret deal with Vespasian.'

Josef, who had studied with the Yachad and with Bannus, knew the skills of Ossaean prophecy. He prophesied to Vespasian that he would become emperor—well, that was convenient—and so the general kept him in honourable custody.

'Yochanan, by contrast, is bravely holding out at Gush Halav,' the messenger said. We said to each other, 'When the Romans finish with Galilee, Secacah and Jerusalem will be next.'

The next messenger carried worse news. Gush Halav was taken.

311

'The citizens opened the gates to Titus, and Yochanan and his rebels fled south, crying bravely that 'even had they wings Titus' legions could not surmount the walls of Jerusalem. Even the small towns of Galilee gave Vespasian and Titus headaches as they broke their engines of war against our walls. The walls of Jerusalem in all their magnitude, they could never fall.'

The whole population of the city turned out to meet Yochanan and his Galileans.

Yochanan of Gush Halav, the new Messiah? I hoped it to be so.

'As long as he wins,' said Uzziel.

The new messiah arrived in a city where power was already shifting away from the Herodians. Junior priests in service at the Temple were wearing white in the Sanctuary, according to the Way.

Emboldened by the entry of the Galileans into the picture, the House of Hillel mounted a coup and overthrew the Pharisee High Priest Yeshua son of Damneus, and replaced him with their own Yeshua, the son of Gamaliel, the rebel priests' candidate. Supporters of each Yeshua threw stones at each other in the streets.

Sha'ul and the Idumaean Costobarus, both kinsmen of Agrippa, got together a band of Herodian thugs and used much violence against the people.

The Kanaim in our fortress were close to mutiny in our restlessness.

'It is too late to do anything about Galilee, but now it is certain the Romans will turn on Jerusalem,' they said. 'We must concentrate our forces. If indeed we should attack them regiment by regiment, we should do it all at once, fight many battles on the same day in different locations, make them divide their forces.'

I overheard things like 'We must leave Secacah like we left Jericho'; 'They will not steal the riches of our lands'; 'Our wealth is in our strong fighting hands'; 'As strong with the sword are we as with the plough'.

The augurs were kept busy, but ultimately it was down to the commander.

I had troubling dreams. Visions about defeats, about fire and death, about betrayal. The assembled company was less inclined to accept the word of a woman than the Yachad had been, particularly when I gave prophecies they didn't like.

Then, I had a dream so strong in portent that it woke me in the middle of the night. I saw walls and walls, at every turn another wall, I couldn't get out, stones falling into my path. The walls of Secacah? Of Jerusalem?

On awakening, I invoked the Four-Letter Name of Tiferet, as Abba Nehunniyah had taught us, envisioning the letters engraved in the white and red fire of glory. I concentrated on the white at the edges of the letters, making sure to keep all four letters in sight at once. The Dreaming Self descending into me, and I felt a sudden equanimity, flying, swooshing, into the Name. Out of the red—sunset?—came a fox before me, saying, 'do not perish'.

Now I felt an urgency. We must leave the fortress. HaShem had commanded it.

One needed no divine vision to see that the Romans were coming for Jerusalem, and the battle was foretold by every seer in camp and by almost every wandering desert messiah who came through Idumaea and Peraea.

On this occasion, though, even my fellow sectarians would not heed my vision, though the ones who were masters of dreams did listen for a moment or two. The soldiers had instead listened to a desert messiah who filled their hearts with ancient prophecies from the Orient.

The words of this prophet, as I heard them reported, seemed also, I thought, to point toward removing all our troops to the city, but I could not convince them.

Reinforced by the confidence of my vision, I spoke to one of the lieutenants. They wouldn't let me speak with a commander.

I had lived long enough with soldiers to note that arguments about armoury, water supplies, numbers and health of baggage animals held more weight than the turnings of the stars or visitations of the Holy Spirit. But before I could say more than, 'We must march to Jerusalem. This fortress will fall,' he pronounced, 'We need to hold Secacah. Between our fortress and the ones at Machaerus and Masada, we can form a triangle of territory where the Romans cannot tread.'

Uzziel, the only soldier among those who would listen to me, said, 'Then we shall be divided in three places and the Romans united in one. They can march from one corner of our triangle to the next, and knock us from our foundations.'

I was unnerved when everyone ignored me, and in my confusion, I couldn't compute the calendar, I had no Abba Lilyukh to consult, and I could not determine the day. Did the prophecy regard the Kanaim? I consulted the Ossaeans at camp, but they were unable to help me. I prayed, but confusion filled my head, and I heard nothing. I berated myself heavily, falling, as is usual post-prophecy, under a black cloud.

I felt the urge, yet again, to flee, but I stopped myself. It was wrong. My own experience also tempered my confidence. Whether my prophecies are true or false, they are always followed by the black cloud. The clarity of God's vision seems to open a door though which the demon Ahriman can enter. Once he is in, no spells or exorcisms or healing herbs can avail me. I must simply wait until the demon passes.

# Chapter 20
## The Copper Scroll

One evening during the late autumn planting, I was called by the Inspector to assist a large delegation of priests and civil servants from the Holy City.

Anna and I and some other women were returning to camp bringing baskets of olives in from the storehouse, and on entering the main gate, we saw a string of militiamen carrying in pots from the Pottery.

The delegation had arrived earlier that afternoon, carrying much baggage on donkeys. We girls had all been agog to learn what was happening, so I was excited when, before I'd even had time to put away the olive baskets, I was among those summoned to the unclean quarters set aside for travelers. I joined the group, noticing that those called were the ones among the company who were skilled with documents, the Levites, scribes and anyone who knew foreign tongues.

With representatives of the new arrivals at his side, Pinhas ben Clusoth the commander addressed us. They stood outside the pottery workshop so we could all gather around the steps, and people could also hear from the refectory. These days we were always anxious to hear news from revolutionary Jerusalem, but our interest was further on edge wondering what was in all those saddlebags?

'Ananus ben Ananus runs the government, but Eleazar and his Zealots hold Temple Mount. Now, with our sacred treasure in the hands of the people and out of the hands of Herod and his corrupt priesthood, nothing must be risked that passes our treasures into the hands of our enemies.'

He asked one of the representatives to speak: 'The Sanhedrin huddle in the Court of the Hewn Stone, sending their lackeys out through the tunnels, fleeing the Holy City with our precious legacy. The hills are crawling with them. Priests and scribes are scurrying across the Judaean wilderness as far as Jericho looking for caves and wadis to store all our scriptures, our sacred and historic literature. If the Romans are so disrespectful of our sacred offerings to steal from the Temple Treasury, how ready will they be to pillage our holy books?'

What the visitors had brought with them to Secacah, all that baggage on donkeys, was bundles of documents from the sacred archives of the Temple, nothing less than the entire Jerusalem library—scrolls from the days of the Maqabim, the writings of Pharisees, Tzaddikim and Ossaeans, the words to ancient prayers and holy psalms, the prophecies predicting the Day.

These they desired to store in a secure location. They were in possession of funds, and their travel had been sponsored, as many wealthier private citizens in the city also wanted their documents stored.

'Our guests have asked for assistance in safeguarding this heritage,' Ben Clusoth said, 'and thus we have summoned you among us who are skilled in archiving.'

The Jerusalem library, founded by Nehemiah, who collected all the books about kings and prophets and the letters of kings about sacred treasures, was to be hidden in the hills.

When he came to me, I was bashful to address the commander face-to-face, but he put me at my ease, 'Sister Sophia, as well as the stylus, are you also skilled in the care of documents?'

317

I responded eagerly that in Babylon my father had taught me everything about the qualities of writing materials, and that at the Yachad, I had learned about the storage of scrolls under these desert conditions.

So, I was selected to go with the delegation to the caves. This one was much larger than the one with which we sent our Yachad library. Every spare jar or amphora we had in the Pottery was filled with scrolls wrapped in linen and tied to a donkey. Anyone who knew anything about document storage helped with the packing.

Compared to this, the Yachad library had been but a few saddlebags. I peeked in one of the bags and mentally calculated the number of scrolls and codices. There must have been over 200. I hadn't seen so many books in one place since I left Babylon.

My regret over seeing the posterity of the nation depart from the hands of scholars was deep. There was a complete scroll of the Book of Isaiah. One of the items I packed was from the days of Simeon the Just, a section from the Book of Samuel.

I was not the only scribe on the trip; there were two official scribes among the Levites who handled our correspondence and archives. Those who knew anything about the geography of the land were along for the second time, as it had been they who had helped transport the Yachad library.

They led us toward the same caves, north from the fortress. Zealots had occupied caves in this range as military hide-outs over the ages. I could also see evidence that some had been used as prayer caves. But we chose a group of caves further south, nearer to Secacah.

It took an entire day to maneuver around the rocks and

crags.

The Jerusalem documents safely stored, I wondered what had happened to the rest of the treasure, the coin, the gold and jewels, the sacred ornaments. If Zealots held the Temple, then they must also hold the Treasury. Was the glittering Treasure of Solomon sitting in some vault waiting to be seized by Romans, reclaimed by Herodians or burned in the course of the war to come?

Shortly after our return, a man arrived at Secacah from Jerusalem, identifying himself as a civil servant, an under-scribe from the Temple. The Temple was now, we were sure, under the influence of the Levites in white, the Shammaites and Yochanan of Gush Halav. But were the Tzaddikim still in power?

We eyed him with some suspicion—came he from the Herodians or from the Zealots? We figured he must be trustworthy if the gatekeeper let him in. But later when the Overseer called me to him, I asked him why I should have business with a servant of the abomination.

'He asked for you by name, Sister Sophia,' he said.

I met with the traveller in the unclean quarters reserved for visitors, just behind the gate under the aqueduct. I brought him a loaf of barleybread and some pomegranate juice. He looked shifty, always looking to left and right, which only increased my earlier suspicion.

'Are you Sophia the Ossaean?' he said.

'I follow the Way, yes; now I am with the Kanaim.'

'We fight together. I also follow the Way; my affiliation is with the Sicarii.'

'Welcome, Brother. What news have you from the city?'

It would hitherto have been considered quite inappropriate

for a maiden to converse privately with a man in such a frank manner. Things were different now; we were all soldiers.

He continued, 'Our forces are greater than ever, but Yochanan's militia merely adds one more faction.'

'Is it to inform our garrisons that is the cause of your journey?'

'Yes, and of that I have already spoken to your commanders. But I have another. I know you to be a friend to the revolt. Can you copy Hebrew?'

'As well as any scribe.'

'Then I have a mission for you.'

I asked him who sent him to me. And he replied, 'a slave by the name of Athanasios'.

The sudden recall of my Greek patient startled me down to the pit of my stomach. My Feeling Self betrayed me, and my hair bristled all over my head. 'He is known to me, and I am glad to hear of him.'

'He says you saved his life.'

'He is generous with his words. He performed a brave service for my people and sorely suffered for it. The Brethren are in his debt.'

'He calls you an angel.'

I turned away with a jerk, surprised by a gush of feeling. Imagine the surly Greek using such a word!

'How do you know him?'

'He is active in our works. His duties allow him free time while the master pursues his leisure. Sister, do not mistrust me. I come to you on urgent business.'

'Your mission must be grave if a copying job should be such an urgent matter when the Holy City is under threat.'

'It is. And it is for that threat that I prepare.'

He drew something immensely heavy from a bag and placed it in my hand. It was pounded copper rolled into a cylinder–a scroll–a scroll made entirely of copper. Any kind of metal was a prohibitively expensive commodity these days, but copper! The metal in this sheet must have been worth a year's wages. A section of the inner surface jutted out just far enough from the cylinder to reveal the chiselled rough, linear marks of a Hebrew script.

'On this sheet of metal is inscribed a record of the treasure of the Temple of Jerusalem,' said the Sicarii, who called himself Yona bar Hakkoz.

So, this was what had become of the Treasure of Solomon.

'What is written therein?'

'Everything. What the treasure consists of, how much there is of it, where it is hidden, how to find it.'

'It's a treasure map?'

'Alas, a map to bury a treasure and not to reveal one. The Romans will take Jerusalem as they will take Jericho. Our lives will be lost, and our nation will be no more. Our history will disappear into the dust of legend. But we cannot let the treasures of the house of the Lord fall into unclean hands.'

'You would bury the Treasure of Solomon?'

'It is already buried,' he said. 'Our treasure is in the hands of the people. At last our sacred first fruits are taken from the mouths of the Hasmoneans.'

Somewhere also were hidden, it was written, more ancient treasures from the First Temple–the Holy Ark, the incense altar and menorah. To save them from Nebuchadnezzar, King Josiah buried them 'under the wood house', wherever that might be.

'Why did you not send this map to Secacah for safe storage along with the rest of the library?'

'There are those among that company whom we do not trust. They must not know of this. The sacred treasure must not fall into the hands of our enemies, be they foreign soldiers or our own priests.'

I could see that. Our Ossaean sacred literature contained evidence of sedition, which would be dangerous in the wrong hands, but only if those who found it could read the code. Furthermore, seditious evidence would be of no more danger were we already to be defeated.

A treasure map was different. Kings and soldiers die, but treasure lives on, enriching whatever hand may hold it. The Romans had plenty of treasure; to give them more would impoverish the whole world. If the Herodians regained the treasure, they could forestall the Restoration forever longer.

I said, 'What would you require of me?'

'Hide it, and let none but our circle know of its location. But first make a copy, and let me take that along my way.' He also had some Ossaean writings from a family collection he wished to bury for posterity, a midrash on Isaiah, some hymns of praise and angelic descriptions.

'Indeed, Brother, I know just the place for it. But you place great trust in me. My teachers were no friends to the Temple, nor my brothers and sisters with whom I now reside.'

He was of the same opinion. 'The priests will not stand up for the people. Many Jews and Zealots will fight, and they will look to the Temple for leadership. They will die for it.'

'How came you by this treasure map, then, if you are not sent by the priests?'

'I stole it. They have no knowledge that I am a Sicarii.'

'But they may well suppose you are the thief.'

'Of course, but I left the Temple in a state of chaos. By the time they realise the Copper Scroll was not taken by one of them and can ascertain my route, it will be hidden, and only you and I will know where.'

'They cannot connect you to me?'

'Athanasios speaks to none but those within our circle. As you know, he would take the lash before betraying a comrade.'

'How did he know of my transport to Secacah?'

'Your cousin Yitzhak is also of our circle. The Brethren in Jerusalem are apprised of your departure from Ein Gedi.'

He put it diplomatically. 'I see,' I said, and this time, my blush was from shame. And still you trust me?–I thought.

'Why me?' I said. 'Surely Athanasios knows loyal scribes in Jerusalem?'

'Athanasios knows you to be a friend to scholarship as well as to freedom. As for scribes in Jerusalem, the city is no safe place. If this one scroll should be destroyed, no record of our wealth will remain, and the treasure itself lost.'

'But why do you not take your treasure to Masada? The fortress is impregnable, many times more formidable than our fort here at Secacah. All Sicarii share your distrust of the high priests. Surely your brothers there would keep it safe?'

'Indeed, it is to Masada I am bound, but transporting such a heavy, valuable object across the wilderness was treacherous enough this far. Better to hide it in a cave somewhere.'

Bar Hakkoz said the Sicarii had weaponry at Masada laid up a hundred years ago by Herod, enough to equip 10,000 men, and not only that, but provisions which in the mountain air have not spoiled.

'They must be brought back here,' I urged, 'for the final battle.'

'No, all the prophecies have failed; I am going to my brethren at Masada. Small though it may be, we will build the Kingdom there.'

'You don't believe we can fight in Jerusalem?'

'Zealots and Sicarii are few in number in Jerusalem, and we have few friends. We are ravaged by foreign oppressors and enemies of the Ebionim. We have no land. Jews across Palestine are being slaughtered, burnt and crucified by the Greeks and their legionnaires. Yet the Kittim bring good trade along with their oppression, and there are many who prefer silver to freedom, especially the priests. The Temple bureaucrats will prove their mettle, and the revolt in Jerusalem will fail. And thus, may we all end,' he sighed.

I watched him pondering the insignificance of two pursued Jews scuttling across the Roman-occupied desert clutching secret treasures as against a coming apocalypse of defeat.

Never in my life did I meet such a gloomy Zealot, Sisters. I was annoyed. I understood the urgency of his mission, given the chaos in Jerusalem, but his catastrophic pessimism was insulting to one about to undertake a dangerous mission.

I said: 'As an Ossaean, I have no love for the wealth the Temple has tithed from the Many for generations. And as a Zealot, I rejoice that the treasures should return to their hands. You speak truly that as a scholar I revere history and tradition.'

I agreed to make him a copy. I do know something, after all, about secret scrolls. This I would enscribe on ibex skin, discreet and light enough to fit into his travelbags, for him to keep clasped close to his breast and destroy, if defeat should be ours.

I would also make another copy, a copy written in a code few scholars could read.

'There is one who knows it,' I said—my former suitor Guryon—'but our enemies would not know him.' The coded copy I would likewise keep clasped close to my breast, the more easily to be destroyed if necessary.

He continued: 'What of the key to this code? Will it not disappear like our golden cities?'

'Surely the resistance shows some hope for victory,' I said, 'if we plan our battle wisely.'

'Sister, I meant no offence. I only mean, if you and your brethren should not have the chance to teach someone. The End of Times brings no good news for the world, I fear.'

I knew what he meant. He meant—What if we both are killed? It was of concern to me, as well. I thought: This ancient treasure is of no use to us right now. Only those who know the Lost Wisdom can know what we have lost. Only they, we if we survive, will ever be able to find it. If the future holds not this promise for us, then it is gone, disappeared into the desert sand.

I told him: 'I will leave my own treasure map, that those who know the key may find it.'

'Make your coded copy, then,' said Bar Hakkoz.

I promised him, 'Someday when Jerusalem is free, we will search again for the Lost Wisdom, and when the Kingdom is in our hands, we will take up again our hidden treasure.'

Utmost care must be taken with such precious metal and such an important document, so we enlisted the aid of a goldsmith I knew in Ein Gedi. 'Never fear for your secret,' I said. 'He is a Zealot and no friend of the Temple, and cannot read anyway.'

I begged permission from Commander Pinhas to travel. I told him the Sicarii had enlisted my help with a translation job, and we needed to see a scholar in Ein Gedi about it.

So as not to attract attention with our cargo, we took the low road close to the Salt Sea rather than travel along the cliff. It stank horribly. The hot sun burns away the water at such a rate that the sulphurous residues of Sodom and Gomorrah remain in greater concentration. I could not adopt the nose of my desert fox, as Bar Hakkoz engaged me in conversation.

He continued the account of his escapade; the Temple archives had been emptied. 'It was in the general confusion that I managed to procure the scroll and make my escape.'

'How did you do it?'

'My clan were once Temple Treasurers in the days of Zadok.'

Now I recognised the name. 'The house of Hakkoz? Eupolemus?'

'Yes, my ancestor. He was ambassador to Rome under Judas Maqabi. So, you see, I know secret ways of access into the treasure rooms that they have all forgotten, deep down in the southern sector.'

Goldsmith by profession, Adiel was arms-maker by occupation in these revolutionary days. The goldsmith's trade was no more. Indeed, normal commerce was almost at a standstill. Like every other metal worker, Adiel was continually pressed by this or that farmer into melting down his ploughshares for swords or knives. There was never enough metal, but whenever they could lay their hands on some, every apprentice was immediately pressed into activity making spears, shields, knives. Even for those afraid to fight the Romans, the streets, roads and hills were dangerous places these days. Everyone wanted weapons. Most were only able to repay Adiel's work by gifts of food and news.

He shoved aside a pile of newly pointed spears, their tips engraved with tiny letters 'Shining Javelin of the Power of God', to lay the copper upon a heavy, straight board, fastening it tightly with padded clamps, and stoked his fire as he examined the metal.

'It's extremely high quality,' he said, laying his irons upon the coals. 'I would guess only one part tin to ninety-nine parts pure copper. This was made by a very rich man.'

'The trick will be to heat both the interior and the exterior surfaces evenly,' he explained, 'so neither side will crack.' He accomplished this by holding four irons instead of the usual one, evenly spaced, two above and two below the fold. Though illiterate, he didn't need to be told he was working with a valuable document. He softened it slowly, holding the irons a good distance from the copper.

'We only want to soften it, not to melt it,' he explained, 'neither to damage the inscription nor to cause cracking.'

With his free hand, he began to smoothe the solid folds, a white linen cloth that had been washed many times wrapped firmly around his fireglove. 'Using wool would leave oil spots on the metal, causing unevenness where those spots would burn hotter than the surrounding surface,' he explained.

I began to form sense from the scratchings; it was old Hebrew, in a square script and in a colloquial style:

> below the portico's southern corner in the Tomb of
> Zadok, under the platform of the exedra; vessels for

tithe sweepings, spoilt tithes, and inside them, figured
coins

This was no esoteric tract; it was a true treasure map, and an
explicit one, obscured though it was by encoded language. The
text listed treasure hidden and buried in and around Jerusalem,
in wadis, in secret places, under the Temple, each location
which was identified. One item was twenty-four scrolls, buried
under the foundations of the Temple as near the Holy of Holies
as possible. Then there were tabulations of gold and silver. I
copied onto an ibex skin:

> in the cavity of the old House of Tribute, in the plat-
> form of the chair, sixty-five bars of gold
>> four talents of silver by the dam at the mouth of the
> Qidron gorge
>> in the sepulchral monument, in the third course of
> stones: one hundred bars of gold

As Adiel softened the folds, he straightened the sheet using
a series of padded clamps, and the copper flattened onto the
straight board. As the scroll unfurled, he repositioned the four
pokers with perfect agility, keeping them the exact distance
from the metal.

There listed were sacred objects:

> nine cubits under the southern corner: gold and silver
> vessels for tithe, sprinkling basins, cups, sacrificial
> bowls, libations vessels; in all 609

And talents:

in the stubble field of the Shaveh, facing southwest,
in an underground passage looking north, buried at
twenty-four cubits: sixty-seven talents

In all 4,630 talents of gold and silver were listed; I had ample
time to count. Of course, that was before applying the cipher.
I knew the code; it was Aegyptian, from the days of the second
Rameses. For smaller numbers, it used vertical strokes, and
multiples of ten represented larger numbers. Even with the
numerical adjustment, it was prodigious wealth. The text
seemed to refer to tithes collected from across the Diaspora
during some period of political unrest.

It took the smith much longer to soften the metal than it
did me to write, and during the intervals I transposed the text
onto a second skin into a Chaldean code Guryon had taught
me, etching with a stick in the sand on the floor to establish
the pattern of translation of the Hebrew consonants.

I accomplished this code by taking all the place names in
the document and substituting for them euphemisms familiar
to us from Hebrew scriptures. The resulting text made little
sense, actually, but one might think that was simply the effect
of its being ancient.

'You are right,' said the Sicarii looking on. 'Though a junior
scribe, I can't read a word of it.'

'You wouldn't know the meaning if you could read it,' I said.
'A Babylonian would read this and think it referred to a treasure
altogether more other-worldly.'

A keen Zealot, Adiel talked much with Bar Hakkoz about
the size of the resistance's arsenal, a small part of which he was
himself crafting. We were also making our own coinage by

then, stamped with our victory cry, 'Freedom of Zion'.

Adiel quizzed Bar Hakkoz on the state of Zealot forces in the city, but the Sicarii's pessimism concerning what he saw as an inevitable coming apocalypse kept pulling the conversation toward his expectations of a last defeat.

He told the smith: 'Sicarii troops are garrisoned at Masada. If we can't hold them there, it will be the end of Israel.'

'There are still our Kanaim here at Secacah,' I countered. 'You will fight, Adiel? The people of Ein Gedi?'

'Yes, we will fight. The Lord will be on our side. We patriots will fight, but the People of the Land will not fight beyond their own villages, as the further they are from their own fields, the closer they feel themselves to being seized by the enemy.'

We talked about the forces and movements of Roman garrisons in the region and Secacah's water system. Adiel knew the manufacture of the pipes; his guild had worked on Pilate's aqueduct.

We didn't need rely on Pilate's unclean water, he said. 'Our fortress's system of wells and cisterns,' he told Bar Hakkoz, 'can hold water enough for 750 people for eight months after the winter rains.'

It was King Hezekiah who built the water tunnel over 1000 cubits long from the Gihon Springs. Desert peoples even in those ancient days knew all about water.

Adiel said: 'The Romans are numerous. All they need is a good water supply line and they can lay siege. And they are rich. They can turn their Roman gold into water.'

'Magi, are they?' I laughed.

'No, conquerors. And what their swords cannot win them, their gold can. Gold and silver will defend the spear. Barley from my brother's field was once enough to barter with for whatever we needed to fill our stomachs. Now, everything has to be paid for in coin. Even if we kick the Romans out of Palestine, we'll still have to use their money.'

I copied the final entry:

> In the pit adjoining on the north, in a hole opening northward, and buried at its mouth: a copy of this document, with an explanation and their measurements, and an inventory of each and every thing

'So, there is another document?' I asked Bar Hakkoz, not wishing to reveal my full question before Adiel.

'Those who buried it are trusted,' he said enigmatically.

Adiel looked a bit perplexed at this intrigue over documents, but he asked no questions.

Completely unfurled, the copper scroll was about two *ells* (eight feet) long. He had finished straightening the sheet, and began the process in reverse, rolling it back into a cylinder. Halfway through the process, however, we heard a crack, and the sheet split in two. The three of us let out a groan, and Adiel exclaimed, 'I'm sorry, there was a fracture line. It couldn't withstand the bending.'

'Do not fear,' said Bar Hakkoz. 'The text is not compromised. We still have our document and its facsimile. It will be easier to carry now, one on each side of the donkey.'

After Adiel finished, I asked the men to be silent for a moment while I tuned to the vibrations in the copper, and channelled the energy from the metal to the ibex skins. The vibration of a semi-precious metal is very different from that of the skin of a dead beast, but the energy of the content was not compromised. We said a prayer of dedication, 'O Lord, the God of Israel, there is no God like Thee'. We also prayed for Bar Hakkoz' safe journey: 'Lead us in peace and direct our steps in peace...'

'Now this treasure,' I said, 'will rest together in safety with the treasures of our holy works.'

Adiel said: 'And will future scholars, as you, know the tongues of the ancients?'

'I hope for it. But do not flatter me, Adiel. It is your metallurgy that has accomplished this mission.'

'Well, never before have I used my skill with the metal for a scholarly purpose.'

I told him: 'Generations will remember you for it.'

On our parting, Bar Hakkoz gave Adiel a few shekels, though he was not in need. Skilled craftsmen earned more than legionnaires. The Sicarii offered some to me, but I asked him instead to give them to Adiel for the works of the Secacah forge.

As an Ossaean, I am content to rely on the goodness of God and the collection boxes for my sustenance. Zealots in these times lived like that, too. I had no need of coins and wished not to take any back with me, to have to explain to the militiamen the nature of my undertaking, as we had sworn to tell no one. Adiel was glad of a double payment for his work. The funds would undoubtedly be put to immediate use.

He made me a parting gift of a beautiful pair of *tefillin* phylacteries (boxes to contain prayers, worn on head and arm during morning prayer), bronze with little glass doors, still simple enough to please my Ossaean taste. Behind the little glass door of one I placed my coded copy of the treasure scroll.

In the other, I placed the transcription of my stolen tablet.

On our trip to the caves I asked Anna and Uzziel to come along, especially as Uzziel had been one of the scouts on the earlier trips, so he knew the route. On my assurances, Bar Hakkoz agreed to take them into our confidence. A group of four was safer than two, and a man and woman traveling together would be suspect, as well. I wouldn't be able to shape-shift in company.

With two donkeys—one was needed for the Copper Scroll alone—we headed north from the fortress. Uzziel and I led the group past the cave where the Jerusalem library had been stored and further north along the ridge past the one where the Yachad and Zealot scrolls lay, considering a suitable repository.

Uzziel chose a suitable cave, just beyond the last of those holding the Yachad scrolls. Men had used these caves since the days of the Great Beasts, though we could tell by the smell its more recent occupants had been bats. Only one who knew the history of our forefathers would find their location. This was a fitting and propitious hiding place for this treasure of the Lost Wisdom.

We deposited Bar Hakkoz's private collection—there were about fifteen pieces of parchment—in the cave, and further back, in a cranny obscured by shadow, on a little rock shelf we hid the Copper Scroll.

When Bar Hakkoz reached Masada, he would record its location for our heirs, but until then, I made him to learn the route by mouth, and only he and I and my two friends would know it.

He departed from there southward, and we joined some Kanaim militiamen homeward bound to Secacah.

They reported bad news. Fearful that Jews would rise up in their cities, the Greek citizens of Qesarya and Askelon had carried out pre-emptive strikes, and risen in violence against their neighbours. More crosses on the hill of the Ebionim.

# Chapter 21
## Heroes and traitors

I remained with the Kanaim at Secacah for a year, day after day waiting with excitement for news from Jerusalem and Galilee. It was nearing the day I would reach nineteen years when events in the land led me to return to the holy city.

The call came from Jerusalem to Idumaea and Peraea. We received a letter by messenger. 'Ananus has betrayed the capital to the Romans,' it said. 'Come to defend the Glory of Zion against our own corrupt priests and rulers.' It was sealed by Eleazar ben Simon.

This was not a call from a corrupt commander from some far-off and soon-to-be-defeated siege. It was from the revolutionary leader of the New Jerusalem. We were called upon now not simply to defend the fortifications of this or that town; this was an appeal to defend the very heart of the revolt.

Furthermore, when it came to defence of Jerusalem, the argument that 'we can only defend the terrain we know' no longer held ground. Any zealous Jew will have visited the holy city many times since the age of twelve. Many adults knew every street. I myself, after only one trip, was familiar with the route between my cousins' and Athanasios' master's households, and the whole area between the Upper Market and the Jaffa Gate.

I'd abided the decision of the commanders while the war was in Galilee. We had to till the land, and anyway, as a girl I was bound to be of more use farming and cooking than fighting.

But now it was Jerusalem under threat. The very name of the holy city stirred something primeval in my heart. I had myself witnessed the victory over Florus, and the memory was fresh before my eyes. If we could defend anywhere, it would be that ancient mount. The final battlefield for the Kingdom of Heaven would be there.

A miraculous event further forced the hands of the Secacah commanders. Over the delta from the Jordan came a large body of men. Our scouts had spotted them to be Jews. The sound of their horses splashing echoed all the way to the top of the cliff. The sight electrified us; we all ran up and leaned over the edge of the wall.

The leader was carrying a ploughshare to which a bar of wood had been strapped to form a cross with the plough blade for a tail. It was Nethanel bar Tholomi the chief of the Notzrim in Armenia. They had responded to the call. As soon as we realised who it was, we broke into cheers.

He wore a splendid white robe with a purple stripe, and a white tzitzit cloak with purple gems at the four corners. He was very hairy, black curly hair covered his ears, and his beard was long and grizzled. He had white skin and large eyes.

Along with his band of believers Bar Tholomi drew with him hordes of the People of the Land, and they had rich booty, as they'd long beleaguered the emperor's men on the highways. We didn't know what news he brought, but we knew it would be big. With the Armenian enforcements to our Idumaean garrison, we would have a formidable army.

By the time we welcomed them and heard their news, it was even better. The princes of Adiabene, royal proselytes to our faith along with their mother the Queen, were on their way to our alliance as well.

The rally to Jerusalem was decided. A contingent would remain to still guard the fortress, but the garrisons would march en masse to defend the city.

Anna and I asked permission to join the company of the militias and received it.

Though we were from all over, they called our alliance 'Idumaeans'. We marched on the city, a large force under four commanders–John and Jacob sons of Sosas, Simon ben Cathlas, and Pinhas ben Clusoth.

But the traitorous slave Ananus would not open the gates. It was illegal and scandalous! The Holy City is always open to Jews, especially now to defend against the idolatrous enemy.

Ananus' second in command Yeshua ben Gamala spoke from the walls, 'Why should you Idumaeans in your shining armour come to help these scoundrels? These reports of treason are false. You must now either act as neutral judges or help us eliminate the Zealots.'

Simon ben Cathlas replied for our side, 'You prove that the city is in the hands of treasonous people. You close your gates against fellow Jews, and we can't make our offering. You imprison those among you who desire liberty. The Zealots should have killed Ananus first.'

Of course, we refused to take up arms against the Zealots, nor would we lay aside our own weapons. We were forced to sleep out in the open, in front of the gates, and a storm broke. It was a bad omen. Was this the interpretation of my dream? Were these the walls I saw?

Nevertheless, Zealots on the inside under cover of the storm managed to saw through the bars across the gate and let us in.

We trudged up to the Temple, where our garrisons flooded in upon the soldiers in the Outer Court. Uzziel and the other men joined the Zealots in the fighting, which continued all night through the storm, while we women huddled under the porticoes.

At dawn 8,500 were dead. Among the martyrs was the Armenian Nathanel bar Tholomi—may his memory be a shield unto us.

As soon as it was light, Anna and I made our way to the old house near the Jaffa Gate, where sure enough, Abba Jairus had set up the clinic with some of the same volunteers.

The Upper City was captured, and our commanders set up a tribunal on Temple Mount and started putting the Herodian priests on the stand.

First to be executed was Ananus ben Ananus—may he be hurled into the Great Abyss! Thus, did the Wicked Priest reap Miryam Maga's curse. Then was his cohort Yeshua ben Gamala— they murdered him in the middle of the Temple and threw him into the valley. The executioners mocked their corpses and flung them outside the gates without burial.

They had all collaborated with the Kittim.

At the Ebionim refectory, Joanna bemoaned the 'senseless violence'. But we knew this was the necessary next stage of the revolution.

Athanasios later said, 'Even if, like Caesar, they had just cut off their hands, still with their feet they would have run to Vespasian.'

The radicals among the Poor overthrew their corrupt rulers, yet they did not know what the next stage would be. Not an unreasonable desire for change, simply a desire without yet a direction.

We were at a crucial point. The situation was much different from the last time I came up. Now, anyone who was not with us was against us; collaborators were as much the enemy as the Kittim.

Yet my heart grieved over the barbarity of their treatment. This was not proper trial and execution. It was vengeful murder, and right in the heart of the holy city. Lawfully, even the cruci-fied are taken down and buried before sunset.

The street battles with Florus' soldiers had done nothing to offend my sensibilities like this sight. That had been honorable fighting against the foreign oppressor. This was man against man, Jew against Jew. And it all happened so quickly you didn't even get a chance to hear the evidence.

At least Anna agreed with me; at that moment we did not feel–This is the beginning of the New Jerusalem. We thought–This is Satan's abode on earth. The New Jerusalem cannot be a holy city of peace without the rule of righteousness. However evil were these men and their works, profaning the corpses of Jews like that–it was an offense against God.

Uzziel disagreed, 'The Sons of Darkness practice crucifixion and scorching and all manner of torturous killings. So, must we exact revenge when we take the hill. Leave only enough alive to tell the tale of our victory. Or else, they will come back in force.'

One among one of the Fifties said, 'Steadfastness is no longer enough, Sister. Too much is at stake.'

The rest remained with the Idumaean encampment, but I sought out the house of the Inspector of Ossaeans.

My cousins no longer lived there. They had sold their prop-erty and left Jerusalem. The brother, Yitzhak, remained in the city, the Inspector said, and he told me where he was abiding. He pointed me to some houses of other brethren, but made no signs of planning to seek hospitality on my behalf. At one point he muttered, 'Hospitality is difficult these days.'

I was happy to find Yitzhak. His mother and Shulamith had joined their brethren across the Jordan in Pella, escaping the coming conflict. Many of their Jerusalem brethren had emigrated further afield to Alexandria.

Yitzhak's father having gone to those who sleep, his duties as head of family were impressed upon him, but he had refused—something unheard of for a Jew, and remained in Jerusalem for the fight.

So were the divisions in the world causing ruptures within families. Every city in Palestine and every household was divided into two camps, those with the revolt, and those against. In every household in Judaea there was at least one who had joined one of the militias.

Yitzhak had married, and lived with his young wife and her widowed mother in the Ossaean Quarter near the theatre. Bruriah was a Zealot girl through and through, and I was glad to meet her. Her mother Mara welcomed me to lodge with them.

Yitzhak said that he had been a Zealot two years hence when he'd accompanied me at the healing; the letters were stitched into his cuff even then. He had not wanted to speak of it at the time, suspecting that my Pharisee parentage would not incline my sympathies toward rebellion. A tendency toward capitulation was normal in the Diaspora. 'That's where Agrippa gets a lot of his men,' Yitzhak told me.

I wished to see my old patient again, especially after he had sent me the mission of the Copper Scroll. We went together to the household of Avichai, taking care to call when the market boy Menelaus said the master would be absent.

Menelaus led us down the hall. 'You can wait in here. It's quite safe. Master's away in Qesarya, and Athanasios' services are not required.'

He had what virtually no slave had–freedom at night. His services could be required for business in the morning, and he could be called on at dinner for interpretation when there were Greek guests, but when there was no banquet, he had no duties. The merchant preferred to travel alone, with only a manservant. Athanasios was only needed for business in Jerusalem or when trips were made to Greek speaking cities. In the meantime, he copied books to earn his master money which would eventually, the promise was, buy his freedom.

So, I saw my patient again, this time, no trace of the pain on his face that I remembered from before. The old scar on his face was matched by the more vicious ones on his back which I had treated. They were all healed now, and the collar of his tunic rested across them comfortably.

All this killing seemed to agree with him. The colour of health was on his face. Not a handsome face, granted, but sober, honest, a face you could trust. This was a man who almost never smiled. Nevertheless, I could tell he was pleased to see me.

'It looks as if we will be fighting a war after all.'

I noted how he said *we*.

Yitzhak commented, 'If we can stop fighting each other long enough.'

Menelaus moaned, 'After this, they'll send the legions.'

'Sure, but the Idumaeans have changed everything,' Yitzhak

said, nodding in my direction. 'We're unstoppable now.' He clapped Athanasios on the back jovially, and I could see that in my absence their friendship had grown.

As well as the factionalism in Jerusalem, civil war and banditry throughout Judaea was swelling the rebel ranks, they told us. Countryside militias crept into the city, grouping either under Yochanan of Gush Chalav, the Sicarii or Eleazar.

I told them, 'Our commanders set all the prisoners free, 2000 of them, and they immediately ran off to join Bar Giora in the countryside. It's looking as if we'll have plenty of garrisons, but too many princes.'

Athanasios looked at me; I could see he agreed with my interpretation, 'too many princes fighting for themselves and not for the people,' he said.

When no one else was within earshot, I thanked him for sending us the Copper Scroll. I blushed a bit behind my veil when I said the words, remembering what he had said about me being *an angel*. I called him 'Tasios'.

I said, 'Again, you do a great service to my people.'

'It was one thing I could do,' he said, 'and you have already repaid me.'

Quickly, too quickly, he returned to Yitzhak's side.

There was great pressure to side with one militia or another. Three years before, or even one maybe, I would have been searching the registries myself for the heir of David or Judas the Galilean. Now I looked for a commander. As Uzziel said, someone who would win.

I would have sought out my fellow sectarian Yochanan the Ossaean. He and his brethren had fought bravely in Galilee and Askelon, someone told me. I see the revolution has dragged even peaceful Ossaeans into war, I thought. But he had no following in Jerusalem.

Then there was the question of what to do with my copy of the Copper Scroll. Who in Jerusalem should guard the key to our buried treasure? Should I entrust it to Yochanan? Or Eleazar? Or the Idumaean commanders? I remembered my promise to the Sicarii: 'when Jerusalem is free'. We were not free, yet. In the end, I kept it with my Chaldee transcription in the tefillin the goldsmith crafted for me, which I hid at my lodgings.

Despite the chaos, it was exciting to be in revolutionary Jerusalem right at the apex of the struggle. It lifted me from my fear of the demon. Perhaps the Feeling Self hoodwinked me into a selfish adventurism? Too much was happening me for to remain under his spell for long, and I was well supported by those around me.

Yitzhak's perpetual energy was contagious—he could ever make me laugh. I warmed with a new friendship with Bruriah, and her mother Mara gave me much maternal comfort in a city of warring men.

The hope of the Many lay outside the city; that was certain. Civil war in Rome could only delay the conquerors for so long. Most looked to the Nations; we needed to rally the garrisons from the Diaspora—deepening. Mara counseled us against this hope.

# Chapter 22
## Sons and Daughters of Belial

It was a quiet moment one morning in the widow's small room when I came upon Mara readying herself for a trip to the well, and she was taking out her cosmetics box. A woman always wants to look her best at the well.

'Shall I comb your hair, Mother?' I offered.

'Yes, thank you, dear.' She took the box onto her knees and removed the toggle to open the lid. I admired the box, a fish carved in ivory, with two sheaves of river reeds at each side. One functioned as a hinge, the other as a toggle, with an ivory dowel behind it to fasten the lid.

'This is the treasure of a princess,' I marveled.

'Indeed,' she replied. 'My sister gave it to me, and she was given it by the princess Shulamith, daughter of the tetrarch. My sister was one of her handmaidens.' Shulamith was now queen of Chalcis and Armenia.

She handed me the comb, and I fixed her hair while she applied to her face perfumed unguent from a glass vial. It was pigmented with some whitish substance, and left her cheeks looking ghostly, I thought.

'You are lovely enough without all that stuff,' I said.

'No, no, girl, I couldn't go out without my face on,' she insisted.

From inside the box she pulled out a small stone bowl and an ivory spoon with a carved palm leaf on one side of its handle and on the other a woman's head flanked by doves—the ancient

344

goddess. Taking the spoon, she dipped from other small bowls kohl and oil and mixed them in the stone bowl.

'Have you yourself met any one of the royal family?' I asked.

'No, and I would never want to,' she said. 'A traitorous, idolatrous lot they are.'

'Your sister, has she told you tales?' I angled for gossip.

'Many. What you might find surprising,' she said, 'is that the women are every bit as disgusting as the men.'

She told me about the Herodian women, while she applied the kohl around her eyes with a small ivory wand.

'Princess Shulamith was the daughter of Herodias and Herod Philip.'

Herod Philip, the son of Herod Magnus by Mariamne, the daughter of the High Priest Boethus, was tetrarch of Galilee and Peraea. Herodias was daughter of Aristobulus son of Herod and the Hasmonean princess Mariamne.

'After he killed her father and his brother, her grandfather Herod married Herodias to Herod Philip. His brother Herod Antipas, son of Herod Magnus by Malthace, was married to Phasaelis the daughter of King Aretas, but desired to marry Herodias.'

I'd heard this tale from Abda. The 'niece marriage' had been opposed by the Baptist, and the whole issue had provoked a war with the Nabatu.

'She divorced him of her own accord, without permission or sanction, while he lived, to marry her uncle,' I said. 'She brought two nations to war.'

'Child, you don't know the half of it,' said Mara. 'These women poison their husbands, telling them it's a love potion, in order to lie with the husbands of others. They don't care if

345

they're circumcised or righteous as long as they are rich and wear crowns. They don't care if they eat pork or meat sacrificed to idols as long as they are served on gold plates.'

'Well, they're all scuttling back to their friends in Rome now, aren't they?' I said. Soon we would be rid of all the Sons and Daughters of Darkness. 'Herodias ended her days in Gaul, didn't she? Exiled for her treachery.'

Now exiled from Jerusalem, Herod's riches were now in the hands of the Ebionim. Simon still had vast stores of booty from Beth-horon in hand, but he didn't control the food. The distribution of provisions was ruled by the widow Joanna.

She had the wealth of three patrons behind her. Ben Kalba Sabbua, Ben Tzitzit Hakeseth and Nakdimon ben Guryon, three rich disciples of Yochanan ben Zakkai, had promised her grain, wine and oil enough to feed the city for up to seven years and wood for cooking fires.

Ben Guryon—for whose sake the sun continued shining— was a benefactor of the Ebionim, and Joanna told me, 'It was Nakdimon who buried our Lord,' she said.

Joanna also had the political clout of the house of Hillel and the strong arms of the men of Simon the Patriarch, the son of Gamaliel the Elder. Outwardly, her authority was challenged by no one, and all the workers, we clinic volunteers as well, would have defended her with our lives. The high priests wanted to be seen to be supporting the people, and Gamaliel regularly sent his slave Tavi to check up on the supply lines.

Joanna had taken the organisation of the Ebionim kitchens in hand and broadened the operation into a revolutionary refectory. I was among those who collected the daily provisions for the clinic. This was often on our way back from Noon

Contemplations, as there were always enough of us.

There, food from the communal stores was parceled out by lot according to garrison or residential quarter. The lots were drawn from potsherds inscribed with each person's name, only it was usually our nicknames—'Fat Man', 'Longlegs', that sort of thing. At the clinic, we had our own system of lots; despite my new associations, they inscribed my potsherd 'Sophia the Ossaean'.

In the New Jerusalem, silver drachmas, gold candelabras, rich fabrics meant nothing. Food and armaments were the currency of the people's need. Coins could still purchase anything at the markets, but that would mean dealing with the Romans. These days, conversations with Romans or Greeks who had dealings with Romans, even the suspicion of commerce meant immediate execution.

Joanna gave the Zealots their lot. Indeed, the militias and our clinic received provisions first. But she supplied the townsfolk, the enemies of the Zealots, with equanimity.

To accusations of 'feeding the collaborators', she would retort, 'feeding the people, feeding the children of God'. She and her donors rigidly refused to let the distribution be influenced by sect or faction. 'The gift of God for the people of God,' she said, 'divided by head, not by what is inside the head.'

No amount of gold or silver could buy an extra lot.

Joanna was the widow of Chuza, manager of Herod Antipas' household. She was elderly, much older than me, and we formed a difficult friendship. We both greatly desired female companionship and were associated with each other through our works.

She looked to the Kingdom of God, and she did earnestly

support the people. Nevertheless, at every moment she urged capitulation to the Romans.

Joanna said, 'What are we complaining about? The tribute is not heavy. The harvest has been prosperous lately.'

'Precisely, Mother. The People of the Land believe God is granting us our Day of liberation.'

'So, we show our gratitude by canceling the tribute and electing our own government?'

'Strictly speaking, we have only banned the foreigner from our Temple and cancelled sacrifices to Caesar.'

'Why should we so protest? Alexandria is filled with images of the emperor. The Temple is filled with gifts from foreigners. The gold table for the shewbread was given by Ptolemy Philadelphus when he commissioned the translation of the Law. Would you have them throw that in the streets?'

'It's true, foreign rulers have oft shown reverence for the house of our God,' I said.

'The Romans have always been soft on us,' she continued. 'Pompey didn't any take booty. Jerusalem is the only place in the empire they don't force their religion. The Kittim, as you call them, have been giving us honours, gifts and preferential treatment for centuries.'

I remembered something Abda had said–that Palestine paid tribute to Rome according to an antiquated exchange rate. 'The Romans don't know it, but the Jews are paying the lowest taxes in the Empire,' he told me. But I didn't want to tell Joanna that.

'With one hand they proffer gifts, with the other they smite us to our knees,' I said.

'You do exaggerate, Sophia. This whole thing is all about the tribute, you know. We should have simply paid it. The treasury is rich enough.'

'And sometimes they need not smite us, we fall to our knees of our own.' I sniped.

'By which you accuse me?' she retorted. 'Well, why should we all get dragged into war because one bunch of people wouldn't let another bunch of people have some money?'

'For one thing, it isn't one bunch of people, it's the whole town of Jerusalem and surrounding People of the Land, and we were preceded by the heroes of Galilee and Peraea. It's not just about Florus, Mother Joanna. It's about being on our knees. These kings' meagre crumbs of gifts and preferential treatment blow away in the wind as we stand at the gates of the new Kingdom of God.' It was an analogy I'd heard from Abba Ahissa.

'But you are right, it started with Florus,' I continued. 'He profaned the house of God and tried to crush our desires for liberty. With the attack of Florus, they have forced us. If they would only leave us, we would be no threat.'

'Well, they won't leave us this time. And you can hardly blame them, they're only defending the Empire. Rome is surrounded by enemies.'

'We are not attacking them,' I argued.

'It's all the squabbling of the sects that started this,' she complained. 'Shammaites and Herodians, Boethusians and Gamalielites.'

'The Many are crying out so for righteous leadership, and all we get is men trying to build their own little empires,' I replied.

The consensus of opinion at the refectory was more in line with 'death to the transgressor' than 'love thy neighbour'. But appeasers like Joanna seemed to think there was a third way:

Give them a fright, but then show the mercy they never, with all their lofty civilisation, showed us. Give them back the keys to the gates, but demand our own terms.

They underestimated just how much the Romans hate us.

Whatever the battle portended, we were on the defensive, not on the attack. We could only wait for them to come.

It was at the refectory that I again encountered Athanasios. He, Menelaus and other slaves of the document merchant were sent by their master to assist the cause, and on many days when I arrived, they were working.

Avichai–that mattress-fluffer of the Kittim–was certainly no Zealot, but as a rich person, he was expected to do his bit. Sending a few slaves, for whom he had no use anyway now that there was no commerce, would look good for his reputation. Though sent by their master in hypocrisy, Athanasios and Menelaus were sincere in their works.

Yet Athanasios would have nothing to do with Joanna, and would address her only as a slave would address another slave's master–that is to say, never.

The clinic was not the place for political discussions. We just listened to the preachers while we worked. But there were many impassioned conversations at the refectory. When Joanna wasn't looking, the slaves discussed with us as freely as the militiamen.

My companions were surprised that a non-Jew and a Greek would flock to our battle, particularly after the violence in Qesarya, but Athanasios explained to them what he had before said to us about fighting the same enemy.

'You can hardly expect equality in the world of commerce, Athanasios,' said Menelaus.

'Not if we're expecting it to be given to us,' he replied.

'But equality is not something that's going to happen on Earth,' Menelaus insisted.

One of Joanna's slaves said, 'I think, if I am a good man, I am truly free. Though we may not be equal on earth, we are equal in the sight of God.'

But Athanasios argued, 'Free is not free if it is not on earth.'

Yitzhak backed him up; he often accompanied us. 'God made us equal to begin with. It's the Kittim and the Herodians that corrupt us with their commerce.'

'We were corrupted long before that,' was my belief. 'The legions are only effective where merchants have corrupted the people and created a market for foreign goods.'

'The Greeks,' said Athanasios, 'the noblest of all people on earth, pay six bundles of rods in tribute. Even we are subject to Rome, and the subjugation is more onerous than the tribute.'

'And we are all slaves of Jews who are slaves to Rome,' one said.

Tavi, Gamaliel's slave, had something to say, 'Come, it's better now, isn't it? In the days of the Hasmoneans when they had rivers of captives from wars of subjugation, there wasn't an atrocity imaginable they did not inflict upon us. But now they are quite decent. Selling a slave to fight the beasts is illegal, we're allowed our own *peculium* (property rights) and wages, and we're even allowed to marry.'

Athanasios was silent, but one of the others said, 'That's easy for you to say. You enjoy as much luxury as your master.'

'Rights and payments make little difference to the fundamental injustice of it,' I said. 'I would prefer death to slavery.'

Athanasios turned to me and snapped, 'We who are slaves were not given the choice.'

That comment kept me out of the conversation for a few moments.

'You must be realistic,' said Menelaus. 'The Empire is built on the labour of slaves. Their world wouldn't function without us.'

'Precisely so. Think,' Athanasios proposed, 'if the slaves' labour, rather than feeding the luxury of their masters, were used to transform the poor.'

'It would bring in the Jubilee we were promised by God,' I said.

One of Simon's militiamen, there to requisition his garrison's lot, joined in, 'Liberty for slaves and rewards for the free—it's a good policy.'

'Yes,' I said, 'under that banner, we can rally all the Ebionim.'

Before strangers, Athanasios never spoke unless spoken to, the habit of the slave. Among friends, when he would speak his mind, he tended to contribute a broader perspective than most of us on the topic at hand. When the topic didn't concern him, he was simply silent. One tended to listen more closely when he spoke.

He was surly, but never aggressive. He oft said, 'You must win your hearer not by opposition but by persuasion.' There was a toughness to him that frightened me. He never spoke of his own feelings, he only spoke of larger things, history, wars, Greeks and Jews, human beings in general.

Athanasios' character was so different from Yitzhak's effervescent soul. His inner brooding was brightened by Yitzhak's outward-facing energy. Even physically the two men were entirely dissimilar. Athanasios was tall, thin and wiry, where Yitzhak was shorter than many militiamen, and shaped like a cowbell, his chest and shoulders being muscular and so much larger than the rest of his body.

And yet the bond between the two was ever-growing. Acknowledging Yitzhak's open affection for him seemed to soften the slave's ferocity; he responded with unswerving loyalty to the young Zealot.

There was a discussion during the food allocation. I remember it so vividly after all these years because of Athanasios' part in the discussion. And because I was still regarding him in those days with eyes of wonder.

Someone had again mentioned the surprising presence of a non-Jewish Greek in our midst. Someone else began to praise the Greeks, their antiquity, scholarship, their might in warfare, perhaps in defense of Athanasios.

Before anyone had a chance to begin a lesson in history, a militiaman noted, 'The Greeks made bows of wood from the castle walls of Syracuse, but we have no wood for many *parsa'ot* (10 parsa'ot = an average day's walk). The Greeks have shields of bronze; ours are made from skins. Cestius' war engines from Beth-horon are in our hands, but our men don't know how to use them.'

One of the women began to wail, 'What do we have that can defeat such force?'

These were the answers that we gave:

Yitzhak was defiant. 'We have nothing but our passion to call none master than the Lord.'

I said, '…the knowledge of our divine destiny'.

Bruriah, '…our fearless warriors of God'.

Athanasios, seemingly aware neither that he had been defended nor that he had needed defense, said sternly '…our

353

steadfastness in unity'.

'But how far does that unity go?' said the militiaman, one of Simon's. 'Will the Parthians invade? What about the Gauls, what if they revolt?'

'What if they don't revolt?' I said. 'What if they sell their swords, join the legions?'

Yitzhak argued, 'We need not look to the Nations.'

I said, 'They are not striving for the same thing we are.' I still believed they would come, though.

Yitzhak said, and I think he was the most correct of all, 'We've had three victories, defeating Florus, then the king, then Gallus. Under Ananus, we've had nothing but defeats. With the loss of Galilee, our territory has been reduced by half. What we need now is one big victory.'

Athanasios agreed, 'What we need is another Beth-horon.'

Not a talker was Athanasios, but when he spoke, he almost always turned out to be right. Before this day I had thought about him, 'what a brave man', but today I thought, 'what a good man'. I thought, 'if there were a right thing and a wrong thing to do, this man would always do the right thing.'

I said to Bruriah that night, 'Accommodation is the path of darkness, the Lord showed me in my prayers.' I had not spoken of it thus that day. I had said what I needed to say. I simply expressed it using different words, words we can share. The only word I left out was God. Perhaps there are feelings within us that all people share, yet our souls express differently. Or even, religion may be only one point on which we differ, where we agree on other things.

It was the language of our revolt, religion. We strove for freedom from the foreign oppressor and from the tax collector, but the fire that drove us was the zeal for God. Athanasios shared our aims, yet he did not put God in the middle. He may have done what was required on the special days of the Greeks gods, but he never spoke of them. His world was ruled by what he saw on the Earth, not what he looked for in the sky.

I gave a reading to someone at the refectory one day. It was one of the volunteers, who was visiting her injured husband. A Shammaite, he'd picked an argument with some of Yochanan's men in the wrong part of town.

As we came back to the company the supplicant was visibly consoled and some colour back in her face. I'm sure I didn't reveal any secrets to her, and if God spoke it was mainly by giving me a feeling of love and desire to shoulder a bit of the burden of her grief. I think that's what she needed, just the knowledge—even for just a half hour—that she wasn't alone.

We went back to the tables, and Athanasios looked at me with a look I had never seen before. Partly approval—he was relieved to see his fellow worker comforted—but there was something else. My Feeling Self whispered that suddenly he understood me.

Indeed, there is no man in the world like Athanasios. There were slaves and non-Jews who fought for our cause, but they only united with us in part. They had separate agendas. The slaves only wanted their masters dead and a bit of coin they could call their own. The non-Jews with us tend to be people who, for personal or historical reasons, had cause to hate the Romans. They fought to purge their grudge, not because they had a vision.

What made Athanasios so remarkable was the largeness of his world; this enabled him to ally with us all the way. I think he would have fought with us to the end; his heart so loved the New Jerusalem; he would have burned in the Temple. It was only for love of me that he left the battlefield. But again, the old crone jumps ahead in her tale.

There was always time at the refectory, while we waited for the slaves to load up the donkeys, to catch up on gossip, but in the New Jerusalem the seriousness of the current situation intruded upon our frivolous girlish pleasures.

One day that winter, a friend of the widow's visited the refectory, and we girls whispered in the corner.

'Who is she?' said one of the girls, Ahat, a Babylonian Jew like me. 'Someone rich by the look of her robes and the size of her retinue. I hope she's come to contribute funds.'

Cypros, a princess, we were informed, the wife of Helcias, Herod of Chalcis' master of horse.

'Is she one of the fornicators they won't allow in the Temple?' I asked.

'Ssh, Sophia, keep your voice down,' said Bruriah.

More days than not Bruriah volunteered at the refectory. She said, 'Cypros is blameless herself on that account. Unlike most of her sisters and cousins, she's never been divorced. But her children are apostates. Her son Julius Archelaus married Mariamne the daughter of Agrippa. Her grandson Julius Archelaus Epiphanes wouldn't be circumcised to marry the king's sister Drusilla.'

'Isn't Cypros the sister of Sha'ul and Costobarus?' I said.

'Yes,' said Bruriah. 'Her mother Cypros married her first cousin Antipater the son of Costobarus the Idumaean and Shulamith.'

'How do you know so much about the royal family?' asked

Ahat.

'My mother's sister used to serve Princess Shulamith in her youth. She keeps Mother informed of all the gossip.'

'Herod's sister Shulamith, she's the fornicator, isn't she?' The girls were still giggling, so I kept up the fun.

'All the sects consider her relations a scandal. In Rome, Shulamith fell in love with an Arabian, King Obodas' minister Sylleus, but he refused to be circumcised. She divorced three times and married four. One of them was her own uncle. According to your rules, Ossaean, she is certainly unlawful.'

'It was political, though, wasn't it?'

'Herodian princesses do not marry for love, Sophia,' she continued. 'She divorced Costobarus because he was an ally of Hyrcanus. She had children by him, though. One of her daughters married her stepson by her fourth husband Alexas—he is of the same family as Cypros—and one of them married Herod her own brother.'

I shuddered as I considered the possibility of having to marry my uncle.

'Most of them live in luxury in Rome,' Ahat told me.

'Who?' I asked. There were so many of them. Herod Magnus had ten wives. None of us had even counted how many grandchildren. But Bruriah seemed to know the entire dynasty.

'Aristobulus of Chalcis and his sons Agrippa, Herodion and Aristobulus. They've never set foot in Judaea. The kings of Palestine spend the whole of their days in Rome, living off the wealth of our land and our labour. The king; Archelaus the Ethnarch; Herod Boethus, the son of the High Priest Sireoh's daughter; Herod Antipas the Tetrarch—they were all brought up in Rome. Cypros' granddaughter Berenice who married

Alabarch Demetrius lives with her son Antonius Agrippinus in a luxurious villa at Pompeii. Cypros herself lives in Alexandria.'

'You wouldn't think there would be royals still willing to show their face in the Holy City,' said Ahat.

'The ones who can be bothered with Jerusalem now are hardly friends of the Many,' Bruriah commented.

'So, what's she doing here? Surely it won't be just to visit Joanna,' said another of the girls. 'Maybe the alabarch is sending a donation.'

'Don't count on it. More likely it will be the other way around,' said Bruriah. 'Maybe you should sniff around, Sophia, and try to hear what she's saying to the widow.'

I was slow to move, though. I was enjoying the gossip.

Then Tavi, the slave of Gamaliel, came up, and we hushed. It was not only the people in power who were beginning to reveal themselves. At the clinic, Jairus was steadfast as ever, but at the refectory, we met people of all stripes.

I had realised by then that slaves were more our friends than people like Joanna, but Tavi, due to the exalted position of his master, was high ranking. Some of these slaves had lands and slaves of their own. You were never sure of what was being reported back to the House of Hillel.

As Bruriah had suggested, I became the Cat and purred discreetly next to Cypros to listen in to her conversation with Joanna. I had always suspected that sooner or later the widow would reveal her cloven hooves.

I overheard her telling the princess that her husband Chuza's men 'could still get letters and things to the Romans' if they wanted.

'You're joking,' said Cypros. 'The Zealots have all the roads

358

blocked.'

'Sure, but there are wadis and tunnels. The bedouin know them,' said Joanna.

## Chapter 23
## The myrtle canopy

I had suspected Joanna was a collaborator, despite her noble works for the Ebionim, and now I believed I had proof. I spoke with Athanasios. 'She implied that her husband's clients are planning to sell documents to Vespasian.'

'It's my master they're referring to,' he said. 'His bedouin contacts certainly know the wadis, and he is the only documents seller who hasn't left the city.'

The last time I heard of his master wishing to sell documents, it bade ill for my people. And so, it was again.

I decided to pay a personal visit to Joanna. The executed Ananus ben Yonathan was her kinsman. I should officially offer my condolences. I would go for a girlish chat and very politely speak my mind. Maybe I would learn something.

She had no way of knowing that Athanasios and I were acquainted before meeting at the refectory. And so, she was unaware that I had any knowledge of the document merchant. But she knew of my Zealot sympathies.

I called for her at the gate to Chuza's house, but the gate-keeper said, 'Her Ladyship is no longer in residence. She has moved to the late lord's family in Bezetha,' he said, muttering about 'these End of Times'.

Joanna hadn't told me this. I pondered that she and I were so unfriendly that she would keep her domicile a secret from me.

I didn't ask where the house was. Everyone knew. It had escaped the Roman torches. Bezetha was the richest quarter of Jerusalem, anyway, but the villas of the Herodians were the most impressive of all.

The gatekeeper called Joanna from the back of the villa, and she courteously ushered me into a room with a view of the courtyard full along one side. The courtyard had been cleared of ornamentals in favour of utilitarian fruit trees, and the fountain, fed by aqueducts from the highlands of Hebron, was still spouting.

The tiles beneath the couches were black and white checkered. All along the sides of the room, the wooden panels were painted in gay colours. No images or animals, of course, just stark stripes and geometric shapes, diamonds and ovals in bright red, blue, yellow. Her house was the height of modern fashion and luxury.

She gestured to a couch and clapped for a servant to bring refreshments.

'In my own house, I would serve you myself, but here there are so many servants. The slaves have run off to join Bar Giora, of course, but there are so many others at the gate desperate for work.'

I tried to smile as if to compliment Domina's generosity.

The servant returned, placing fig juice and roasted pistachios before me.

That there were still houses in Jerusalem serving up such luxuries! I ate as many as I could without seeming a glutton.

I was never very good at girlish chatting, so I was soon out with my purpose. 'What is Cypros up to? Are you saying your husband had dealings with the Kittim, Joanna?'

'Not he himself, but people he used to do business with.'

'What kind of business?'

'Not treachery, Sophia,' she grimaced condescendingly. 'Commerce. They're simply selling some documents.'

It took Athanasios less than a day to search Avichai's shelves. He found letters from Chuza's clients and other nobles, offering deals to Vespasian on behalf of the Rich. I looked at the names on the seals, Guryon ben Joseph–a respectable aristocrat, and Niger of Peraea–the hero of Beth-horon!

These men, formerly our heroes, now offered our shining revolution for sale, and for nothing more than to be allowed to keep their own bits of land.

The land is the gift of God to his Chosen People, to be divided equally by lot, not to be parcelled out by emperors. These Rich, when have they ever given us our Jubilee? Now they sell off our land to Greeks, and the Poor of the Jews can no more even beg the gleanings from the fields.

Along with the incriminating letters was a map of the wadi system, indicating for Avichai egress to the Roman camp. For his percentage of the traitors' wealth, all in the name of commerce, he was willing to open the gates to Vespasian and Titus–two pairs of buttocks in one pair of pants.

We should have reported it to Simon, but Athanasios acted too quickly. He brought me with him to confront Avichai directly, in the forecourt of his house, where I was shocked to see him grab his master violently by the throat.

'Again, your treachery betrays you,' he growled.

I held the letters up in evidence. Avichai knew he was a dead man. I was more than arm's distance away, even were he not restrained, and we might have already gone to Simon. The rumour of treachery alone was a sentence of execution. With hard evidence like this the Zealots would probably not even allow burial rites.

He looked at his slave pitifully and said, 'Have I not been good to you?'

Athanasios said, 'You whipped me twice, I need only kill you once.'

Avichai said pathetically, wriggling like a fish in a trap, 'I have that money of yours, from your scribing.'

'Yes,' Athanasios said. 'You have everything that is mine—but no longer.' He pulled out a curved sicarius knife and pierced the man deeply in the throat. Blood gushed all over Athanasios and pooled in the forecourt.

I looked at him, how boldly I looked at him; I did not flinch. I looked at the growing pool of blood, and I looked at him. My veil had fallen from my face during the scuffle, and I did nothing to replace it.

He held out his hands, still dripping with the horror of his act, as if to say, look what I have done. I didn't look at the blood; I clasped his hands in my own, looking into his eyes fearlessly.

He didn't say, 'Sophia, I had to do it.' He didn't say anything. His eyes held mine for what seemed like an eternity. He didn't ask for approval, nor did I need to show it.

The merchant and his lot are not with us; they are nothing but Kittim with a Hebrew name. Athanasios did not do this work in hate, nor in revenge for being forcibly circumcised and whipped, nor in recompense for his enslavement. It was a political act. Avichai and the Rich had attempted to sabotage our revolution for the last time.

The collaborator crumpled against the wall. Breaking away from the gaze that had transfixed us both, I stuffed the letters in the sleeve of Avichai's robe, so everyone would know of his crime, but we kept the map.

'The money?' I said.

'What?' he responded.

'Your money from scribing'.

He shrugged, 'He will have it banked in some Temple vault, with a row of bureaucrats in front of it. He'd no intention of ever giving it to me. I didn't do this for money.'

'I know that.' As I looked at him, I thought of the treachery of Chuza's rich friends trying to sell off our Kingdom for their bits of land, the corrupt rule of the Sons of Ananus and the high priests, they who had closed the gates against us.

I remembered, *over a pool of blood.*

I said a prayer to the Angel of Love, 'Descend upon my Feeling Self and purify my feelings.' If there was a question there, the Angel had answered yes.

I pulled Athanasios' blood-soaked sleeve into a side room.

'You're cold,' I said, and moved to put my shawl around him, but instead he drew me to him. He held me solidly as a rock against his chest for a very, very long time, and my whole body melted into him, slipping in the blood on his garments.

The smell of his body masked the stench of Avichai's blood. The heat of him filled every part of me and radiated outward until it filled half the room. Called forth by the fire of my own love, the warmth filled my soul and shone forth into the shadows of the alley.

At that moment everything changed for me, that such magic could be generated. A virgin bride of God, yet God sends me these feelings.

Twice before had I felt the heat of a man's body upon my

shoulder. Before, that heat was a sword reaching to stab at my soul. This was the fire of the sun, the fire that heals.

Yet from him, I still felt no coming forth. He still looked for no approval for the deed. He didn't need me for anything. He did not kiss me. I knew that he felt my desire, and I felt ashamed. His actions seemed to promise something that he did not want to give.

I should have beseeched God to heal him from the horror of murder and to forgive us both for rejoicing. But all I could think of was the heat of his body. My hands rested on his shoulders and felt the radiating warmth. The very colour of his skin seemed to generate heat.

I stared transfixed at his skin, the patch between the neck and shoulder blade, just above the beginning of his scars. A natural bronze, untouched by the sun, just that patch, such beautiful smooth skin—and the rest a tangled mess of discoloured welts. The tortured suffering betold in those snarled lines reflected on the smooth patch, and it shone ever more beautiful to my eye. The beautiful patch generated a heat of its own, several fires higher due to the sanctified light. I touched it with my finger, sticky with blood, and the heat moved up through me, the roots of my hair tingled with fire.

We broke away without a word, but I knew that I had been blessed.

We threw our bloodied cloths into the alley. These days they would hardly earn a remark. And we washed our hands in the fountain, turning the water pink.

I passed the day boiling herbs and tending wounds, trying to behave as normal. But all day long, I felt the heat. My hands healed well that day; I think it was from the sanctified light.

But my wits were nowhere to be found. The physics and helpers asked me questions, and I responded idiotically. Patients called for me, and I did not hear them.

Anna arrived at the clinic gate. I was not yet ready to tell her about my new love.

'There have been more executions, Sophia—Guryon ben Joseph and Niger of Peraea. They found one of the conspirators murdered, with letters on him.'

'What letters? What was the crime?' I had to pretend ignorance.

'Collaborating with the Romans. They offered to open the gates if Vespasian let them keep their land.'

'Traitors!' I cried. 'Niger the Peraean, who would have thought he'd betray us?'

As he died, Anna said, Niger cursed them, 'the vengeance of Rome be upon you, famine and pestilence. You will be slaughtered by the citizens among you.'

In the end, though we feared it, the murderer of Avichai was never sought for. From this point on, most murders and other crimes in the city went unpunished. The government could no longer protect the rights of the citizens.

A relative of a patient came begging for our prayers. Yet I believe that I received more guidance from those prayers than my supplicant, although she parted with a smile.

There in the sanctuary of the household where our clinic was accommodated, I sang for her a sacred song—there was something in it about a wall—and as I closed my eyes, I saw an image. Here is the record I transcribed:

The queen and the prince reaching hands out to one

another across a wall, which had been breached from the prince's side. But was the prince reaching after all? I couldn't see his hand anymore. His face was turned away. I became the queen, and I saw myself hold her hand out ever firmer, turning it over in offering.

I told my supplicant that she must care for her loved one diligently, as he was not caring for himself. However, you may understand, Sisters, that I took this to be a sign for myself as well.

In gratitude, she gave me a chicken. The chicken was a great gift, but the clinic was well supplied. I asked permission and received it to take the gift to the supply lines. I would give the chicken to Athanasios for the militiamen.

But I didn't find him at the main refectory. I should not have been surprised. Of course, he would not be able to show his face after what had happened. Menelaus was not there, either. In fact, Athanasios had endangered all the slaves of Avichai; normally, according to Roman law, all would be executed for his crime.

A maiden was in no danger of violation in territories under Simon's jurisdiction. He strictly forbade the dishonouring of womenfolk. However, the possession of food made me a target for marauding militiamen.

I became frightened for Athanasios' safety. I tried deep breathing to calm my fears for my beloved and called upon my shapeshifting skills to sneak around the Lower City in the fading light.

Someone told me there was an abandoned residence in the western sector where runaway slaves lodged, and that is where

I found him. Also there were Menelaus and several people I did not know, mostly men but a few women.

They started at my arrival, but when Athanasios did not jump, they relaxed.

I handed the chicken to him as if it were the price of my admission to the company. The others, excited by the acquisition of food, went into another room to prepare it and heeded not our conversation.

'You do not condemn me?' he said. Finally, he asked my approval.

'Simon's men would have done worse.' There was no need to say more. We both knew the danger collaborators like Avichai posed for the city. He looked at me like he had in Avichai's forecourt, and I realised how seldom he had ever done so before. His deep brown eyes looked soft beneath the sharp, straight eyebrows and that long early scar. I felt the sanctified heat again in my cheeks and hair. I had to say something; I was burning up.

'You're free now; now everything is different.'

'Sophia, you fight by my side, but now that...everything is different, you wish for more.' Then he turned away and spoke to the darkness in the room behind him, 'This tortured heart would not be enough for you. I've never thought that I could love a woman, and I do not know that I can now.'

It was just like my vision. I reached out and touched his shoulder. I couldn't believe my audacity. Unfortunately, neither could he. He jerked away, and the rejection was an agony as if a spear had pierced me. What had I done? Just because I felt the heat and I knew I'd been blessed didn't mean he felt the same.

Just then—oh, the bad timing—we heard a banging and

crashing some rooms away, and we had to leap into action. Perhaps it was some of Yochanan's men, and they'd found us out. They'd get the chicken, and maybe kill us for it as well. Someone wrapped it in a palm leaf and tucked it under their robe and we joined up with some of the others, hurriedly gathering up supplies and making our escape out the back way.

The whole time it seemed, although in reality it was only the very end of the afternoon, Athanasios was sharp with me. He whispered directions, telling me to do things I had already done. Adonai, forgive me, but I did think—What, is the slave giving me orders? I felt that it was only me to whom he was speaking in this manner, although everyone was frightened and speaking harshly. I didn't say a word all evening.

I couldn't tell whether he was angry at me, or just frightened by the situation. But why be frightened? Our escape was perfectly orderly. We didn't leave anything behind, and we still had the chicken. I could not see what he was upset about.

Surely, he was angry at me for revealing my feelings in such an unmaidenly way. I felt ever more ashamed. Yet why should I be ashamed? I had revealed my feelings, and he might now speak his mind to me. I wished not to force anything upon him, only to let him know of my offering. I had asked the question, now I awaited the answer.

As soon as we established a new refuge, in the confusion of getting settled and the excitement of cooking the chicken, which we had to heat in coals underground to avoid making a fire and attracting Yochanan's men, he gave me his answer. Athanasios pulled me into a corridor. My heart beat in my throat. I was without speech.

'Sophia, I'm glad that you approached me. But you must

be clear. What do you want? A slave makes a bad husband, you know.'

I remembered my first conversation with Abba Ahissa, when also those little words 'you know' had reassured me.

'You are no longer a slave, Tasios. You are master of your own destiny. This is the New Jerusalem.'

'All my life I have been a slave. My parents were slaves as well. I don't know how not to be a slave. A slave is not permitted…' His face showed an expression I had not before seen him bear, conflicted; he averted my gaze. '…such feelings. For they cannot have expression. Knowing of your vows…to your… god… I'm also afraid that you do not want a man's love.'

Was that his concern? I could find words for that. 'Whatever you can give me is exactly what I want.'

How joyful have I been to be a Nazirite virgin, yet how joyful would I now be to break that vow. She who was once a bride of the Lord was now a bride of the Revolution.

Then, O, thank you, Adonai. He pulled me into a backroom and kissed me.

A girl's first love bed is a joy that comes only once. You will forgive me if I reveal openly what were my thoughts in this newly awakened state. Virgins among you, I do not apologise, for one day you will know my happiness.

Thoughts of love filled me with certainty of the sanctity of my action, like the torrent of a spring rain washing away any hesitancy. This love which had been ordained by the stars and was the very consequence of the New Jerusalem, I opened to Athanasios's arms like a flower to the day.

As we knew each other and he comforted me through the pain, we whispered into the night. He was very gentle. I found myself able to tell him the tale of my uncle before morning. I joked about how I might burst into prophecy at his merest touch, and we laughed–it was the first time I had ever seen him smile–and he touched me some more. In our lovers' bed, my soul was healed, and I was able to feel safe near a man.

I had feared that I was to commit an offense by lying with an uncircumcised man, though to be honest, thoughts of love more than drowned out any doubts. But I discovered to my surprise that Athanasios was circumcised.

'He made me a Jew, but he could not make me a eunuch,' he said.

It was the messier cut of those circumcised in adulthood–I hope I do not offend you virgins–messier even than is usual, so I understand, because the proselyte struggled. Avichai had been heard to boast, 'all in my household are Jews', but that is not how Athanasios told it.

'He whipped me, but still I refused.'

'The old scar?' I asked, and this time unabashedly, lovingly stoked the scar on his face.

'You may be called upon to serve at table'–were the words his master had said–'and I'll not have my guests served by an uncircumcised barbarian.'

'He thinks God can be delivered at the point of a knife,' said Athanasios, 'and Master called ME the barbarian.'

In the gentle, fresh intimacy of our first night, he spoke to me with great emotion about it. Never again would he mention the incident in my presence.

How lovely it was to wake in the morning to see his face next to mine on the straw. Though not a beautiful face, it was one I had come to respect. Oh, how beautiful it looked to me that morning. In sleep, his face looked so broken. Yet I was accustomed to seeing only his integrity. Where was that secret pride with which I was so familiar?

His face showed none of the Athanasios I knew. Then I reflected that I'd never before seen him with his eyes closed. All his pride was contained in those deep brown eyes, concealed then to me on the straw behind black eyelashes beneath the old scar. I had seen Athanasios' soul through his eyes and experienced love from them first with that long glance the previous night. As he slept, I looked at his face and body with love.

He lay face down, still asleep, his scarred back facing upward into the cool morning air. My eyes surveyed him in my love, from the beautiful patch of skin above his shoulder blade over his scars and down to his legs.

There he lay, broken and spent, blood sticking to his thigh, dry and caked now but fresh enough last night to have picked up smudges of dirt and bits of straw. Next to it, on my thigh, the fresher blood of deflowerment. From maiden to wife in a day and a night; my head spun—this day that had brought us together, from the blood and horror of murder to the rapture of a lover's arms. I hoped that he was healed; I was.

I know there are those among you, perhaps Christian sisters in your hermitage who have chosen the Nazirite way. That is your calling. In Jerusalem, I knew that my calling was to Athanasios. All the important events in my life had led me to him. The Yachad, the spilled ink, the Copper Scroll in the desert, the chicken. That, my dears, is the love of the young, and you only have it once. The overwhelming feeling that this and no other is my destiny; this is my mate, and I will no longer be alone.

During the day, I was all aglow. Changed was I, now made a woman. No longer did I walk on the earth alone with only God at my ear. Now my betrothed was by my side.

The scent of our union was all over me, under my robe, between my legs, in my hair. And it stayed on me until the evening's bathing. Surely everyone would know. I felt as if my very skin told the world, here is one who has known a man. I was so active that day, running here, running there, as if I wanted the whole camp to witness my new womanhood.

I don't know if they saw, but Athanasios certainly seemed not to. I encountered him three times during the course of the day. He seemed unchanged, and his behavior toward me was no different to that which had gone between us before.

By the third meeting, I had become so disturbed by this that I asked him, 'Is something wrong?' When he started recounting some argument he'd had with one of the Greeks during a provisions search, I was dismayed.

How painful it is to be a woman. With the smell of him still wafting up to my nostrils from under my robe, I had happily thought of nothing else all day long, but his mind was fully occupied by the daily tasks.

'No, Tasios, I mean between us.'

He snapped back, as if angry at me for distracting him from the important business of the supply lines, 'Nothing is wrong between us. Why do you think so?'

I actually had to say it, 'I don't know if you wish me to come to you tonight.'

His face remained hard and dark, portraying nothing, but when he looked at me with his deep brown eyes, I saw into his soul for some moments as he said, 'I do wish it.'

This was as it was in our household, Sisters. During the day, I was his comrade like any other, and he barely acknowledged me, certainly never revealing our intimacy. It was as if during the day we reverted to our former relationship of Greek slave and freeborn Jew. At night, I was his lover, and he held me body and soul. He did not invite me to his bed, but I went and was received. I became accustomed to this.

On the way into the refectory for the food allocation Bruriah hooked elbows with me possessively, 'We haven't seen you at home these evenings. And yet a little pigeon tells me it's a reason for celebration?'

She raised her eyebrow in the direction of Athanasios, who was further along, queuing as inconspicuously as possible with the other runaways. There was no separate queue for slaves in Joanna's kitchens. Freeborn and slave, Greek and Jew, all received the same plate of food under the banner of the Ebionim.

I felt the colour rise to my face in a flash of mixed emotions—the flattering one of a girl whose new love has been revealed and a fear for Athanasios being exposed and a shame as to what he might or might not have said about me.

'Which pigeon...?' I ventured.

'Yitzhak might have had a word,' she said. 'He's overjoyed, you know. As far as he's concerned, you couldn't have chosen better if you'd picked the prince himself.'

At that point Yitzhak marched up to join us with his squadron of Tens, and he overheard our last exchange.

'Yitzhak?' I said, wondering how he knew. I was certain that Athanasios had not told him.

'I've been watching your eyes and his eyes for a while now,' he said, 'wondering if I needed to do any encouraging. You've been dancing around each other like courting swans.'

As it happened, Athanasios had happily confessed to his friend the murder of Avichai, in full bloody detail, but as for the bedding of his cousin—not a word.

We girls are so transparent with our feelings, are we not, Sisters? But who can understand the discourse of men? Then, of course, with Athanasios, it was two or three times more so.

So it was that throughout the war, I spent my days tending the clinic and my nights in my lover's bed in the company of the runaway slaves. I was happy, but I pressed Athanasios to marriage.

'Under which law would we marry?' he said. 'Is it *confarreatio*? Is it *contubernium*? You, a freewoman, I would be freed, but where is my master to give his approval?'

'That's Roman stuff, Tasios,' I said. 'That's not our law.'

'According to your law, I am a foreigner as well as a slave.'

'My love,' I said, 'it is the Kittim who make those rules. This is the New Jerusalem. The People make the laws, not the priests and kings.'

The old law forbids marriage with Greeks or Phoenicians—but with Athanasios I thought not of it, and the priest, if he thought it, didn't mention it. There were many of the junior priests among us, and they were as willing as I, with apocalypse at our gates, to overlook such conventions.

We broke bread in the company of friends and those who wished us well—Yitzhak, Bruriah and Mara came, and Anna and Uzziel. I had a half-broken roof for a bridal canopy. Someone managed to deck the beams with myrtle branches.

Yitzhak spoke the words as Athanasios would not. 'O Sister!

375

May you grow into thousands of myriads.' Our comrades performed the ceremony, and we were wed in the battle-torn quarters squatted by the runaway slaves, with all the chaos of the new world around us. No *ketubah* (marriage contract) signed we. We married according to the law of the New Jerusalem, with love in our hearts and freedom in our dreams.

During the war the rabbis had forbidden bridegrooms to wear crowns, but I laughed to think that Athanasios would have considered doing so. Though he would not convert to our faith, he did not mind sitting the Jewish rite for my sake.

'Religion is the realm of the woman,' he said. I felt ashamed to hear my beliefs explained thusly, and ashamed again to be belittled as a woman, but I was pleased that he provided for me to be wed in the sight of God. He even allowed me to place a *tallit* (prayer shawl) across his shoulders.

O, the romance of those days, the days filled with agony of waiting, but the nights filled with love. Physics and volunteers would note my silly mood towards the beginning of an evening. The expectation of a man's arms to hold me at night, the very expression of life, helped me endure the chaos around me.

However certain I had once been that celibacy was the path to spiritual purity, now it seemed instead that marriage was the spice in life's stew. My husband's love gave me physical vigor. I lifted patients and put on muscles. I felt the gift of God, my humanity, in every pore; every part of me danced in His glory.

It was not always lovely. Athanasios' grim moods and quick anger grated. I was wont to take as personal affront something he had not intended as such, and cried many tears over a comment thrown away in a brief fit of selfish gruffness. But I awoke in the morning refreshed and forgiving.

I came to understand what Athanasios had meant that night when he spoke of his fears of not being able to love a woman. Now that he is gone, I may write it. He was tortured by the idea that he could not return my love. It also agonised me. But what he gave me was enough. I knew what he had suffered.

I knew that until a few hours before he became my betrothed, he had lived his life behind the mind of a slave. His pride as a man with a woman was tortured by the perception of our difference. From time to time, God forgive me if I complain of it, he spoke cruel words to me. My respect for him led me to forgive, but often he made me feel ashamed to be a woman.

These, I believe, are the words you virgins should be shielded from, yet I still tell them to you. You will have your own lessons to learn. Despite my love for him, I often needed to be away from him in order to be myself.

I stepped into new waters at every moment. Learning to be a wife and to be with a man was a skill new to me, and I had no tutor. Bruriah and Yitzhak were such a perfect match, her experience was too unlike mine. My lessons were trials and mistakes, and the mistakes hurt. I often remembered my old thought that I was not good with men. I think Athanasios, too, was not good with women.

There was a part of him that would never soften. The inner pride I so respected kept his soul locked inside him, and he never gave that away, even to me. Still, there is no one by whose side I would rather have been. I fought the war in Jerusalem by his side, and I have fought the war of life holding his hand.

Sisters, does it look like this inside each of our hearts? Perfection is of God; it is not to be had on this earth. Look to yourselves to strive toward the perfection of grace, but look upon your husband's imperfections with love and tolerance. In this way, your love will grow along with your love of God.

I ceased to practice magic during this period. I either lost my touch, or perhaps I was simply too busy with the war and my nights with Athanasios to bother with what he called 'mumbo jumbo'.

Once I would have said my magical power resided in my chastity—I had certainly believed that during my training with the Yachad—and that opening my heart to Athanasios had necessitated the sacrifice of that gift. But I am rather embarrassed by the thought now. Magic was simply not a part of my life. My life was fighting the war and being a woman in love.

At the clinic I still used the knowledge of herbs and gave readings and prayers, to Athanasios' disapproval. On war matters, though, I found military strategy a better teacher. Looking at what was in front of us—arms, food, water—that was a more urgent task.

Athanasios' absence was noticed at the refectory, and Joanna quizzed me, 'We haven't seen your friend the Greek slave recently.'

I looked around nonchalantly. Only my distrust of the collaborators kept the colour from my face as I pretended disinterest in my beloved. 'Oh, haven't you heard from the master?'

'We've received nothing.'

'Perhaps he's gone away on business?'

'What, now? With Zealots guarding every crossroad?'

I said, 'Well, I haven't received any messages either.' I almost said, 'Your husband, Joanna, he was the one with the contacts.'

That evening, I happily regarded the crew around me in the domicile we'd carved out of the wreckage of the city. Only in the New Jerusalem could slaves be free like this. Before, where could they run to? Who would feed them?

Under Joanna's equitable distribution—slaves, citizens, priests—they all received the same rations. Table fellowship freed them from the chains of the household. As for Athanasios, if order were restored in Jerusalem, whether under the Sanhedrin or under Titus, he would be punished for his crime. Only a new world where slavery didn't exist could save him.

And if the slave's world were turned upside down, everything would be upside down. Commerce would turn to table fellowship; war would turn to peace; inequality would turn to justice; sin would turn to righteousness.

We would fight for it together, and we would save each other. I would rather die than be a slave to Rome, but I would rather save my life than die needlessly. Now I had something to live for—my love with Athanasios, a pearl of beauty in all the ugliness.

# Chapter 24
## Prophecies and secrets

I was still aglow with new love when one evening Shulamith, returned from Pella, appeared at our doorstep. We had so much to talk about, everything that had happened in Jerusalem since Florus, but instead, she dragged me outside. It was getting dark and no time to be in the street.

'Come, Sophia,' Shulamith said, 'you must see this.' I was frightened by her urgency. Bruriah and I gathered some within the neighbouring households, and Shulamith led us up the city walls.

People were gathering as the stars appeared. Here and there were lamps and candles which they tried to shine toward the speaker. Simon's men had closed the gates for the night, but they were letting some people in, respecting them as supplicants.

'He prophesies at night,' she said.

'This is another full moon prophet, Shulamith, Yeshua ben Ananias. He's been up here every night for years,' I complained.

'Yes, every night since the killing of the Just One,' Shulamith said.

'He's taller than I expected,' I said.

'Yes, he's not even standing on a stone. See how his head rises above the crowd?'

'I also see his dirty robe and unkempt beard. Probably hasn't changed or shaved since the killing of the Just One.'

There was a hush in the gathering, as I whispered to Shulamith, 'I thought you shunned these Asian heretics.'

'He is no heretic. Listen.'

And the prophet began:

> A voice from the east, a voice from the west, a voice
> from the four winds, a voice against Jerusalem and the
> holy house, a voice against the bridegrooms and the
> brides, and a voice against this whole people.
>
> Woe, woe, is Jerusalem. Leave Jerusalem, for she
> gives a cup of bitterness to the Sons of Light.
>
> When ye shall see the Abomination of Desolation
> stand where he ought not, flee into the mountains. For
> the days shall come upon thee, that thine enemies shall
> cast a rampart about thee, and compass thee round,
> and keep thee in on every side, and shall lay thee and
> thy children even with the ground. And they shall fall
> by the edge of the sword, and shall be led away captive
> into all nations.

It was late when we reached our bedrolls. I was too moved to
pray, although I was more used to these prophets than was
Shulamith. Thanks to the encouragement of Abba Jairus, we
heard at least one or two a day. Not only did we entertain every
passing Shammaite who felt like making a fiery speech, but
people from every sect and every political persuasion came to
pay comfort to the wounded. I knew that prophets could not
foretell the future, but if they purported to do so, I thought,
their words should be of victory, to give heart to the Many.

On the morrow, I heard from Shulamith the reasons for
her urgency.

'We received a letter of warning from Antioch,' she said. 'The

Kings of the Nations are gathering against us.'

'Of course, they are gathering,' I said. 'What would you do in their place? The throne lies empty, and the royal genealogies have been burnt.'

She insisted, 'Bandits are swarming to get their hands on the Kingdom of God; and our forces will not hold it.'

'You are wrong. The militias swell with pilgrims and People of the Land. We can call upon the Kanaim again, and we can surely expect support from Babylonia, maybe Alexandria.'

'We also received a warning from Mattathias of the House of Ananus. The followers of the Just Ones are in danger again.'

'Cousin, that is the case for us all. I can barely get to Noon Contemplations without worrying whether I'm crossing Yochanan's or Simon's quarter. Stick with the Ebionim and you'll be as safe as anyone else.'

'No, Sophia, Jerusalem is doomed. You heard the prophet Yeshua.'

'The man has a demon, Shulamith. I felt it on him. His words are potent, but they're not true; it is only your fear that leads you to heed them.'

'My brethren are leaving the city, joining us with our proselytes across the Jordan.'

The Gentile proselytes, along with the seven deacons, the benefactors of Ebionim during the famine of Claudius, had been caught up in the persecution of the Shammaites. That was Shulamith's community in Pella, a city in Peraea, well away from the madness of Jerusalem and off the road from invading armies.

I argued vehemently, 'You've just come back, Shulamith, and at the best of times. How can you run away again from our destiny and our liberation? How can we fear anything when Heaven is at our fingertips? You want to leave the field just when we have victory within our reach. I never took you Notzrim for cowards.' I said cruel words, perhaps, but I was tired of losing friends. All the heartbreak of parting with Shu'dat welled in my throat.

I conceded. 'So, you've come back to escort them?'

'Well, partly. But the main reason I joined the delegation myself was to see you, Sophia. There's no point in asking Yitzhak—he's determined to die—and Bruriah will naturally stay with him, but I was hoping to convince you. Join us in Pella. The New Jerusalem is not a matter of geography; it is what we create in our hearts. We have Godfearers among us, and non-believers.'

I bristled at her including me among 'Godfearers and non-believers'. Perhaps she was taking revenge for my implying the Notzrim were cowards. Thinking about it afterwards, though, I do not think she intended it that way. She sincerely wanted to save me.

She agreed to volunteer with me at the clinic while she was in the city, and as we made our way there in the morning, we continued our argument.

'Our Lord said—Watch, for you do not know what day He will come.'

'So, do they all say, Shulamith. If he is needed here today, he should come. Or else he leaves us weakened.'

'That is in God's hands, not ours.'

'Yes, of course, but the kingdom of God is on our doorstep. If your Just One is the Messiah, he should come now. If he were here now delivering us, then we would know he is the one.'

'Well, it hasn't come yet. You don't see the resurrection of the dead, do you?'

'It will come when we make it come.'

'You're wrong. Sophia. Everything has gone wrong. The proselytes banned by the Shammaite edicts, it's an outrage. They are devout, like you and me. They observe all the laws, circumcision and everything.'

'I cannot attest to their devotion, cousin. But I agree with you that it is an outrage. The Shammaites want to exclude the Sons of Darkness. There's no need to ban Gentile Godfearers, earnest supporters of the Ebionim.'

'And now they and the Zealots are whipping up a war with Rome.'

There is one place on the journey from our lodgings to the clinic which goes through some territory usually claimed by Yochanan of Gush Halav's men, and at this point we crossed paths with a clump of Galileans, one of whom, seemingly having overheard Shulamith's last statement, chimed in with, 'War with Rome has been coming for long time, Sister. Better get your prissy little head round it.'

She turned up her nose at him, and I didn't want any arguments, but what I said to her next I could easily have said to the Galilean.

'These swords we should be turning on the Kittim, we are turning on each other–Jews and Greeks, Greeks and Jews. We give the Romans an easy target. If they weren't so vengeful for the reputation of their empire, they could simply enjoy their circuses and gymnasia while we destroy each other. Shulamith, we need you in Jerusalem to help us unify our new Kingdom. We need your voice and we'll need your arms.'

'No, Sophia. The final fight will not be here.'

'Where, then?'

'Pella, perhaps? The Saints say it may be Cyrene.'

'If the Cyrenians are ready, let them come to our aid now,' I said.

'No, we must await the revelation of the Day.'

'The Day is delayed and delayed. It will not come just from the waiting for it.'

'You have your prophets, and I have mine,' she said. 'You will see that the son of Ananias has spoken truly.'

As we walked through the clinic gate, I said, 'Oh, that's the solution, is it, wait for the end of the war to see whose prophecy bears true?' and I banged the gate shut.

Maybe, Sisters, it was a prophecy I should have heeded. We are bound, I think, to heed prophets whose words we want to hear. Yet I believe to this day that it need not have been so fated. We could have won. We could have.

Later when she departed, I pleaded with her again, 'We need to hear messages of hope, Shulamith.'

'What you need to hear, Sophia, is the truth,' she retorted.

Yitzhak, Bruriah and I argued with her, but Shulamith's group was in a hurry to depart.

I did suggest, 'Ought you not to pass on any information you have to High Priest Yeshua and the house of Gamaliel?'

She said, 'We have done so. But they are staying; they're crazed with zealotry like you three.'

So again, my friendship with my cousin was torn by differences of belief. I am sorry to say that our parting kiss was not one that would leave a warm memory.

This was a sad business both because of our earlier friendship and because it was the last time I saw her. The disagreement meant that we parted frowning at each other, each throwing arrows of sectarian dispute. The sour note on which we parted was to stay unhealed forever.

Saying goodbye to this Sister of the Ebionim with a loving embrace and a kiss of peace, as was right, was something I had to do in my dreams, over and over, as I had failed to do it in reality.

I had warm relations with other Notzrim during the war, but I never saw Shulamith again. I heard that the Pillars and the Pella *ekklesia* (assembly) returned after the war, but I never heard whether she was among them.

My tears needed to fall for my beloved friend and cousin, but they were blocked by uncomfortable reverberations from the antagonism of our exchange. So had the war caused divisions among family and friends, planting a sword between the love of one to another.

I later found out that most of the Hebrews in her community had remained in the city. The ekklesia on Mount Zion still held its Assemblies.

Jews from Asia, Sha'ul's converts claiming to be disciples of Yeshua Messiah, preaching all kinds of capitulation and laxities of the Law, came into the clinic, too, but they could rarely make speeches outside in the city without causing a riot. Their message seemed to be that we must recruit Greeks, Persians and Aegyptians to the Word of God by any means necessary, even to allowing uncircumcised men and menstruating women into the Temple.

'Our Lord commanded: Go to the highways and the hedges, bring back whomever you find,' they said.

I whispered to one of the girls, Doris, 'Who would follow the instructions of a commander who is already dead?' But we volunteers were not allowed to argue with the preachers.

Looking for volunteers to help at the clinic, some of us skirted round the Old City Wall to the top of Mount Zion, where was located the Tomb of David, to the Notzrim prayer house they called the Upper Room, and there Joanna introduced me to Tabitha.

Tabitha was from Joppa, a matron and a deaconess, many years older than I, and, though she never convinced me to gainsay my allegiance to the Saints of the Yachad, every time we met, I was the loser. She had words and scripture for every occasion. I would come away feeling that though, surely, I was right, she had taken the prize.

Tabitha was wed to a man named Yeshua ben Thebutis, a junior priest at the Temple. I had heard his father speak from the porticoes during the Florus campaign. She and her husband lived together as if unmarried.

'We've vowed to remain pure until the day of our salvation,' she explained, 'when we shall gain the reward for our chastity. By breaking the chains of childbirth, we loose the coil that binds us to mortal suffering.' In her accent, the words sounded more like 'chasti'y' and 'mor'al'.

I said, 'Many of my brethren as well are avowed to celibacy in readiness for the judgement. They say that at the End of Times, no more babes will be born.'

'That's already happening, don't you think?'

It was true; there were so few births in those days. Athanasios and I had not even mentioned the possibility of a child. The Lord closed our wombs to the strife around us, but there were many marriages. We cleaved unto each other and wildly embraced love in the anticipation of martyrdom.

'Yes,' I said, 'why bring a new child into a world that is coming to an end?'

Even today, many Jews and Christians take their faith to the renunciation of the flesh. We used to look to the Final Deliverance as a liberation of suffering here on earth. Now so many just look forward to death.

I told Tabitha about the preachers at the clinic.

'There is no question of laxity of the Law,' defended Tabitha of her order. 'These preachers are those who followed the Spouter of Lies, apostates. That is not what the Christ meant. He never welcomed insincere supper scroungers. He meant that we should bring all to our table, under our holy Law, to liberate all the Nations at once under God's rule.'

I agreed with her, though by that time I considered questions of strategy regarding the enemy more important than debates about table fellowship.

'You are quite right that the son of Ananias is a false prophet,' she assured me. 'Our Lord said they would come in his name to lead men astray. We follow his command—to stay in the city until clothed with power from on high.'

'Deaconess, I am glad to hear you say it. Much have I regretted my differences with my cousin, and I have suffered with the feeling that your Saints had betrayed us. Have not our traditions been united in the past? Now more than ever when the liberation of Jerusalem is at hand...'

'Do not blame the proselytes for escaping,' she said. 'They were persecuted, and by our own people. Near the sword is near to God, but the interpretation is to strike the enemy, not each other.'

Everything Tabitha said was eloquent and well supported by references. It seems that Scripture can be turned to any purpose. But I think what is important is to look at what is happening and what has happened on Earth.

We went back to the clinic with three new volunteers and an amphora full of coins from the Notzrim collection boxes—shekels stamped 'Redemption of Zion'. Tabitha jibed, 'Though you declined support for Cephas, you see we support the Ebionim.'

'We were forced to it, Mother.' I explained to her what the council had ruled. 'We did send a letter of support.'

'A letter of support? But then, he died,' she frowned. 'Forgive me, it is quarrelsome. Under the circumstances, I think you were probably right, though it is sad for me. You see, it was he who raised me from the dead in Joppa.'

One of the first things I spoke to Tabitha about, when we had gained each other's trust, was her fellow sectarians, Shulamith and the widow Joanna, the organiser of our refectory. She and Joanna were not table fellows.

'She was one of the few who knew our Lord in the flesh,' she said, 'and she supported our collection box with her means while he rallied the Fifties and the Hundreds, so I would count her among the heroes of the Ebionim, but the woman is a collaborator at heart.'

I had already formed a similar opinion of her.

As for Shulamith, I regretted parting from her in anger.

'She understands, Sophia. Our Lord said that he would create differences.'

'It was not the mission of your prophet that I disputed with her. It was the question of the war,' I protested.

'The question of the war has created differences everywhere. Many of those in Pella are coming back, you know.'

'What about the Pillars?'

'They follow the Way across the Jordan.'

'What about supporting the war, though?'

'They are supporting the war. The men from Pella and Ephesus have not hesitated to shed their blood, and revolutionaries among the Ebionim remain in the city—the Barjonim fight alongside the Zealots and Sicarii.'

'What about Alexandria, Cyrene, Babylonia?'

'The Saints' fund-raising for the Ebionim has accelerated throughout the Diaspora. So many have sold all their goods and abandoned their lands to wait for the Day, postponed and postponed again, they're becoming a burden on the collection boxes. Even those who shy of arms may contribute their works.'

'But the question of arms is essential,' I argued. 'We cannot defeat the Kittim with collection boxes.'

'You and I agree on that, but believe it or not, there is still much support for the rule of Rome, even among the Ebionim. The Poor depend on Caesar to check the greed of senators, not to mention the stipends of Aegyptian corn. When you've got bread and circuses, what more do you really need? I tell you, it's often the Rich who are most devoted to our works. They're the ones who most protest against subjugation.'

'Only when their lands are taken away and given to other rich people.'

'In every assembly and every meeting hall, opinions are widely divided, Sophia.'

'In the Seven Sects, too?'

The preachers of the Seven Sects came to the clinic, all

the sects of the circumcised. Ossaeans, Hemerobaptists, Masbothaeans, Kutim, Tzaddikim, Pharisees, and the Sons of the Galilean. They were in constant argument under the porticoes of the Temple.

'Not only the parties of the circumcision,' she said. 'Now there are more than seven. In our ekklesia in Corinth, for example, there are four factions—Rechabites, Christians, Barjonim, and those of the Christ. The only thing they agree on is the collection boxes.'

The Rechabites were followers of the Baptist, the Christians followers of Sha'ul, and the Barjonim followers of Cephas. The Christ faction supported the brothers and sons of Yeshua and Ya'akov. In Ephesus, there was a faction who supported their widowed mother, and in Asia there was a group who revered Yeshua's widowed wife. Even those who believed they had found the messiah could not agree on a leader.

'But Mother Tabitha, giving money to the Poor is not the same thing as defeating a powerful enemy,' I said.

'It is by rallying around the collection boxes that we organise the widest crowd and by the distribution of food that garrisons march,' she said. 'But you are right. It's not enough.'

'What about the garrisons, those who stay to fight, who will be king?' That was the key question. Tabitha's sect was ruled by Symeon, their Lord's cousin—may he lead a good long life—but he was in Pella. He had left the battlefield.

'Symeon won a large part of the Brethren to Pella, but my father-in-law prevailed against many.' In fighting Jerusalem, there remained a faction supporting Thebutis.

'The Antioch congregation won't be on our side, of course, but we have presbyters overseeing garrisons in Salamis, Cyrene,

Cilicia, Pella, Ephesus.'

'But will they come up? Or are they just defending the strongholds?'

'It doesn't matter if we fight different battles, as long as we fight the same enemy,' she said.

'No, what matters is winning the final battle. Surely it will be Jerusalem. Will the generals stop fighting each other long enough to fight the enemy together?'

'Or Cyrene, or Cyprus. How can we know which will be the last if we do not fight all of them?' She sighed.

'And if we are victorious?' I said.

'If we are victorious, the people will rule, and only HaShem will be king.'

# Chapter 25
## Charms and relics

I had a reason regularly to visit Mount Zion, as the deaconesses, by the hand of Tabitha, were generous donors to Joanna's kitchens. I was often sent with a donkey and one of Gamaliel's slaves to collect provisions.

Tabitha seemed unusually interested in the secret teachings of the Ossaeans. She asked me about Mem, and I told her what I could. In return, I asked her about her initiation, for she was of higher order in her sect than I was in mine.

There were two baptism ceremonies, she explained, immersion with signs and miracles, and immersion with a descent of the Holy Spirit. The higher orders, of whom she was one, those who were ready to teach, were, it seems, further initiated with a laying on of hands and a magical breath from the apostle.

'Being raised from the dead by the Holy Spirit is the Gate to Salvation, Sister Sophia. We must make ourselves righteous for the new world immediately, and open the garrisons to the people. Now is the time to raise even the dead soldiers from the Underworld.'

One subject that really set her eyes alight was the Ossaean knowledge of the true names of the heavenly hosts.

'Is it true you know also the True Name of God?' she questioned me. It had been a while since I had concerned myself with ancient Names of God, Chaldee or otherwise.

'I have been taught the Seven Letter Name.'

'Tell me it.'

'Tabitha, you know I can't. They only taught it to me after two years of tutelage.'

The second time she mentioned it and I again refused, I retorted, 'and your order, don't you have secrets?'

'Yes, of course. And one of equal value to one who is a friend,' she said, and winked. I blushed to realise she was offering me a bribe.

I don't even know what I replied, yet afterward I thought—knowledge of the Name of God, spoken once a year only by the High Priest of Jerusalem, in fear of his life, in the most sacred Holy of Holies—could there be a secret equal to that?

'It is one that only the deaconesses know,' she told me, 'after at least two years of service—ten years in my case.'

She bargained with me, but it wasn't just a trade. She believed in magical hastening. She wanted knowledge, and she wanted to give me knowledge, and she wanted the exchange to take place quickly.

'The world is coming to an end,' she said. 'We must hurry our works. Who knows but that we might put to use our charms; we must use every weapon we have.'

'Tabitha, to know my charm is one thing, to speak it is blasphemy.'

'I seek only the knowledge. To invoke my charm, also, would be blasphemous.'

'Then why do you flaunt it? Should you not conceal it?'

'As you hold yours with pride, so do I mine. It is only in knowing the route to damnation that we know the route to righteousness. Anyway, as you said, the knowing of it is not blasphemy.'

The third time she approached me I gave way. Tabitha won

me to her works with the passion of her will.

'Sophia, to pledge to you my sincerity, I will add to my offer. I will go first and reveal to you another secret, similar to yours.'

'Similar?' I said—to the Name of God?

'Our Saviour Yeshua had a secret name.'

'Yes, of course, most magi do.' I would have received mine upon my seventh-year initiation.

'I know this name; the Saints in Ephesus revealed it to our Sisters on Mount Charaxio. I will tell you it.'

'You would tell me, an unbeliever, the Name which must surely only be spoken by the highest among your order?'

'I will tell you it. It is: *IE ieus EO ou EO Oua.*'

I blinked at her. Was she joking with me? Had she just revealed to me, with no more ceremony than that, secret knowledge known only to those above the rank of deaconess, a secret which, though it was of no value to me—I had no interest in magicians' battles—was surely a precious treasure to her?

She smiled, 'I know what you've been taught, little sister, that the cosmic powers are so very dangerous, and knowledge of the power of God should be so closely guarded.'

'Well, it's not only my school; all the sages say so.' It was one of those things you just assumed.

'If the sages are such authorities on the fate of the world, shouldn't everyone receive their wisdom?' she argued.

'Supplicants have to be worthy first.' I found myself echoing the words of the Fathers and Mothers, things I had always argued against. 'I'm always trying to learn things too fast, and I get into trouble.'

'With your masters?'

'Yes, and with demons, as well.' I had not spoken of it to

her before, but she was unsurprised.

'I will protect you from demons,' she said. 'I get into trouble, too. I am of a faction among our ranks who favour speeding up the attainment of worthiness. Ya'akov the Just ordained that proselytes should be baptised only after six years of instruction. But I myself, and some of the presbyters here, will baptise right now any we know are righteous who repent and believe. Men like my husband and his father are with us. Let he who is thirsty come. Let he who desires drink freely from the water of life. I tell you, I've even donned the black robes when I needed to make an impression.'

The robes of a high priest? 'Deaconess, you would present yourself as a Saint without sanction?' Not only was the disregard of hierarchy shocking, but why was she so keen to divulge all her secrets to me?

I couldn't even think of a similar infraction from my camp. Spitting in Assembly was punishable by thirty days detention; I couldn't even imagine what punishment would be heavy enough for impersonating a priest. I did remember, however, the times I happily undertook vows when punished for defending Imme. The punishment weighs lightly when you know you are in the right.

Tabitha said, 'I do not consider that I have done wrong. I am being candid with you to persuade you of my conviction. The world is coming to an end, and we must save as many as we can.'

'What you say is new to me, but what does your quest for hastening have to do with magical names?'

'As for that, Sophia, I don't know magic like you do. I just want to bring in the Kingdom by whatever means we can, quickly.'

I bargained with her, 'I know you have shown your trust in telling me your first secret. You keep insisting that what you have and what I have are of parity, yet I haven't the slightest clue about yours. A charm the Sisters possess, rumoured to have been used by Yeshua–that's all. Whereas, you at least know the nature of mine.'

'Very well, then, my secret regards a charm which some say our Lord used in his magic. I can show you this charm.'

I was disappointed. 'We all have charms. I have a hawthorn wand given to me by my junior disciple. My master had a staff...'

She stopped me, 'I promise you. When you see this charm, you will not deny its importance. If I'm wrong, I'll lay my garments at your feet.'

Her assurances compelled me. So, I spelled for her the Name and explained the breathing and head movements. Rendered into Greek it can be seen to have expanded from an earlier Five Letter Name.

Though it must not be spoken, the Name itself is not secret. Even Ananus, the Tzaddik who usurps the Throne of Melchizedek, knows this word. The secret is that it spells the invocation to a goddess.

To you, Sisters of Alexandria, I also reveal whatever secrets of God and Man that Wisdom has granted me to know. The word is sacrilege to write, so I revealed it to her in the gematria code of Mount Carmel.

20-15-10-5-1

It is a title taken from the Goddess in her five-fold emanations: Birth, Initiation, Consummation, Repose, and Death. The conquering God reversed the order—as you might do in an exorcism, to counterbalance the power. Reading to the left the letters spelled an invocation: 'White Barley Goddess, Queen of Heaven and Earth, who gathers all under your Destiny'.

Tabitha was delighted; this was just the sort of revelation she'd hoped for. She went straight away to a cabinet where she opened a drawer and removed a key.

'Come with me,' she said. She led me up through the Assembly Hall, where we mounted to the Upper Room.

I took a peek into the Assembly Hall downstairs. There was the great Throne of Ya'akov—empty. Indeed, who could fill that seat today? Would we ever see the Just One rising up newly armed to lead the Fifties and the Hundreds? It was of solid black basalt, carved in symbols of the Oblias (Bulwark)—the peaked mitre of the High Priest, the crosier staff of the Shepherd of Men.

Across the Upper Room we entered a corridor, off to one side was the Tomb of David, and from the other side of the corridor she opened a tiny room.

'Don't be frightened,' she said.

I scoffed. I the maga, frightened of a magical charm? Yet when she shone her lamp on the thing I nearly jumped out of my skin. In the middle of the tiny room atop a wooden stand was one of those plaster-covered skulls the magi used for necromancy.

She closed the door and locked it behind us, positioning the lamp where it reflected best the outline of the macabre object.

'Don't step over Him or cross your shadow,' she whispered.

I know that much—I thought, but I couldn't say a word.

My first thought was—the mystery of the Empty Tomb? Proof that there was a body? But the actual identity of 'Him' was hardly less shocking.

She explained in a whisper, 'He was the...'

'I can guess whose head it is,' I said. For some reason, I didn't want the name spoken in the presence of the thing. It might give it power. Power to do what? Whose power did Yeshua wish to possess? Him, she called it; it was bizarre.

I was too awed to speak further in the room with the head, and pulled her back into the corridor.

'So, Sister Sophia, do you now acknowledge the parity of our secrets?' she teased.

Had I been inclined to deny it, my shocked reaction would have betrayed my hand. I was quick to admit. Her secret was fantastic. Mine—an old secret, hers—a newer one, but one as equally concealed from the novice—it was more than a fair trade.

I had to find my tongue; I had so many questions.

'Your master used the head of his teacher as a magical talisman?'

'So they say, and hence He has been preserved among our relics. The Sisters call him Baphomet, and we invoke him by singing, Yalla, Yalla,' she chanted softly.

'Baphomet?'

'You should not be so perplexed, Sophia.' She bent down to the floor and scribed with the doorkey letters written in our Zealot Code. The Hebrew letters, rendered into Greek, were those of my name, Sophia.

Again, the sense of awe overwhelmed me. I thought—a talisman? but checked myself. I imagined myself and Imme conjuring with Ima Miryam's head and felt sick in my stomach.

'How came you by it?' I challenged her.

'Herodias' daughter was one of our Saints; she begged Him of Herod Antipas.'

'She betrayed the Baptist?'

'No, no, this was after he was already beheaded. She went to her stepfather in tears and confessed her faith in the resurrection of the righteous, begging for Him for to join the body in burial. She humiliated herself before the king, dancing for his favour.'

'To win the head?'

'Yes.'

'And why was it not joined then in burial?'

'That, I do not know.'

I was determined to get her to tell me of the magic. 'Will you tell me, then, how is it used? What is its power?'

'They say that He sings in prophecy.'

'Have you heard it?'

'Of course not. If I had, I'd be leading the Fifties and the Hundreds.'

'Did Yeshua hear it?'

'He heard the call of the Hundreds from somewhere. But perhaps not from Him.'

'The Rechabites, are they aware that you hold the bodily relic of their prince? The brothers of the Baptist, who buried him at Sebaste, do they know?'

'I am certain they do not. Otherwise, they would demand Him from us.'

'You must explain to me, then, why you hold it.'

'I know not what happened with Herodias' daughter. But I

can suppose the deaconesses before me safeguarded Him not only because they half believed our Lord used him magically.'

'Why is that so?' She locked the tiny room and we started walking back down, and I was glad of it. It was time to return to the world of the living.

'Sophia, you and I know the importance of rallying ALL the Ebionim. I think our sharing of that opinion is what brought us to this contract.'

'Yes, that is so....and the deaconesses?'

'They felt, I'm sure, that our guardianship would confirm our Lord as the Baptist's apostle.'

'I see.' Yes, if he could speak from the grave, a great many people would be influenced by whomso the Baptist served.

'Not that I agree with them,' she continued. 'I would never that He should become an issue of conflict.'

'What about those of Simon of Gitta, the Sons of Dorcas? Would they not desire to guard the relic themselves as heirs to Yochanan's teachings? It would surely be a talisman of more power for the Kutim than for your sect?'

'Certainly, they would. And we could not allow that. They are our enemies.'

'Enemies? Said you not that we must unite ALL the Ebionim, Mother Tabitha? That must apply to the Kutim as well.'

'Your desire for it to be so is as mine, but remember it was only six years ago the Galileans had that unholy row with the Kutim in Lydda.'

'Yes, Dorcas and four of the Kutim were crucified for it,' I recalled.

'I fear our differences with the Dositheans are increasing rather than diminishing. Likewise, there is no love between the Brethren of the Lord and them of that magus.'

'Surely war with Rome will force us to unite,' I believed.

'I think it will; though it is not certain whether there will be time enough.'

'You are right,' I agreed. 'We should be fortifying the city instead of fighting amongst ourselves.'

'You can understand why we do not want another issue over which the sects may fight. He has wisely been kept a secret known only to our inner orders.'

'I will join you in the secret, then,' I said. 'Perhaps when the Day arrives, all truths will be revealed.'

I must say to you, Sisters, if I sinned in revealing secrets of the Kedoshim to an outsider, the Lord never struck me for it. And if I sin in revealing them to you, I remain here at my writing bench unscathed. At the time, I had to keep the secret, but now it no longer matters. I can reveal you all, and you may use the information as you wish.

I was coming to Tabitha's point of view. Time was running out. We must hasten the Lord's hand.

We waited then, and there were ever too few of the righteous. Now, still we wait, as I rush to paint my life's stories on this scroll, in a hurry, so you may know them if you will. You, Sisters, must not miss the Day.

It was on the Eve of Pesach. We received news of the Sicarii at Masada.

Eleazar ben Yair's men, the heirs of Menachem the Messiah, Bar Hakkoz's comrades, had left the battlefield and remained isolated in their mountain fortress. There, they created their own little New Jerusalem–Jerusalem in one fortress, and of no interest to Titus–may his eyeballs burst–while he had the real

Jerusalem yet to conquer.

Our messenger was a Novice from the Yachad. Though shame does lose its force after years pass, I was glad he knew not my face.

He came to report the latest incident of revolutionary banditry. Ben Yair's Sicarii had rampaged rich houses in Ein Gedi, and their madness had led to massacre. They returned southward drunk with booty, the messenger said, and began attacking homes along the Wilderness Road as well.

There had been much sentiment among the company in support of Ben Yair, especially from the Ossaeans. His cousin had been our King Messiah. These men stood in shocked silence, but the women wailed. The violence in the land—Greeks killing Jews, Jews killing Greeks, Jews killing Samaritans—now it had extended even unto Jews killing proselytes? It was not our idea of the Kingdom of God.

'Which homes? Which roads?' I demanded.

'Most roads south of the Hebron Road...'

'The road to Qiryat 'Aravaya?' I heard my voice tremble.

'Yes. They massacred them all.'

The heritage of Judah, the sons of Job and proselytes alike, the pensioned retainers of Herod, women and children, they killed them indiscriminately. Some from the Yachad had gone down to bury them, the Novice said.

'The children, too?' My cherubic pupils, their righteous parents?

'All.'

That was when I released my wail. I shouted at Uzziel, as if it were his fault, 'Is this what you calling winning?'

How could I understand this despicable action? The mount

403

of Masada was so high, perhaps they could not get down to till the soil. Fortresses would normally be provisioned by the surrounding farmland. It was a common problem. The harvest in Palestine that year was the poorest it has ever been, with the demands of the militias on our hands. There was no olive harvest, the Romans had cut down all the trees. The first fruits offerings even ceased.

The Sicarii must have run out of food. Maybe Bar Hakkoz's tale of provisions perfectly preserved since Herod was a fiction. Yet Joanna's kitchens had supplies enough to last seven years. They needed only to have sent a messenger to one of the Inspectors of the Ebionim. The collection boxes in the countryside were still full. Believers were giving everything they could in hopes of getting aid up to Jerusalem, in hopes that coin would make an acceptable offering when they had not offered their lives. I hoped to myself that it was hunger that drove their knives and not hatred.

Perhaps in Eleazar's eye these people were not innocents, so many of them proselytes of Greek or Arab descent, converts who diluted the power of the Kingdom, they weren't real Jews, but upstarts who wanted to inherit the prize without paying the price. And they were Rich. Perhaps he was angry that they had not fought in Jerusalem. Perhaps it was in revenge for Menachem.

In a flash I saw a wicked vision. I told Bruriah about it that night as I poured out my grief.

Calantha, Clio and Cynthia were drawing pictures, and Calantha recited, 'We are killing our neighbor.'

Bruriah consoled me, 'Our Kingdom, Sophia, is not one where your little pupils would be so vilely done.'

This is not the interpretation of tzedakah–Kill that Greek or Arab whose neighbour hates thy neighbour. This has no end point in liberation, but only reciprocal bloodshed.

We must hope for a unity of all peoples of the Ebionim–Jerusalem, Samaria, the Greek cities and the wilds of Edom. And, Sisters, Athanasios says that even those boundaries are too narrow. Our Kingdom must extend even to Babylon and Rome. The Poor know no nation, and it is we who shall inherit the Earth.

The massacre of the innocents of Ein Gedi was a turning point for the Ebionim movement and for me. It wasn't just that I had known the victims of the violence. It wasn't just that despite all the banditry that had taken place up to now, this was the worst atrocity–killing our own converts. It wasn't just that Menachem the Sicarii leader had been our messiah.

It was a sign that we had given up the battle for the Kingdom of God.

The revolutionary potential of the Ebionim collection boxes collapsed. No longer did the law of tzedakah–Love thy Neighbour–strengthen our hand with the righteousness of God's Law. Our Kingdom of bounteous justice was reduced to pockets of resistance, resorting to atrocities in order to keep our children fed.

In embattled Jerusalem, people had already chosen their allegiance. Yochanan issued orders like a lord, and the factions rivalled. Their fighting was at the expense of the people, as the militias battled to see who could bring home the most loot.

Anyone caught outside the city was assumed to be on his way to the Romans and killed. Yochanan ben Zakkai–scholars bless his name–by a ruse perpetrated by his sister's son Abba Sikra, the leader of the Sicarii in Jerusalem—escaped to the Romans in a coffin, feigning death.

When they reached the gate, the Zealots wanted to test the coffin with a lance, but his disciples cried, 'Shall the Romans say, they have pierced their master?' The Zealots wanted to give it a push. But they said to them, 'Shall they say that they pushed their master?'

We accused him of desertion at the time, but it was good that he escaped, as he lived after the war to teach the Way of Righteousness in Yavneh.

# Chapter 26
## Crosses and tombs

Around town public notices were written on the walls in three languages. There was too much treachery for partisans to communicate directly. But there were places one could go to get news delivered. Womenfolk gathered at the wells, and passed ostraca—shards of pottery—inscribed with images and letters.

Code images functioned as passwords to identify the righteous—a fish, for example, or a flock of quail; the wheels of Ezekiel could signify dates and times by the numbers of their spokes. The garrisons developed code languages, *tongues*, in which they coded written messages. They looked like rows of square snakes.

Scratched in the dirt at market, behind corners on walls, painted on ostraca with messages handed from sleeve to sleeve, you'd see the graffiti of crosses. Sometimes they would be in a group together—the crosses of the martyrs, the symbol of zealot suffering. Or the three crosses of Yeshua and his Galileans. Sometimes they'd be solitary—these were usually the newer scratchings—the cross of the Messiah, the symbol of unified leadership. Alas, there was none such in Jerusalem.

The sects and their garrisons were not the only ones using coded means to communicate across the dangerous city. From inside courtyards children flew kites of different colours, as if sending out surrogates to play in the freedom of the skies, since no mother would let her child onto the streets in those days.

Tabitha and I between the two of us used a Zealot Code, one unknown to the Herodians; as women we could not always travel safely alone between the clinic and the Mount Zion. I couldn't read their tongues, so we expanded on the code to include letters and figures to represent certain basic concepts. This is the second code I have taught you, Sisters, after the Chaldee code of Guryon.

Every first letter of the alef-bet is exchanged with the last. So, every *alef* is written as *tav* and every *tav* is written *alef*. Thence every second letter is exchanged with the penultimate letter. So, every *bet* is written as *shin*. And so on. The same encoding can be used in Aramaic or in Greek.

A slave whose face I knew begged entry to the clinic and presented me with a basket filled with five barley loaves resting in barleyseed. Tabitha didn't need to send me barley; the harvest had finished, and the clinic had already received our daily stipend from Joanna's kitchens. And if she had wished to give me some, she could have waited until I visited her, when I would likely have a donkey with me to carry it and a slave to load it.

The five barley loaves were a reference to one of their scriptures, meaning the message had something to do with Tabitha's sect. A dove would have been reference to the Barjonim, builders' tools a reference to the Ossaeans as Diggers of the Well.

I presented the gift to the matrons, but had no trouble in first retrieving a shard of pottery from under the loaves.

On the ostraca were inked symbols of a fish, a mountain, and a wheel with no spokes. This I knew to be a message telling me, 'Come to my chamber on Mount Zion whenever you are able to do so. I have a mission for you.' I was free of duties, so

I went back with the slave.

Hardly pausing for me to finish the cup of fig juice she gave me, Tabitha burst forth, 'All the city is filled with smears against my Lord.'

I waited to hear the mission.

'They say He was a tool of the Herods hired to subvert the Jewish zeal with heresy, a sorcerer seducing the People of the Land with idolatrous Aegyptian mysteries. He was caught by the cohort practicing sex magic, naked man with naked man.'

'A wine-bibber who dines with rich sinners and Greeks,' I put in.

'That is no truer an accusation than the others,' she snapped. 'You may look to communities in the Diaspora for sinners and uncircumcised Greeks, not here, Sophia. Anyway, I have not asked you here to defend the earthly reputation of my Lord, but rather to defend the unity of the Ebionim.'

'I am sorry. I should listen before I argue.'

'You and I share a secret, do we not?'

'How can I forget it?' I was the only person outside the deaconesses on Mount Zion who knew that the Saints of the Notzrim possessed the mummified head of Hanan the Hidden.

'And you must not reveal it; now is the worst time of all. On top of all the other problems, a charge of necromancy, however false, would cause much harm. He could cause conflict between the sects just when we need unity the most. In fact, Sophia, the deaconesses regret our own knowledge of Him. I have offered to procure secret burial.'

'You want me to bury...Him?'

'No, I will bury Him myself. They must not know I have divulged the secret. What I want you to do is to record the location; I will write it for you in our code. Then you must guard it for the future. If you ever make it out of Jerusalem, hide the record where those with eyes to see and ears to hear may find it.'

The intrigue of it appealed to me enormously. I was experienced, was I not, in the business of hiding secret documents.

'One more thing, friend,' she said.

Ah, now she was to tell me the mission for which she called me. If her goal had been merely to bury the head, she could have accomplished that by herself.

'Would you not like to consult the oracle? We, the last two to sit before His earthly presence until I slip Him beneath the stones?'

'You mean, invoke the…Him…for a prophecy?'

'That's just the sort of trick you have hidden in your sleeve, isn't it, Sophia Maga?'

'The head of prophecy was cut off with the Baptist. It's ancient, forbidden magic.'

'Perhaps the ancient magic will work now, at the End of Times, more than ever?'

'But Ima, necromancy? It's the most forbidden of all.'

She said, 'Sister Sophia, the outward form of this world is about to pass away. We shall all be dead. What more is there to fear?'

'I have read of the magic of these heads. But I am only a novice maga, Tabitha. I am not qualified.'

'You must make yourself qualified, as this opportunity lies before you and no one else.'

'We must send for my master Ima Miryam. Can we send a letter…?'

410

'No,' she said, 'no one must know.'

'You will not inform your husband?'

'No. You and your master know as well as I that magic is the realm of the woman.'

'I only worry that you and I will be the only bearers.'

'You mean, if we die?'

It was like the conversation with Bar Hakkoz.

'I will let the deaconesses also know of the location,' she assured me. 'And we shall record the burial in our own code.'

The atmosphere of conspiracy tickled my fancy, and I felt giddy. 'I shall do it, and you shall be the supplicant.'

Tabitha could talk me into anything. She knew it, and I knew it. By now it had become a joke between us.

'You amaze me, Sister,' she said. 'The Baptism of the Holy Spirit is the deepest of anathema to you, yet, a bit of necromancy? No problem.'

'Again, you corrupt me, Deaconess,' I giggled.

'And you me, it seems.'

I chose the day as best I could, consulting the Jubilee calendar. Tabitha cared nothing about choosing a day; whatever it was, she always wanted to do it today.

We both fasted and prayed for three days in preparation.

Athanasios and I were not spending much time together in those days, having differing works, but he couldn't help but notice my fasting. Though truly magic is the realm of woman, I felt ashamed to conceal something from my husband. In any case, I was pledged to secrecy, so could only tell him it was due to a vow I'd taken with one of the deaconesses at Mount Zion.

He said, 'I wouldn't trust them if I were you. They're on the side of the Rich.'

I certainly could not imagine Tabitha in this light, but as I didn't welcome his probing, I said nothing.

Tabitha and I met up again at the Mount Zion ekklesia, where she led me to the Assembly Hall. We sat before the Throne of Ya'akov while we made our plans.

'Do you know what will be our question?' I asked her.

'Of course, the question we all want to ask–When, O Lord, will we be saved?'

'Is not the question who rather than when, though? Who will save us?' I argued.

'Yes, it is both.'

'If we know who, then we will know when.'

She conceded, then asked, 'By what name shall we invoke Him?'

'What is the most secret or ancient name you know?'

'Probably Yahya. It was the name he was called by the Arabs, to whom he was Adam Paghia, Adam the First Man, the incarnation of Elijah.'

The name was agreed.

'Whom shall we invoke? The earthly Yahya of our grandfathers?'

'No, we need not consult Him over questions of history; it will be the shade of the prophet as He visits us today.'

Tabitha led me to the tiny room that housed the head.

She procured a thin sliver of gold leaf–she wouldn't tell me from where, and I carved into it 'Yahya' in Aramaic. Solemnly she oiled and salted it according to my instruction and handed it to me.

I placed the token inside the jaw–it was supposed to be under the tongue–and hung Him, the head of Yahya, on the wall. Tabitha positioned the lamps, and we prostrated ourselves before the teraphim.

I chewed laurel leaves and breathed the smoke from aromatic incense on a small brazier, and clapped three times, once to alert the mind, twice to awaken the soul, thrice to free to spirit. Together we chanted, 'Yalla, Yalla'.

> A star flew down into Judæa, a star flew down into Jerusalem. The sun appeared by night, and the moon rose by day. The priests in the Temple did woe, fire burned in old father Zakhri and Enishbai did conceive, and the king was born in Jerusalem.
>
> I beseech you, Yahya, Hidden One, descend to us on Mount Zion, that a seat to your disciple, the Throne of the Bulwark, may here receive you.
>
> You bade us repent, and we repented. You warned us against fornication, and we remained pure.
>
> I summon up Yahya, the spirit and the power of Eliyahu. Give direction to our works as you once did in the days of Antipas. Then may we know the Day of our Deliverance.

It was much longer than this. It takes only a brief spell to bind a spirit once you have him, you need a long one to capture him first. When the incense had filled me fully, I said:

> You promised the coming of one whose sandals you were unworthy to unloose. Who among us now wears those sandals? O Yahya, whom do you serve?
>
> I, Sophia, invoke you. Hear our supplication and respond. Whom should we serve?

413

The flame burned red, not white, and I feared I was not entering the gate of prophecy. Nor did the blue flame appear; Yahya was not going to descend.

I rocked before the teraphim humming a holy song until I lost sense. On reviving, I had nothing before my mind's eye but the flash of an image of crosses, broken crosses, all in a pile. Tabitha said the only thing I'd uttered in trance was, 'Nooo'.

I had to sleep after that, but as soon as I could I visited her again.

'Nooo WHAT, then?' She demanded.

'I am as mystified as you. No, He won't tell us? No, He serves no leader?' I told her of the vision of the crosses.

'Does that mean the martyrs will all die? or No, don't follow martyrs? Or No, don't be martyrs?'

'I don't know. And as I'm sworn to secrecy, I cannot go to Jairus or any other sage for guidance.'

Despite my blindness, still did the deaconess trust me. She said, 'You have bravely addressed my supplication, though I have not understood the answer. And you have asked for no reward. Sophia, I have something to show you, another secret to tell you in thanks for your works.'

'The burial place? of Yahya?'

'No. That will be somewhere underneath the Temple, whose sanctity he defied the king to defend. I will write it for you. But I will bind you in our subterfuge by the telling of a further secret.'

'As with the former, my lips shall be sealed.'

'What would you say would be the question most asked about our sect?'

'Let me see...Do you really hold love-feas...?'

'Not that one.'

'Or, who was the naked man with nak...?'

'Nor that one.'

'Very well. What really happened when the women rolled away the stone?'

'That's the one.'

'You're going to uncover to me the mystery of the empty tomb?'

'I am.'

On the pretext of going to market, we enlisted Menelaus and another slave. She led us up to the city inside the perimeter of the Second Wall. Leaving Menelaus and the slave at the Damascus Gate market, Tabitha and I progressed around the wall southward beyond the old City of David, where we sneaked into a storehouse.

Under one of the floorboards was the entrance to a crypt. On the lintel was carved a symbol in tongues, a circle with an upturned chevron cap above it. We moved aside the stone, and as she took me down the stone steps, I could see that the tomb was part of a warren of burial chambers, maybe of several families, or of a large extended family.

'There, the mystery of the empty tomb revealed,' she said, and shone her lamp into the corners of the crypt. There were six limestone ossuaries, each carved on the front with two six-petalled rosettes.

I looked behind the one she illuminated first. I was as astounded as I had been by the head. On the back of the ossuary was carved in Aramaic 'Yeshua bar Yosef'. The next one, a fresher grave, was 'Ya'akov bar Yosef'.

It was the family tomb of the Just Ones, the heroes of the

Ensigns Protest, the Bulwarks of Jerusalem. Yeshu's bones were not risen from the grave like Ezekiel walking around Jerusalem newly armed. They were resting beside those of his mother Maria, and brothers Ya'akov, Matya and Yosa, his son Yuda and wife Mariamene. On her ossuary was written MARIAM H KAI MARA.

'Also called Mara?' I translated.

'Or?' she prompted.

'Also called the Master.'

'She was first among the deaconesses,' said Tabitha.

I spake no more in the presence of the entombed, but as we walked back up to the city, my Acting Self seized what my eyes had seen.

'Tabitha, you are telling lies to your proselytes. How can you do that?'

'I had you for a hastener, Sister,' she said.

'I am not averse to a bit of magic, but...an outright lie? And regarding the central tenet of your creed!'

'Sophia, the central tenet of our creed is that the Kingdom of God is upon us now.'

'And I agree with you there, but I just saw...'

'Believers have so accepted the Resurrection as proof of the coming of the Kingdom that to dispute one would be to refute the other. The belief strengthens the hearts of the Many, deficient as we are in armaments.'

It was good that she did tell me these secrets, Sisters, as she was soon to join with her messiah in useless martyrdom. Now, I, who live, pass these secrets on to you.

416

# Chapter 27
## The New Jerusalem

The anemones were popping up on the hills; it was the start of the spring campaign. The Romans were ravaging Idumaea.

Aristocrats from Jerusalem, deserters and traitors, went to Vespasian—may Balaam's angel drown his enemies—to beg him to invade the city. Yet for a second summer he delayed. Instead, he attacked Gadara, a town in Peraea. It fell without a fight.

With news of an uprising in Gaul, Vespasian felt the danger to the empire, and stepped up the campaign. Thamna, Lydda, Yavneh, Emmaus, Bethleptepha, Betaris, and Caphartoba—all fell to his engines.

Now the Jews held only the three Salt Sea fortresses.

The Tenth Legion—may nails lodge in their horses' hooves—was on the march, and either Secacah or Jerusalem would be next.

There is nothing like the expectation of bad news to divide men. What should we do? Suddenly, there was a myriad of opinions, and for a few days the commanders lost all authority. Some soldiers argued for a last stand at Secacah, some wanted to join the Sicarii at Masada.

I cornered Joanna at the refectory, 'Mother, the patriarch is going house to house with the principal men holding anti-Zealot meetings.'

'And so?'

'They're urging the people in the city to expel the Zealots

from Temple Mount.'

'And so they should,' she said. 'Those innovators have wrecked everything. Lady Cypros was here yesterday, and she said her brother has been persuading them that abolishing the sacrifices to Rome is impious and seditious.'

'As I heard it, the citizens remarked upon how the Zealots are well armed and trained, numerous, young and courageous.'

Joanna continued, 'These villains execute our nobles, and now they have captured our Holy Temple. Of what use is it to fight the Romans if we are to be ruled by the scum of our own nation?'

I shouted at her, 'The Poor shall inherit the Kingdom of Heaven.'

I had no need to inform anyone of the information I learned about this treacherous meeting. The Zealots found out immediately, and attacked first. Injured Zealots stained the sacred pavement with their blood, and we were immediately called to the clinic.

We were fortunate to hear all the ins and outs of revolutionary politics from an entertaining source. We called him The Messenger. He was one of the ones who regularly brought news to the clinic.

This is how I met him.

I assisted Jairus administering to a sick girl with a serious fever. My role was to attend the physic and afterwards to sing for her, so during much of the procedure I had little to do. The mother, father and grandparents were in hysterics over the little girl—they had lost two young ones through illness and famine—and no one had given a thought to the older brother, a boy of about nine years named Malachias, who sulked in the corner.

I sought his ear, explaining what the physic was doing and how that was going to help his sister. He seemed to appreciate the information.

The girl had been administered a tonic–anemone flowers, I believe it was–but she worked herself up so it could not take effect. She absorbed the hysteria of her parents and grandparents, which, frankly speaking, the nature of the illness warranted not. The tonic was making her Acting Self sleepy, which she needed for the healing, yet her Feeling Self was keeping her buzzing with anxious thoughts. I worked some Ossaean magic, explaining to her that the two things–the sleepiness and the buzzing–were coming from different places, and they could be separated.

Later, as the physic showed the parents how to apply the cold compresses, I calmed her by singing a hymn. It had a strong repetitive chorus, and each time I returned to the line she calmed a bit more. I taught them the words and melody so they could sing together.

We said a prayer together of thanks to God. Father, mother, grandmother, boy–they all shed tears and regarded each other with smiles. The adults' smiles were those of relief at the girl's improved prognosis and the gratitude to God for protecting these two of their children.

The mother, father, and grandma (the grandfather being rather too elderly) all in turn kissed the girl, who was all smiles, the fire cooled on her brow. They then reached for the boy.

The boy tried to hide his tears, until he saw that the entire company was overcome with emotion. For just a moment, before he joined the family embrace, he threw me an odd glance, one of confusion having been comforted.

Later I found out that while sulking, he had been plagued by feelings of jealousy towards his sister, and these blackened his heart considering her illness. He had already lost two siblings. Was it due to his evil thoughts?

By addressing him, while others were in hysteria over the sister, I had simply given him the attention he was craving, and his better feelings for her triumphed. The shared experience reunited him also with his family.

I left feeling that the whole household had been healed.

It's funny how certain things can so impress a young person. I remember how I was so struck with fascination for the Chaldee spell. Words, even, can strike a child's fancy.

I didn't know this then. All I knew was, the next afternoon he appeared at the clinic, overspilling with news from the city. Thence began a regular relationship of great value to me. He would exaggerate, but he did provide us with the latest news and presented it so entertainingly. His regular visits were always a welcome break. Indeed, his stories never suffered from working while listening. The patients enjoyed the stories, too.

'The aristocrats are on the attack,' Malachias reported. The Zealots fell back to the Inner Court; the moderates seized the Outer Court. Ananus would not enter the Temple unpurified, but he set 6000 men to guard the porticoes.'

'He put his arm around Yochanan,' the Messenger said, grabbing one of the slaveboys as a prop. 'He's been going everywhere with Ananus, pretending to be on the citizens' side. They're plotting something.'

'Now our brave men face a third army,' he said. 'We beat back the Kittim at the Upper Market; we chased away the king; now we have to fight the Rich.'

From this point on, the city was permanently divided into quarters. The rebel forces of Eleazar and Yochanan each had their own territory. The next we heard was that Yochanan had gone up to the Temple and whispered to Eleazar that Ananus–that Wicked Priest–had invited Vespasian to take the city. I had no trouble believing it.

Throughout that whole year the Romans were more concerned with their own squabbles than with ours, and Qesarya as well as Rome remained convulsed in the revolt of the generals.

Taking advantage of trouble in Rome, Gaul, Spain, and Africa revolted against the Empire. When the army hailed Galba as Saviour of Mankind, Nero–may the Beast be devoured by beasts–fell on a sword. I heard, Sisters, that followers of the Way were involved.

Nero was dead, and the race was on. Who could make it first across the stadia from the provinces to Rome with a big enough army to defeat all other pretenders?

Four emperors in a year and a half. An empire that stretched from Carthage to the Balkans could not keep an emperor in place long enough to rule it. The turmoil in the Mother of Whores was the final sign, we were certain, of the End of Times. Surely now the trumpet would sound and the clouds of heaven would descend.

I may now bring you back to New Jerusalem, freed of her chains. For while the cat is away, Sisters, the mouse is free to form her own government. Unfortunately, though, as in old Rome, the mice were fighting among themselves.

Not only was there strife between the militias, there was conflict between every religious sect and every political faction.

Not only Pharisees, Tzaddikim and Ossaeans, there were Herodians, Hebrews, Hellenists–Mannaseh and Ephraim–Shammaites–blue striped hypocrites–Gamalielites, Boethusians still hoping to creep back to power, Aegyptian Jews–history's middlemen since the Hyksos–Kutim, Diaspora Jews who were almost Greeks, uncouth Galileans and Edomite bandits–fundamentalists versus innovators.

Each of these factions was further divided between those for war and those against. Every hearth was riven with disputes between Zealots and collaborators.

'The son of Giora has been driven out of Acrabatene by the Zealots to his fortress at Nain. But he came back with a larger force and camped at Tekoa.'

Whenever Malachias recounted a story, he would put on an imposture of the person involved. It was a gift, I joked with him, 'like shapeshifting'. His talent made the most serious of tales comical, especially upon a body so young.

His representation of Simon was tall, as a man aware of his masculine comeliness, the dashing young prince.

Simon bar Giora was a messiah of a new breed. He proclaimed 'liberty for the slaves and rewards for the free', and slaves were running away from their masters in Jerusalem to join his band, including most of the released prisoners. Many of the prominent men also joined his camp outside the city.

'With the secret aid of an Idumaean general...' Malachias didn't know which one, but he adopted an imposture that could have been Pinhas ben Clusoth–stern, dictatorial, never smiling. 'Simon marched into Idumaea unopposed with a force of 60,000. He captured Hebron'–back to tall and dashing–'and much booty in corn and supplies. The Zealots, however, captured Simon's wife'—a brief pose of damsel in distress— 'and Simon advanced upon Jerusalem like some wounded beast'—tall and dashing with a crazed look— 'torturing everyone he saw, vowing to break down the walls to recover her. He cut off their hands and sent them back to Eleazar.'

'The Zealots' he concluded sternly, represented as one-handed strict men carrying scrolls, 'gave her back.'

I said to Malachias, 'We do enjoy your visits. Why do you so honour us?'

He giggled raucously, but replied, 'Now I am your messenger.'

'So you are,' I said, and giggled too.

I introduced Malachias to Menelaus, and they became friends and regularly swapped news. Other adults listened to his reports. I even conveyed some of his opinions to Athanasios and the militiamen.

I watched his ability to circulate the news blossom, as he became more skillful at picking out and describing the important details. He stopped chuckling idiotically and grew in stature. He's growing up, I thought as I looked at him, tall as a cedar. He caught my eye, and gave me a strange grin.

Soon after he was given a position with Simon's militia as an official messenger, an honour for one so young. My reliable informant entered enthusiastically into this work, proudly calling himself 'a militiaman', the closer proximity to the heart of the action adding greater detail to his reports.

He had to be trained not to embellish the story, but his new sense of duty inspired him to develop a new style of reporting, all military and efficient, completely different from his former campside style. Fortunately, he still entertained us in the old manner when he came to the clinic.

We saw much less of him then, of course, but my heart felt proud.

Around this time, just before the Romans came, Tabitha again pressed me into magical works.

She sent no messenger. The deaconess came herself to the clinic. She was buzzing with enthusiasm, greeting me as 'Sophia Maga'.

'There are reports that the martyrs are rising.'

'Rising from the grave to join the garrisons of the Zealots? Truly, Deaconess?' I whispered, 'Like those in the not-so-empty tomb?'

She ignored the gibe, 'Just reports, but people want to believe it so badly that the word has gone around the city. At our Assembly on Shabbat, no less than five men spoke in tongues in the voices of departed heroes, promising to return.'

'Really, Mother Tabitha, we must look to our more real assets.'

'Of course, but our hearts can hasten those assets to greater purpose.'

'Perhaps.'

'So, magic—though only symbolic of a spiritual state, as you always say, Sophia—can have a real effect...indirectly.'

'So we hope.'

'If the righteous martyrs are not rising to defend us, who would you have, then?'

'The townsfolk, the royalists mainly. Great numbers of them are against us and would open the gates to Vespasian without a fight. Yet they remain in the city, fearful to go or to leave their property. And that's not a matter for magic, but for persuasion.'

'Yes, we meet them at our assemblies,' she said.

'And you haven't persuaded them, have you? Likewise, here at the clinic and at the refectory...It's at the point now that the more they are argued with the less they are convinced.'

'We need someone to persuade them.'

'Everyone I know has tried, but...'

'No, we need someone new, someone uniquely–divinely qualified.'

'Mother, I've given up looking for messiahs.'

'Not a messiah. I want you to create someone.'

'Create someone?'

'A creature.'

'Creature! You mean a *golem* (clay figurine brought to life by magic)?'

'A golem,' she confirmed.

'Are you joking?'

'No, I'm not. Do you know the limbs (parts of a magic spell)?'

'My master Miryam taught me the permutations.'

'Do it, Sophia, please. The Kittim are marching southward, and we stand with death and obliteration before us.'

'A golem is usually created in order to perform some work...'

'Perfect. His task is to turn the collaborators. If the words of the living cannot accomplish it, we must give a voice to the unliving.'

The supplicant had come to me. How could I refuse?

After the fasting, we met up in front of the Throne of Ya'akov at the Mount Zion ekklesia with the ingredients for our conjuring. Tabitha had sent a boy to fetch a basketful of virgin clay from the mountains where no man had ploughed–the female element of creation–and I brought an amphora of living water from the Pool of Siloam—the male element.

The impatient Tabitha, after lighting the lamps and incense, rested patiently on her knees as supplicant. I began forming the golem, in the shape of a little man about the size of a year-old child, but rounder. My fingers fashioned the creature, kneading the clay into a shapeless husk, and my voice gave it life. It was an Aramaic spell.

I recited the long invocation, permutations of the alphabet opening the 221 gates—different strings of letters generating each limb, and each balance by a letter of the Ineffable Name. Ima Miryam had taught me to memorise them by visualising wheels inside wheels of letters.

'*Rava bara gavra...*' I wrote it in Hebrew on a piece of vellum and placed it in his mouth to give him life. And I wrote on his forehead *golmi* (my golem) so that he would be mine to command.

When I got to the end of the recitation, the Dreaming Self took me, the source of prophecy, and I saw our little man crowned in the light of creation, infused with a little piece of God, just like us Children of Abraham.

Tabitha later told me she could feel it, too, the ugly thing in front of us becoming the focus for our consciousness as our hearts soared upward.

We had to give a name to it—him, as Tabitha would have it. Adam was the obvious choice, but it reminded me too closely of my little brother. Remembering my Mem name of Chava, the name also seemed to conjure up unbearable images of me mating with the thing. So, we chose the name Yehuda.

Of course, the creature didn't physically leap up and begin to go around town visiting the loyalist hearths. The golem is only symbolic. It only gave us heart.

The Ossaeans among us, sometimes even Jairus, unless there was an influx of injuries from faction fighting, were still excused to go up to Mount Zion every day for Noon Contemplations. Indeed, we tried to get others to come with us, as noon prayers were open to all ranks and proselytes.

If any of the patients were of our sect or wished to attend, we insisted on some volunteers coming to assist. We are all facing our Maker, we argued, but for these, that day might be today, and so they have a greater right to their prayers.

By the same argument, teachers of every sect and persuasion were allowed into the clinic. We insisted on purity—anyone entering the compound had to wash their hands and feet at the door—and we allowed no faction fighting, but we encouraged the preachers. And not only the chiefs of congregations, we welcomed even the itinerant Levites and the desert prophets. It was good for the patients and took their minds off pain and death, Jairus said.

There was one the wounded soldiers liked very much, who told stories of Yeshua, Tabitha's messiah. His name was Leucius Charinus, which I remembered because he later wrote one of their goodnews books.

Not only had Yeshua been seen alive after death and ascended into heaven like Elijah, these stories we had heard. But when he died, Charinus said, he had descended for three days into Sheol, from whence he raised the dead from their sepulchers. 'Many of these have been seen walking in Jerusalem,' this man claimed. 'As it is written, those who died righteous zealot deaths would rise again in vengeance upon the Day of the Lord.'

427

Yeshua died and descended into Hades. Satan the prince of Tartarus said: Why doubtest thou and fearest to receive this Yeshua which is thine adversary and mine? For I tempted him, and have stirred up mine ancient people of the Jews with envy and wrath against him. I have sharpened a spear to thrust him through, gall and vinegar have I mingled to give him to drink, and I have prepared a cross to crucify him and nails to pierce him:

Hades said: Who is the King of glory, that cometh down from heaven unto us?

I have cast fire upon the world, and look, I'm guarding it until it blazes.

'Was it Yeshua leading the dead?' I asked him.

'I know not,' he said, 'those who saw it said they were led by a small boy.'

'About the size of a year-old child?'

He looked at me, astonished, assuming that I must have been among those who witnessed the event.

We volunteers nodded amongst ourselves as if to say—we see more of ours joining the ranks of the dead, actually, than dead ones coming back to life. But I hoped I would have the chance to send to Tabitha to suggest that our magic had been accomplished.

Jairus permitted the speaker, and anyone who would offer the patients healing, whether physical or spiritual, but he quietly commented to me, 'These gospels should be burned; even paganism is not as dangerous as these heretical sects.'

Shortly after that we found out that, though I was nowhere

near correct on the timing, my prophecy at Secacah had, also, been accomplished.

The camp of the Kanaim had fallen to the Tenth Legion. Some Zealots had gone out there to bury them. All who had stayed behind when the rest of us marched to Jerusalem had been totally slaughtered, they told us on their return, as if our comrades had fled into the Romans' arms open-hearted, expecting to prevail by miracle alone. Vespasian–may the angels of Himat torture him for all eternity–threw the bodies into the Salt Sea, where they all bobbed up to the surface unsinking.

We clung to each other in tears, Anna, Uzziel and others of the Kanaim all the more, as we knew those fallen. Gadriel the Angel of war between nations banished our tears, and we prepared for the fight.

New coinage was minted, stamped with the slogan 'Redemption of Zion'.

Yochanan and the Zealots now refused to hospitably comply with Joanna's regime, and the two factions competed in commandeering supplies from the people. Their uneasy alliance began to unravel.

Throughout the winter strife continued between the Idumaeans and the Zealots, and by the spring the Idumaeans were losing.

Some of our Kanaim could bear Yochanan no longer and mutinied, driving his forces to refuge in the Palace of the Adiabenes, seizing their goods along the way, but Eleazar's Zealots rushed out to defend them, threatening a major attack.

Partisans fought each other in Jerusalem until the arrival of another militia. A few days after Pesach had finished, Anna arrived at the clinic with a gang of people to report to us that

Simon bar Giora had arrived in Jerusalem.

He came up to cries of 'Saviour, Protector of the People'. Zealots from the Edomite countryside flocked to the banner of Bar Giora. Tens of thousands were in arms.

In a panic, the chief priests, the Idumaeans and the Rich citizens had sent for him, promising to open the gates if he would restore order to the city. Some of these men had been with him at Masada.

'High Priest Mattathias summoned him, but he just went straight to join our militia,' Anna said. 'Now they're warring with Yochanan's men. From his stronghold at Phaselis Tower he commands the city.'

During the month of Xanthicus (April), Simon besieged Yochanan who in turn was besieging Eleazar in the Temple.

It was no longer possible to be a rebel in Jerusalem without allegiance to one or the other of the militias. We needed a messiah who could lead all the Fifties and the Hundreds. Instead, we had three. It was a sorry situation, but that was the way it was.

The Zealots were too narrow a group, too demanding in their zeal to rally all the Ebionim. Yochanan was two-faced, and would betray us to the Herodians. During Purim, he and his Galileans dressed in finely dyed cloaks like women and killed with their right hands (fighting while dressed as women was a violation of holy law). After this, the Kanaim and other Idumaeans who'd come up with us split from Yochanan.

I was beyond looking for messiahs by this point, Sisters, but we had to pick a side. Yitzhak, Bruriah, Uzziel, Anna and I and others we were friendly with at the clinic and refectory sewed into our sleeves allegiance to Bar Giora. Athanasios, Menelaus and the ex-slaves had long since worn those stripes.

Simon plundered Eleazar's stores and led the Rich against the Zealots in the Temple, but they beat them back from above with catapults, ballistae, stone-slingers and archers erected on the four towers.

That spring, Vitellius, coming out of Germany, plundered Rome.

With all their wealth and might, these foreigners are no different from us. Men focus their eyes on the mightiest of the soldiers corrupted by the hope of spoils, forgetting their dream of a New World. So was the great Rome in the same sorry state as Jerusalem, soldiers wreaking havoc, demanding at swordpoint sustenance from the populace.

You will know, of course, the final winner among the Four Emperors, Sisters—Vespasian—may buzzards scatter his bones. That is where my story of Roman politics comes back to Judaea.

Vespasian had lurked outside Jerusalem, unwilling to commit to attack while each new messenger brought news of a new emperor. His reticence paid him well.

The prefect of Aegypt at Alexandria proclaimed him emperor, and naturally, his own Qesaryan troops agreed. All the legions in the East pledged their arms to him. Thus, did the soldiers seek the most bloodthirsty of candidates to elevate.

He sailed back to Rome in triumph.

Now the whole world knew; emperors could be made elsewhere than in Rome. This one had been made in Judaea.

I was happy to see Anna and Uzziel again one day in the month of Tammuz. I was at Yitzhak's house when Malachias brought them to the gate with some others of the Idumaeans, but their news was sad to me. With the threat of Vespasian supposedly gone, they were going home to what was left of Secacah.

'The spring wheat will have rotted on the fields by now, Sophia, if the Romans didn't burn it,' said Uzziel. We need to get back to our land.'

Just at the dawning of the New Jerusalem, everyone was leaving.

'We have done the job,' he said. 'We've brought in righteous government.'

'The high priests aren't betraying the capital to the Romans, after all,' said Anna. 'One of the Zealots spoke secretly to our commanders,' she said. 'Yochanan's accusation of Ananus, it was all a ruse. Ananus wasn't a traitor.'

I didn't believe it. Neither did Yitzhak and Bruriah.

'He is the leader of the Herodian priests, of course he's a traitor,' Yitzhak said.

'But we have found no evidence of treason. Where are the armaments?' said Anna.

'We may not have found them, but we know they have them. It was our ironmongers they got them from,' said Bruriah.

'In any case, if he has not betrayed us yet, he will do so later,' I argued. 'He is not among the righteous.'

'There's no invasion on the horizon now, Sophia,' Anna maintained. 'The Zealots told our commanders we should all go home.'

I spoke boldly, 'Sister, are you mad? We await the wrath of newly laurelled Caesar.'

The Messenger immediately backed me up. 'Your lands must wait until after our final victory. The final battle will be here.'

And so did Yitzhak, 'Uzziel, you must not leave.'

432

I pleaded with them that their sustenance was guaranteed. 'Your children will be fed. Widow Joanna's refectory and the collection boxes of the Ebionim could support the entire city for seven years.'

There was a buzz of agreement among the company, but it remained more an expression of regret at parting than a pressure they would succumb to. Many Idumaeans did stay, but the bulk of the contingent went down from the city. I was sad again to part with beloved friends.

Once the Idumaeans were gone, the Zealots were in full control. The stream of refugees dwindled, as it became difficult for anyone to leave the city. Zealots guarded the road and killed deserters.

The winter rains were coming. The Romans were nowhere in sight. Only after his armies had secured his laurels did Vespasian send Titus–may his seed be cursed–to resume the war against the Jews.

In the city, a few weeks after Hanukkah, Eleazar ben Simon and a number of prominent citizens broke away from Yochanan and the Zealots. Eleazar took the Inner Temple and planted weapons atop the gates from which they threw down missiles upon Yochanan.

His men returned fire upward, but caught in the middle between the two forces, also barraged Simon's forces at a lower level, with catapults, slingers and archers. In doing so they caught scores of pilgrims who were there to worship at the Temple.

Joanna ran shrieking to pull me from the clinic, 'Sophia, your Zealots have burned the Ebionim warehouses–all that food.'

Yochanan had continued sallies into the city against Simon, and his last atrocity had been to set fire to the warehouses—the ones near the Temple that stored all the refectory supplies. The whole area surrounding the Temple Court was filled with smoke.

'How can you explain this atrocity?' she wailed.

'Sister, I cannot. We will all starve.'

The trouble was, I could explain it. The refectory served collaborators as well as patriots. With this supply gone, the people would have to turn to the militias for sustenance, and this the Zealots could use to rule them. But I could not say this to Joanna. It was too cruel a tactic.

'But do not tar me with the same brush as those Galileans. I am no partisan of Yochanan.'

'He hasn't stopped there, you know. He's seized the sacred timber to build towers so he can attack Eleazar up in the Temple, and he's melted down the gold vessels given by Caesar Augustus.'

'Raiding the sacred Treasury? We fought a war with Florus for that.'

'Stealing from HaShem and stealing from His people? That food could have fed the people for years. The result will be a famine that will destroy the city,' she said.

For once, Joanna spoke truly.

# Chapter 28
## Titus

During the first days of Pesach we watched for them every day. First someone would go up to the wall, then when they came down, someone else would go up. When the hour arrived, Doris came rushing down to the clinic. She didn't say anything; she just stood there with her mouth open, and we knew.

There were no more injuries. The fighting had stopped in expectation of the arrival of the real enemy. So, all the workers in the clinic climbed up to the roof, and we heard a huge shuffling and padding as, all over the city, the three militias and the entire population of Jerusalem climbed up steps and ladders to the walls and rooves.

Doris clutched at my sleeve and pointed toward the horizon. It was one huge horizontal band of dust as thousands of soldiers marched in formation. We saw their dust and heard their feet for over an hour before we saw the first sight of them.

The city watched in fear the terrifying sight of the Flavian army marching up to Jerusalem.

I have already said that the army of Florus was a frightening sight, but the army of the Flavians was four entire legions—many times huger than Florus' few cohorts. Each legion was more men than any of us had ever seen.

Vespasian—may his bones be crushed—marched from Emmaus with the Fifth Macedonica, joined by the Tenth Fretensis from Jericho. His son Titus—may his bones join his father's—joined him from the north with the Fifteenth Apollinaris and the Twelfth Fulminata. It was the Twelfth Legion under Gallus whom we had defeated at Beth-horon, and they were eager for revenge.

The noise of thousands of feet marching and millions of clanking plates of armour was the most horrible sound I had ever heard. It was slow but unhalting, relentlessly approaching, accompanied every few minutes by horns and trumpets blowing, proclaiming the armies' power and magnificence. Flags and banners bobbed up and down above them, shimmering in the heat, like colourful cloths floating in the sea.

We counted—6,000 in each legion, plus 6,000 auxiliaries—in all nearly 50,000 soldiers. First the Kittim in their standard armour, then the men of the client kings in the livery of their nations. Rows and rows of soldiers neatly organised, stretching like an armour-backed snake all the way back to the horizon, moving slowly forward, first one row of scales, then the next.

Nothing could have stopped that forward momentum, the might of each scale fortified by the weight of the entire animal. Any blocking manoeuvre would only have allowed another section to progress ahead of them.

It continued for hours and hours, so long we had to keep sending people down for water. You would think that the rapid advance of an invading army would terrify. Actually, it was their very slowness that chilled the blood. The inevitability of our destiny approached over the horizon like the progress of the sunset. Heavy, slow, hot, immense, unstoppable.

They all marched in perfect formation; our disorganised and ill-equipped faction-fighting militias were a sorry comparison. Though we were peoples on the same earth, great were the differences in our conditions and our chattels.

They had siege engines, battering rams, trebuchets. The soldiers had metal breast-plate armour, arm and shin guards, swords, spears and javelins. Our clothing was ragged; our knives and staves crafted roughly from converted rakes and plough-shares; our armour was leather at best.

We could never face an army like that—four legions—on the battlefield, full frontal infantry against infantry. Their weapons were superior, their military training formidable. Our victories had to be small, stolen moments, subterfuge under cover of darkness, stones flung from caves and crags, a lucky boulder rolled down a cliff. Our only advantage was our inventiveness and our zeal.

Titus—cursed be his luck—was hoping for an early victory—*dreaming of Rome, wealth, and pleasure*—but he would not attack on the first day. He could save his father's sponsors in Rome much gold if he could win our surrender by threat of terror rather than battle, so they would surely begin with an invitation to negotiate.

The militias had hastened to their posts by this time, but all the women stayed on the walls and rooves. Mothers put their babies to sleep under awnings, hoping the heavy noises wouldn't awaken them. We were up on the roof so long, the matrons brought up food.

As the legions drew closer to the city, they became confused by the terrain. The suburbs were all steep hills with olive orchards terraced in levels and divided by a complex chain of low walls. Furthermore, the entire area under and around the city was networked with underground tunnels and wadis, and militiamen could carry out ambushes from them, leaping out as if from nowhere for quick sallies, then running back down for cover.

Titus was dressed in finery to impress, not geared for battle. He had neither helmet nor breastplate on, so all could admire him. As his horse pranced here and there, it began to falter, and he became separated off from the main columns.

The first of our heroes, a great body of militiamen jumped out from the Women's Towers through the gate next to Queen Helena's monument and blocked his horse. They showered him with darts, as we women cheered, overjoyed that our men had not remained crippled with terror.

There was nothing in the Roman books of war that instructed them in how to deal with situations like this, and for a short period, the army did absolutely nothing to save their general. For a few moments, it looked like we were going to capture the young general before even the first battle. A triumph like that would be heard around the world. But somehow, he remained untouched until his men could rally.

Though the Lord denied us that victory, in the first days we had some initial successes. Titus decided to shift the camps, moving the Fifth opposite the Western Gate and the Twelfth and Fifteenth opposite the Psephinus Tower, and our men greatly harried the transfer of baggage, ambushing from the tunnels and then disappearing again unscathed. There was still nothing to do in the clinic, so I watched from the roof.

The legions set about in an orderly fashion constructing three encampments, the Tenth, Twelfth and Fifteenth on the western side, the Tenth on the Mount of Olives to the east. They began cutting down trees in the vicinity and constructing platforms for their battering rams.

The tunnels meant we could still get in and out of the walls, and though the city was swollen with Pesach pilgrims, we were still looking for recruits, and I was still in daily expectation of the arrival of the Nations. It was at this point that Yitzhak demanded an introduction to the Notzrim.

'We need to find out once and for all where these Minim (apostates) stand,' he said. 'If there are any collaborators among them, you must urge your friend Tabitha to expel them, send them across the Jordan with the other traitors.'

'Yitzhak, you know most of them, like Shulamith, aren't traitors; they merely left the battlefield when we wished they had not. Then many of the Greek proselytes, not wishing to be circumcised, became victims of the Shammaite persecutions.'

'That was then, Sophia,' he was firm. 'Now anyone who is not a fighter is a collaborator. Shulamith, too. I've written this letter...' He brandished it like a lance.

'I'm going to ask the ekklesia to send it to her. She can sit at the right hand of God for all I care after we sleep. Now it's time for her to come home and fight like a Jew.'

Issuing orders of expulsion may not have been Tabitha's role at the ekklesia, and I did think branding all the Godfearers of Pella as traitors was too harsh. However, I agreed with him on this course of action, and I, too, wanted to send a letter to Shulamith, so I sent ahead a request for an introduction to her husband Yeshua ben Thebutis, his father having joined those who sleep, and the other presbyters.

After Noon Contemplations, as the place of its celebration was nearby, we went up to the Upper Room.

On arrival, I left the men downstairs, noting that one of the presbyters was a woman–Yitzhak would be pleased to see that—and mounted the stairs to the Assembly Hall to find Tabitha kneeling before the big black Throne of Ya'akov.

At first, I thought her in prayer and remained respectfully silent at the back, but then I saw her elbow popping up and down energetically and heard her muttering curses under her breath. I heard, 'Oblias…Spouter of Lies.' She was ferociously writing onto a scroll, so vehemently that it was quite messy with ink blots in the margins.

'I'm writing to Symeon,' she announced. 'They can leave the proselytes and Godfearers to their heavenly tablecloth (Peter's vision that it was alright for Christians to eat non-kosher), but the Pillars must now return to the city. We need them to rally the Fifties and the Hundreds. The battle for Jerusalem is beginning.'

Upon rejoining Yitzhak, I learned, as I had suspected, that any collaborators had long left of their own accord.

'They are patriots to a man,' he said, 'and there was even one woman among the leaders, befitting in this New Jerusalem.'

'So, no expulsions?' I teased.

'They had a major schism at the time of the royalist purge.'

'Shulamith told me that some of the proselytes were in Herod's employ, like Philip bar Jacimus.'

'They all got run out of town when we stoned the king,' he said. 'Then there was some friction at the time of the riots in Qesarya, they said, and all the proselytes took off. Some joined Shulamith's lot in Pella, some left for the Asian synagogues of the Cilician. I know you have your doubts about Chuza's widow, Sophia. She hasn't attended Assembly in ages, they said.'

'So, where you expected traitors you found a hall full of Zealots.'

'Yes. Most of them supporters of Gush Chalav and not Bar Giora, but then, I suppose, since so many of them are Galileans...'

'The first apostles were disciples of Simon Cephas, himself a Galilean.'

'That's how we started. They gave me a history lesson expounding the heroism of Judas the Galilean. At which I heartily agreed. Then it was the ensigns protest in Qesarya. At which I heartily agreed.'

'I told you, Yitzhak. It was Yeshua the Just who led that protest.'

We skirted along beneath the First Wall, though we had no longer to fear from Yochanan's partisans. Zealots, Sicarii and Galileans were now of one blood in the face of the invading Romans.

He continued gaily, 'So, I started on freedom for the slaves, at which point they heartily agreed.'

As we crossed back into the Lower City, Yitzhak's laugh was good to hear, but it seemed to echo across the vast spaces that had once held walls, gardens, olive trees. Now all had been turned into weapons of war in the hands of our enemy.

Simon had been training the men relentlessly, but they'd been given a brief reprieve—some whispered it was 'to say good-bye to their families'. I could see by the way Yitzhak walked that his leg muscles were sore.

'Many of the proselytes are slaves, I hear,' I said.

'Yes, and some of the presbyters, too. A few of them know Tasios, said they'd follow him into battle any day.'

I considered how often did I speak of Tabitha to Athanasios, or Shulamith his best friend's sister, yet he had never mentioned to me his Notzrim comrades.

'They ended up inviting you and Tasios, me and Bruriah to join them in table fellowship after Yom Kippur—if we're still alive then, someone noted. Whether we heard the goodnews or not, we'd be welcome, they said.'

'If we're still alive then, it will be good news for the whole world,' I said.

I left my letter with Yitzhak's for the next messenger bound across the Jordan. We had had all the arguments; my letter only said, 'Come home. We need you. Be well.'

At the Feast of Unleavened Bread, even with four legions of Romans at the gates, thousands came up to worship at the house of God. So righteous was their love they faced the army of the Kittim on either side as they walked up the road.

Festival time was often a tricky time for enemies of God in Jerusalem. Nothing bar death would keep the devout from continuing the religious practices of our forefathers, and the crowds and the rejoicing and the abundance of food at these occasions whipped us into patriotic frenzy at any threat to deny this our freedom.

The gates were open to all Jews at festival time, but the guards were hardly going to require everyone to drop their breeches in the road. And these days, a circumcised foreskin was no guarantee of a circumcised heart. Once the gates were opened, anyone could enter, claiming to be a pilgrim. So had Ptolemy son of Lagus conquered Jerusalem by deceit on a Sabbath, welcomed through the gates as if on his way to offer sacrifice.

Eleazar opened the gates, and we watched the pilgrims come up. Among them were some of Yochanan's Sicarii with curved knives in their sleeves. They attacked Eleazar's men, who fled into the tunnels.

We heard the story later at the clinic from the Messenger, 'Yochanan took the Inner Temple, and the rest of the Zealots joined him, led by Eleazar and Simon son of Arinus,'–he characterised Yochanan as a shifty schemer–'Simon's forces included the Idumaeans led by James son of Sosas and Simon son of Cathlas. Now Simon holds the Upper and part of the Lower City. Yochanan holds the Temple and the eastern Lower City.'

Where there had been three militias, now there were two.

We wore Bar Giora's mark inside our sleeves, and unless on neutral ground like the refectory or clinic we had been careful to remain within the territory of his dominion, within the western part of the Lower City–that was necessary just for personal safety–but none of us had raised a hand during the faction fighting. Even Yitzhak, a ranked partisan, had managed to stay out of it, as Bruriah and I had begged him.

Now Athanasios' band of runaways, too, began to function as a loose militia. The ex-slaves took up swords, sticks and slings. They each managed to pilfer a full set of military equipment–armour, dagger, sword, javelin, spear, crossbow and arrows, pickaxe, scythe and digging tool–from dead Romans or rival partisans.

The efforts of their tiny number were scrupulously attuned to the strategies of Simon, though Simon knew it not. When Yitzhak and Athanasios reviewed their day's fighting, they always found that they had been carrying out roughly the same operations.

I told Athanasios what Ima Miryam had said about Tsuiyah and me, how one may work together without liking.

'I agree,' he said, 'though I think if I met this prince, I would

443

like him.'

Though Athanasios' zeal inspired his companions, he wished not to lead. As a result, though they fought fiercely in their small way, the band was quite disorganised. He would offer advice or suggestions, but then stand aback, as if waiting for orders. He took on tasks as a good slave obeys his duties, and executed them soberly and intelligently.

He was not a soldier; his skill was more in organisational matters. Thus, he was a vital element in our resistance force. But he indulged in little of the glory the soldiers revelled in and relied on to keep their courage up. One of the unsung heroes of our revolution, he was. And is it not the unsung who are the real heroes?

Titus had put pressure on our supplies by allowing pilgrims up to the city to celebrate Pesach. Now he refused them to leave, and for several days I was more needed at the refectory than the clinic. With our stores gone, we had to rely on requisitioning the citizens, and they did not donate willingly.

# Chapter 29
## Victor

The Romans continued constructing platforms for attack towers and for battering rams and began three ramps out of earth and timber. The walls of Jerusalem were too high for ladders.

So afraid were they now of harassment from our men, they guarded the operation with three ranks of infantry, a row of archers and three ranks of cavalry behind them.

Still our men attacked the ramps. They ambushed from the Western Gate and managed to light the thatch roof of one of the platforms with firebrands. Titus' revenge was fierce; he crucified one of the commanders he seized in front of the walls.

Before the dawn was light, we heard the trumpets. Romans blow trumpet three times, each commander shouting three times in the native language of the battalion, 'Ready? Ready? Ready?'

All down the columns, the soldiers raised their right hands and shouted in four or five different languages, 'We are ready'.

It was an enormous sound, after which they fell quickly into battle formation, each slipping effortlessly into his position like coins rolling into a collection box. Once in place, at a signal, they began to march, utterly silent but for their heavy footfalls.

After the terrifying call to war from the triumphal trumpets, the silence of the march was ominous, deadly. Our men scurried in a panic to their own posts, shouting at us women to get out of the way. We shivered in fear and shushed our children as we found safe places to await the charge.

Six bulls the Ebionim priests sacrificed. They wailed and wrung their hands over the unfavourable entrails, and the Lord remained silent while they agonised over the meaning of the auguries.

A sacrificial cow gave birth to a lamb in the Court of the Temple. Fish jumped out of the wadis and flapped gasping on the sand, calves were born with split hooves, and young brides aborted in pain, their wombs releasing untimely infants into the storm. Nature itself seemed to be screaming that something was wrong. The priests wailed in bewilderment, not wishing to see what the signs were showing them.

In my readings, the signs were there as well. 'The Lion is rising, and the Shepherd is on the cusp,' the Magi said, catastrophic omens.

The sky was an unholy colour—red, brown—and it got darker by the minute. This was the worst day the skies could give us. The omens were wrong for a battle. Yet on this day would begin our war. My entrails churned like those of the sacrifices. I rushed around frantically grabbing at people's elbows. They looked anxiously at the sky and groaned.

The earth was so silent. Townspeople groaned silently in the anticipation of something, all the more frightening in its mystery. The animals were deadly silent, as if they knew what was coming.

Militiamen rushed here and there. There must have been skirmishes going on outside the gates; every few minutes I heard noises in the distance of swords clashing and victims crying. Wives and daughters began to beat their kitchen pots in fear and protest, and men, young and old, ran to the gates to find the skirmishes.

The skirmishes escalated and came closer, and as the sky got blacker, the fearful silence of the earth was replaced by the more certain, but more dreadful sounds of battle.

We'd been sent to market with two donkeys to gather crucial supplies, Bruriah, Doris, me, and some of the matrons.

On the steps to the Temple, a half-dozen or so Zealots—some of Yochanan's Galilean rebels, I could tell by their accents—had gathered clutching an amphora, drunk.

'Shame on you, brothers,' I jeered.

'Where is God now? Where is Elijah?' said one of the men, losing his balance in the passion of saying it.

'Elijah will come when swine have wings,' said another, as if it were my fault.

Bruriah chided me, 'Have a mind to your safety, Sophia, angering men like that, and a mind to judging people in their suffering. When people have no food, they lose all care for everything—even God.'

Indeed, I regretted my scorn, I who had been nourished from the collection boxes of the Ebionim. And it is not as if I don't have my own demons. Is it any wonder that people in their misery seek redemption through Dionysus, trying to cheat their way into the Kingdom of Heaven? Have I not tried to cheat my way in though magic? I thought of Yahya and the golem and blushed at the memory of the follies Tabitha had pulled me into.

We were at the market when it came, the moment our fears had been anticipating for so long. The largest of the Roman's battering rams—Victor—attacking our walls. The thud was heard throughout the city, echoing off the mountains around, a heavy, overpowering, terrible sound.

The whole city let out a wail. We watched the whole market-place reel in one huge wave. Women blocked their children's ears and huddled them under the stalls. Animals bolted.

From somewhere—was it from Yochanan's quarter?—a tribune called, 'Free passage to all partisans. All fighting men to the walls.' Then other voices started calling the same thing from other quarters. Simon and Yochanan had finally called a truce. They could wait to vie for the throne of Jerusalem until after the foreigner was expelled.

Militiamen among the crowd scuttled outward to their posts, and Bruriah grabbed my elbow, 'Can you believe it takes this to rally them together?'

'Better late than never,' I said.

'All this time, two years it's been. We should have been manu-facturing arms and renewing our fortifications,' she moaned.

The wave of movement in the marketplace had settled, and there was a moment of strange silence in the crowd.

Just then, one of Yochanan's Galileans came running in, shouting, 'Who has '*mar* for sale?'. In the silence, hundreds of heads turned toward him, and some of the stallholders began mocking his accent. 'Oh, do you want *ḥamor*, a donkey?' Another cried, 'or is it *ḥamar*, wine?'; 'you must mean *amar*, wool'; 'no, no, *imar*, lamb for slaughter'.

After the terror of the ram, we stood open-mouthed at the levity of it.

Surprisingly enough, the market regained its bustle. Subsequent thuds from the ram provoked shudders from the crowd, but everyone bravely returned to business. We were able to make our purchases and take them back to the clinic.

'Even under attack, commerce goes on,' I said.

Bruriah commented, 'People have to make a living until they die, up until the last breath.'

Joanna was right. With the food storehouses destroyed, famine soon broke out, and desperate people scuttled outside the walls at night to forage for food. We became used to sleeping with the pitiful cries of suffering families in houses around us. Athanasios and Yitzhak came home at night so exhausted they couldn't speak.

After one week, Victor, their biggest ram, breached the Third Wall. It was the Seventeenth of Tammuz.

Our forces had to pull back to the Second Wall, while Titus began levelling part of the Third Wall. Anyone caught by the Romans would be executed in the usual way. The hills around the city were littered with thousands of crosses of crucified Jews.

For those who still cherished hope of a miracle from the clouds, there was no more concourse between man and wife, no more studying of the Torah, no more shaving, cutting hair or wearing cosmetics. Ordinary life came to a permanent end; there was nothing between us and the world but our vows.

The smell of blood and disease and the cries of people in pain made me long desperately to escape the clinic. I convinced Jairus to let me assist with the carrying of the wounded. The horror of battle was hardly worse, but at least the battlefield was exciting, and I got to see the progress of battle firsthand, without having to wait till the end of day when all the bad news was circulated. The Messenger was too busy with official duties to visit.

There were other reasons I wanted to join the ferrying teams, though. It seemed a comfort to hear bad news early on. Seeing

449

a friend's death was less upsetting than hearing the news of it.

A bit of shapeshifting came in handy. Never once during the war was I targeted by a missile, lance or sword. They simply didn't see me.

Some of the younger militiamen soiled themselves, losing control of their bodies in the first experience of mortal terror. We tried to deal with these young men in dignity without drawing attention.

We suffered no shortage of hands in the clinic that we didn't suffer in the field.

The physics collected some bodies for demonstrations and when there was a lull, would teach us this or that detail about the brain, stomach, or the blood. We only objected when the specimen had been known to us.

Even had I sat at the feet of the Ossaean Therapeuts, I would not match the knowledge nor the courage of these men. Daily the physics showed us this new fact about blood flow or that new fact about organs.

We workers quickly became equally skilled at the procedures we performed many times a day. Within the first few weeks of the war, new volunteers learned everything I knew about blood, breathing and broken bones—which formed the basis of the cases we dealt with—and gained a fairly good appreciation of what happens in the few moments before death.

All the workers in the clinic—at least all those with no extra family ties—were keen to learn everything we could. At every moment in the field or on the plank, our knowledge could save a life.

There were many things my magical knowledge or the medical knowledge of the physics could have added had we treated them in peacetime. Death stole our patients away before we could try our hand, and war kept bringing fresh cartloads of bloody skin and bones to replace them.

We performed the same operations over and over—clear the breathing passage, stop the blood, dig out arrow tips and spearheads, wash and stitch the wound, set and bandage the bone. We rarely had time to do more than that. Most of them, if the wounds didn't kill them, the infections did. We rapidly ran out of ways to help them with pain.

I learned many things I had never had reason to learn from the Yachad. To take a pulse to feel the body's heat, to dose with both poppies and henbane for amputation. The more serious cases required several people to hold them down while the physician operated. They were cruel lessons, every one of them, but at least I was not alone. Each time a procedure was done, there were a crowd of students watching.

We learned quickly, but we had so little effect. I longed for the luxury of bringing a patient back to health, and I had dreams of soldiers coming to me for an elixir or one of Imme's infusions or a reading to restore their courage. All we ever seemed to manage was to hold back Death's evil hand for a few hours or days.

Bruriah was on the burial team, which was a separate operation, but naturally our works overlapped. I touched corpses so many days running I rarely ever got the chance to complete the purification process.

Even if one wanted to go to the Temple with sin offerings, there were no more red heifers in the land. Jairus still strictly insisted on full mikveh after contact, though. 'Cleanliness is essential,' he said. 'If it were not the Law of Moses, it would

451

be the law of physicians.'

In the clinic, my task was to take instruction from the physics, but when I had a free moment, I looked to the needs of the heart. Sometimes I was able to use my magical knowledge when I had a receptive patient.

Healing was the realm of the Acting Self. A physic's instinct was to address the wounded by asking the pertinent questions: 'Where is the wound?', 'How much blood has been lost?', 'Are any bones broken?', and then base the treatment on the answers to these questions.

In the field, I seemed to have the gift for a certain sort of diagnosis, though it was unfounded on medical rationality. I addressed the wounded with my Feeling Self. It is difficult to describe. I bathed the battlefield with the force of my love, and received emanations in return. Those destined to die seemed to emit a weaker emanation.

There were others skillful at choosing on medical criteria. I could not teach them my skill; it was a question of listening with more than the ears and seeing with more than the eyes. The captain of the ferrying team told Jairus I was more valuable in the field than in the clinic. I seemed to have a knack for picking out those whom Death had claimed and those for whom Azrael (the angel of death) would wait.

'Again, you succeed in second-guessing Death,' he said once as I marked out those ready to give up the ghost.

'I cannot claim such.'

'Yet you do have a talent. I would wish you could teach it to the rest of us.'

'What is my talent, then?'

'You can look a soldier in the eye and see his destiny.'

I wasted much of my power regretting my lack of knowledge of the physician's science, but after this, I began to see that I did have a gift, and was able to use it.

As I stepped through the blood and the bodies, inspecting each soldier for no more than a moment or two, deciding which ones to carry off first, I felt in my heart that my judgements were correct. We saved so few of them, but I can honestly say that of those who could be saved, we didn't miss many, at this early stage of the war.

There were hundreds of cases where a soldier would insist on having a minor injury treated on the spot so he could continue fighting, only to have the wound fester and kill the man days later. It was not our treatment at fault here but rather the soldier's zeal. I could not fault them for that.

As we assessed the gravity of each injury, it seemed fairly obvious to me, physic or no, which ones were mortal. Most often the amount of blood was the telling clue, and any untrained eye could gauge that. As we packed the planks, shouting to each other, passing bandages back and forth, I also looked each soldier in the eyes.

While the physics looked at the wounds, I looked into their hearts. If their eyes were shut in pain, I told them to open them and look at me. Those whom Death had already marked seemed to show it in their eyes. I saw a kind of film over them, as if they couldn't quite see me, they were already looking past me over my shoulder at the Heavenly Host.

There were prayers for moments like this, but even they were rationed. Each soldier received a few words to comfort his passage, no more.

So many died in my arms that I prepared a brief prayer to

comfort them. 'Life is the trial for man, death provides the release... death gives freedom to the soul, washes us clean... only the mortal self knows pain and suffering.'

The body is a tomb, was the idea, and how uplifting it would be to fly free from that. But I hardly believed it myself anymore. None of the deaths I witnessed were uplifting in the slightest, and yet we sang songs when the souls passed amid the din of battle.

On a few occasions, I spotted Death in the eyes of a militia-man I knew and put him on a plank anyway, influenced by my own feelings. I was dishonest in doing so. Without exception these all died, and I'm ashamed to have wasted our clinic's efforts for my own selfish sentiment.

There were no smiles on the faces of the people, all crammed into the Market Quarter and Upper and Lower City, no idle chatter in the streets, but there was still hope of victory. The loss of the Third Wall was not crucial. It did, however, put great pressure on provisions. The refectory was in chaos.

I rarely saw anyone apart from Bruriah and other clinic or refectory workers during this period, even my own husband. Yitzhak was always at his post, Athanasios and his runaways were usually somewhere close by, fighting too.

Though I was never particularly chatty with her, I had no longer any reason to distrust Joanna. Her royalists were totally defeated. She had heard Victor's first thud, too. Now for all of us, survival was what mattered.

When I returned from Noon Contemplations, a woman was speaking with the head matron. She was the wife of Cabi son of Lenthius, a prominent Boethusian. Some collaborators had been caught up in the slaughter, and he was one of those we'd saved, and she wished to give thanks for his rescue. There were loads of people around, and we heard every word.

She volunteered to attend her husband in his convalescence and help our effort in any way she might. While there were those who doubted the wisdom of allowing one of these traitors in our midst, the physic agreed. Our clinic, like the refectory, served zealot and collaborator alike.

While she was here, however, the physic said, there would be no back and forth between clinic and town. Naturally, we all kept an eye on her.

After four days, the ram broke through the middle of the Northern Wall. The garrison on the towers of the Second Wall fled, but our men barricaded the breach and fought for three days. Both sides passed the nights in arms.

A soldier, wounded in the leg but not seriously, hobbled about trying to help his comrades. He was picking his way carefully through the corpses, approaching any he saw moving and using his stave as a staff.

There were so many dead, forming a motionless carpet from Bezetha Hill to the breach in the wall, that from where I stood it looked like he was stabbing them in the face. I thought, the prophets of old could restore life by the laying of a staff upon a dead man's face. Alas, there was little this soldier could do.

We soon convinced him, though he protested that his wound was minor, to lie on a plank. Better to treat his wound soon to have him fight another day than to spend our efforts on those who may as well already be lost.

On the fourth day, the Kittim broke through again, and Titus began levelling the Northern Wall.

Everyone had to pull back to within the Second Wall, and

we had to rapidly move the clinic to some disused houses in the Lower City—quite an undertaking, as by this time there were mountains of wounded.

Partisans huddled in corners of the ruins and jumped on would-be deserters. You couldn't go anywhere without seeing corpses.

It was the wife of Cabi who made us the offer; the houses were owned by her family and their neighbours, but most had fled.

There were no more trips to Noon Contemplations. We prayed the Eighteen at the new clinic, but only in shortened form.

Yitzhak, Bruriah and her mother had to leave their house and so did Athanasios' band of runaways and I. We rounded each other up and found another bunch of refugees to crowd in with in a warehouse on Ophel Hill.

We skirted around the edge of the walls, where here and there cluttered stones from ballistas, broken arrows and even bits of armour no one had scavenged yet, making for hard walking. Fortunately, the reprieve from fighting had provided each side an opportunity to gather up the dead.

Of the aristocrats at the refectory, only Joanna and Gamaliel's people were left. All the others had defected or been caught up in the purges.

The refectory was in a constant state of chaos, the procuration of supplies near impossible, and the distribution of supplies to the crucial fighters often required armed supervision. We girls with neither strength nor arms had to defend our mission with nothing but our sharp tongues.

Many died of hunger. The famous priest Zadok—may the

memory of the holy be a blessing—who had fasted for forty years so that Jerusalem might not be destroyed, was so thin that one could see the food he ate as it passed down his throat.

Even the Rich were starving.

Martha the daughter of Boethus, the wife of the High Priest Yeshua ben Gamla, Doris told us, had sent her servant out to purchase some fine flour, but he was unable to find a single *se'ah* (about one bowlful). He reported, however, that there was still some of inferior quality to be had.

'Buy some for me at once,' she said.

But by the time he got to market, there was only barley flour left.

'Go get it, quick,' she said. But again, it was too late.

So, she put on her slippers and went to market herself, where she slipped on a piece of dung and died.

'Couldn't take the rough food we're dishing out,' said Doris.

'These once-a-year Jews,' I commented.

'The Boethusians are as pampered as the Herods,' Bruriah said. 'That Martha was so rich she had her servants lay carpets from her door to the Temple on Yom Kippur, just so she wouldn't dirty her golden sandals. She died with them covered in dung.'

'She was only where she was because she bribed her husband's way into the high priesthood for three *qabs* (one qab=1.276 litres) of gold,' Doris continued. 'As she died, she threw all her silver and gold in the streets, saying "What is the good of all this?".'

Ahat said, 'She should have given it to the Ebionim like everyone else.'

'Little good it would do us now,' Doris commented.

# Chapter 30
## Heartache and hunger

Somehow, during these days when men were all fighting, the women still held life together. We ferried supplies to the front of the battle; our hands distributed the meager food; we carried the wounded; our arms comforted the terrified children. When a mother, watchtower of the household and bulwark of the community, lost her life, often the rest of the family expired along with her in hopelessness.

Such was the mood in our little household when we lost our own matriarch.

Bruriah's mother Mara was with a group transporting water to the men on the wall, when she was caught by an enemy missile and fell to her death.

It seemed obscene that her face, battered and bloodied, was still carefully powdered with white pigment and her eyes perfectly lined with kohl. Though her neck was fully broken, the lines around her eyes were not even smudged. She had even gone to her death 'with her face on'.

Most everyone had sold everything of value, but we, nourished by the bounty of the collection boxes, still had Princess Shulamith's exquisite ivory cosmetics box, which Bruriah took with her when we fled to Alex.

Yitzhak hadn't been home for days; and the Messenger was always at official duties. If we wanted to get messages to the militiamen, we had to go ourselves. It was I who went in search of Yitzhak to inform him of the sad news.

The place was a vile drinking hole frequented by the Zealot party. Where women go to the nice clean well for their messages, men seem to have dirtier, more mysterious sites for their company.

I entered by the side. No passing trade would have seen this as a door. They were irregular planks of wood nailed to a frame, which slid sideways along a groove. It used to be made of iron, someone said. They must have melted it down for staves. The wooden frame was wet with rain, and I had a bit of a time sliding it.

Once inside, I went up to the proprietor, an old man, very hairy, who was huddled next to the pallet with a mate, even older than he and more whitely hairy.

He nodded, 'What will you have?'

I was not about to have wine or ale, and he didn't have anything else; nor did I carry any coin. 'Water, please.' He began to frown that my order was to earn him no payment.

'I'm looking for Yitzhak,' I flashed the inside of my sleeve to show the stripes of a partisan of Bar Giora, 'one of the captains of the Tens.'

His face lifted at the sight of my stripes and the mention of a name that told him my business.

'The battle continues. Another hour, he'll come,' he said.

I took my pitcher and mug of water to the nearest bench and waited. The proprietor, old and hairy, mentioned not another word to me. He went back to his mate, who was equally taciturn.

Installed back in his place, they both became immobile, and sat there like statues, every few minutes saying one or two words to each other in some language I'd never heard before.

Bithynian, perhaps?

There were no paying customers for his trade. The only other person in the room was an old, old man, even more ancient than the two at the pallet. He was bent sharply at the back, and his white hair and beard touched his knees.

He clutched a broom hard with both hands, as if more for support than for sweeping. And indeed, his sweeping was of little industry. In the entire time I'd been there, he had moved the straw barely a hand-breadth.

If I hadn't known I was among partisans, I'd have been very nervous as a woman in such company. Naturally, I couldn't regard them directly, and there was little to look at anyway. The two old men sat motionless and almost wordless, the sweeper moved so slowly, one wondered if he was still alive. Maybe he had simply frozen dead, propped up by the broom.

I had nothing to do, so I kept refilling from the pitcher and drank mug after mug of water. About halfway through what must have been the hour I was to wait, I realised to my horror the consequence. Not only would I have to approach the strange proprietor, I would have to do so under the gaze of the other old man and the ancient sweeper. Furthermore, who knew what kind of facilities they had.

I only had to pull my shawl tight over my face, however, for him to deduce my purpose. He said not a word, pointing me the way.

I walked awkwardly straight past the two old men, through another wooden frame that slid sideways into another room.

The next door, open this time, led almost backwards. I went through a hallway, then another room, then more hallways and more rooms, each older, dirtier and more decrepit than the

460

last. At each juncture, I seemed to move further back in time.

At some point—I'm not sure where, I'd lost my direction in the maze—I exited the building.

Here were walls, as ancient as the city of David, yet they seemed to join with what I presumed were the walls of the inn. The strange establishment seemed to have been built into, grown out of, ancient walls inherited from the Jebusites, and so had marked the evolution of drinking establishments since ancient times. Jerusalem had been here since before King David. Would it endure until the end of this month?

Skirting the enclosure of the walls, I crossed next to a small patch of farmland, punctuated here and there—in no particular design—with barren fruit trees and clumps of unweeded vegetables. I stepped across planks of wood laid in the wet soil to the hut. A huge, ugly rat poked its nose out from behind a fencepost, one of the few that hadn't yet been caught for food by starving citydwellers.

The latrine was horrifying—the whole area stank; the hut's wooden door wouldn't close. Flies buzzed all around, and worms crawled beneath my sandals. The facilities consisted of a pallet of wood with a hole in it set over a long trench.

The trench was one of a series dug all the way through the patch of land. The fruit trees—an irregular old fig tree and a clump of quince—and the vegetables—beans with lots of weeds and squash dotted here and there—had all been stripped bare of anything edible.

They seemed so undesigned as not to have been planted at all, but perhaps to have grown of their own from seeds expelled amid ripe eliminations. I think the latrine hut had been moved round and round to fertilise the area with the sewage. I hurried my purpose. Elimination and fertilisation are equally acts of nature, but the thought was repulsive.

Perhaps the land had been so used for generations. I was transported back further into the past, to a time when men first came out of the forests and dug trenches in the muck for their refuse. And here learned the accident of agriculture.

After returning to my bench I splashed the rest of the pitcher over my hands and feet to cleanse me, my head reeling from the revolting journey. The ancient sweeper seemed not to have moved at all throughout the ages of time.

A short moment after, I was relieved to see Yitzhak enter through the side door.

Cascading onto my senses, already overwhelmed by the filth, sewage, and rot from the latrines of history, came the smell of Mara's blood, and the memory of her crushed body. I fell upon him in tears.

From every corner, the Sons of Darkness attacked our souls. Pain and death afflicted our bodies, fearful and tragic sites disturbed our eyes, foul smells invaded our nostrils, slimy putrid things offended our fingertips, terrifying noises penetrated our ears.

Bruriah had no time to sit *shiva* (a period of seven days' mourning), nor we with her. We had to use any water we could find—all the pure water had long been used for thirsty militiamen, and there were certainly no more red heifers (to purify after contact with a corpse)—for sprinkling on the third and seventh days; I'm not even sure if we counted the days correctly. We worked every minute of every day.

Before this Bruriah had mainly been occupied with the disposal of dead bodies, but thinking this too cruel a task for someone recently bereaved, I asked Jairus to shift her to helping me with putting wounded men on planks. I hope it helped her to feel we were saving some.

On the Third of Sivan, we had happier news. Yitzhak came to fetch Bruriah and me at the clinic's new location. 'Come, get up to the walls, and you will be in time to see some fun. We've had the word from Yochanan's men.'

We looked down on the ramps, complete after only seventeen days, those of the Fifth and Twelfth facing Antonia ominously side by side.

'Yochanan sent some sappers down the tunnels. They've built a long mine under the platforms, propped up with timber and stuffed with bitumen. They've gone to set it alight now.'

'Yes, look, smoke,' I cried. From one or two of the wadis, curls of smoke were creeping out. The Roman soldiers scurried around in bewilderment as in one or two places crevices opened up, emitting black clouds.

Soon the Market Quarter and Tyropoean Valley were filled with smoke. Wafts of a sour odour entered our nostrils from their useless damping down the towers with vinegar-soaked straw. Flames burst through from crevice to crevice, and the platforms began to slide into them and catch fire. Soon the whole operation was in flames. The platforms and engines were utterly consumed.

There were cheers all along the wall, and we embraced one another. We needed a victory like this after the two walls had been breached.

'We have just destroyed two weeks' work of four legions,' cried Bruriah jubilantly.

It was enough to lift the lines of grief in her eyes, but was it enough to turn the hand of history, was it another Beth-horon?

Two days later, Yitzhak and some of his best men–Tephthaeus, Megassarus and Caegiras the Lame–bravely attacked the ramps.

'It was the most audacious fighting I have ever seen,' Athanasios told us, clapping his friend hard on the back. He and Yitzhak were forever saying the other one was the braver. They kept a running tally of who had wounded and killed more Kittim, but were quick to afford the other's exploits the greater glory.

'They tarried boldly, fighting off missile and swordthrust while their firebrands took light, till they made sure the whole engine was in flames,' Athanasios acclaimed.

Yitzhak could not deny the praise, as his mission had been such a success, but he bade us thank heaven for his luck and not his prowess. 'As for bravery,' he said, 'a sally like ours is different from open battle. In the field, front line men need the boldness to be first, but it's the second line that requires bravery. You know, don't you, Tasios?'

It was a backhanded way of returning the compliment to Athanasios, as he and his runaways could be called 'second line' troops.

'The first wave withstands the shower of arrows,' he explained. 'The second wave has to climb over their fallen and crying bodies to face the full force of lances, swords and battle-axes. Atop their dead and dying comrades, they teeter between the hope of victory surging forward and devastation of defeat manifested at their feet.'

The Romans had captured the Second Wall, securing the southern egress, and Titus called for the building of a new siege wall, as too many of us were managing to smuggle in supplies through the tunnels.

Shulamith's prophet Yeshua ben Ananias was still up on the walls. He joined the debate, 'Woe to Jerusalem, woe to the people and to the Temple.' But at that moment, he was struck by a stone hurled from the ballista. 'And woe to me, also,' he said, and fell down dead.

For four days, Titus rested from fighting, wishing to appear unperturbed by the destruction of his siege engines. During this period, he paraded his army before us in all their armour as they collected their pay, boasting their riches and the sumptuousness of their armaments.

His soldiers were so laden with plunder that the value of gold in Syria had dropped by half. Their supply lines were secure, and they flaunted their wine and food from the frontline. The show had devastating effect on our soldiers. Our starving men stationed all along the ramparts of the First Wall watched murderously.

Titus sent the defeated commander in Galilee, Josef the turncoat, to beg us to surrender. The townsfolk still wanted peace, but those holding the keys to the gates scoffed at him, 'traitor, turncoat', we Zealots shouting back and spitting.

We waited while Titus held a council of war.

During these days we had further heartache, as Bruriah miscarried of a child she had not even told anyone she'd conceived, even Yitzhak. During the days of fighting, he had been constantly in barracks, and was only now around—at home, if you could call it that—when it was all over. She was refusing to speak to him, pleading reasons of confinement.

The city was in too much chaos to call a midwife. Between Ophel and the clinic, there were many more crucial patients in need, and as for other skilled matrons outside the clinic's works, with the entire population crammed inside the First Wall, everyone was scattered. People became separated from their loved ones and comrades and went to their deaths, to the lions or to the slave mines without finding them.

I had come into the warehouse that was our lodging to find her lying on her own in a bedroll, her garments filled with blood. No wounded soldier ever so grieved my sight.

'It was an aberration, a freak of nature, like the sacrifices in the Temple,' she cried. 'How could the Creator bring a child into a world that's coming to an end?'

With her mother gone, poor girl, I tried to console her, but though she cried about 'all the blood', she refused to grieve. At any urging to speak her heart, she would talk only about the Kittim and the battle.

Even with this compounding of tragedies in our personal world, the daily travails of the siege outweighed anything else in the realm of our existence. Our lives seemed of nothing next to the enormity that was all around us.

Once the bleeding had stopped, Bruriah was up transporting water, sticks and stones like the rest of us. She was brushing shoulders with men, her confinement—for the sake of which she had shunned her husband on his recent reprieve—no longer considered.

The only consideration was surviving unto the last breath, the only objective to give up our lives rather than to be a Roman's slave. We looked minute by minute to the clouds. How long, Adonai, how long? What must we do to unstay Your hand? We can protect Your house no longer without Your help.

The Romans had destroyed all the gardens outside the city,

razed and burned them to the ground, and all along the route though Judaea, they had cut down our olive trees to build their platforms and make way for their roads. 120,000 olive trees they chopped down, chopped down like our sons. The hills were stripped bare; there was no timber nearby, but Titus sent men to cut wood from far away, and they began constructing new platforms.

There was no chance of escape from the horror. Whomever the Zealot guards at the gates didn't kill with their sicarius knives, the Kittim would hang on crosses. Most of us realised by now, there was probably no chance of victory. There were only two paths in our future, slavery or death.

Foraging was an essential work; there were no more stores of food in the city. But the only area now accessible for foraging was southeast toward the coast. Even the priests were starving. But no one wanted to go, as it was so dangerous. Being captured by the Romans meant certain execution.

We four and the runaways still lodged together in the Ophel warehouse, though with us there were many other refugees from the occupied parts of the city. Between the lot of us, we had one lamp, as someone had enough oil kept back.

One of our runaways didn't return from foraging one night, an Arabian. His name was Shakil, but he was called 'Handsome'; it was both the meaning of his name and because he was a very pretty boy. We knew he'd been captured.

This event sparked greater turmoil amongst our group than all the deaths we'd seen. A captured forager was not important enough to be crucified; he would be shipped to Delos (to the slave market). We knew what type of slave they would make of him.

Menelaus raged that we had sent him out alone, 'You women should have gone with him.'

But I pointed out, 'If we'd sent more, it would have been their destiny as well; we'd have lost more than one.'

Stephanos muttered, 'It's always the slaves who are put in the front line.'

Athanasios was furious, 'You dare to say that in front of Yitzhak, who has scars on him from head to toe?'

With the entire population of the city crammed inside the First Wall, Titus began constructing a siege wall all around the city, intending to starve us out.

'The strategy of Alesia won't work in Jerusalem,' Athanasios believed. 'The tunnels provide endless egress.'

'And we'll die ourselves before we send out our women and children as sacrifice to Azazel (to be scapegoats),' Yitzhak agreed.

'Caesar's success at Alesia depended on walling in the newly-come allies, did it not?' I said. 'When the Nations arrive...'

As I said the word 'nations', Yitzhak yanked my sleeve violently and pulled me down onto the bench, so hard I later found a bruise on my rear. Bruriah opened her eyes wide with amazement. Even in these Last of Days, even in the New Jerusalem—when distinctions between man and woman, young and old, Jew and Greek had all but melted away—to lay hands upon a man's wife... But I knew better than to hope that Athanasios would admonish him.

'Stop saying that, Sophia,' Yitzhak said. 'They're not coming. Alexandria, Babylon, Cyrene, they're not coming.'

It took the Romans just three days to build the siege wall. Refugees fled from the city in droves, rushing out before they would be walled in.

It was past the first hour of night, and Bruriah had long since undressed Yitzhak of his armour and tidied it onto a chest near the warehouse doorway ready for the morrow, as militiamen trained every day whether there was fighting or not. We were still waiting for Athanasios, in the dark, as our oil had run out. Only the Temple, refectory and clinic had lamps at night.

Usually the two men would cross paths at some point and come home together, congratulating each other on brave fighting they'd seen or mourning defeats and martyrs. He hadn't come to us on a plank, and I hadn't heard of any fighting, as the Romans were all building walls.

But Yitzhak and Bruriah could feel the worry coming off me in waves, and they tried to cheer me, Yitzhak talking about the small victories we'd had, Bruriah telling me where foragers had found unexpected sources of food.

Finally, he came through the door, grumpier than was usual, and I threw myself upon him in relief.

'Stephanos deserted,' he announced, 'and Balak.' Another of the runaways.

'Are you sure? I can't believe it,' I cried. 'They were among our bravest.'

'They just streamed out with the rest of them,' he said.

I think the capture of Handsome for them was the tipping point. If the slave markets were their only future other than death, perhaps they hoped to win better conditions by giving themselves up. When there are only crumbs left, people will still grab for the better crumbs.

'We also lost volunteers from the refectory and the clinic,' I admitted. From what I heard later, it's likely they were enslaved or thrown to circus beasts.

The common distribution literally collapsed; the widow and the Gamalielites took the cruel decision to cease the common bread and continue to feed only the militias. The people would have to fend for themselves.

We were now compromised by the treachery of desperation as well as military defeat. Anyone would do anything for a bit of food. Famine was so far advanced in the city that people were chewing belts to glean nourishment of the leather; they were selling old hay for four drachmas, four days' pay for a labourer.

The Rich were selling everything they owned for a mouthful of food. If women concealed food to save for their children, marauders would pull out their hair. Women and children lay dead on the floors in their houses, and the streets were full of corpses of old men. They didn't even get thrown into the valleys. People died with their eyes fixed on the Temple, where the priests still ate fresh lamb.

We clinic workers fared better than most, as the refectory still fed us, and relatives of the wounded brought us food, but the fare was poor—rarely more than a bite of bread and a few spoons of barley gruel.

But at the Ophel warehouse, we could see the famine first hand, and we could do nothing to help, as we, too, were starving. No family gathered round an oil lamp at night. No one set a table; they ate pieces of grain uncooked or snatched food from the fire and consumed it in a frenzy. Even though there was nothing to seize, during the day, the women huddled there had to fight off marauders.

So desperate for food were the people of Jerusalem that every kind of vegetation within a hundred stadia was brought in for possible consumption. A lot of the illnesses we saw at the clinic were due to people eating inappropriate things, and we did treat these cases. We also identified plantstuffs for people, teaching them which were edible and which would bring illness.

We ate a host of vile things—broth from bark, slimy stew of fenugreek, boiled aloes, lizards, and worms. We would have eaten swine, snakes, mice, lizards, any unclean thing if we could have gotten it.

So irregular was our diet, there were many digestive complaints, and people queued at the infirmary daily for fig syrup to loosen the stomach or meadowsweet to aid the digestion of strange things, until our supplies of both were used up.

There were hundreds of complaints, from noncombatants as well, of stomach and elimination troubles. We found that almost all of these were due to hunger, which we could do nothing about. We turned these people away, sent them foraging.

We gave out no food; we had none to spare. Our supplies went first to the clinic workers, secondly to the wounded. It was difficult not to begrudge the wounded soldiers their brew, as they'd only die anyway, but Jairus scolded anyone who put these thoughts to words.

A woman named Mariam daughter of Eleazar from the village of Bethezob, who'd moved all her property to Jerusalem fleeing the troubles in Peraea, killed and ate her own son, saying she'd rather see him a sacrifice than a slave. She offered half her dead child to the starving marauders who'd broken into her house for the second time in the same day.

Deserters, if they were Rich, were welcomed by the Kittim. If they were poor, they were enslaved or crucified. Rich or poor, they were so swollen with hunger, often they would gorge themselves on the first food they saw, and burst a gut.

It's hard to believe there was any gold left in the city after all the looting and the depredations, but the townsfolk had been stashing it away for generations, knowing hiding places the Galileans and Idumaeans knew not.

Doris, ever one to relish a salacious tale, told us that deserters were swallowing their gold pieces so as to avoid detection when searched. Once they reached the Romans, on the next trip to the latrine they'd have money with which to buy their comfort and bribe their way into a secure situation.

'One of the Syrian centuries found a deserter picking coins from his own crap,' she recounted, 'and word got around among the camp, spreading to the neighbouring Arab century. The two camps grabbed up 2000 refugees and ripped their bellies open.'

'They turned out to have been as poor as all the others,' she cackled. 'The soldiers were no richer, though they were much filthier.'

# Chapter 31
## The Siege of Jerusalem

I dreamt of Ima Miryam often. I think it was the constant noises outside intruding upon my sleep, reminding my Dreaming Self of the tap-tapping of her lectures. It was as if across the stadia over the hills of Judaea, over the Mountains of the King, her angel continued my instruction. In the ethereal tent of my dreams, my lessons progressed.

The angel of Miryam chose to instruct me on the oddest of matters. There were predictions of the glory to come. We all saw those visions; how could we have continued the awful fight had we not? Then there were everyday matters that concerned us all, how to judge if water was clean for drinking, where in the chaos to find things one had lost.

The dreams for which I truly felt blessed were those where my teacher tap-tapped into my sleep messages about people whom I had encountered awake. My dreams revealed to me insights into people, to trust them or not, what words they were thinking but not speaking.

Tragically, our visions of immediate future glory were false ones. I know now that we will have to wait longer for that.

One morning, I awoke in a sweat while it was still dark and Athanasios slumbered soundly in the straw. An aweful vision had come to me. I was a warrior, treading knee deep in blood—red, sticky, stinking blood—and under my feet were the skulls of the enemy. I heard them clicking as my feet hit them against one another.

The warrior brandished a Roman sword engraved with Hebrew letters, which was hit by many arrows but undamaged. I looked closer, and there were also Chaldee wedgeletters.

All around me hands reached out madly—the living enemy seeking to destroy me? my comrades-in-arms expecting something of me?—touching me, flicking all over my body like locusts. Despite the horror, I forged ahead boldly, sword-arm raised, a shout of anger in my throat, the action of which awakened me.

I breathed in the night air as the drops of my perspiration cooled. They had been the horrible locust hands. The birds began to sing, I first heard them, the coo of the white doves at the Western Wall, waking me into the world.

Shaken, I changed into my whites quietly and went to mikveh before the battlefront arose. The dark solitude of the sacred well, while rebels and Romans alike remained a bed, I could better hear the voice trying to reach me. The cold of the holy water cleansed me of the locust hands, and at the appropriate point in the prayer, I reflected upon my dreaming and waited for divine guidance.

It was a true dream—one involving more than the Dreaming Self. I saw and smelt the red blood. I heard the clicking skulls. I felt the locust hands. The waking feeling was one of horror, but the dreaming feeling had been of anger and boldness.

By the time I got to the clinic, the physics were treating the day's first emergencies. I seized Martilla's ear after she finished dressing a wound. If I asked for any time off to pray, she would complain, but she comforted me, stroking my arms.

Was it just a dream? All of us awoke in the night. Some screamed, some flailed their limbs, some ran about in the full moon shrieking prophecies. The clinic itself was a never-ending din from the wounded and dying. We all had terrible dreams and interrupted sleep. Our days were no less horrible.

In the last days, I started to address the horror of the war as the warrior of my Dreaming Self. In the field, I wasted no time bemoaning the dead or irretrievable, leaping straightaway into choosing and collecting hopefuls. Nor did I spend any precious moments analysing the battle; that waited for the evening. Instead, every evening I strained to understand the ins and outs of the battle. Only once her mind has rationally analysed the situation can the maga's heart be harnessed.

In the clinic, I did my best with all the patients we managed to get to, but I spent my emotion on only those we saved. It lightened the constant air of tragedy around the place. I am not certain, though, if following the divine advice was good for me in my heart. The only guidance I heard those days was my dreams. I heard no music but the clash of arms, the shouts of pain and the crackle of fire. The angels came not to me. The Elohim did not sing.

When the spirits of heaven don't allow access, it is usually due to a decision of the maga's own will, so I searched my conscience ruthlessly. I cried sometimes at night, but felt some-how thus unpurged, and my mind was confused.

It took him three weeks, but Titus had worked his way up to the Temple Mount.

From the First Wall I looked upon the breach and the two ramps up against Antonia, wondering–Why, oh, why is His chariot so long in coming?

I began to hum the Song of Devorah, a song of war: 'Hear, O ye kings, give ear, O ye princes…' Bruriah set down the plank she was carrying and began to sing the words, 'Awake, awake, utter a song. I, even I, will sing unto the Lord…'

The women and children and everyone on the ferrying team, one by one, began to sing. Even the fighting men and wounded joined in, 'The earth trembled and the heavens dropped'.

When we reached the line, 'The mountains melted from before the Lord God of Israel', a matron came frowning up the steps, ordering tasks for each of us. Comforted of our fear, we jumped to them with enthusiasm.

We had even the children carrying planks now. So many families had been torn apart that we had to turn one of the big empty warehouses near the Damascus Gate into a giant orphanage. The aunts and mothers were often supporting the battle during the day, so there were many in there who were not yet orphaned.

These children were all distressed and angry to varying degrees, and simply caused trouble if not given something to do. At first, we did our best to keep them from the blood and stench of war, but now we needed all hands. Nothing that needed doing avoided the horrors, so the children just had to brave them as we did.

Naturally, we tried to shield them from witnessing the deaths of their own family members, but in the heat of the moment, we sometimes literally forgot who was related to whom. Some of our little heroes had to watch their own fathers or uncles being carried bloodied from the field, and we had few moments to spare to ease their anguish.

They were horrible days for the children, horrible for all of us. Rich or poor, Levite or peasant, Zealot or Pharisee, father or son, we all end up on a plank.

By this time more people were dying from hunger than from combat. Children who at this time of year should be playing in the streets, their faces and hands all sticky with pomegranate juice, instead were gaunt and smileless, lurking in corners of half-wrecked houses protected fiercely by their mothers, those who still had mothers.

We had to convince the mothers not to forego nourishment themselves for the sake of giving every morsel to their offspring, but they did so anyway. Mothers of young children were in such weakened condition they barely had the strength to put out their hands to beg for alms. But though they gave every grain to the children, still the children were dying.

Nor did we limit our works to medical means. We tried everything in the compendium of magic of Moshe and Solomon. As long as we didn't slacken in our medical treatments, Jairus sanctioned the use even of heathen spells.

We retrieved the enemy swords and arrowheads that caused a wound, to clean and oil while the soldier mended, and all bloodied bandages were immediately tossed on the fire lest they fall into the hands of necromancers. Fervently also we invoked the Angels of Darkness against the enemy.

Boys too young to fight were employed to mark the hoof-prints of Titus's horse into which we hammered nails to unseat the Dreaming Self of the beast, and when there are was no more metal to spare for this purpose, we use jagged rocks. Still, the Angels came not to me.

We could have used poison. There were quite a few toxic substances native to our land that would be unfamiliar to the nose or tongue of the Kittim. But the only ones of us ever in close enough proximity to the enemy were Simon and

Yochanan.

I don't know whether it occurred to them to try slipping the generals a potion, but whenever they were together in negotiation, they were heavily guarded.

I had just been pulled by a supplicant into the sanctuary to sing a song for her starving child, whose belly was hard and swollen and whose eyes had no life in them, when a group of us were called upon to go fetch some patients. I was about to delay the supplicant, but she began to wail mournfully, as if only my song could keep her child alive for one more hour.

So, I nodded to the others and ducked into the sanctuary. Out of the corner of my eye, I saw a few of them, Martilla included, make a face.

When the supplicant left, I was called over by Jairus.

'With all this,' and he waved his hand in the direction of the fortress of Antonia, 'you are still doing readings.'

I knew I was being reprimanded, but I ventured, 'The hearts of the Many are troubled.'

'The Many are troubled because they are dying,' he said.

'Perhaps my prayers can help strengthen them for the fight.'

'The time for prayers has passed. That child's belly needs your help more than does his heart. You will do well to consider the needs of the militias as your priority,' he scolded.

'If I have neglected my duties...'

'You must not only do your duty, but be seen by others to be doing your duty.'

'Is it not my duty to use my knowledge of magic when it can help?'

'Your magic has not yet won us the war. Let us put our efforts to that.'

The words stung me to the quick. I kept hearing the words in my head—Your magic has not yet won us the war—and cried into my straw. Though Athanasios soothed me, I know he agreed with the censure.

'Look upon it more as guidance from a master than as reproach,' he counseled.

I was wounded by Jairus' words at the time, but afterwards I was mindful to follow instruction obediently. Perhaps I had finally, in these last days, learned the lesson of humility the Kedoshim had preached.

Titus had by now built four new platforms; it had taken them twenty-one days, bringing timber in from far away. They had turned our beautiful Judaea into a desert of olive stumps. After the terrible weeks of resisting, the Kittim launched an all-out attack on Herod's Palace and Antonia.

Our fighters managed to set fire to their engines and stop them, but the deaths mounted, and the burial committee could no longer cope. Bodies couldn't remain within the city unburied after sundown, so they just threw them over the walls into the valleys.

As they piled on top of one another a brown stream of decomposing flesh and blood oozed from underneath them, and the unclean vapours wafted up to defenders in the Temple and on the wall to cause diseases.

The clinic effectively ceased to function. Jairus and the physics still toiled tirelessly, but the stream of incoming injured, not to mention the starving and diseased, was so enormous, they started on one patient only to find thirty more queueing behind him.

We on the ferrying teams put only those from the front line

on planks. Otherwise, we instructed loved ones and comrades to treat them on site.

'Keep his head upright to keep him breathing; stop the bleeding, and get him to drink some water,' and if they could manage to take the patient to Jairus, he could join the queue for the physics.

We clung ever more fiercely to our vows. There was no more eating meat nor drinking wine nor wearing leather shoes. No more washing or bathing. No cutting of hair or paring of nails. Every aspect of survival from minute to minute was chaos.

In a last-ditch attempt to cleanse Jerusalem of treachery, Simon bar Giora arrested High Priest Mattathias and his three sons, two high priests and fifteen aristocrats, and a commander and ten men who had tried to defect. It had been Mattathias who'd invited Simon into the city. His men stoned them threw them over the walls into the valley.

In a desperate last gasp, the rebels destroyed the remaining vestiges of the aristocracy, a minor terror hoped to counteract the major terror at the gates and the avalanche of counter-revolution.

I was not tempted to solicit Joanna's opinion on the violent demise of her fellow sectarians. Now that the refectory was no longer operational, there was no way of knowing where to find her. And it had been several months since I had been able to visit Mount Zion, nor even to send a messenger to Tabitha. Everything was in too much chaos for anyone to bother with the usual niceties.

It was two days after the Fast of the First Born at night after a heavy rain. We all heard the horrible sound, for a moment thinking the Romans had broken though, but the truth was even worse.

We ran to the Temple and climbed atop the wall above the Royal Porch to see. The Romans had their campfires here and there, so we got a clear view.

The mine the sappers had dug two months earlier had collapsed, taking part of the northern wall of Antonia with it. Herod's fortress, which had housed the Roman garrison for a hundred years and during our war had been our strongest fortification against the invaders, now crumpled into the hole. Our own inventiveness had backfired upon us!

After this, Titus began the assault on Temple Mount. But due to the excellence of its masonry, they rammed the wall all day long and only managed to dislodge four stones. Yochanan's men had built a secondary wall inside that one to strengthen it.

There were no more visits from Malachias the Messenger; news of what was happening travelled in waves through the population like ripples from a stone in water.

Titus took volunteers for a frontal assault. This I heard from Yitzhak. Only twelve stepped forward. A Syrian auxiliary climbed the wall, but he tripped and fell and was immediately buried in a shower of missiles. Three soldiers were killed on the wall, and eight were injured in front of it and were pulled away by their comrades.

We had little time to cheer this brief victory.

A few days later, in the early hours, we awoke to a trumpet blast from one of the watchtowers. It was one of theirs.

Yitzhak, like most of the men, was stationed overnight on the Western Wall, but the rest of us were in our quarters on Ophel Hill. The sound of shouting and clattering of armour descended from the direction of Antonia as Malachias appeared with the news:

'They snuck into the fortress at night–twenty men, a standard bearer and a trumpeter–and killed the sentries.'

By the time we got up to the front line, Kittim were answering the trumpet, streaming into the Outer Court. Jews were fleeing in panic into the tunnels, and the soldiers were trying to follow them. It was a situation of crisis; within moments the Kittim and all their foreigners could be in the Holy Sanctuary.

The Zealots cried from the Temple Wall, 'to enter beyond this mark is instant death'. They shouted at the Kittim, but it was meant for the ears of our fighters, to give them courage, to remind them what we were defending.

Yochanan's and Simon's men staunchly blocked the tunnel entrances. Athanasios and his band ran to join them on the periphery of the battle. I spied the ferrying team and got to work with the planks.

The Romans were in a disadvantageous position, blocked from behind by the crevices of Yochanan's sappers, and blocked in front by continuously refreshed rows of Zealot fighters.

A centurion from Bithynia, driven crazy by the legions' persistent set-backs, rampaged ahead toward the Temple. No one followed. His boots slipped and he fell, buried in missiles.

After eleven hours, Titus pulled back. The first Battle of the Temple ended in our victory, but we only had a few days to celebrate it.

The fortress of Antonia was captured and burned. The soldiers began to take down the walls of Antonia in order to create a wide breach.

Bruriah and I struggled to find the courage to leave our warehouse for the clinic each day. At each sunrise, we thought today would be the end of the world. We helped our menfolk don their armour with tears running down our cheeks unbidden, fearful that they'd be martyrs by nightfall.

The city of David was laid to rubble by the Sons of Darkness. Ordinary life no longer existed. Women didn't stop to cover their hair; mothers didn't change the cloths from their babies soiling. Children didn't speak. People crumpled in starvation in corners of the square, and no one helped them. We didn't even shed tears at each progressive event in our ensuing destruction.

The priests in the Temple could no longer continue the *Tamid*–the perpetual sacrifices. There were no more lambs for the offering. It was the first time they had ceased offerings to God since the riot following the trial of the Temple Eagle martyrs. Even during Pompey's invasion, the priests had been unfailing in their devotion.

The people wailed, 'Even God will leave the battlefield now.' Most had given up hope of victory, and only continued fighting to save themselves and their loved ones from death or slavery. There was no longer any denial of the coming defeat. The New Jerusalem was vanquished.

# Chapter 32
## Leaving the battlefield

Two weeks after the fall of Antonia, Titus began the assault on Temple Mount.

It was the Third of Av according to the Jubilee calendar, the day when the Yachad celebrates the Festival of the First Fruits of Wine, and I thought back to those happy days of plenty. Here in Jerusalem was nothing but ruination and starvation.

But in my sleep, I saw a different vision. From each side of the Temple rose two rays of light, which curved around the mount and met each other in front. As they crossed, they diminished the other's light by half. Just at that point, the two arcs met an onslaught by a shaft of fire and disintegrated, shattering globules of fire across the land.

Then I saw a repeat of the same scene. The two lights above the mount joined together in a dual column, but now the light doubled its force, and turned to meet the shaft of fire, which exploded into flames, dispelling the clouds with glorious sunshine.

In the flames, at the point where the firebrand would have been set, was a menorah, the seven-branched candlestand symbol of the light of God on earth and the mark of Jewish sovereignty.

I suspected that my Angels were not speaking of my feelings for the Temple sacrifices as an Ossaean, nor my hatred of the high priesthood. My Dreaming Self spoke of my feelings as a Jew.

Not only is the Temple the altar for our offerings to God, the repository of the wealth of the Jewish Diaspora, it is also the symbol of our history and independence, the very essence of our Jewishness.

We bow to the emperors, but our Lord bows to none. They have their Roman laws, and we have our sacred law. We pay their taxes; yet they dare not to lay their unclean fingers on our sacred offerings. Though they subjugate our nation, we would die like rats before we allowed their idols within our holy sanctuary.

I begged God's forgiveness that I had admonished the Angels for their silence. Was this instead a clear prophecy? It was a seeing dream, not a hearing dream. Throughout the noisy activity of lights and fires, there was no sound.

It was the story of our war. The Romans were united; we divided. Our forces caught between two camps that didn't even permit the crossing of their territories. Could the import of this image be any otherwise? Defeat was not imminent if we strengthened our hand.

It is suspect to trust in the divine origin of dreams. Sometimes an element in the vision has no greater import than having been something we saw that day which was unusual, or the last person we met before going to bed.

But this was a true dream. I knew because I saw the colour of the fire. I knew that I had received divine guidance. I asked permission to be absent for the afternoon, permission that was difficult to win.

I wandered around Ophel, speaking poetry. I found Bruriah and said, 'The Temple will fall. We must call for the Nations to rally for the defense of Zion.'

'It's a bit late for that, Sophia.'

'We must rally the Nations, we must! We have to leave the city,' I screamed at her.

'You know the Sicarii will slash anyone entering the tunnels,' she said.

'I know a way,' I said.

'You do?' her mouth hung wide.

'Yes. Find everybody.'

'Is this another prophecy?'

'It's more than that. It's a strategy.'

We were all so terrified by then that she was easy to convince. 'I won't go unless Yitzhak does, Sophia. I'll meet you back at Ophel once I've managed to speak to him.'

I couldn't find Athanasios.

I remembered from that night on the walls with Shulamith the words of Yeshua: 'when you shall see the abomination of desolation, flee into the mountains.' What had the crazy man said? 'A call to the East, a call to the West.'

Perhaps that was indeed a true prophecy. Without support from Jews in the Diaspora, Jerusalem would fall. We must get out of the city to get messages of urgency to all the communities to rally a rear-guard action.

I would write to Ima Miryam. And Secacah, the Kanaim, had they returned to an empty fortress? Anna and Uzziel, were they still alive? Who was left that we could contact?

I needn't try to write to my father. There would there be no time for a delegation to reach them. Moreover, the Jews of Babylon had already shown their stripes when they marched against us with the Kings of the Nations, as did the patriarch of Alexandria Tiberius Alexander, and he a Jew!

If I could have reached Tabitha, she could have given me letters for the Pillars and presbyters of the seven Notzrim communities of Asia, but there was no way of getting across the city to find her. Though I assumed her husband Yeshua was with the Zealots in the Temple, it had been five months since I'd been able to contact Mount Zion.

The tunnel system might now be less guarded than before, with so many frontline demands on the men, but the main entrances were right in the heart of the battle. How could a messenger get out? Was there another entrance into the tunnels? An access from the wadi system outside the walls?

I found the Messenger Malachias and swore him to secrecy, but he refused to help me.

He said, 'I can't believe I'm hearing this from you, Sophia, and if you urge me further, I shall report you as a deserter. I've pledged my last blood to the king of Jerusalem and the captains of the Hundreds. I'll be your messenger, but I will not desert the battlefield.' He was only eleven years of age, our brave Zealot Messenger.

I approached a few others I wanted with me in the Final Days. I had intended to be calm and present my argument soberly, instead I rambled incoherently, finding my words falling upon deaf ears. Everyone continued preparing for the final battle.

The more people rejected my pleas, the more hysterical became my tone. Some of the women comforted me, bewailing with me the plight of our city, but few heeded my words.

People were too accustomed to prophecy. Some predicted the Son of God descending any moment in his chariot to smite the Kittim. Some saw eternal damnation in every turn of the soupspoon. Furthermore, most had long ago faced the prospect of defeat and were firmly inclined toward fighting to the death.

Some listened. Some came because they were seeking a party with whom to flee, some because they knew me, saw that I was agitated, and were concerned.

Malachias did give the message to Athanasios, and he came with Menelaus and the runaways, and some others who'd listened, including some who had come with us from Secacah, those who still lived.

'Well did we harken last time to your dream,' one of them said. They hadn't, actually. They only believed it now that it had already happened.

I was surprised to find a willing ear in Martilla, whom I had never really trusted as a true ally. She approached me as I left the clinic, and I thought surely it would be to remonstrate with me for not treating the patients lined up on planks.

Instead, she addressed me kindly, 'Sister, I have seen you in such state before. Have you had another dream?' She sweetly tucked an unruly strand of hair under my headscarf. 'Take my arm. I will stand by you.'

'Will you really, Martilla?' I cried, and I dragged her out with me.

We congregated at our quarters on Ophel Hill. Bruriah arrived with Yitzhak. 'If Tasios votes to go, I'm in,' he said, 'but I will bring some of my comrades. They deserve to be saved.' He named them, the three men who with him had braved the attack on the ramps.

'Would they not go to the general?' Menelaus worried. He was also deeply suspicious of my rash inclusion of Martilla in the mission, but I told him—it's a debt I owe to a fellow disciple, to trust someone who had been willing to trust me. If I had never won Tsuiyah's friendship, here, Martilla, who was not previously well disposed toward me, was willing to give me her confidence.

Yitzhak was certain, 'No, they would rather die than betray me, and they certainly want to save themselves.'

'We're not trying to save ourselves,' I said. 'We're trying to save the revolution.'

'I am certain they support that mission,' said Yitzhak. 'They're no cowardly deserters. But regardless of the motives of their hearts, cousin, I am pledged to them as brothers in arms. We have fought together all this time. I cannot leave them now.'

Out of the corner of my eye, I could see Athanasios assessing the conviction of the group.

'Are we determined, every one of us, to leave the battlefield?' he said.

They agreed. He looked for a few moments in the direction of the Temple under siege, then at me. 'We must save ourselves if we are going to save anything.'

I had formed a plan.

'Someone told me once about a secret entrance into the tunnels.'

'Where?'

'Inside the Temple'.

What was it Bar Hakkoz had said? *deep down in the southern sector.*

'You're crazy. How could anyone get inside the Temple, even if there were such an entrance?' said Menelaus.

'I think you ask the wrong question, there, Menelaus,' said Bruriah. 'Our little desert fox would have no trouble sneaking past Simon and Yochanan. The question is—how would the rest of us get in?'

'The same way Yochanan's sappers did,' I said, 'by digging from the inside out.'

Menelaus scoffed, 'Somewhere under the noses of Simon and Titus you're going to shapeshift into the Sanctuary, get into the tunnels and quarry your way out with your little Ossaean digging tool?'

'That is exactly what I am proposing,' I said.

'You'd have to go in with someone,' said Athanasios.

Yitzhak said, 'With no disrespect to your bravery, I don't think you would be much help, Tasios.'

'The safety of Sophia is certainly my concern (he never called me 'my wife'), but I am suggesting someone of skill, a sapper.'

'Do you know any we can trust? Any of Yochanan's?'

No one did.

But Yitzhak said, 'There is one of the commanders who supports the strategy Sophia suggests. He wants to rally the Nations. We could win him to our plan, and he could select the man.'

We sent for Malachias. He had promised he would still deliver messages.

'Can you get a message to Judah ben Ari, in confidence?' I said.

He responded, 'What do they call me?'

'The Messenger, that is right. Here is what I want you to say. I know of an unguarded access into the tunnels. Tell him my intention is thereby to summon the garrisons of the Nations, and I know he desires the same would that Simon's guard permitted it.'

I was summoned almost immediately. Ben Ari stepped away from the battle to speak to me, and I found myself addressing one of the captains of the Hundreds.

'What is this?' said the commander.

'There was once someone who mentioned a passageway into the Treasury known only to those of his house. He did not tell me where, as I never suspected I might need to know, but I have a feeling where to look for it.'

'True, what is an access into the Treasury is also access out. If we could get into the Treasury, we could access the internal entrances to the tunnels. But you suggest an undertaking of great danger based on a feeling. What makes you to come forward now? It is not only I, but many commanders would defy Bar Giora.'

'It came to me in a dream,' I said, which was not a lie. 'And I have something that may help.' I took out my tefillin.

'I hardly think your prayers will be any surer than your feelings...' he said.

I stopped him, 'No, it's not that.'

I opened the glass door and pulled out the map of the wadi system Athanasios and I had taken from Avichai.

He grasped it gleefully.

'You'll need a sapper—we'll get Hilkiah. In fact, if you could create a new opening somewhere Simon wasn't looking, we could get several men in.'

'Then every would-be deserter in town will be traveling in our wake,' I protested.

'You realise, Sister, at this point, the people who would volunteer for this sort of mission are going to be the deserters,' he said.

He was hardly going to take his entire garrison; their arms were needed. But he was in charge of the mission, so I had to agree to his bringing anyone he liked. I was planning to bring my loved ones, why shouldn't he?

The agreed group was to number twenty one, comprising: Yitzhak and Bruriah; Athanasios and me; the runaways including Menelaus; Martilla; and the people from Secacah—nine in all; Yitzhak's comrades: Tephtheus the Galilean, Megassarus queen Mariamne's ex-servant, Chagiras the Lame from Adiabene; Judah and his picked men: Artanus ben Barnadus one of the most ferocious of the guards, a priest Ananias ben Masambalus, and Aristens, the scribe of the Sanhedrin, an eminent man from Emmaus; and Hilkiah the sapper by whose guidance we would select a spot to dig upward to create a passage for our companions.

We gathered at the Ophel warehouse to plot our mission. Judah showed us maps of the Temple he'd obtained from Ananias ben Masambalus.

'The southern sector, you say? That would be the area where the private storerooms are. Is there any way of knowing which direction the tunnel would take, once you've found it?' he asked.

We turned to the sapper. 'No, but I have some experience in feeling my direction down there.'

'All the combatants are crowded around Antonia, the towns-folk and pilgrims are huddled wherever they can find in the Lower City,' said the commander. 'The priests have mostly fled. It's likely that whatever noise you make would not be overheard.'

The main tunnel system ran from Temple Mount to Siloam

ending up in the Kidron Valley, constructed firmly of stone with ceilings up to forty palms (ten feet) high. Simon's men guarded the entrances, but as we were entering by a secret entrance, our tunnel would intersect with this system somewhere below the Temple. Hilkiah pointed to the spot on the map.

Judah marked three or four places where we thought it would be safe to come up. 'Once we're down there, we'll target one of these,' said the sapper.

'How long will the digging take?' several of us asked at once.

'Three days, at least,' said Hilkiah.

We all groaned, but it was the only way. We couldn't bring along more diggers. Even getting two people in there was risky.

This mission would be much more challenging than slipping past the Antioch Gate, There, I only had to dodge one guard, who was looking for thieves and trouble-makers, not little girls.

Here, we would be trying to slip past a crowd of battle-mad Zealots, all on the lookout for just such saboteurs as they would suppose we were. The urgency our entire group felt for the mission was tempered by the awareness that to be caught was certain execution.

There was no time to consult calendars or to school the sapper in more than the basics of the technique—at any moment Titus could break through into the Temple courtyard. On his part, Hilkiah was so terrified of the task he was willing to take advice from a girl—a tough Galilean, he hid it, but I could tell.

'From the time we start out in the morning, you must forget that you are yourself,' I taught him, 'truly believe and behave in every way as if you are one of the Temple guards. Behave this way even when you speak to me, though obviously we must not speak unless necessary.'

Normally, you would fast and pray for three days before-hand, meditating upon the subject. We couldn't afford three days—Titus' men had already breached the Northern Wall of the Temple itself—and I felt that the military aspects were more important than the magical, so instead Hilkiah and I reconnoi-tred the position, checking the steps to the Temple, to study the subjects in advance.

I did insist Ben Ari grant me one day fast. In the flights of my meditations, I went through the changes in form that I learned from Ima Symacho and remembered them according to the seasons as she had counselled.

As my Dreaming Self progressed through the seasons—Lion, Goat, Serpent—the last spirit to descend into me was the Fox, so I knew the augurs were good.

Ben Ari sent Megassarus to fetch me at the agreed time after I'd broken my fast. I was to carry the provisions and digging tools as I was least at risk.

We went in the morning. We worked out in advance a cover story in case we were challenged, and an alternative plan and retreat strategy if anything were to go wrong. But nothing did.

The plan went perfectly. The sapper and I, both dressed as Levites, walked straight up to the Temple, completely unchal-lenged. At every point where we passed people, we slipped by just at the point when they were occupied with something else.

I remembered—lock up the Feeling Self...I am merged with the earth...I am merged with the crowd.

Once past the Levite guards and the mikva'ot at the entrances, we went straight across the Court of Women to the Beautiful Gates.

Around the periphery were the trumpet-shaped collection boxes for the sacred offerings. They were not guarded; no one would dare touch the profits from God.

Normally a woman would not go higher than this point, but today, I wasn't a woman, I was a shapeshifter. I thought not of the beautiful, high carved ceilings starred with eight-petalled rosettes nor of the multicoloured tiles paving the floor; I thought—I am the sneaky accomplisher of my own designs.

We were not entering the Sanctuary. We weren't going up; we were going down.

I heard a priest laugh to another behind us as we breezed effortlessly past them.

'What is it?' the other said.

'A couple of foxes.'

'What's funny about that?'

'This place is death to any stranger who enters, yet now foxes prowl freely.'

'More a reason to cry, isn't it?'

'That's why I laugh,' he said.

We slipped around the side and took a staircase down into the Treasury, three stories of vaulted storerooms below the esplanade, stuffed full of treasures laid up for the consumption of the Rich.

They hadn't fed the Ebionim; they hadn't armed the militias. They had been frantically stashing away their wealth since the siege began, in hopes that the Holy Temple would protect their private wealth, planning to reconstruct their villas atop the rubble of our revolution and the skeletons of our sons.

Inside, we located the southern sector and went further down the corridor until we found the storeroom of the House of Hakkoz.

On the storeroom next to it, I recognised the seal; it was the treasure of Avichai, Athanasios' master. There were no rows of bureaucrats in front of it, all the guards were outside; the entire southern sector was deserted.

I said, 'Wait for me a moment.' In a flash I slipped into the room next door, and there I regarded pouring out before me the treasure of the traitor. Amphorae were stacked against the walls, and rich furniture was piled with sumptuous cloths.

There was a woven bag full of coins, and I grabbed it without hesitation. They were sure to be Roman sestertii, but I wasn't planning to touch the unclean things myself.

We slipped quietly into the Hakkoz treasury.

I pointed Hilkiah to the hole. You never would have found that door unless you looked for it, but looking for it, we found it in no time.

Down there in the tunnels was an unworldly experience. I would have been utterly useless without the sapper. I could barely tell up from down, much less south from north, but Hilkiah seemed to find his nose.

We had to crawl without light, smoke from a torch would have suffocated us and might have been seen above by a guard. It was no problem for Hilkiah, but I was entirely blind, and bruised and cut my arms and legs many times.

When the passageway turned direction, he whispered back to me, 'southeast toward Kidron'. After a short distance he stopped me, 'This is far enough. Otherwise, we'll be beyond the wall.'

Hilkiah chose a central spot where the ceiling was highest, and we stood upon the bag of treasure to gain height. We dug at that ceiling for, sure enough, three entire days, though I was utterly ignorant of time down there.

We worked in complete silence; what was there to say? After the chaos of the battle above, the silence gave me much time to ponder, and I could barely sleep.

Compared to the silence down here, my life above seemed a long noisy confusion. Running away from home, travelling with a gypsy caravan, joining the holy Yachad, marriage and war and murder and a few bits of necromancy.

I bound like a fox straight from one life to another. When I take on his glassy emotionless eyes, I am not myself. I am the sneaky accomplisher of my own designs. Yet my designs have shifted more than my shape across these lives.

Indeed, who am I when I'm not shapeshifting? Women will always look to their beloveds for the answer to that question, won't we? If they can love us, surely, we can love ourselves. Yet so much of who I considered myself to be was utterly alien to Athanasios.

Strange, I thought, that in these End of Days no one had considered it inappropriate, a married woman three days underground with another man. My husband had even been the one to suggest it. 'The safety of Sophia', he'd said.

I could not imagine Athanasios in a public situation, stepping forward to claim rights over me as his wife. If I had leaned over and kissed Hilkiah on the mouth in front of everyone, Athanasios wouldn't have blinked. He wouldn't have said a thing.

It was like going down into the Underworld, and indeed the dead haunted me. My Feeling Self saw the sight fresh before my eyes of Bruriah's mother crushed, shot and fallen from the wall, her beautiful face still carefully powdered and painted. Justa and Mattai, Vespasian shattering their dreams of a Samaritan Kingdom of God with obscene ease. If our mission could save the city, nothing could bring back our dead from out of the earth. Unless one believed in the resurrection of the righteous.

When we finally saw the light peeking through, we discovered we'd come up on Ophel Hill just below the Southern Wall of the Temple. It was early evening, still light.

'Perfect,' said Hilkiah. He'd gauged the location just right.

'I know how Niger the Peraean felt,' I said to him. 'Coming up from down there is like rising from the dead.'

We hadn't heard it below ground, but the assault on the Temple had begun. In the distance we could hear the thud of the ram and the clattering of armour from the north; all the action was happening around the other side of the Mount. We blocked our hole with brush and ran to collect the others, he to Judah ben Ari, I to our lodgings a few streets up.

Bruriah was there, and she fetched the rest of our companions. Before anyone had a chance for a word, I shoved the bag of coins into Athanasios' hand.

'What?' he said, astounded, seeing the seal.

'The payments for your scribing.'

He let out a funny sound. 'Sophia, I see you will always liberate me,' he said, and in front of all those people, he kissed me. Even Yitzhak was shocked. The runaways grabbed the bag and started gleefully counting the loot.

Sisters, you will know that it was this bag of treasure that purchased our safety in Alexandria and funded the first shelves of our Academy.

I had committed fornication by marrying a Greek; I was an

accomplice to murder; I'd practiced necromancy and now had with my own hands committed theft, if I was not guilty of that sin already with the Chaldee tablet. Yet on all these accounts, I am certain that God guided me in righteousness.

Athanasios was disturbed by my demeanor. I was delirious from lack of sleep; my eyes rolled, the skin on my face twitched, and I could not look him in the face. They later told me some of the things I was saying–I would never have remembered myself, I was in such an excited state–'here in the court of the wrath of the Lord, the people heed not the word', and again I spoke of fleeing 'toward the West'.

'The underworld has addled you, Sophia,' he said. Over and over, he said to me 'you must sleep'.

That night Athanasios put sleeping powder in my soup–how did we still have a supply of it?–but I could barely eat it.

I wanted to spend every moment questioning him–What did he think about this? Did he agree with me about that? What about this? that?

Every time I spoke in prophetic words, he argued with me. 'We're escaping, we've agreed? I don't see what your mad prophecy has to do with it.' I became upset that he didn't understand.

I pleaded with my husband, desiring him to hear the same message that I heard. 'Please pay heed.'

He calmed me, 'I am. We have agreed. We leave in the morning. Look, there, our travelbags are packed. Now sleep.'

He tried to discuss practical things. Yet, when we lay together, my Acting Self scuttled like rats and I could not sleep; catching only an hour or so before dawn.

When I awoke, quiet as a dream Athanasios had everything ready. I encouraged him to take a cup of last night's soup, without the powder of course, as we walked.

At sunup we removed the brush from the hole Hilkiah and I had created and entered the tunnels.

Our destination was the Forest of Jardes, where many refugees from Jerusalem were gathering. Thence we would despatch our letters all over Diaspora.

'Jews across the land, arise. Take up the sword, for the final battle is now. Come to defend the glory of Zion and the house of the Lord.' That was the plan.

I was quite sullied. I had bathed after the three days in the underworld, but anxiety left beads of sweat all over me. They felt like locust hands. I could have bathed before our gathering, but I felt too confused, agitated, and unholy.

Emerging from the tunnels into the desert above, following the map of the wadi system we took from Avichai, we were all covered head to toe in dusty white chalk. The elation of escape congealed into a cold anxiety of the future.

Then, right before us in the furrow was a bad sign. A dead fox—not a good augur. Athanasios and the commander walked straight past the creature, but I clutched at Bruriah and emitted a little shriek, which stopped everyone. I frantically calculated the direction in which it lay and the direction in which it must have expired.

Some of the troupe thought I was ridiculously trying to bring the animal back to life.

'Come on, Sophia,' said Menelaus. 'We've got enough to worry about for ourselves.'

Some others were desperate enough from hunger they thought it sensible should I be intending to eat the creature.

'It's bone of carrion, Sophia. We'll find nourishment once

we get to the forest,' someone said.

It was Martilla. As it turned out, I was very glad to have brought her with us, not only because trusting someone who trusts you is the right thing to do, but because she was such a comfort to me. I think she found that having won my friendship by comforting me in times of distress, my friendship was actually something good to have. So, she was ever saying words of kindness.

Bruriah was shunning me, and had walked on ahead. She was annoyed with me for stopping for the fox.

'No, no, this is a bad sign,' I mumbled. Could it be that I had brought these people into danger? The whole tunnel of Hakkoz idea was no divine revelation, after all. It was merely the scheming of the demon who hung over me. My blood drained as I feared a tragic conclusion of our mission, and it would be my fault. We had no pillar of fire directing us in the wilderness.

I thought, I must quickly do something. I took some blood from the body of the fox on a leaf and began to shake it as if sprinkling, to the north, east, south—but before I could finish the ritual, Athanasios grabbed me quite roughly.

'It is not a sign, Sophia. It is a dead fox.' And in a lower voice, he said, 'People are depending upon you today.' Here, in fact, was Athanasios in a public situation, stepping forward to claim rights over me as his wife; yet I was not happy for it.

Later, though, I considered it the right thing for him to have done. He did not put it into words, but I knew him to know what he was thinking. It was foolish of me, and even selfish, to occupy myself with fox-magic when twenty-one lives were at stake. These people had all risked their lives on my devise.

I owed it to them to remain straight as the fox toward the destination. Even in the face of a defeat or a bad sign, the task at hand must be—what to do next?

And of what use was it all anyway, if this final escape plan didn't work? To our west, Titus was besieging the Temple of God. The three walls of the City and the fortress of Antonia had already fallen to the Sons of Darkness.

I knew not what had befallen the Saints of the Yachad; it had been many moons since I received a letter from Ima Miryam. Perhaps she, somewhere, was fighting still, ever keen to hasten God's Kingdom. Or perhaps she lay somewhere buried in the sand.

Of what use was the Lost Wisdom of the Magi, when all the beauties of the world of today were gone? Of what use had been my magic, or that of Yeshua, Ima Miryam, or any of the magi to us? He who knows all had not heard our cries.

Once we reached the forest, Athanasios busied himself with the practical things. We needed to join with the refugees already gathered there and find our roles within the camp, collecting firewood, obtaining food or cooking, before resentments flared up.

Then there were bigger questions: Where should we go? Should we all split up? Many of our company had relatives and acquaintances in Alexandria, but factions within the group wanted to lead splinter groups to Tabariyya or Qesarya. Some wanted to join the Sicarii at Masada; some wanted to flee to anywhere there were no soldiers. No one, no one was talking about going back for the final battle in Jerusalem.

Everywhere I turned, whenever groups of refugees moved from one place to another, I could hear a scuttling of rats that no one else heard, and I thought, what was the message? We left Jerusalem like rats in the night. Was God telling me we are all cowards?

While I agonised over the wisdom of our escape, everyone, rather than berating me for leading a desertion, congratulated me for finding the tunnel. They were all overjoyed to have escaped. Athanasios the brave fighter, though concerned over my behaviour, was certain we had done the right thing to leave. But I could not accept it. The possibility of Jerusalem defeated was too terrible to believe.

What strategy was left for us? Athanasios' commitment to our fight led me to abandon sharpening. Now I know that even those who don't follow the Way may be righteous.

Full moon messiahs looked to hastening, enacting prophecies to stir HaShem's hand. Ima Miryam, like the Notzrim, was a hastener, but her training led me to believe the right path was broadening—converting non-Jews to the Light, and the Zealots had so hoped for deepening—winning Diaspora Jews to the Fight.

The Pharisees and Notzrim had even looked to widening—spreading the works of the Ebionim among the Rich.

Broadening hadn't worked. With all the violence between Greeks and Jews, proselytes were leaving in droves. Deepening hadn't worked. Only Adiabene and Armenia heeded the call to the Nations, and their leaders were purged in the tribunals.

Widening hadn't worked. Rich Jews just moved to places like Pella and Apamea, and their leaders were purged along with the royalists. Rich Greeks joined in the pogroms.

The enemy of my enemy could never be anything more than a short-term tactic. They'll just trade you off to some other enemy; for them you're a temporary means to an ultimately different end.

The Kutim rose up alongside us, but they chose the Day according to their own calendar and neglected to consult us about it. The common enemy is less threatened when the battles are fought side by side and not together.

The hastening of faith—Tabitha's magical martyrdom—was nothing but a recipe for funerals. If the Zealots' hastening of works may indeed have been the best strategy, I guess God didn't approve of our timing.

To whom could we write? Babylon betrayed us, as well as Commagene and Emesa; Alexandria had sent Tiberius Alexander to command Titus' troops. The Armenians and Adiabenes were unlikely to still wish us well after their leaders were executed in the purges, and they were too far away. We sent messengers on the run to Alexandria, Antioch and Tabariyya, and we waited; but the messengers did not come back.

The openers of our letters, community leaders and wealthy Jews, hid their faces behind the Sons of Darkness.

## Chapter 33
## Judaea Capta

Woe, woe to Jerusalem. God's spirit has departed.

It was the Ninth of Av–O cursed day–when we saw the line of smoke in the sky. In just three weeks and nine days, Titus had conquered and destroyed the house of God and the holiest city on earth. We couldn't see the city from the forest. I had only the vision of it from my dreams.

The terrible news was spread by signal fires. From the top of the Mount of Olives the smoke signaled to Sarteba, and from Sarteba to Agrippina, and from Agrippina to Hauran to Bet Baltin in Babylonia. From there the fires went up north and south and across the whole of Diaspora in a rolling wave of smoke, as if they could burn away our tears. As if the pillar of fire in the wilderness pointed us to flee, flee, away from Jerusalem.

In the morning we awoke again in tears, aiming our morning prayers, instinctively not toward the East but toward the smoking Temple. The practice so remains among all Jews today.

Hundreds of survivors had flooded into the forest, no fighters. They were all pilgrims from elsewhere caught up in the Pesach crowds or townsfolk who had not been allowed to desert before, to whom Titus had granted clemency.

During the day we began to receive some of the fighters; they'd found their way into the tunnels. They reported: 'The Kittim fired the colonnade between Antonia and the Outer Court while we looked on doing nothing to stop the flames, preferring to create a clear attack and escape route,' they said.

'After surreptitiously preparing the cavities between the columns with firewood and bitumen, we tricked a large body of soldiers up onto the western colonnade and caught several hundred in the flames. But the legions slaughtered so many that their blood put out the fires.'

The Temple burned for a week. We pitiful refugees cried from the forest, 'Help, oh Lord, for the faithful are no more.' 'Nobody seeks, and nobody asks, "upon whom shall we depend?"'

The militiamen who brought news of the fire decided to remain in the forest for a few days, hoping to rejoin with any straggling refugees who might arrive from the final fall of the city. Talk was that they would rally forces and join the Sicarii at Masada.

That was not for our ragged band of widows, orphans and runaway slaves. No one wanted to travel in a small group anywhere. So, it was decided to march together.

Judah ben Ari ordered that the injured and all the women and children would depart with him within three days. Our letters were too late; now we had to save our lives.

The men would wait to see if any more refugees came, and they would send them quickly after us. Within the week, the fighting men would depart for Masada. The Sicarii were still undefeated.

The next wave of refugees continued the sad tale: 'The Temple of God has been razed to the ground,' they wailed. Simon bar Giora and other brave men withdrew to the Royal Palace, and some of Yochanan's men fled there. Thousands were still in arms.

'On the viaduct, our doomed king negotiated with the general. He would have his freedom on the promise of laying down weapons, but this Titus mockingly refused.'

In a fury over the request for terms at this late stage, Titus—wicked man, son of a wicked man—torched the Lower City—our lodgings on Ophel would have burned—and over two days arrested every Zealot in sight. A noble Zealot death his only option, Simon renewed the fight.

I was heartened to see among this group of refugees the Zealot priest Yeshua ben Thebutis, Tabitha's husband. I threw myself at his feet, kissing his hem, but he was in no mood to be welcomed.

'She burned with the Temple, Sophia. They all burned, the deaconesses, the righteous congregation of the Upper Room. I heard their screams. I couldn't reach her, and had to watch from the Temple Wall where I was stationed with the rest of Eleazar's men.

'On the word of one of the junior priests they gathered on the roof of one of the outer colonnades. I don't even know who it was; they had all decided at the last minute he was the Messiah. "Now is when God will intervene," he promised. The prophets foretold that after our terrible tribulation would come the Day of victory. We all believed it, didn't we, Sister? The Day just never came.'

'Nooo,' I heard myself say. The sound came from somewhere else—the oracular head of Yahya, I presume. That was the interpretation of the teraphim. Nooo more martyrs to hastening. Nooo more Zealot deaths.

'As my wife and brethren burned, they raised their arms to Heaven and glorified in the victory, salvation and happiness to

507

perish thusly, eager to leap into Everlasting Life.'

'May the Kingdom of God blossom forth from their sacrifice,' someone said.

Tabitha–may HaShem avenge her blood–was on her way to the resurrection of the righteous.

She died in the flames with 2000 others, certain that now, at this last moment, the clouds of heaven would finally descend–another 2000 martyrs departing the battlefield for expectation of the Day.

Yeshua bewailed that he knew it not until after the flames began. 'We should have been together,' he cried. 'Now we are forever apart in the Kingdom to Come.'

We assured him his resurrection was guaranteed.

The tale was continued by another, as Yeshua was thinking only of his wife in flames.

'The soldiers held back from entering the Sanctuary,' the man said. Perhaps they were aware of its holiness and superstitious of its antipathy toward their race. It was in Greek so they could read it, but they already knew what that sign said: death–by magic or by the knife–to any uncircumcised.

'But Titus threatened them with military execution, so they crossed the threshold. There was Titus, the Abomination of Desolation, standing where he ought not. Our courageous men still managed to kill a good number of the Kittim as they crowded in.

'The first division of Jehoiarib was serving. Meirus ben Belgas and Josef ben Daleus, the last of the priests, threw themselves into the fire. To cries of, "Imperator, Imperator, Imperator", Titus sacrificed an ox, a sheep and a pig at the Eastern Gate.'

'A pig in Jerusalem!' I cried.

'The rage of Mattathias was for less than this,' said Bruriah.

There was not a Zealot in any city or village in Judaea who would argue that the kingdom of the Jews could yet be won.

The Romans fired the northern colonnade. They set fire to the gates, silver melted and streamed onto the ground, soldiers lifted the molten mess with sticks into their helmets.

Women gathered by the Western Wall, weeping like one huge family at a funeral. They sang a song of lament, every verse punctuated with the names of the fallen.

The Upper City was taken and Herod's Palace captured. After a siege of 134 days, the New Jerusalem was no more.

'As the Temple burned, we heard a pop, pop, coming from inside the walls themselves, like corn popping on the fire,' said one refugee.

'I thought it was some new engine of war,' said another.

'It was the *Shekinah* (Divine presence) leaving Jerusalem,' said another.

'No, it was the Shekinah remaining in the stones of the Western Wall.'

'I thought it was the last judgement of the Lord,' said Yeshua.

Athanasios said, 'It was the water within the cracks of the stone exploding from the heat.'

I frowned at him. Yeshua and the rest needed to express their feelings of anguish.

Yeshua continued his painful confession:

'For their royalty they spared the kinsmen of the king of Adiabene, and Josef their interpreter. Pinhas the Temple Treasurer bought safe passage with tunics and spices, and woe is me, with my own hands I gave over the treasure to the hand of Caesar—lampstands, tables, bowls, platters of solid gold, sacred ornaments, bags of coin. Only the holy Books of Law did we keep.'

The women comforted him, 'It wasn't your fault. What could you do?'

I did not say anything. Why couldn't he have maintained steadfastness unto death?

'They haven't got all of our treasure,' I told him.

I took him aside and told him about the Copper Scroll. My copy of the treasure list was still hidden in my tefillin.

In addition to Athanasios by my side with his gruff love, it was Yeshua's arrival more than anything that snapped me back to the earthly world. The loss of a loved one we shared made me to concentrate on his feelings rather than the smoke inside my head.

I said a prayer for him, but I couldn't read him. My Feeling Self was blocked by thoughts of anger–anger against my supplicant for buying his freedom with our holy treasure. Anger against a dear friend who died a painful death!

Well did Tabitha die happy, then; she was ever one for useless martyrdom, I thought. I could not banish my Feeling Self, and the angel guarding the gateway blocked my ascent up the ladder of consciousness. But I had to pretend some ability to heal, as Yeshua was in need of it.

And so, it came to pass that the prophecies were fulfilled. The Messiah–Menachem, that is–had been pierced in his prime by the hand of Jews. The holy Temple burned, and by an unfortunate backfire of tactics, the flame that began the fire was lit by our own hand. Not treachery, it was the tactics of desperation.

The seeds of our own destruction were sown by our own hand. Indeed, this enemy was on our soil at Jewish instigation, invited in by the self-appointed Herods to back their wars of usurpation.

As my prophecy had portended, it was not the might of Rome that defeated us, it was our own internal dissension. Though it was no consolation at all that my prophecy had proven true. Indeed, that threw my soul into further turmoil.

Had my previous visions, visions of victory, been false, then? Had we who had seen victory encouraged the Many to fight a doomed battle? Why have we laid down the blood and lives of our nation, if God was not to grant us victory? I looked back upon all the times I had hoped for victory and seen the promise of God in prophecy. The words of encouragement I had given my comrades and they had given me—divinely inspired, I was so sure.

I sang from the Songs of Sabbath Sacrifice with tears running down my face, and the refugees around me huddled close. 'Praise the God of the lofty heights, O you lofty ones... Let the holiest of the godlike ones sanctify the King of Glory.'

Today forty years on in the Roman city of Jerusalem, the great Temple of the King of Glory lies in ruins, and our hearts lie with it.

Sisters, I fell into the blackest of clouds I had ever known. I could barely speak. I couldn't put food in my mouth, which took me close to death, as we were all little but skin and bones by then.

I told someone, 'the Lord's sustenance has gone; the food will not nourish.' Nevertheless, Bruriah and Martilla put spoons of gruel in my mouth, perplexed by the memory of seeing me doing the same thing for patients in the clinic.

I was completely smothered in a show of grief, dejection,

frustrated zeal and self-hate, and the wails of grief throughout the forest did nothing to dissuade me from the mood.

As news came in with each new group of refugees, I felt ever more dejected. Where once I had tried to look at each turn of fate from my Acting Self rather than my Feeling Self, now I had given up. Each piece of news was to me another confirmation of our failed dream. Instead of discussing events and considering what should be our next step, I wailed and moaned over the tragedy of it all.

We heard each refugee's personal story along with news of the city, and I was of no help to these people. I had no love to give, so lost was I in my selfish dejection.

Many in distress asked me for readings, but I was out of grace. I had to explain to them that I heard nothing. It was I, the supplicant. I turned to Athanasios, pitifully, everyone who loved me, for support, but I could not feel their love.

Athanasios stood beside me, frustrated and powerless. I am sure he felt dejected by our defeat, too, but he was thinking practically—What must we do now? What is the task at hand?

The desperate need for physics and cries for comfort began to pull me back to life. So again, I owed the lifting of my terrible spirits to the call of the Many, and to the love of the people around me.

Especially Athanasios. I know my behavior was bizarre to him, particularly for someone who believes not in prophecy and divine words. He endured me, talked sense to me, and still loved me at the end. He even gave me a gentle smile when I started giving readings, sensing that I needed it as much as they. Thus, we established between us a new pattern of understanding, which I am happy to say we were able to maintain.

I insisted upon it.

'Great are the differences between us, so that to love me you must love my differences,' I told him. 'You need not to agree with them, but you must love them.' And so, he did.

There were no astronomers nor augurs among us. I knew the basics–bad luck if the heart is found diseased, good luck if the liver is folded–but even Yeshua didn't know how to read them. Ben Ari consulted him anyway, but I avow that he must have been as dejected as I. He only said, 'go, go, the haste is too important for the augury to matter.'

Tears running down our faces with sobs of 'Jerusalem, O Jerusalem,' we departed for Aegypt.

Refugees joined our party even across the desert along our route to Alexandria, our numbers grew as the terror spread. Militiamen, pilgrims, refugees–all who were captured were enslaved.

The slave market was so flooded with our brethren, we later heard, you could buy a Jewish slave for less than the price of a horse. The Roman roundup included a boatload of Jewish children sent to Rome for immoral purposes. The children were told to jump overboard and drown themselves before the ship docked.

How would you in Aegypt, where gold is like dust between the toes, look upon our wretched condition? How could we impose on our friends and relations a sudden influx of starving and war-defeated refugees?

In any case, we had little choice. The Kittim would be on our backs soon scouring the countryside in their customary roundup of survivors. Those siezed would be massacred or sold as slaves. Prostrating ourselves at the mercy of Alexandrian

Jewry seemed a milder option.

We prayed for the generosity which you did indeed show to us, Sisters, and in a situation of great adversity.

Athanasios gave me much comfort. He begged forgiveness for his cruel words, as truly, it had been after his remark—I don't see what your mad prophecy has to do with it—that I had stopped eating and speaking. Yet even in the midst of my pain, I assured him that his words were only one of the reasons for which my heart bled with pain, only the trickle of a breeze on the water in the midst of an enormous waterfall.

I knew he was feeling deeply, as well. Yet the more I approached everything with raw emotion, the calmer and more practical he became, as if to provide a counterbalance.

I was as terrified of prophesying as I was of the events prophecy seemed to import, as the flash of light is always followed by the black cloud. Even as I fell off the edge of the chasm, I remembered my history.

The black cloud of Gehenna and the fire that is not extinguished follows the bright light and ecstasy of prophecy, whether the message be divinely inspired or false. Though he refused to use the word 'prophecy', Athanasios was untiring in reminding me of this.

I made an infusion of winter aconite which I drank, and it settled me. But when I look back, it is always love that has pulled me back into the world. On the caravan trail from Babylon, it was Shu'dat's friendship and attention that cured me. Now it was Athanasios' love that pulled me back from the deep.

Also, strangely, his disapproval of my religious mania seemed to keep me from floating off into the clouds. He did help me look upon what happened inside my head. I talked much in proverbs, as usual, and he would brusquely tell me when the connections I drew were verging on the twisted.

If this had happened in the midst of battle in Jerusalem, he would not have been so kind. It may be correct that that should be so. I still stung from his jibe—I don't know what your mad prophecy has to do with it—and Jairus'—your magic has not yet won us the war.

Here, Athanasios was patient and slow. His love shone over me, though I struggled to feel its rays. His grim face, which never smiled and only withheld its habitual grumpiness in deference to my weakened state, did not cheer me.

He loved me, and I loved him for his effort, but I could not bring myself to fulfill my wifely duties. I felt too unworthy for the joys of the world. Coupling and the reproduction of life seemed meaningless. If our individual lives were worth nothing, so of what worth is love?

The matrons spotted the tension between us, and placed me in the company of pleasanter people. Fortunately, I was feeling better, or this might have distressed me.

Once the troupe set out, my spirits lifted a bit. I thought of the Nabatu and the comradely feelings I had so newly experienced. These memories also brought tears of missing Shu'dat, missing those happy days, the innocence of our days in Palmyra. I went to the stream and cried, my sweat poured out the pain; I begged forgiveness for my fall from grace and prayed until my hands were wrinkled from the long bathing.

When I returned to camp my eyes were red and swollen, and the matrons bade me drink a tonic and go to bed. They clucked and said they understood my grief. This soothed me, and tonic or not, I slept like a dog and woke up to find the birds singing.

I realised how vigorously Athanasios was trying to steady me, and I thanked him. This pulled me out of my selfishness, and I could begin to think about how others were feeling. This was my first step on the way back to grace.

Soon, I was reconciled with my husband and participating more energetically in camp life. I began to help with the ill, the wounded and the malnourished. Then again, the camaraderie of caravan life and pleasant associations of the desert pulled me up from the cavern of dark thoughts, though unlike the Nabatu merchants', it was not a happy camp.

A voice from the East and a voice from the West warmed me back to God's grace—the voice from the East of the caravan and the voice from the West of Athanasios' love.

Years later in Alex an Ossaean suggested to me that perhaps my prophetic dream was not about foretelling the manner of our defeat. What could I have done that thousands of others did not try to do? Perhaps my Dreaming Self had been trying to make a decision which my Acting Self had feared. Though the Temple may fall, I would live. All our good works since then, Sisters, have helped me to hope that it was not the cowardly choice.

We were past Azotus, almost at the coast, when another large group of refugees joined us.

'The whole of the Upper City was torched,' they reported. 'The Romans have razed the land all around; not an olive tree nor a vine remains.'

'Yochanan the Ossaean,' they said, 'still commands some resistance from Jerusalem to the coast, part of the last defensive network. But the Romans have arsenals at every ambush point from Aegypt to Syria.'

'And it's open season on Jews in Jerusalem.' They'd found our tunnels; they rooted out all the stragglers and all our hideaways. The most important prize for them was Simon bar Giora.

'Yochanan surrendered, but Simon resisted to the last, fleeing into the tunnels. For three days he hid from the terror above, but hunger drove him to emerge. He was wrapped in a white shroud and gave the soldiers a fright.'

'On the third day, risen from the dead, like Niger,' I said to Bruriah.

'They seized him and took him to Titus, who reserved him, along with Yochanan, for his triumph in Rome.'

The most immediate news for us was next.

'They found the wadi system into the Forest of Jardes and massacred your militiamen.' They never made it to Masada.

It would have been time for the olive harvest were our trees not all cut down. Titus feted his brother Domitian's birthday in Berytus by throwing 2500 Jews to the beasts in the amphitheatre—our sons, our sons.

Three years later at Masada, our final citadel fell, and 960 died, the Sicarii and their families.

There were some from the family of the prince, Menachem's line, who hid out the slaughter in a cistern, that the dream of Judas the Galilean might yet have seed. Five children and their father's grandmother, the matriarch of the Zealot princes. The Sicarii had committed mass suicide to a man, woman and child.

Like a lamp when given a burst of oil flares up and then extinguishes, the Sicarii blazed in desperate fury, women fighting too, and children throwing stones. Each embattled group fought to the death.

When faced in the end with capture, the men turned their knives on their own wives and children and themselves rather than face a future of slavery to the foreigner. To die rather than to call anyone but God Lord, it was an honorable zealot death.

After Masada, the grim signals went up, fell the forts at Herodium and Machaerus.

All over the Diaspora, Greeks wreaked their revenge on the Jews; mass pogroms took place in Alexandria and other cities. These were the very Jews who had refused our letters and stayed with their Greek friends. They had said to us, 'No, we are Greeks'; and now the Greeks said to them, 'No, you are Jews', and killed them for the name. Thus, did they pay the price for their betrayal of Jerusalem.

We spent so much of our hearts and arms and lives during the war waiting for the Messiah, computing and calculating the signs, interpreting and reinterpreting the prophecies. Sisters, this matters little, and the auspices of the day even less.

Defeat is not undignified, however chaotic. It is simply a defeat, a mistake of history, tragic and not to be repeated. What we must do is correct the mistakes. Look to magic and ritual if it gives you courage, but it will only be when we have won the victory that we will know that the Lord has spoken. He gives us guidance from within ourselves, and not from without. We can only shape history by ourselves understanding the balance of cosmic and earthly forces, and above all, not making mistakes.

After the terror, not only were relations between Greeks and Jews at the absolute peak of bloody vengefulness, relations between Jews and Jews were worse as well. We had a name for it—*sinat chinam*—the senseless hatred of our own.

The seven sects splintered into a myriad of factions, each

blaming the others for starting the war or collaboration with the Kittim, betrayal of the war or of the Messiah, or betraying others into slavery, blasphemy against God or disobedience of the Law, unrighteousness and sexual license.

I wondered about the Yachad; the only group of rebels about whom I hadn't so far heard disastrous news was my Brethren. If the Romans had crushed such a renowned band of scholars, they would surely have broadcast the news. We heard nothing, and as far as I knew, no news was good news.

It wasn't until later in Alex that I heard the story, one of the few pleasant stories I heard in the aftermath of the Fall of Jerusalem.

The Romans had indeed raided the Yachad camp in their countryside roundup. All set they were to imprison and humiliate these high and mighty desert rebels who said their God endowed them to be above Roman law. Yet they found not a soul there. Someone near Secacah had given the Yachad an estate in fulfillment of a vow, and they were departed thence.

The Tenth Legion, the story goes, marched into the Yachad camp above Ein Gedi 'to arrest the cursed holymen' and found the camp 'absolutely deserted and cleaned spotless'. The buildings were immaculately stripped of goods and materials; pottery wheels were disassembled; animal pens were empty; the fires were cold.

The town of Ein Gedi was destroyed, rooves they had tiled with pitch from Sea bitumen made all the houses flame. Tel Goren lay in ruins.

I heard this from a Christian, who was one of the soldiers. He said, 'Perhaps they were carried up to heaven, their holiness too pure for this sinful earth.'

A lovely thought. But I prefer to think that the Brethren in transition to their new property and the Kittim in their scouring, they managed to just miss each other.

The Jewish Revolution was defeated. The war—the greatest of all those not only in our times, but of those that were ever heard of—this victory legitimised Vespasian throughout the empire. On all the coinage—gold, silver and brass, even down to the smallest quadrants—they all bore the terrible words *Judaea Capta*.

# Chapter 34
## Revelation

Here is where my two stories join, Sisters, as here is the point at which the young Sophia and her husband, refugees from the Jewish War, were accepted by younger versions of yourselves and your families into your community, even putting yourselves at risk of the violence that confronted us. Now the old Sophia seals this gift to you, knowing that she sits among scholars.

This was a sad tale, and the continuance of it is not finished. I have not written about the signs–the eruption of Vesuvius, the famine in Pisidian Antioch. It was written that the Fourth Plague would precede the overthrow of the great. Were these portents of the end of Roman rule?

I have not written of Yavneh–blessings upon the Sages and their works.

The scrolls fill my shelf now; my tale becomes long. I have written all my broken and crushed heart can bear to tell of the war, and I have fulfilled your request for my private testimony on the matters of my personal experience.

I have written of magic, of the treasures and great works of the Jews, of the Lost Wisdom and of the secret traditions of the Yachad. You, who are of our inner circle, will know how to translate my tale for the Many if that is your wish.

I have lived through the most significant of times. Jerusalem, our shining Holy City, fell to ash. And I fell in love. These events, the tragic and the joyous, gave me Wisdom. I could not have survived everything—the war, hunger, crucifixions, pogroms, blood and injuries—if I hadn't found this Wisdom. But if I hadn't fallen in love, I wouldn't have known those eyes that loved me and believed in our future, too.

My people have been destroyed. Yet I have a belief and hope for the future. When you read my story, you will understand. Then we will have much work to do. There could be no better place than Alexandria for our works. If not us, who else will? And if not now, when?

Though we ban no works from the Academy, I cannot recommend the Greek work of Josef, Sisters. I wouldn't buy an old camel from that man. One of you girls skilled in Greek would do a good work to make a new translation.

King of the Jews no longer has any meaning. High Priest of Jerusalem no longer has any meaning. The whole world uses Caesar's calendar. Yet still the people look for the Day and the coming of the Son of Man.

Most Jews today believe God judged us for our sins. It was wrong to fight, or it was the wrong day or place, or the wrong Messiah. Sisters, it is our common belief that none of these are the lessons God wishes us to learn that has directed our works together at the Academy, as much as it is our love of Wisdom.

If religion is to be our motive, it must be motive for creating a better world, not for following Caesar's rule.

Even when Jerusalem was ours, we did not win all of the Jews. The priests and property owners stayed right where they were, seated next to the Kittim and the Herods. Even our own army was divided, Simon and Yochanan and Eleazar competing for prominence.

Instead we fought against not just Rome and Herod, but all

the other client kings who answered their liege's call. Nor did we win the Nations; aside from Athanasios and some other internationalist heroes, we had no foreign allies. Even our brethren in Diaspora did not come to our aid; our kin from Babylonia and Alexandria fought on the other side. Excepting Armenia and Adiabene, we received no reinforcements from other lands.

The Germans did yet again fight, but it was too late for us. Britain, Germany, Judaea, there was not a single messenger between us.

If only your fellow Alexandrians had come to our aid. By attacking their subjects piecemeal, in our own towns, with their well supplied armies, the Kittim forced our fight to remain only defensive. We were left to be picked off one after the other, the battlefield chosen by the enemy.

Those among you who have seen Jerusalem in its glory, who have seen a glimpse of the Heavenly Kingdom, to us it is to recreate the possible, remaining unblind to what is evil. We remember how they united the Sons of Darkness in their infamy.

We have seen with our own eyes how kings and their backers whip up the mob to wage their wars of greed; how they use the cry of 'terrorists' to spark pogroms across the Diaspora; how they created an empire of commerce, which they rule with their armies; how they provide riches and armaments to the Nations, then demand from them a vassal's support to attack their own brethren.

Every generation learns things afresh, but you young people, who never knew our glory and our defeat, are different. To you, Rome is the world, and we are her people. Deceived by empty words like 'citizenship' you are, and bought by a few crumbs from the table of Empire.

When I was young, things were different. Rome was the enemy. The battle was coming, and we had God on our side.

Today, still, senators pile our gold in their cellars, while everywhere their privilege goes unchallenged. Today, commerce rules the world. Rome is all-powerful and has no insurgent.

I must reveal that it is for the purpose of setting you a task that I impress upon you the dejection and utter degradation we suffered. I remind you to remember that all of us who experienced this, our hearts remain cloaked in the timidity of remembered loss.

People all over the world, tribes and client nations, who even simply heard about it, were disheartened for generations. Rome's power holds a firm lock on our chattering knees, and we cannot walk.

It must be to you the task to remember what there is to gain, and to seek out with whom to work for it. When we see you flying, our old hearts will gain the courage to forget our knees.

When I join my husband in the arms of God, my Sisters, let me know that you will continue this work. Spread knowledge—mathematics, literature and architecture, the stars and machinations of the heavens, science and metallurgy, herbs and medicaments—all the jewels of civilisation.

My husband left me to join those who sleep not so many years after we came here. Though never a believer in destiny, he was ever convinced that he would die young. 'A slave's heart is not meant for long life,' he would say.

The Lord's hand did not bless us with children. Perhaps I had the same scarring on the womb as my mother. Though I did not experience pain when lifting things, my moonblood has been more irregular than most.

However, because of this freedom, I have been able to fill my days with other than a wife's tasks. Perhaps God had touched my husband in that way, denying a slave a man's nature, blocking even that most basic expression of God's provenance. Or perhaps it was I who was touched; I was wanted for other works.

You may ask me what happened to the Copper Scroll? You know of my copy of the Chaldee fragment—I never did manage to translate it—it is in one of Adiel's tefillin lodged on the Academy's shelves in the Alexandria Library, and, as I have revealed to you alone, my coded copy of the Copper Scroll is concealed in the other. You may see them there to this day.

I can reveal to you, Sisters, you who know all my secrets, that it is in keeping the two documents together that is my treasure map. Thus, thought I, may our future scholar know that there is some connection between the two, giving a hint of the key to one who knows for what to look. We are safe in knowing that our treasure remains enshrined through time without end in that magnificent abode.

I leave it to you and your menfolk to let our fighters know about the caves. It is the treasure of our heritage, and must not pass from our hands. But remember that the real treasure is people, land, sheep, olive trees. And Wisdom. Tell the princes what we have learned.

The interpretation of tzedakah—Love thy God—is never to cease in the struggle for liberation. Till the fields and nourish the poor, but keep your swords ready. The interpretation of chesed—Love thy neighbour—is Jews, Gentiles, Samaritans, even

Romans. Do not fight each other; fight together against Satan and the Rich.

You must learn the New Wisdom. Not a Lost Wisdom, but a newly found one, one we know because we ourselves laid the building stones, the Wisdom of the future. Why were the victories and why the defeats, the corruption of kings and generals, the treachery of collaborators, the strategy of revolt.

And then teach every pearl of this to your brothers and sisters. With them you shall form an enormous army, and then we shall see the New Jerusalem and the Kingdom of God on earth. That is your task. Remember it, learn it, and teach it.

May our apprehension of the significance of our past enable us to find the path to redemption. The Wisdom is there for us to seize; we need no prophecy. What we need, sisters, is courage.

Love your menfolk and put courage in their hearts, but give a second hand to your sisters. They have an extra cross to bear, for their hearts hold up the world.

We must strive for the unity of peoples the Samaritan magus preached, but it must be a wider unity, not only Jews, for the battle will not end with the Jews against the Romans. We must look to a more universal movement. You must have the love to unite with your brothers and sisters, anyone under the feet of the foe. We will rewrite the war songs and use new words.

I share with you, Sisters, one last tale, something Athanasios said to me at the beginning of our flight to Aegypt. We were standing on a hill having departed the Forest of Jardes, watching the smoke from the Temple of God.

I was still caught in the depths of the black cloud, and poured my tears onto the sand with evil prayers. I saw the